Marilyn Heward Mills was born in Switzerland and brought up in Ghana, the daughter of a Ghanaian father and a Swiss mother. She was a practising lawyer for twelve years and now lives in south London with her two children. Her first novel, *Cloth Girl*, was shortlisted for the Costa First Novel Award. *The Association of Foreign Spouses* is her second novel.

Also by Marilyn Heward Mills

Cloth Girl

THE ASSOCIATION OF FOREIGN SPOUSES

Marilyn Heward Mills

SPHERE

First published in Great Britain in 2010 by Sphere
This paperback edition published in 2011 by Sphere

Copyright © Marilyn Heward Mills 2010

The moral right of the author has been asserted.

*All characters and events in this publication, other than those
clearly in the public domain, are fictitious and any resemblance
to real persons, living or dead, is purely coincidental.*

A CIP catalogue record for this book
is available from the British Library.

ISBN 978-0-7515-3814-4

Typeset in Caslon by M Rules
Printed and bound in Great Britain by
Clays Ltd, St Ives plc

Papers used by Sphere are natural, renewable and
recyclable products sourced from well-managed forests and certified
in accordance with the rules of the Forest Stewardship Council.

Mixed Sources
Product group from well-managed
forests and other controlled sources
www.fsc.org Cert no. SGS-COC-004081
© 1996 Forest Stewardship Council

Sphere
An imprint of
Little, Brown Book Group
100 Victoria Embankment
London EC4Y 0DY

An Hachette UK Company
www.hachette.co.uk

www.littlebrown.co.uk

For my fabulous mother Elisabeth Heward-Mills,
with much love and admiration.

Acknowledgements

I am indebted to Christine Green my amazing agent for her unfailing faith in me, and to Joanne Dickinson, my brilliant editor, for understanding this story and for waiting patiently until I was able to tell it. Thank you also to Rebecca Saunders, Zoë Gullen and everyone else at Little, Brown who helped this book on its journey.

Thank you to Karen Botchway, Rebecca Clouston, Beatrix Heward-Mills, Zoë Lloyd-Ewart, Caroline Pickering and Jane Stone, whose unfailing love and support during bleak times illustrated the meaning of true friendship with enduring and astounding constancy.

Jamie and Serena
you wonderful two,
I am proud, so proud of you.

Chapter One

Eva rolled out of bed with care so as not to wake Alfred, and pulled on her dressing gown. Her bare feet flapped on the cool terrazzo floor as she walked to the window. She looked behind the curtain and saw that the Harmattan winds had arrived overnight carrying fine desert sand which would cloak the sun, making it appear benign, winter-like, almost. Already, the lightening sky was filling with the white dust. Harmattan heralded Christmas, at least what Eva had learned to make of a West African Christmas. The dust made it dry, a pleasant change from the tropical damp, and a degree or two below the usual temperatures. For the next few weeks, all activity, even sleeping, would seem altogether easier.

A quiet street ran in front of the house. There was no pavement so pedestrians ambled down the middle, moving aside unhurriedly only if a car tooted at them. A couple of uniformed workers sauntered past towards the junction of the main road up ahead to wait for a *trotro*. Eva watched the girl sweep the yard across the street, as she did every morning, gathering every little leaf from the large neem tree that shaded their yard and parts of the house, into a neat pile. Some hens pecked at the ground, and the girl shooed them away when they got too close to her pile. Every now and then she stopped, stood upright, and re-adjusted the cloth she wore wrapped around her body, tightening it underneath her arms.

The bed moved. Eva turned and saw that Alfred was watching her. He smiled sleepily, his face soft. She went over to his side of the bed and sat. She rubbed his bare torso, his tight abdomen. He took her hand and pulled her into a hug, kissed her on the neck. 'Happy anniversary, babe.'

She pulled away, to show him the longing in her eyes.

He smiled and whispered, 'Later?' He traced his finger along her face, across her mouth.

Even though he made it sound like an invitation, she felt rebuffed. 'Ten years! Can you believe it? Only you don't seem to have time for me any more . . .' She raised her eyebrows at him, grinning. 'Promise?'

He winked. 'I do, Mrs L. I do. And,' he added, looking deep into her eyes, 'I'll spend all day thinking about exactly how I'm going to pay my debts later.'

She leant forward and kissed him. 'I do love you Alfred.'

On her way downstairs she poked her head around the open door of the children's room and saw that they were still sound asleep. She had enough time for a quiet coffee and an amble in the garden before they all woke up and raced about without pause until tonight.

As she walked through the hushed house, warmth spread up and through her. She smiled and savoured the peace that flooded her mind. She hadn't set out in their marriage counting years, and yet they had reached here comfortably in the end. Everyone had convinced her that ten years was something to celebrate, to shout about, so they were having a lunch party with their closest friends, a celebration of their life together. She had been hoarding food for a while now, and had bought some new blue and white, tie-dye tablecloths and cushions to replace the old, sun-faded sets that were wearing thin. She felt a flutter, excitement at the prospect of everything coming together so beautifully.

Raised in a reserved household, she had initially struggled with the constant social comings and goings of Ghanaian households. Now she too enjoyed hosting friends, feeding them, passing time in their company. Back in the UK, there would have been shopping centres to visit, dates at the cinema, theatre, concerts, new restaurants to try out. None of that was available in everyday Accra life, and gathering in friends' gardens with or without the entire family was how friendships grew and were strengthened. She liked the chance to showcase her family and her home, and was always surprised how much she enjoyed the process. And today she felt rather celebratory. It was remarkable really, but whenever she decided to think about what good things she had, she saw lots to shout about everywhere she looked. Three amazing children: Abigail who was nine, Simon, seven, and the baby Joseph, her unexpected, unplanned joy, who would soon be one. It still made her shudder to look back, aware now of how low she had been, how frighteningly real her bleak outlook on life had seemed. That last pregnancy, unwanted at first, had turned her thoughts and emotions on their head, left her reeling, and it had taken several months of his life for Eva to accept with joy that she had a third child. The guilt had been the worst thing, and it had prevented her from sharing her darkest thoughts with her friends, or even Alfred.

Then one morning she had woken feeling more clear-headed than she had in months, a tingle on her skin, her eyes brilliant. The sun seemed brighter, the sky bluer, her heart lighter; the baby blues had eventually gone for good. Time was all it had taken after all. And she was relieved that she could cherish Alfred and the children once more.

She hummed a tune to herself, smiled, unlocked the kitchen doors and threw them open to let in the morning air. The usual

3

moisture had already been sucked out of the atmosphere leaving it dry and pleasant; everyone would perspire less until the desert winds passed.

She walked to the sink, shut her eyes so tight that they twinged. She turned the tap, a little first, then all the way. She heard a gurgling, as air was pushed about in the pipes. A trickle of water flowed into the dented, stainless steel sink. She gasped in anticipation, leant forward slightly, willing the water flow to increase, trying to entice it. She turned the tap some more, but it wouldn't move and she watched as the trickle reduced to a few drops and then ceased. 'Oh blast!' she said out loud, puffing and hitting the tap with the palm of her hand. How she had hoped the water would be back on, but here, in typical Accra style, was the foil to her perfect party plans.

There had been no water for three days now. Not a drop, no matter how often she turned on the taps and willed it to flow. Yesterday Alfred had teased her about her tenacity and, in her defence, Faustina the maid had said, 'Anyway madam, *I* under-stand, because a positive thought brings a positive result.' Eva had looked across the room at Alfred struggling not to laugh and couldn't help smiling, when only a moment before she had wanted to scream in frustration.

The water tank which sat on the roof of the house was nearly empty now. She stared at the sink and wished that as she stood there the water was making its journey from the distant reservoir through the miles of clay pipes just for her. 'Please God,' she whispered, wishing she believed in Him as fervently as Faustina or Gladys, her mother-in-law, or just about everyone else here did.

She shook her head. There was nothing she could do about this now. She filled a pot of water from the drum and put it on the stove to make some coffee. Thankfully, she thought to herself as she waited for the water to boil, they had several drums and buck-ets filled with water. Flushing the guest toilet would be a bore, but they had managed that many a time before and they would again. All her guests were used to the frequent lack of running water. She made a note to herself to put some fragrant flowers on top of the cistern.

The drawn lace curtains shrouded the living room. Outside, Zachariah the night watchman was working to ensure the garden was tidy before he left for his other job. A simple nod of the head was often the only acknowledgement of her instructions or her presence, which made Eva question from time to time whether he had understood her, but without fail he interpreted her wishes faultlessly. He was under the golden cassia tree, ablaze with grapelike clusters of resplendent blooms. He watered the orchid, a purple *dendrobium* hybrid, a gift from dear Margrit, which she had planted nearly a year ago. Long wavy tentacles covered in fragrant flowers now grew out of its waxy green leaves.

Zachariah removed browning roots and leaves from around the lustrous blooms. His brow was furrowed in concentration, but even from here she could see how gently he moved his large hands around the delicate plant. She observed him often from behind the partly shut louvers in the living room. His skin shiny and glinting with perspiration, his lean muscles tensed and flexed as he dug and weeded in the flower beds, the expression on his face unchanging as he wiped his brow with the back of his hand.

He handled the plants and the flowers as someone who understood them, yet she was in no doubt that these species didn't thrive in the north where he came from. From here she could see his prominent jaw grinding on a cola nut, which reddened his spaced-out teeth and tongue. She wished he wouldn't chew the red nuts all the time and allow their juices to disfigure his smile.

Did he get any enjoyment from the work he carried out with such diligence? She had wondered on countless occasions. And what made him get up and carry on day after day, living a life with no hope of things changing for the better. Like every other ordinary Ghanaian, his monthly wage didn't cover his weekly

5

outgoings. No wonder corruption was rife. Increasing inflation had eroded purchasing power, and it seemed that just about everyone had to turn to illicit means of making ends meet, even if they had two jobs like Zachariah.

It happened at the very top of society and filtered down; public officials stole or abused government property to help themselves and now it seemed that all moral integrity had dissolved. Anything was fair in this game of endurance. It infuriated Eva, this idea that what belonged to your employer was yours to steal, use, sell, so long as you could get away with it, and it had taken a while for her to understand that dishonesty was not a national trait, but a means of survival. Truthfulness was a luxury that few could afford, even Zachariah. Nonetheless, Eva had a soft spot for him, and his face etched deep by life, occasionally tugged at her heartstrings. Somehow she had learned to overlook it when Zachariah took plantain and pawpaw from her garden without asking, hiding them in the colourful woven bag he carried slung over his shoulders, or when Faustina cooked extra rice or yam so she could give some to her children or friends. But anything on a grander scale was inexcusable.

Her own husband, she had to admit, was not even entirely innocent, not entirely honest, no longer in her eyes completely morally upstanding. None of the husbands were. They were all doing things here and there that they wouldn't have thought to do back in Europe, where they had paid their bus fares and put litter in bins without fail.

Back in the kitchen, she poured herself a cup of coffee and added a drop of evaporated milk. On the radio, which buzzed almost constantly in the kitchen, there was yet another discussion about last week's budget. *'Where on earth is this country headed?'* asked an agitated panellist. Eva stirred her coffee. It was all anyone was talking about this week, the fact that inflation was now well over 100 per cent. And they could certainly talk, the Ghanaians, thought Eva, sighing again. If progress could be made by analysing or debating alone, this country would be a real paradise. The men on the radio seemed to agree about the fact that since independence there had been little real economic growth in Ghana. '*State-owned industries are woefully unproductive, foreign debt is growing, and the government is riddled with corruption,*' said the same frustrated man. It was true, increasingly so, that there were shortages of basic items, and that what was available was sold at over-inflated prices. '*And world price for cocoa continues to drop while foreign debt is increasing out of control. So, how, I ask you, with this reduced productivity and the cocoa revenue continuing to decline, is it any wonder that the budget is hopelessly undermined . . .?*' She stopped listening. In a minute they would lament the lack of a proper manufacturing industry, the lack of leadership, vision, entrepreneurship . . .

What was most depressing to her was that there would be an even further reduction in investment in education, health and transport, infrastructure that was desperately in need of funds. How far could things go before they completely fell apart, she wondered. This government had been in charge for a couple of years now, and once again the media was voicing the increasing discontent of a populace struggling to make ends meet in a country where investment had stalled and development was on hold. The evidence was everywhere; in a climate where uninterrupted investment was necessary to prevent decay, buildings were crumbling, roads melting and people grumbling.

Alfred thought it was inevitable that the discontent would lead to another coup d'état, another set of military leaders without any experience of government, but Eva didn't want to dwell on that prospect. A further set of armed officers with their own band of intoxicated militia wasn't what this country needed. But maybe a real dictator would do the trick, she thought, someone who could whip Ghana into shape. There were occasions, she was ashamed to admit to herself, when she secretly thought it made sense that some colonial masters had used canes on their servants in order to

7

get them to behave. Because, as far as she was concerned, until there is any real consequence for wrong behaviour, how can you expect people to do the right thing when doing the right thing can mean choosing death over life?

She went into the garden as Zachariah was finishing with the orchid. She watched him step back and admire his work briefly.

'Good Morning Zachariah. It is lovely, isn't it?'

He nodded at the orchid. His face was lined and bony and registered no emotion. He stepped back and moved away from her silently to continue with the garden.

She stroked the glossy green leaves of the orchid. The blooms were magnificent and smelled wonderful. The damp soil around the tree was intoxicatingly fresh, infused with the scent of rain she longed for. She filled her lungs and looked around the garden, which today was as neat and tidy as is possible in such a hot, dry land. She smiled again. 'Thank you Zachariah. You have made the garden look lovely.'

He was preparing to leave in his wake a swept, sparse lawn, blades of grass combed into submission, irregular patches of barely moistened soil around her most loved plants, weeds and fallen leaves cleared away. The sort of order she needed, that made her heart lift a little.

The garden was best at this time of day. The greenery smelled of the night, the sky was still untroubled by the brilliance of the sun. Walking in her grounds soothed her if she was upset and cheered her up if she was down. The intense night-time scents could awaken her more dormant emotions. The beauty of a single flower could bring untold delight. She never ceased to be excited when a shrub she had taken as a cutting in a friend's garden thrived, when an unusual flower bloomed.

And here she could charge her soul for the day ahead, fill up on peace and quiet and keep at bay the old dismal feelings that were trying to linger in step with the festive ones. Anniversaries always brought up other less joyous milestones and a deep, unresolved regret that demanded to be acknowledged. Here she had the room to heal, to meditate, the time to think about nothing greater than the smell of a flower, the shape of a tree, the length of life left in a dying blade of grass, the absence of new, green shoots forcing through to fill the gap left behind.

Beyond the spiked wall that surrounded their plot, a wall so high that no one could see over, life in Adebenya Estate had begun in earnest. When she first came to Africa she had found the incessant clamour hard to bear. But the high wall protected her from the chaos and arbitrariness out there, and now, from this safe distance, she found the noise comforting; the clunking of metal buckets filled with recently fetched water, the scrape of lazy flip flops on the sandy street, animated conversations, loud, mournful singing, conflicting radios, tooting cars. No one carried on in the stillness that she felt the dawning weekend deserved, or with regard for neighbourliness, for those who might yet wish to sleep.

But she was safe here. She could forget about the long petrol queues, the empty shop shelves, the dirt and the cloying stench of clogged drains, the undereducated, half-naked, skinny children who played on the streets, laughing and waving as she drove past, the disfigured beggars, the decay, the frightening lack of progress. The hopelessness that was beginning to be imprinted deeper on faces. Outside, on the mainly treeless roads of this part of Accra, the stuffy, sultry air could be overpowering, making thinking a chore, shortening tempers, adding an extreme level of physical discomfort to the most simple of tasks. But here, amidst the swishing tree branches, the rustle of lizards on crisp grass, the breeze that swirled around the thick vegetation within her white-washed, garden walls, here, she could dream, and still hope.

She looked up at the hazy sky. She could sense the dust that was infiltrating every crack and corner of her house. It would continue to seep in even if she left the louvers at an angle all day and shut them at night in an attempt to defend her home. The daily cleaning schedule that she had devised for Faustina would be all the more purposeful now with all the dust, and Eva found that satisfying. They would have to be resourceful and moderate, though, given the water situation, and she would have to be strict with Faustina, make sure she didn't neglect her regular chores.

Back in the house, Faustina had mopped the floors, cleaned the windows and laid the table for breakfast. She was polishing the furniture as she sang.

'Madam, please good morning.'

'Good morning, Faustina. I am glad you are early. There is a lot to do today, we need to . . .'

'Don't worry about anything today madam. Today I will take care of everything. I will not let you and Architect down. And if the childrens misbehave today, madam, I will beat them well. I warned them yesterday.'

'Yes, Faustina,' said Eva laughing. 'I would like to see that.'

'Madam, in fact, I am not joking,' said Faustina heading towards the kitchen.

Eva often thought how blessed her children were to grow up in an environment where they were indiscriminately and generously parented by so many different adults. Faustina had come to work for them when Simon was a toddler, and had almost immediately proceeded to murmur frequently about the need for more children in the family, reminding Eva that two was not enough. 'If something happens to one then only one left. That is not good,' she would say in front of Eva. When Eva had pointed out that she too only had two children, Faustina responded, 'Yes, but my case is a different matter, madam. Their father has got many, many childrens, so my childrens have already got plenty brothers and sisters.'

When Eva told her that she was pregnant again, Faustina had

said, 'My prayers are answered!' Then she clapped her hands as she danced about the kitchen. She picked up Simon and jiggled him on her hip while Eva watched filled with a lovely, warm feeling that allowed her to glory in her maid's approval.

It was as if Faustina knew that Joseph would be the last baby in this house. She had cradled him, rocked him and carried him at every opportunity. During the day, at the slightest sign of restlessness, Faustina would pick him up and sing to him. She cocooned him in tight sheets tied to her back while she went about her duties, and in the evening she walked up and down the garden singing to him in Ewe while he drifted into sleep. When Alfred heard her the first time he asked, 'What are you telling my son that I don't understand? Sing in English please.' Then to Eva, he said, 'Watch her. These Ewes have some peculiar manners.' After that, whenever Alfred was around, Faustina would sing the Ga lullaby, *Baby kaa fo*. Don't cry baby, where's your mummy gone?

Eva was delighted to have someone amiable around the house to help her. They had caught their previous maid stealing from them, and then when they had dismissed her, she had walked up and down the street outside the house shouting profanities and alleging all sorts of unexpected things against the Laryea family. The entire neighbourhood was entertained for about half an hour while Eva remained inside embarrassed, hoping she would soon give up and leave. None of what the maid said was true, but how *would* her neighbours know that she wasn't mean and nasty, that she hadn't cheated her maid, and she and Alfred didn't treat their servants as though they were slaves?

Faustina was still singing in the kitchen. Eva smiled, thankful that most of the preparations were complete. Faustina had cooked the *jolof* rice yesterday, and made a pork stew with a thick, oily tomato and onion gravy. Eva had baked rock cakes and biscuits. Today they would fry the chicken, which Faustina had boiled yesterday with onion, garlic and bay leaf to tenderise the meat;

the chickens were broilers, strictly not suitable for frying, but there had been nothing else. They had already cut several fingers of ripe plantains into slithers, which now lay in the freezer ready to be fried when the guests arrived. She had no idea how many would come, had no idea who Alfred had invited in addition to the agreed guests, whether the people who had promised her they would come would in fact show up. She shrugged. There would be enough food, which was the main thing. She tried not to fret about guest lists, numbers, punctuality; there would be plenty of food and drink, enough chairs and space, and no timetable. And there would be fun. She knew now that if you seat a group of Ghanaians together, preferably with something to eat and drink, their laughter would quickly come true and deep, their conversation would not cease.

Faustina stopped her singing when Eva walked in and started to hum instead. Eva got out the vegetables from the fridge: green peppers, cabbages, spring onions and carrots and began to chop them up. She wanted the right mix of colours. In her head she ran through the things they still had to do, adding to a neat list that lay next to her chopping board. Faustina had to wash and wipe the plates and cutlery they used for parties. Despite her fastidious cleaning, Eva knew geckos and cockroaches roamed her cupboards. Eva would check that her tablecloths and napkins didn't need to be ironed. The garden furniture looked pretty against the blue fabric and Zachariah had wiped all the tables and chairs before leaving, saving them one task. The guests could sit outside amidst the many trees she had planted over the years, where they could enjoy the shade, privacy and scents of the garden. There were various palms, banana and plantain plants, a large, spreading flame tree, and pink and purple bougainvillea which clambered over the white walls.

There was also the chest freezer to pack with bottles of beer and soft drinks, more ice to be made, several large plastic bottles to be filled with cooled boiled water and then popped into the freezer later to ensure that there was enough cold water for the guests. At least there was electricity. She dispelled the urge to go and check the taps again.

She was deep in thought, comfortably aware that she was well prepared for her guests when the gate bell rang, followed quickly by a loud car horn. Eva looked at the clock in the kitchen. It was only seven-thirty, too early even for unannounced visitors. And the clock couldn't be far wrong; she had reset it just last week and it only lost a minute or so each day. The bell rang again and she heard a woman call Faustina. Eva's heart sank as she recognised the voice of her mother-in-law. Why was Gladys here so early? Although Eva was forbidden from calling her Gladys out loud, she referred to her as such in her mind, to her friends and to the children. 'Only her peers can call her by her first name,' Alfred had explained the first time after Eva's faux pas. 'You must call her Auntie Gee, like we all do.' When Eva asked him why he didn't call his mother by some term that indicated their relationship, he simply shrugged and replied, 'I don't know. I have always called her Auntie Gee. I suppose that is what I heard everyone else call her when I was little, so I copied them.'

In fact, Eva had broken a great many rules in the early days. It had seemed Alfred was correcting her continually: never sniff food that is handed to you on a plate; never use your left hand to give something to someone, that hand is reserved for dirty work, the right hand is for clean work; on no account call someone 'silly' or 'daft'. And, anyone older than you is owed more respect than you; you must not argue with them or contradict them. She had learned even more just from watching him. He smiled and nodded politely to older relatives even if they were talking utter nonsense, and he said 'yes', even when she knew he was thinking 'no', and agreed with them to their face, just to express the opposite view later. Eva had struggled with this unwillingness to question. It was too close to dishonesty and plain lying. She couldn't do that, it was one step too far. Instead, she had perfected

13

the art of smiling and saying nothing whatsoever when she didn't want to contradict someone or to lie. She had learned to ask fewer questions too, even, perhaps especially, when things made no sense whatsoever to the ordered way of thinking with which she had been raised.

She stood and watched the commotion at the gate, safe in the knowledge that she was hidden from sight. Finally Solomon, Alfred's driver, found the right key and unlocked the padlock, swinging the gate open. A car edged on to the driveway, and from its egg-yolk side panels, Eva knew it was a taxi. She saw Gladys waving her arms about and Solomon and the driver unloading the boot of the taxi. Solomon put a large crate on his head and began to head down the path towards the kitchen. The taxi driver followed with a weighty hessian bag in each hand, and behind him, Faustina and Akua, Gladys' young maid, followed with large, shiny aluminium pots balanced on their heads. Eva peered in astonishment as they approached the kitchen like a troop of farmers returning with a bountiful harvest, smiles of victory on their faces. Now that they were closer, Eva could see the cage on Solomon's head contained a huddle of fluttering feathers, and over the chatter of Faustina's loud directions, she heard the desperate clucking of chickens. Her heart sank. She wiped her hands on her apron and went outside.

'Surprise, surprise, Eva,' said Gladys, beaming. 'I told Alfred not to tell you.'

'I am surprised,' said Eva. 'What is going on?'

'Have you forgotten that you have a party today? *Atoo, atoo*, let me hug you.' Gladys said, wrapping her arms around Eva and ignoring her daughter-in-law's discomfort. 'How are you today?'

'I am fine,' said Eva easing out of Gladys' embrace. 'But why are you here so early? What are all these chickens for?' With her heart sinking, she hoped that she was mistaken.

'For good fried chicken you need freshly slaughtered fowls. Yes, yes Solomon, put the chickens there. Akua, no! Don't put the food on the ground. Ah! But are you stupid or what? Driver, thank you.' She held Eva's arm, 'Eva, what is the matter?'

'We have no water!' said Eva emphatically.

'Oh, don't worry, we don't need much water. And Solomon is strong, no? He can go and fetch water for us if it finishes.'

'I have already cooked two chickens . . .'

'Only two? That is not enough. You know what our families are like. As plentiful as sea sand and as scattered as the stars in the northern sky. But they gather where there is free food and free drink. They can smell it wherever they are. Don't worry, they will come, we just don't know who and how many, or even when, so we have to be prepared.' She patted Eva's arm as they walked into the kitchen. 'I am telling you, don't worry,' she said, giving the word 'don't' several extra o's to emphasise her instruction. 'I have brought another four chickens. Together we will have enough. Yours can be kept for emergency if we run out.' She untied her headscarf and put it on the formica kitchen surface that was already curling upwards in the drying air. Her short plaits, which were old and coming loose at her scalp, were pressed down to her head by a black hair net. She untied the extra piece of cloth, which matched her two-piece outfit, and laid it over a chair Then she pointed to her bag and said to Akua, who was hovering like a timid shadow, 'Get my house dress. It is in the bag. Solomon, get the last box from the car. But careful please, it is fragile. And after give the chickens some water to drink before we kill them. Taxi driver, you too, drink some water before you go,' she said as she rummaged in her bra for money to pay him. 'Eva, I forgot my money, can you pay the driver? I am going to change and then I will start straight away,' she said, taking off her shoes to reveal pinched feet. 'Ah, that's better. Now all I need is some tea to refresh me. Faustina, can you make some for me?' she asked as she walked off to the downstairs toilet.

Eva looked at the carton that Solomon had placed on the table. It was taped, keeping whatever was in it well hidden. She sniffed

15

long and hard. It had to be something sweet. Perhaps those pink and orange biscuits Gladys often made that left her mouth coated with margarine and tasting of artificial flavourings. Yes, come to think of it, she could smell almond essence.

Gladys returned to the kitchen wearing a floor-length loose-fitting dress. She stood for a moment observing the activity disapprovingly.

'What's in there?' asked Eva.

'Aha! A surprise, a surprise.'

'Well?'

'Ah-ah,' Gladys said clapping her hands. 'Curiosity killed the cat, remember?'

Eva rolled her eyes.

'Come now Eva, let us go and have some tea.'

'I am actually in the middle of something.'

'Don't worry yourself Eva. Come and sit down. You have to learn to relax! Drink some tea with me first.' She walked off into the living room with the certainty that Eva would follow. 'Oh!' she exclaimed suddenly, throwing her arms into the air, making Eva start. 'We had some terrible news last week. My neighbour's granddaughter died,' she wailed as she lowered herself into the armchair. 'A mere baby. And I tell you, a child must not die before his mother. Before his grandmother even? Oh God, show us the error of our ways that we might not wander off your pathways into death and destruction.' She sniffed loudly and sat back in the armchair. She stretched her toes and wriggled them on the rug in front of her. 'Thankfully the child had been baptised, so there is no question about whether his name will be in the book of life eh? St Peter will have no difficulty identifying him, unlike . . .'

'I am sorry to hear such dire news. Send our condolences, will you please?'

'I want you to understand that the baptism of my grandson is not a trifling matter.'

'Let's not talk about that now,' said Eva firmly.

'Hmm.'

'We *will* do it,' Eva said, trying to sound reassuring. 'We just haven't decided when.'

'Tomorrow waits for no man you know. Today is all we know we have. And even then, we don't know what is around the corner of this very day. One minute we are walking along, everything tickety-boo, and the next, we are struck with unforeseen circumstances that shatter our world and make us long for something meaningful to say, but all that comes, again and again is, "had I known". But it never comes at first you know?'

Eva looked at her watch. 'Yes, you have told me.'

Gladys had wanted them to have a church service today before they celebrated their anniversary with 'alcoholic beverages and such like'. 'After all,' she had reminded Alfred and Eva, 'the longevity of your marriage is thanks to the grace of only God.'

'It is good to give thanks Eva,' she said now, looking at Eva imploringly. 'One day you will understand that.' For the next few moments she tutted periodically and chewed her lips to make disapproving sounds, stretched the dress over her knees pulling out any folds and creases and then asked, 'How are the children?'

'Fine.'

'Good, good. We will by all means enjoy today.'

Faustina came with a tray and placed it in front of Gladys. On it there was a cup of lukewarm, sweet, milky tea and a plate of buttered bread.

'Oh delicious,' said Gladys leaning forward and tearing off a piece of bread. She dunked it in her tea and slurped on it hungrily. 'But where is yours Eva?'

'I am fine, thank you. I just had a coffee.'

'No. Faustina bring madam some tea. Bring the pot. I will also have some more'

Eva said nothing while she waited for Faustina to bring them the tea. She took it, had a sip and put the cup on the table. It was disgusting, overly sweetened and with too much milk.

'Thank you Fausti,' said Gladys. 'How are you these days?'

Faustina smiled. Her hands had been clasped behind her back, but she relaxed a little now.

'Please Auntie, I am fine.'

'How is that daughter of yours eh? Is she still at school?'

'Please, yes. Please, Peace is going to Form Three now. Please, she will like to be a teacher.'

'Good, good. Tell her to learn hard. We need more teachers. And what about Harmony?'

'Please he wants to be a mechanic.'

'I see,' said Gladys, leaning back in the armchair. 'Anyways I hope they can help us to fetch water later if we need some more?'

'Please yes Auntie.'

'Good.' Gladys balanced the mug of tea on her belly and sipped it periodically. 'Okay, go and continue your work. We are working extra hard today, understand?'

'Please, yes,' said Faustina, nodding before she walked off.

'And you are still not wearing shoes? Didn't I tell you to wear shoes? This is not the village, you know.'

'Please, yes,' said Faustina, sauntering through the kitchen door without turning around.

'These village girls,' said Gladys, sucking on another lump of bread she had dunked in her tea. 'They come here and they don't want to learn our ways. You must watch her daughter too. She is a bad girl. I can tell. I saw her just the other day when I was leaving here. She was with a man who had his hand on her waist. Hmm! No modesty whatsoever.'

Eva nodded, not knowing what to say. She shifted in the chair. 'Auntie Gee, I think I need to go and get on with things in the kitchen. The children will be down soon and then . . .'

'Oh don't mind me. You go. I will join you when I finish,' said Gladys. 'But you look too stressed up Eva. Don't be worry. It will be hunky-dory-fine. There is plenty of room in the kitchen for you and me. And anyway Akua prefers to cook on the coal pot, so she will even fry the chicken outside.' She clicked her tongue and continued. 'Is the German lady coming? You know, the crazy one, is it Margaret?'

'Margrit, yes.'

'Margaret. Good. And that Russian too? The one who wears the short, short dresses?'

'Yelena, yes, and you've met Dahlia Ejura-Wilson? Her husband was friends with Alfred in London.'

'The West Indian lady?'

'Yes. They wouldn't miss it.'

They wouldn't miss anything she hosted for the world, and their presence gave her added confidence. The four of them spent a lot of time together and had formed a sort of surrogate family unit. There weren't that many foreign wives in Accra, where everyone seemed to know each other, so it was inevitable that they would have met at some point, but Alfred had known Dahlia's husband Vincent in England, and the two women had clicked from their first meeting soon after Eva arrived. They met Margrit not long after at some party or other, and Yelena had come up to them on the beach one Saturday a few years ago and asked to join them. She had introduced herself and told them about how she had recently arrived in Accra to find that the father of her twin boys was married. She told the story in a way that made them laugh with her, rather than feel sorry for her, which Eva had found admirable. Margrit had put her arm around Yelena and said 'we can be just as good a family to you. I am always telling these two how important it is that we foreigners stick together. We don't have to be isolated and helpless, we too can have a club, our own association where we belong without feeling odd and foreign all the time.' Yelena had dabbed at her eyes, smilingly, the first and last time that Eva had ever seen her come close to tears.

And now, most Saturdays the four of them went to the beach club leaving behind their homes for a day, along with everything else they wanted to forget. Paradise Beach Club was worth the hour long journey from Accra westwards towards Cape Coast; it was a breathtaking beach with white sand and coconut palms that leaned towards the surf, tall and heavy with fruit. And the sea was gentle, with cobalt waves, unlike the large unimpeded, brown swell that thrashed the rocky shore of Accra's coastline and made swimming there treacherous. The shoreline formed a large bay that tapered about half a mile out to sea where the breakers splashed and crashed. By the time the water reached the shore's edge, the ocean had lost its ruthlessness.

As soon as their cars came to a stop, the children spilled out and ran to the shore. Shoes came off and were flung towards mothers. Shirts were pulled off, shorts down and in they ran, splashing and shrieking in the cool waves.

They took picnics, which they shared sitting in the shade enjoying the refreshing sea breeze that was so absent in town. Dahlia usually brought brown rice and beans with delicious chicken, Eva took sandwiches and sometimes a cake, and Yelena always made some interesting salad with various beans and pulses and little grated cheese. Everyone brought a coolbox with beer, minerals for the children and water. Alfred was the only one of the husbands who joined them regularly. Vincent never had and Kojo was usually working. Alfred said he liked having the women to himself; he would chat with them a while, play with the kids, then have a swim, invariably going out beyond the waves which Eva hated. It was perilous, she reminded him, even for the strongest swimmers, but he laughed at her and only returned when he had had enough. Then he would settle down to sleep in the shade as soon as he had eaten, leaving the women to sip beer and gossip happily.

They seemed never to have enough time to talk about what they talked about. Husbands, the good and bad sides of them, and the endless question, what to do about Wisdom, the absent father of Yelena's twins. They talked of any news they had had from families back home, the particular things they missed, what they

20

longed for most. Primarily, they laughed. Even about the miserable things. There was always one of them who could steer the conversation back on to jolly ground, encouraging the others so that they didn't become too morose or too nostalgic. They never ran out of things to say.

They could miss home together, more particularly at this time of year. And out of the earshot of those they might otherwise affront, they could safely reminisce about their food, their weather, their own traditions, fostering their camaraderie as foreigners, clinging to what they believed, where they came from, afraid to let go completely of who they were. They were all unwilling and unable to leave behind the women they had been before love had brought them to Ghana.

Later in the day, Eva and Margrit usually had a swim. They played in the surf, trying to withstand the power of the waves, falling and rolling in the sandy sea. Eva was secretly quite proud that she could wear the same bikini she had worn when she first came to Accra. But Dahlia never wore a swimsuit, preferring to remain in her tie-dye dresses and a large floppy hat. She hadn't learned to swim, and didn't fancy starting now. Yelena didn't swim either, but she wore very attractive one-piece swimsuits with belts or buckles or bows, and various bits cut out. She was always fully made up, manicured and pedicured, and looked rather like a glamorous extra on a film set, even trying to walk in her high heeled shoes in the sand.

The same thing had brought each of them to Ghana, a place they had previously known nothing about: the love of a man they had met while he had been studying something lofty in Europe so he could return to his homeland with letters proudly positioned after his name. But when they got here, none of them had found things to be the way they had hoped or expected. Life as a foreign spouse was hard, something they freely acknowledged to each other. It was all so strange and unsettling, sometimes leaving them feeling exhausted. There had been no welcoming committee, no one to hand down guidelines on making a cross-cultural marriage work in an alien land, and no one at home to whom they could turn for help with the problems they faced here.

Even if they had been able to, how could they have described what life was really like? The alien culture, the distance from home, the unimaginable challenges, the incapacitating heat, the collapsing economy, and now, a drought which might mean yet more food shortages. Besides, Eva's parents were not only too far away, they really didn't want to know.

But if she had to have only one regular favourite occurrence in her life, it was this: the journey home after an enchanting day on the beach with her family and friends. The children browner, salty and tired, their little bodies collapsing into sleep. Alfred refreshed, whistling to himself, and her feeling restored and feeling able to face whatever the following week brought. She would rest her hand on his thigh, and enjoy the quiet as the sun began to set.

'Anyway, she always looks nice, even though her dresses are too short,' said Auntie Gee, intruding Eva's thoughts. She nodded and smiled, giving Eva permission to leave. Then, as if she had suddenly remembered something, she said, 'Tell Fausti to fry me some eggs. I am very starving. And you also need to eat. You are too thin, Eva. It makes your face look old.'

Auntie Gee watched Eva go. She muttered, 'You see? If *I* don't do my duty, then who will?' She tutted and asked a little louder, 'Who?' shrugging at the walls covered with masks and paintings, carvings and beads whose significance and potency Eva had no idea about. These Europeans coming here and calling any knick and knack 'art', telling us that it doesn't matter what it means, it is just *simply beautiful*. She could hear their sing-song accent in her head, their naivety and ignorance ringing loudly. Her mouth was twitching, her nose and cheeks moving like a rabbit from the effort of restraining the words in her mouth from tumbling out. After all, he is *my* son. My *only* son. Unquestionably, the possibilities for offence were quite simply endless when dealing with a foreign daughter-in-law.

She put another cube of sugar in her tea and stirred it, rattling the cup and spilling some on to the saucer, which she poured carefully back into the cup. She stirred some more, and then like a child relishing the forbidden, she added a bit more milk, a little more sugar. To hell with her blood pressure! After all the healing services she had attended, that was where that particular ailment should be by now.

She made a mental note to remind Alfred that she needed more provisions. She was running out of everything. She dunked the last bit of buttered bread in her cup and ate it. She watched the melted butter dance on the surface of the tea, then slurped the rest of it in one go. She dabbed her mouth with the hem of her dress and sat back. Although she had sworn that she would resist the urge to reminisce once again, she thought how different it would be if Ignatius were here. How much easier it would be to have him here, giving her reason to hold her head up that little bit higher and confront things head on, not having to resort to under-hand methods like a criminal with something to hide. Sometimes she wished she could wear a badge, a T-shirt even, that reminded people that she too had once had a husband, because having a husband had given her a standing she didn't even realise she had until he went and dropped dead at the stingy age of thirty-seven. A few years ago she had taken off her wedding ring when it begun to cut too deeply into her finger, a decision she repented bitterly to this day, because try as she might, she hadn't been able to get the ring back on. It dangled on a chain from her neck now, but it wasn't the same as having it on her finger, and replacing it didn't seem appropriate. Where would she be now if her life had wound this way instead of that? A different turn here and there, and who knew how things might have turned out. 'Hmm!' she said vehemently, as she sat back folding her arms on top of her belly.

*

23

Eva had slipped back out into the garden. She leaned on the veranda rail and puffed out, turned her head this way and that, trying to loosen the tension that had descended. She wanted to be alone for five more minutes. She needed to restore the equilibrium Gladys had so quickly put an end to, to try and escape the questions and longings that had been plaguing her recently, and which Gladys, completely unaware that she was doing so, had started to trail in with her.

Presumably it was because of the anniversary that she had been thinking rather a lot about how her parents might have played their parts in the drama of her life: mother, father, in-laws, grandparents, roles still gaping after so long.

She looked with tenderness at the fragile earth, loose and flyaway where Zachariah hadn't watered. The trees sagged lifeless, even this early. They would spend the rest of the day dropping leaves and shedding bark like sacrifices to the sun, bartering for longer life. She looked up at the unchanging high white cloud and dust. It would be another very hot day. Rain clouds would be unusual at this time of year, even though they hadn't come when they were due. In spite of the stark reality, Eva still hoped that things had merely shifted badly, that the rain they should have had a few months ago had simply been held up. But there hadn't been a drop here on the coast for months, and it was unlikely that there would be any for another while. A few weeks ago the Accra Metropolitan Council confirmed that the region was experiencing a drought. They began turning off the water supply more regularly, and always without a warning, which infuriated Eva. She could have told them there was a drought. Her records had made that plain weeks ago; she had been recording rainfall for years, ever since they had first moved into this house, when she decided to take gardening seriously. Knowing when there might be rain, when her garden might be allowed to thrive naturally, helped her plan. It baffled Eva that the authorities couldn't warn the residents that the water was about to be turned off. She

imagined some bored fellow sitting in a disorganised office looking out at the water levels of the reservoir and deciding when to
switch the water on and off. She could visualise him going outside
on a whim and turning off a massive tap, then falling asleep and
forgetting to turn it back on. Where was he now? Hopefully on his
way to turn the tap back on. It was Saturday, after all, and the
people of Accra deserved some water for the weekend. As she
walked, she wished her desire for clean flowing water was being
transmitted to him through her slow, pounding steps by some
ancient signalling system, and that by the time she had finished
admiring her garden it would be back on.

Eva was particularly proud and protective of the garden
because it was entirely her creation. Alfred had been so busy over-
seeing the construction of their new house from plans he had
drawn up himself, that he totally overlooked the garden. She had
watched with mounting disappointment as the house grew up
from the ground, a large, square dwelling of the modern style that
she didn't understand, which ate up too much of what initially had
looked like a decent plot of land. She had been startled by his
design. It looked rather like a cabin, with small windows and
square rooms. But when he begged her to demonstrate a little
more interest in their new home, she suggested that she could be
in charge of the garden, and was pleased when he hesitated only
momentarily before agreeing. 'But you will bear in mind the
building's architectural relevance?' to which she had smiled imp-
ishly, making him drop his head into his hands and shake his head
in defeat.

She had set to work immediately, energised, yet daunted.
Suddenly, the garden seemed big and barren, an expanse littered
with rocks and stones that had been displaced by the construction
of the house. She replaced the rubble and grainy red earth with
dark, rich soil and planted indiscriminately, eager to soften the
straight concrete lines and disguise the smell of new paint, transforming it into, in her opinion, one of the most beautiful gardens

in Accra. All this in spite of the fact that she had no real knowledge of gardening or plants. She had enjoyed imposing her taste on some part of her new home and over the years had never overlooked an opportunity to take cuttings from another garden if she liked a plant. Now, the most admired feature of her garden was that it was like a jungle, when it was thriving, in any event. Alfred told her that he was resigned to the 'beautiful mess' the garden had become, but he still asked her regularly to tame it, to cut this or trim that, advice she generally ignored.

It had been a slow, hard job, and in the process, Eva realised how determined and headstrong she could be.

Those were distant days, when Eva had still been coming to terms with her self-imposed exile, when she indulged too often in wondering what her life would have been like if she hadn't gone to London at all. Might she have moved to Norwich? Wouldn't she be married to a nice English man with two children, paying weekly visits to her parents, his parents, gliding through life effortlessly, slotting in wherever she went naturally, not having to squeeze into places she didn't quite fit, uneasy in circumstances still unfamiliar after so many years?

As soon as she and Alfred had moved in, relieved to have their own place, she had set about creating a haven that nourished her soul and soothed the homesickness that manifested itself with symptoms as real and as incapacitating as any physical illness. Now, the fact that none of the houses nearby were similar to hers seemed irrelevant. She no longer felt guilt because of the height of their wall lined with sharp spikes or their imposing wrought iron gate. She had become used to the disparity between her life and the lives around her, even though at first she had been shocked by how easily the haves lived on top of the have-nots in this city. Now she didn't think too much about their driveway, home to Alfred's new Mercedes-Benz and her old Datsun, or about the wall-less, gate-less, single storey dwellings in which her neighbours lived, each of which housed multiple families and which had no gardens to speak of. She no longer let it affect her that her neighbours had latrines instead of flushing toilets, that they cooked outside on coal pots, and that they slept to the hum of the Laryea's air-conditioners. In fact, she rarely allowed herself to wonder what the neighbours thought about her house, which stood in their midst two storeys high and too many rooms wide, like an alien ship that has landed in the wrong place.

Eva was thinking about the things she had to do when Faustina came running towards her with a smile on her face, her voice puffed from the exertion.

'Madam, water. The water is coming plenty.'

Eva felt her soul float upwards. Water? The relief, the joy. She smiled at Faustina. Her eyes were open in disbelief, questioning. 'The water is on? How wonderful!' She could almost have hugged Faustina, but instead she clenched both her fists in triumph, in a gesture far less exuberant than she felt. 'But how did you know?' she asked. She had been sure that she would be the one to find out, she who had monitored the lack of water so closely all this while.

'We leave the outside tap in the boys' quarters on full blast so that we can hear the water hitting the concrete when it comes back,' said Faustina. 'Don't worry, we are filling all the containers already.' As she reached the kitchen veranda she turned and said to Eva, 'Auntie Gee says we should slaughter the chickens now. Madam, if you like you can go inside because of the blood.'

Eva walked back into the house, so reinvigorated by this wonderful news that she was able to ignore Faustina's instructions. There was water when she most needed it. It amounted to a miracle; a magnificent blessing. The tank would fill again, ensuring that there would be water in the house for days. Clean, clear water from each and every tap in her house!

Chapter Two

Many years had passed since Yelena first met Wisdom Tekyi, a charming Ghanaian medical student, in Kiev. This morning, at just past eight-thirty, they sat in the living room of his house on a sofa that was still covered with protective plastic sheets. She had started to bring the twins to visit their father a few weeks ago, and hard as the visits were, she felt a little victorious today. A family of sorts, Yelena thought, with a smile fixed to her face.

They had had to wait half an hour for Wisdom to appear from his bedroom, clearly fresh from sleep, but Yelena didn't mind. She had learned that it was better to arrive when he was still asleep. Any later in the day and, as she had discovered from some of her earlier attempts at 'family time', he might have gone out already, claiming some fictitious appointment when she later confronted him.

The living room was a lot shabbier than Yelena would have had it; dark and dingy and in need of a good clean, the plum-red linoleum floor was lifting in several places, and there were numerous tiles missing. She was dying with curiosity to see the rest of the house. And she had tried taking wrong turns on the way to the bathroom, but the Wife seemed to know her intentions and was always on hand to steer her through the right door.

The house was filled with the scent of cooking palm oil, but Yelena knew better than to expect any kind of sustenance. That was just another of the ways that the Wife could slight her; no self-respecting Ghanaian hostess would allow visitors to her house to leave unfed. Ah, but Yelena didn't care. They were here. For the third time! The boys on either side of her, sitting closer than they normally did, and across them, Wisdom with his legs ajar, his hands clasped on his thigh with a smile, spouting sporadic questions:

'Eh! Have you grown again since the last time, what is your mother feeding you?'

A polite shrug from both boys.

'So, tell me, how is school?'

'Okay,' they mumbled.

'You must not say 'okay', that is American English. Do you understand me? You must say 'all right,' which is the correct way.'

'All right,' they chorused.

And what right do you have to correct them? Yelena asked in her head, smiling from child to child.

'And what is your favourite subject?'

'I don't know,' said Joel.

'Maths,' said Jonah.

He had asked this question before, Yelena thought. But then, he most probably never spoke to his other children. It wasn't a usual sight here, after all, a father interacting freely with his young children. She kept smiling.

'You are studying hard I hope?'

They nodded.

Yelena beamed at them, touched Joel's hands to get him to stop biting his nails. She looked up at Wisdom who was staring at her cleavage. She stared at him until he realised she was watching him and he grinned at her, revealing the gap in his molars that she had always found so endearing. What a mother will do for the children she loves, she thought, as she adjusted the skirt of her dress, moving her legs, which once unstuck, slid with sweat on the plastic seat.

She was tiny, just over five feet tall and slender, but she knew exuded that indefinable thing that made a woman sexy. The soft, pink skin, perfectly manicured pink nails, her wide blue, trusting eyes and her full mouth, almost too big for her face. She wasn't trying to get Wisdom back, after all he was married now, officially this time, and the Wife had four children, yet when Yelena took the boys to visit him, she was aware that she made particular effort with her appearance. Her hair was as he had liked it, her nails freshly painted, her make-up perfect. Today, she knew that she was radiant, her chest smooth and heaving in a frilly blue and white polka-dot dress that was tight in the right places and just the ideal length.

'I am still looking for a husband,' she said laughing, whenever her friends commented with admiration on the care she took over the way she looked. She longed to be a proper bride at least once in her life, to be loved so completely by one man that he married her so he could have her to himself. But she recognised that to be just hot-blooded sentimentalism running unchecked. In truth, most of the time, she didn't think having a husband was all that great, emphatically not if he was as lazy as Wisdom, or as evil as Vincent. There was something about that man that disturbed her, and the way he treated Dahlia, without the faintest bit of respect, made her mad. Yelena often wondered why she put up with him. No, there seemed to be too much at stake in marriage, the odds of making the wrong choice stacked against her.

In the background, the Wife was hovering and doing, watching and listening. She didn't like this arrangement one bit, so Wisdom had said, but Yelena knew that he would use any excuse to get out of his obligations. Nevertheless, during the first visit, Yelena had gone to talk to her in private and assured her that she didn't want anything from Wisdom, definitely not money. Well, she lied, but she had no guilt about such things, not like Eva who seemed to think there was never an occasion when it was fitting to bend the truth a little. No, she had told the Wife with a straight face that she only wanted a teeny little bit of his time so that her boys might know their father, their heritage, their ancestry, 'You know how important that is, don't you?' she had said, smiling at the Wife who maintained her curious expression, part bored, part angry, with one eyebrow permanently raised high above the other.

What on earth did they have in common, she couldn't help wondering whenever she saw her. And why had she, Yelena, not been interesting enough, beautiful enough, sexy enough, just simply enough?

When Yelena first met Wisdom Tekyi, he told her about his country, how no one in his family had ever been to university, and how it was a tragedy that the first president of his country, Nkrumah, had been overthrown; it was because of him that a man like Wisdom, from a family that had not produced a single higher-educated male, could study medicine. She had known from the beginning that she would fall in love with him, and when he said he loved her too, she was ecstatic. She became pregnant unexpectedly and he was pleased. Then, when they found out there were two babies, *he* was ecstatic. Naturally, she assumed she would be going with him when he returned to Accra, but he decided that he should go ahead and prepare for them. By the time the boys were two, he had still not told her to come and join him and she decided to take matters into her own hands. She was eager to escape from the confines of the USSR even though she didn't have a ring on her finger and her destination was one of which she knew nothing, so with the blessing of her mother, she had left her homeland behind and travelled on three different planes to Accra to be with her husband-to-be.

When she arrived eight years ago, Yelena found out that her doctor was in fact already married, and she was heartbroken. She tried to take her abandonment heroically. 'It's happened,' she would say whenever her friends had expressed sympathy at her situation in the beginning and then she would quickly change the subject. It was pointless to dwell on it, after all. She knew that they assumed from her behaviour that she had accepted the way things were, that she didn't hurt as much as she did. But she was like her mother in that regard. She got angry if she felt vulnerable, and she didn't particularly like being angry.

His rejection had come as a great surprise to her. He was so different from the man she had fallen in love with, and it had bothered her for ages that she had made such an error of judgement, wondered how she had made such a big mistake.

She had of course thought about returning to Russia with the boys to be close to her mother when she realised that Wisdom didn't want them. But she had known for some time that she would never leave Accra. There were not many black people in Kiev, and she didn't want her children to grow up feeling like a minority. She and Wisdom had had their own fair share of negative comments when they had been walking about the city hand in hand back then. Besides, she loved her boys too much, and when she said she would kill anyone who harmed them, insulted them, treated them badly, she didn't think her friends realised how serious she was.

It irritated her that Wisdom didn't play his role fully or willingly. Oh, it made her so angry that her boys were living among their own, but had little contact with their extended Ghanaian family. As they approached their teenage years, she was beginning to worry that teaching them Fanti, their father's language, wasn't enough to make them feel like they belonged here, even though they knew nothing else. It frustrated her that they might, in spite of all her efforts, not feel fully Ghanaian, fully at home and might therefore be inspired to go elsewhere to find where they belonged. They too were called 'obronie' because of their brown, mixed-race skin.

It wasn't an easy decision to live with. She had to combat the feeling of being trapped; this wasn't a place one could freely come and go from. The costs of flights was exorbitant. She couldn't afford to go on a visit and hope to build her house in the same decade.

She hated being restricted more than the fact that Wisdom had abandoned her. She told her friends, 'My mother told me that when she used to put me in a playpen so that she could get on with her chores I would bawl until she took me out. She thought that I was not normal like other babies who could sit serenely and chew on rubber rings. She was uneasy until my grandmother told her, "How can you wish for your child to be normal? Normal people don't go to the moon. Be grateful that your baby doesn't sit still. She is impatient. This is a sign to rejoice in. It means she is clever. Very clever." I had a lot to live up to after that. Everywhere I went, I was introduced as Yelena-the-clever-one. "She is almost a genius," my grandmother used to say. "Look at her protruding forehead, very large brain." As soon as I was old enough and suspected that the rest of the world wasn't as terrible as we were told in school I wanted to see it for myself. And I was never going to make it in the ballet or the gymnastics team, despite the efforts of my mother. She spent hours taking me from one training session to the next. And you wonder why I cannot stand exercise in any form now? My poor mother, I think she is still devastated that I didn't live up to her hopes in me.'

For his part, Wisdom had explained that when he returned to Ghana he had informed his family that he had a 'Russian common law wife', but, he pointed out, they had not been satisfied and they had taken it upon themselves to find him a proper wife, a Ghanaian who would bear him Ghanaian children. 'There was nothing I could do about it,' he said to her, as if discussing an ill-timed rainstorm or some other inconvenient natural phenomenon.

The visit ended and Yelena drove fast with gritted teeth, turning corners too tightly, going through lights as they turned red, and mumbling angrily whenever a *trotro* pulled out in front of

33

her, or a taxi swerved off the road to pick up passengers without warning. She looked at her boys in the rear-view mirror. Their questions had dried up a little with age, and today they seemed to have taken the visit in their stride. There had been less complaining about it beforehand, and their facial expressions were possibly less perturbed than they had been the first time. Oh, but they had to have questions. Feelings that they wanted to hide from her. After all, they were 50 per cent Wisdom, weren't they? She didn't want them to grow up thinking that they were by default half bad. Yes, they had to have feelings, and questions, and in their own undeveloped way, reservations too.

She pulled into the car park of the French supermarket. It tried to sell what Europeans expected to be able to buy, and what aspiring Africans thought they needed, all presented in an air-conditioned setting, with gleaming stone floors and clean shelves. She turned to smile at the boys; shopping would help.

Inside, she couldn't believe the sight; the store had been reasonably stocked last week, and now it looked as if the shelves had emptied themselves. Shopping had just started to become a little easier, a bit more predictable, and almost everything one needed could be found eventually, even if it took a few trips. A few weeks ago, she had treated herself to some imported honey and jam because the local pineapple jam and marmalade had disappeared.

She filled her basket with tinned milk and sugar and bought a couple of tins of margarine. There were a few bottles of cheap sparkling wine and she bought two; one for Eva and Alfred, and the other as a gift for their next visit to Wisdom. She preferred vodka herself, but during the first months in Accra, she had realised that alcohol wasn't a terribly clever accompaniment to aloneness and she chose now to drink only in the company of friends.

At the till, she asked the girls why they were so low on stock.

'Madam, we have short everything. And we have not had any delivery for some days now.'

'I can see that, but I have never seen it so empty. When are you getting new supplies?'

'Please, we don't know.'

'Is Mr Tekyi in?'

'The manager?'

'Yes . . .?'

'Please, no.'

'Where is he?'

'Please, he has gone out.'

'Well, do you know when he will be back?'

'Please, he didn't tell us.'

It was looking like it would be one of those pointless trips, one of those drawn out futile conversations. But Yelena refused to give up. 'Is his deputy in?'

The girl turned to one of her colleagues and said, 'Who is Mr Tekyi's deputy?'

'Is it Mr Sowah?' asked her colleague helpfully.

'No, isn't he the chief cashier?'

'Ah! Then maybe she means Mr Quartey.'

'Yes, I think you are right. But madam, please Mr Quartey is also not in.'

Yelena looked at them in amazement. Mr Quartey may or may not be the deputy manager, and he may or may not be on his way in, these girls wouldn't know.

'Anyway, please madam, how are you?' the shop assistant asked smiling.

'I'm fine, but there isn't much to buy.'

'No madam. It's not good, isn't it? Things are falling apart again.'

Yelena shook her head.

'But by all means we will get a delivery if not tomorrow or the day after, maybe then next week, after Xmas. Try and come back. I am told we will get Quaker Oats and Milo and different, different things.'

35

Yelena shook her head again. The shop was empty apart from her. The minute she left the women would resume their conversation. How bored they must be.

'Bye madam,' they chorused jollily as she walked out with her meagre shopping.

She laid her purchases in the boot of her car underneath an old towel and headed to the post office, the only place where she could make an international phone call. She joined the queue of people lined up in the shade of the building, while the boys sat on a low wall that ran around the perimeter of the building. How she hoped she would get through to her mother today.

A number of hawkers paraded with their wares, calling attention to themselves. A pair of young boys carried wooden trays full of colourful combs and sunglasses, a girl came by selling PK chewing gum and Hacks cough sweets, and another carried a large rimmed dish on her head filled with lurid polyester brassieres. Yelena still found this trading interesting and watched and wondered how much any of them had to sell to make any money. On the pavement by the gate, a woman was selling rice and stew from a permanent stall, and Yelena watched her serve a steady stream of customers. The woman wiped sweat from her brow periodically and swished away flies that were attracted by a filthy drain nearby that bubbled in the heat. Whenever the wind direction changed, a sour stench from the stagnant water filled the air and Yelena held her breath in disgust. Next to her, another woman was selling tea and bread. She broke the buns in half for those customers who wished and spread thick, unmelting Blue Band margarine on to the fluffy, white insides before wrapping it in paper. Those who wanted tea received it in purple and brown plastic mugs and stood close by in the shade of a wide tree sipping the weak, sweet liquid. She watched a thin old lady dunk her bread carefully in her tea before each mouthful and slowly chew. When she was finished, she emptied the mug in one swig before returning it to the large tin basin next to the vendor, which was filled with soapy water.

Yelena bought the boys some bubble gum from a lady selling sweets in jars. She watched them unwrap their treat quickly. The gum was incidental to the tattoo that the piece of gum came wrapped in. First Jonas then Joel licked the back of the little piece of paper and then stuck it on to their bony arms, pressing and scraping, then checking that the image had been transferred, licking a bit more, pressing harder and then finally, peeling back the bit of cellophane gently to expose multicoloured pictures that Yelena admired in awe, even though she didn't have a clue what they were meant to be. She smiled happily as they compared their pictures, and then began the tough process of softening their chewing gum and trying to blow bubbles.

After nearly an hour in line, it was Yelena's turn. She dialled her mother's phone number numerous times, each time waiting anxiously to see if the line clicked into life. Finally, it crackled alive, she heard a dialling tone so very far away, and then her mother's muffled voice. Her mother had always hated the phone, mistrusted people who couldn't tell you what they had to say face to face. 'Hello! Hello!' she barked over and over sounding irritated.

'It's me, Yelena.' She heard her voice return down the line a few seconds later. '. . . me, Yelena.'

'Hello?' screamed her mother, followed by a stream of abuse at the stupid telephone and the hollow line.

Yelena continued to call into the mouthpiece until she heard her mother slam the phone down. She stared at the receiver for a while, feeling alone and vulnerable. Then a man in the queue behind her shouted: 'Lady, we are also waiting, you know?'

Yelena stumbled back to the car, calling for the boys to get in. She rested her head on the steering wheel for a moment, aware that they were gazing at her, troubled and glum at the same time. With all the extra difficulties that she faced, she generally managed to contain any cheerless feelings quite well. But the solitude got to her at times; she most hated the evenings or the weekends if she had no adult to talk to. And today especially, for whatever reason, she wanted to speak to her mother, she wanted the opportunity to feel a little mothered herself.

She wouldn't have survived this well without her friends, but all the same the sense of being adrift and so far from anyone she thought she had the *right* to depend on was sometimes crushing. Unfortunately, as she often mused ruefully, she had never realised her family's true worth when they had all lived on top of each other in her parents' two bedroom flat.

Christmas. A difficult time indeed, if she allowed herself to feel that way, when she felt the most homesick. It was a time for family, surely, and close friends. She could feel so very alone, if she let herself even a little. Her mother and brother felt even further away. The nostalgia for Kiev was greatest at this time of year, the cold weather, the warm food.

She wiped her face and then turned around to face the boys. 'Even grown-ups feel sad sometimes. But you know what, I am so lucky to have the two of you and I wouldn't trade you for anything in the whole wide world.' She watched them long and hard until they paused their chewing and smiled back, revealing lumps of pink chewing gum. She smiled harder. Their faces creased, their shoulders slowly fell back into place, anxiety dripped away. She drove off looking at them in the rear-view mirror from time to time. They appeared content, each looking out of a window, chewing gum, blowing bubbles. So like their father, she thought. She gripped the wheel a little tighter. How, with all her talk of 'love' and 'family' and 'there-is-nothing-more-important' could she truly explain to them why *she* remained in this country so far away from all those who loved her the most?

As soon as she got home, she went straight to the kitchen and started to make a chocolate cake. Her last pat of butter, flour she had to sift three times to get rid of all the weevils and bits of unidentifiable stuff, lots of pure Ghanaian cocoa, sugar, almond essence, and one egg; she knew the recipe by heart. She got a cigarette from the packet she kept on top of the fridge for emergencies, and sat at the table smoking and watching the cake rise slowly in the oven. The entire process of baking helped her calm down; whisking the egg and butter, eating dollops of raw cake dough, inhaling the sweet fumes of almond essence that became stronger as the cake cooked. She would eat most of it in one sitting with the boys while it was still warm. They deserved a treat, after all. Only then would she feel ready to go to Eva's.

Chapter Three

Dahlia stroked her cheek again as if she could stop the throbbing. She was going to have to try a lot harder with the conversation today, to rise above the ordinariness of their dialogue, to appear interested in what her friends had to say. All the while, in spite of her continuous attempt to drown it out, to her ears alone would sing the words her father had spoken when she told him she was going to Ghana, his voice gravelled with age and fear: 'I bring you all this way on that boat, an' you choose to thank me by going to Africa? Somewhere more backward than where we from? What's wrong with you girl? Cha! I should have left you with your grand-mother in St Lucia.' In different circumstances she would have reminded him that she hadn't been consulted on their emigration to London in the first place. But since she was leaving them, any additional insolence would have been heartless. Besides, by then, family relations had deteriorated because only six months after they married, Dahlia had had a baby and given up her place at law school, shattering her parents' dream of having a university-educated child. The fact that their daughter had married a lawyer was sorry recompense, it seemed.

She looked in the mirror. Her cheek looked fine, better than it felt. What was she going to do this time? In her bewildered state of mind, it was hard to see what options she had. She found that she kept going back to the very beginning to try and glean some understanding.

Yet, as ever, when she began to remember a smile crept on to her face. She savoured it; it wouldn't last. But for a moment or two, she could enjoy the sting of excitement, the thrill of journeying here, the many challenges of a new life.

And here it was, neatly boxed away, the joy she had felt when she had arrived in Africa proudly jangling a collection of tribal bangles she had collected over the years, laden with expectations of how things would be, looking forward to blending in, pleased that she would finally be somewhere she could really belong. How would it not be better than Norwood, where her parents had settled to give their daughter a good life? Ah the youthful optimism which had allowed her to think how wonderful life would be as part of the majority. A black amongst blacks. Far from London, where she had tired of the question: 'Where are you from?' An innocuous enquiry designed, it seemed, only to wear her down, to make her question her own origins. Until the first time, she had assumed she was as British as her passport. She had been transported from St Lucia as a toddler, her only memories of the Caribbean were those recycled by her parents, who talked with passion about the place they had left behind. The warm, easygoing nature of people, fresh fruit, the coconut milk, the smell of fish – 'no need to freeze, there will be more tomorrow', her parents reminisced regularly. And to illuminate the loss they had suffered in coming over, her father habitually went on to list characteristics of London life that highlighted the good they had left behind. Only once, an impudent teenaged Dahlia had asked her father, 'If it was so wonderful, why didn't you stay there?' He had slapped her across the face quite hard and said, 'An' back home, chil'ren are not insolent.' He then grounded her for a week and made her write an essay on the commandment

41

'Honour thy mother and father so that your life may be long.' 'And don' come to me till you written a thousand words!'

Her smile faded; it always did when she wandered beyond the very beginning. It hadn't taken long before she realised this was going to be a hard life to adjust to. It was nothing like she had imagined; her parents were right. She never would have believed it, although they had tried to persuade her, that she would be as foreign as the next foreigner in this land. She had thought she was coming to the motherland, the continent that she had been fascinated by for years.

From the very start she stood out because of her appearance. The alluring women they mixed with stared at her, some laughed at her loose and ethnically colourful clothing with a headband tied around her head to part her afro in two. Eventually one of Vincent's sisters said, 'Doesn't he give you enough money for your hair? If he is mean, you must take it from his pockets when he is sleeping. It is your duty to look your best or else you will have no one to blame when he strays.' And within months of arriving here, Vincent had given her a gold bangle and told her that he didn't care much for silver or plastic.

Her hair was now straightened, her clothing home-made from local batik and tie-dye; at least her mother would be pleased.

No, when she looked back through the haze of the time that had passed in between, she no longer recognised the feisty, argumentative woman she'd been when she first met Vincent at a social event for the Afro-Caribbean Student Union at Oxford. And now, alone in her bedroom, she felt like a caged pet.

She had to steel herself. At Eva's Vincent would speak to everyone and anyone with smiles and jokes. He would hug and caress, wink and laugh, be witty and self-important. He would stare blankly through her as though she was a flimsy curtain blocking his view to the outside world. His frostiness would be evident to all. Would they feel sorry for her? The idea that they might pity her upset her. She wished for the thousandth time that she didn't have to go, but she would not let Eva down, she couldn't.

She would love nothing more today than to be getting on the tube to visit her parents. To sit in their living room with the television mumbling softly in the background, and converse with them about their week, while her children played with the toys and games from her youth which her mother had stored carefully in plastic boxes for her future grandchildren. She would eat a plate of home cooked food, sip some apple juice, and recharge her batteries. Wouldn't living closer to her family, having access to them, make this horrific life bearable? Wouldn't all this be easier with the unfailing support of family who have no choice but to love you, rather than to depend on the goodness of friends who have their own problems? Was this why her parents had been distraught when she told them she was going with Vincent? Because they had done it this way too? They had uprooted themselves from the bosom of family to live, for better or worse, far removed from the healing tentacles of familial love and support?

Yes, her friends did know some things of her life. She had shared the misery of her marriage with them; the lipstick marks on his shirts, the perfume that lingered in their air-conditioned bedroom in the morning, wafting about with nowhere to go until she opened the windows and let fresh air in. Some days she woke up with floral scents coating her nostrils and throat defiantly, daring her to acknowledge the things behind the scents, as if floating in the air wasn't enough. They listened to the latest dilemmas, sympathised, propped her up and helped her back on to her feet to continue limping through her marriage. Hadn't each of them insinuated at some time or other that she should leave? Margrit had said once, 'there is a limit to what anyone should put up with'. And they didn't even know the whole of it.

She knew she sounded like a stuck record at times. She felt she had used up all their sympathy, and slowly, more recently especially, she had found it necessary not to go into too much detail, at least until she knew what she could do to change the situation, and when.

She had become accustomed to living a lie, in a manner of speaking. On most occasions, she could say 'all is well' in a breezy voice, with a cheery smile, and make her eyes twinkle. It was a kind of self-preservation really, born of out of the need to not think too hard. If she let them, like now, the thoughts came tumbling out, overwhelming her, numbing her mind, crippling her emotionally and draining her of any hope. Frankly, she couldn't afford to think too often. She didn't have the energy to deal with her thoughts as well as everything else.

In recent years, Vincent had been brash and open about his affairs and she had come to accept that everyone knew. It was embarrassing. Why couldn't he simply keep them out of sight as he had done in the beginning? Why didn't he care that his behaviour was hurtful?

Recently, however, his new woman had so distracted him that Dahlia's life had become peaceful and oddly scary all at the same time. If he fell in love with someone else, how easily would he discard her? And what would she do? Where would she go? She was in the process of figuring out what she wanted so that she could discuss it properly with her friends. She always found it so much more productive to discuss a problem when she had some idea of what solution she wanted.

It had started very early, Vincent's philandering. He had begun cheating almost immediately they arrived in Accra, she knew that now. Conceivably even at the start of it all in London. The lies about visiting relatives, about meetings that went on into the night, about this emergency and that; how foolish she had been not to realise.

The first time, she had begged him to tell her the truth, pleaded with him not to leave her, not to see the other woman again, and then cried after he had left in anger. It was only much later as she lay spent on her bed, sweating, exhausted, that she

44

realised he hadn't actually been apologetic, hadn't really explained, that he had in fact left her feeling as if she was the one with something to apologise for. And for what? For falsely accusing him? For implying that he might be unfaithful, an adulterer? Concepts that were not strange to him, no matter how much he liked to pretend otherwise. Was it because it seemed such a common thing here for a woman to be betrayed that she accepted this state of affairs? It seemed to be a national pastime! The men seemed unable to remain faithful to one woman. She wondered whether she was being unfair, whether she had nationalised a generic male trait, not in fact limited to a particular country, race or society. Could it be that she would never know how to keep a Ghanaian man content? Was it down to cultural differences, or was that the simplistic view? Was it a typical female outlook to assume as ever that it was her fault? Did she accept things a Ghanaian woman wouldn't? And why was that?

When, years ago, Dahlia had first confided in Vincent's sister that she had suspicions that Vincent was cheating on her, her sister-in-law had looked at her kindly and said, 'Don't mind him. As for men, that is how they are.'

It still amazed her that Vincent had no shame in fathering children out of wedlock so abundantly. And worse, he seemed to expect her to accept these various children as the siblings of hers. They had started to come and go from the house to see their 'father' as the eldest daughter declared with precocious confidence the first time she showed up. 'My father told me to come and collect my school fees,' she had said with more assertiveness than a nine year old should have. Dahlia had excused herself from the living room, dismayed by the bitterness in the girl's eyes. What option did she have but to grow up in the covetous shadow of her mother, whoever she might be, wherever she might be waiting. Dahlia had wanted, for a split second, to go outside and see if the woman was waiting outside the wall somewhere or whether, as was more likely, she hadn't dared to come, instead sending the

45

child on her own. How could this girl, and the others who later came in her wake, grow up free of resentment when they had to come to their father's house to witness for themselves how his other children lived, in air-conditioned splendour with pretty clothes and a driver to take them to a nice, private school. The children who lived with their father didn't have to walk to a crumbling school which had insufficient chairs, no books and truanting teachers. Was it fair that life would be easier for them simply because they lived with their father and mother under one roof?

Other children, she had lost count now, had been made known to her in passing, by various informants: his mother trying to soften the blow, explaining that these things 'happened', that there was no need to be angry with him, that if she wanted to be angry, she should focus on the woman who had seduced Vincent because of his good name and money; by his sister who couldn't understand why Dahlia was so flustered by a harmless affair, and finally by the driver. They had been on their way to a party, and Dahlia had been absentmindedly admiring her children, saying how beautiful they were, when the driver piped up, 'In fact, not at all like their baby brother.' The driver struggled to shrug off his blunder, but Dahlia extracted the whole story from him later, and as retribution made him take her to see for herself this latest addition to the family.

There was a gentle knock on the door and Jasmine walked in looking insecure. Dahlia looked at the clock on her bedside table. She hadn't noticed the morning pass. Her daughter was on the verge of becoming a teenager and Dahlia loved her afresh. Had her own parents seen her in this light once? A vision of hope for an auspicious future? How would Vincent's shenanigans affect this young girl? Were all men like this? Oh, how she hated to generalise; such an abhorrent laziness, but it was hard not to. Would Jasmine also end up being heartbroken one day by some young man raised to think that it is acceptable to treat a woman badly? She put her arms around her daughter and pulled her close.

46

'You have to stop biting your nails Jazzy,' she said, stroking her hand. Her nails had been nibbled painfully short, the skin on several of her fingers was pulled and bleeding.

'Are you going to get divorced, Mum?' Jasmine pulled away to examine her mother's face. 'Because I would understand. And Cyril would too. I know he would.'

Dahlia couldn't bear to look her in the eye and clasped her tight. She bit her lip, felt her spirit squashed further by Jasmine's question. When is it normal for a twelve-year-old girl to worry about her parents in this way, she asked herself, aware that in the midst of her own confusion she did not appreciate the depth of angst that her children were feeling, she was no longer capable. How does a mother so lose herself, she wondered. She remembered how when she first held this child as a delicate newborn with wrinkled features and sticky, black hair, a bulging belly button and clasped fists, she had felt a gush of fierce love, and had been overwhelmed by the depth of her emotions, had been frightened by the strength of her love. She had believed there was nothing she wouldn't do to protect this perfect being from harm, from disappointment and wickedness. But life had worn her down. Now she could see, as though through winter fog, and hear, as if submerged in water, the reality her children were living with, and yet sit here motionless, a participant in someone else's dream. She hugged her daughter tighter.

'Darling Jasmine, no one is talking of divorce. Have you got homework? Why don't you go and do it now. And tell Cyril to do his too. We're going to Auntie Eva's later, remember?' She shooed her off. Jasmine walked out the door, shoulders drooped further than even a year ago, and Dahlia knew she had to do something. She had to feel a little more, rediscover her fighting spirit. She had to get away from Vincent, who had sapped away the core of her person, leaving her like a mummified insect; still, lifeless, yet intact.

Chapter Four

Margrit had always thought that the meat shop was more like a doctor's surgery than a butcher's. There were a few people seated in the waiting room, and tucked behind a desk, a bored woman – a girl really, thought Margrit – with large, glossy lips was painting her nails. A small blackboard was propped against the wall near the desk. Margrit read what was written on it: Pork Chops, Mince Meat, ~~Beef Cutlets~~. The cold counter stood empty and clean; it had broken down a long while ago, when it was still quite new and had never been fixed. The meat was now stored in the back of the shop where it was cut up, wrapped and brought out to order.

Margrit stood in front of the receptionist for long enough for the woman to put down her nail varnish or at least acknowledge her. Everyone else in the room was looking at her; she was hard to disregard at nearly six feet tall and about two hundred pounds heavy. She was wearing one of her preferred outfits, an overflowing pink and red *bubu*, a traditionally cut dress that was floor-length and essentially shapeless. Her recently hennaed hair was tightly covered in a bold leopard print headscarf because she had been too busy to wash it in days. She wore arresting red lipstick on her thin lips and had arched her eyebrows thickly with kohl.

'Have you got pork chops?' she asked in her loud guttural German accent over the top of the girl's head.

Without looking up, the receptionist gestured towards the seats.

'You should look at someone when they speak to you,' said Margrit, shaking her head disapprovingly.

The girl looked up, her bored expression turning into brief amazement as she took in the elderly, fancily-dressed white woman in front of her, but then her boredom returned quickly and she made a loud chewing noise, shrugged and said, 'If you don't want to sit, don't sit.' She resumed her manicure.

Margrit tutted and shuffled over to sit next to an affable-looking woman who was perspiring profusely in her tight batik outfit. She smiled at Margrit and said, 'Don't worry, the meat is not yet in, but it is on its way.'

'Ach, I know,' said Margrit. But where was the meat coming from, and who had said it was on its way, and when would it get here? The receptionist didn't look as if she had processed any information recently, nor did she look as if she cared one bit. This was precisely the kind of thing that annoyed her overly these days. How had that girl got the job? But this flirty young thing doubtless knew just what to do and say to a man in need of flattery. A woman disdainful of all other women; there had to be others out there more qualified than this rude, lazy, useless, but beautiful girl. 'Her sugar-daddy is probably the manager here,' muttered Margrit. The woman next to her tutted. And all these people accept it! She looked around at them. There was a bespectacled young man reading the *Graphic*, a dozing woman and an older lady who overflowed her seat uncomfortably. None of them seemed affected by the ineffectual receptionist, or had she not been rude to them?

Another woman came in with a baby on her back and a toddler by her feet. Margrit watched with mounting anger as the receptionist gave her the same discourteous treatment. The young mother, looking grateful, nodded and sat down on the edge of one of the seats so that she didn't disturb her sleeping baby. She placed the toddler next to her where he could concentrate on the piece of bread he was eating.

Margrit could bear it no longer. She felt the words gurgle their way to the top of her throat, she could see the frustration cloud her reason, she heard her resolve to try and emulate the same graceful patience of the people around her fading in her head. The words were now too close to her lips, filling her mouth, from where they spewed out uncontrollably: 'Why do you say you have pork chops in stock when you don't have anything at all in stock? What is the point of that? Don't you feel any shame in misleading people?'

'Hmm,' said the woman next to her, a sound of flexible inter-pretational qualities. It could signal concurrence with Margrit, but just as easily, be translated into shock at her outburst. No one else in the room spoke or reacted. In fact, looking around, you would think that no one had said a word.

'But it doesn't make sense,' she continued. 'There is no meat in the shop, so why have you written on the board that you have pork chops in stock?'

The receptionist lifted her head and looked at Margrit with contempt. The newspaper man looked at her and smiled a half smile. Someone said, 'Oh dear!' The young mother shifted her bottom a little and dusted crumbs off her toddler's chest and lap.

'That is the problem with this country. Too many people accept lies.' There she had said it. And they had heard her. All of them turned to look at her quizzically.

'Oh no!' said the older lady in an elongated mournful tone.

The receptionist put her nail file down and glowered at Margrit. 'What makes you think you have the right to come to my office and call me a liar?' She made a loud chewing noise with her lips and rolled her eyes, indicating by her use of these gestures the rhetoric nature of her question.

'Yes,' said the young man looking at Margrit properly for the first time. 'The lady is doing her job and you come here to insult her. Is that what you do in your country? If so, so be it, but we don't do that here. We don't call people liars just anyhow, without foundation or evidence. Lady, you should be ashamed of yourself.'

'Well, can't you see this is ridiculous? She isn't even doing her job properly. She is rude to all of us and we are supposed to just accept it? Why is everyone so weak?'

The man stood up. 'Are you now insulting *all* of us?'

Margrit stared at him and shrugged.

'Are you?'

The large lady said, 'Please, let us behave with some decorum.'

'You should watch yourself, lady,' said the man, sitting back down. From time to time he said something else about her rude behaviour and tutted loudly.

How she wished she didn't care, didn't get worked up by this kind of inefficiency. Like everyone else in the room.

It was just as she and Kojo discussed often. It was these irritating and yet endearing characteristics of Ghanaians – as a people they were peaceable, frustratingly compliant and afraid of questioning authority – which meant that little was ever challenged by ordinary people, little ever changed. She often wondered whether there weren't just a few hundred men and women like her dear Kojo and his fellow foreign-educated professionals who bothered to voice dissatisfaction about things, when in fact the rest of the population couldn't give a damn. As long as they could feed their families and perform their customary rites and duties, ordinary Ghanaians didn't really care what was going on at Christiansborg Castle, the former slave trading post that was now the government seat. Did they even care who was in power, and what they were doing with that power? Nearly thirty years on, and she could still not accept that this was how the people were, or that they might

51

actually be satisfied with the way things were. She looked around. They had all returned to waiting with patience and good nature. They would doze, chat and fidget in their seats for as long as it took for the meat to arrive while the receptionist, who had calmly returned to filing her nails, sat beautifully inefficiently before them. No matter what resolutions she made to herself now to be quiet in the future, confronted with the same set of circumstances she would speak out again. And who ended up victorious? Her fellow shoppers who avoided confrontation, tried to remain polite, accepted the status quo? Or she, who was now all worked up and perspiring and irritated?

For about half an hour she played with her list and surreptitiously watched the receptionist apply an intricate design to her nails. Maroon glossy paint, then a silver line drawn diagonally across each nail with two silver dots on either side of the line. The phone didn't ring once, but the queue grew, and in the end there were several people standing in the room and in the lobby, spilling out into the car park outside. The basket next to her feet started to move and Margrit reached down and pulled out a scrawny puppy.

The woman next to her tutted. 'Please, madam, what are you doing?'

Margrit ignored her, pulled out a feeding bottle and started to feed the hungry puppy on her lap.

'Please, why are you doing this here?'

'Do you know the number of bacterias that are living in your dog's mouth? This is where we buy food, it is not a place to be bringing a dog,' said the spectacled man.

'Pretend you can't see,' said Margrit. 'Anyway it's really no different to feeding a baby.'

'Babies don't smell,' said the woman.

'Or carry bacterias.'

'Ah, a matter of opinion. I never had one, so I think they do in fact stink. Here, I'll cover him with a blanket,' she said reaching back into the bag for a threadbare cloth which she put over her lap. She looked at them and started laughing. 'There, there,' she said to her lap where the noise of wet sucking seemed to have become louder. She looked up at her audience once more and said, 'Just pretend he isn't here.'

A moment later, everyone's attention was diverted by the arrival of the meat. A man in a bloody apron came through the doors behind the cooler and mumbled something to the receptionist. He threw bags of meat into the cooler and went back for more. The receptionist put down the magazine she was flicking through and went to the blackboard. Every slow movement she made seemed to be accompanied by a sigh. She rubbed out the writing on the board and then in surprisingly neat handwriting wrote: *Today we have: Pig's trotters & Lambs Chops.*

Ah well, at least she wouldn't go home empty handed. The butcher came back out and slung some more meat into the cooler. There didn't look enough to satisfy everyone in the queue, and hardly enough to have merited a delivery.

The butcher looked up at the people sitting before him. His face was tired and resigned. He raised eyebrows and said, 'Yes please?'

In exactly the order that they had entered the room, the customers stood to be served. And when it was her turn, Margrit bought the maximum allowance, 3 kilos of each.

Back in the car, she looked at the hazy sky and imagined rain. She began to feel lulled by the hum of the engine, the breeze in her face. It was too hot. Life was exhausting here. No wonder few people had hobbies, pursued passionate interests. She drove by a cluster of neem trees where some women were cooking and selling food. Children played in the dust around them with empty battered tins. Some goats wandered about, nibbling at discarded bits of paper and plastic. One of the women clapped at a goat when it wandered too close to the food. In the background, Margrit saw a man lying stretched out on a bench. She shook her head; here was a perfect illustration of why there was so little progress in a land with so much promise. How can an able-bodied man sleep in the middle of the day unless he is comfortable in the sureness that tonight, a mother, sister, aunt, sister-in-law, or cousin, however many times removed, will provide him with a free meal? Perhaps a man has to go hungry before he really tries to find a better way, she thought.

Later, Margrit and Kojo sat on their home-made veranda sipping lemon grass tea. Over the years, she had transformed the dull grey concrete floor by sticking various pieces of colourful glass and patterned crockery into it; here and there, green pieces of glass from broken beer bottles glinted amongst the floral remnants of cups, saucers and platters when the sunlight found its way through the numerous shrubs and trees that grew wildly in her garden.

At all times of day, the veranda was mostly shaded. Directly in front of the house grew a large mango tree, through which a glossy climber had threaded itself, providing shade for shrubs below with their large heart-shaped leaves of varying sizes and colours. Green leaves with strong pink and red veins, others shiny green, so that they looked polished, and some with light green or white veins. Today as ever, there was the intoxicating, sweet scent of flowering shrubs, and where Kojo had watered the plants, the earth smelled moist and vibrant.

Margrit finished cutting Kojo's toenails and stood to shake the clippings off her dress. She sat back and took his foot again, poured cooking oil into her hand and began to massage his foot. Her red hair fluttered around her face when she bent over his feet.

Kojo sat with folded arms and a smile on his face listening to the radio, which hummed quietly in the background, softly enough not to disrupt the peace. His bare, soft upper body was covered with greying, curly hairs. His stomach, slackened with age, folded and rolled gently towards his khaki shorts.

She rubbed the oil into his skin, kneading his in-step, trying to soften his flat, fleshy soles, the hardened heel.

A gentle breeze rustled through the crisping leaves. Chickens pecked at the hard, bare earth between the various shrubs and trees. Margrit didn't like lawn, not for her the look of a manicured garden, nor the maintenance or water necessary to make something that out of place grow to order. Everything was allowed to grow wherever, and plants flourished merrily, encroaching on each other, so that the overall effect was of an unkempt, lush jungle, an overgrown exciting space filled with unusual plants.

She routinely took cuttings whenever she came across anything with pink flowers or leaves, including many from the botanical gardens, in contravention of all their rules. She had a magnificent collection of large torch ginger and heliconia plants that she confessed she talked to, as well as pink, red and purple denrobium orchids, which grew at the side of her house, on palms and other hosts. At the back there was a fruitful kitchen garden, where they grew pawpaw, banana, plantain, avocado, and various root vegetables, cassava and yam and cocoyam. Recently, with the drought and increasing food prices, their garden had been raided a few times, which Kojo regarded a little more philosophically than she could.

He could overlook the theft of a bit of fruit for a hungry child, but medicines that he needed for sick children that were instead channelled to treat the wives of the influential, cars intended for government work used to ferry their children about, or money that should be invested in schools and roads furnishing houses in London, well all that was criminal as far as he was concerned. But, as they often discussed at length, it was a discouraging situation, since the law enforcers were involved in all manner of corrupt behaviour themselves.

Today he was bemoaning the fact that hospital supply contracts had recently been allocated based on who had been the most hospitable to the minister and his team, so that they were taking delivery of substandard drugs close to their use-by dates and equipment that wasn't suitable for the harshness of the tropical weather and which would therefore be too expensive to maintain. She could feel the anger in his feet and became irritated on his behalf. It was like that latest stretch of new highway between Accra and Cape Coast, which they had all been excited about when it was finished last year. But it had clearly been entirely compromised and the too-thin layer of tarmac was already eroding to disclose defiant red earth. All they needed now were a few heavy rains and the road would be back to its previous state. Too much of the construction budget had been given away in bribes to various officials, Kojo had pointed out. She knew that he was troubled by the greed and corruption of his fellow countrymen, and almost felt ashamed on their behalf.

She interrupted the massage to describe the rudeness of the girl at the meat shop. Kojo opened his eyes and smiled at her. She laughed. 'I know, I know, I shouldn't get worked up, but I do.'

'And you wouldn't be you if you didn't get worked up about such things. But I fear there will be more serious things to be concerned about if the rumours about an attempted coup are true.' He shook his head worriedly. He had intimated in recent days that things seemed to be getting worse, but he was uninterested in politics beyond the impact it had on his work as a doctor, and didn't really follow any particular party or ideology. He looked at Margrit with quiet resignation. 'If there is another coup, we will lose even more of our good doctors. We are struggling at Korle-Bu as it is.'

'They are overworked and underpaid, who can blame them? After all the hard years of study and the expense of attaining their qualifications abroad they can barely earn a living, let alone do their jobs without the equipment or the medicines.'

'Or the morale,' Kojo said, shrugging his shoulders.

She knew that he would stick with it. He often overlooked a

parent's ability to pay for treatment or drugs, using his own money where he could. But the need was too great, the suffering too endless; Korle-Bu, the large teaching hospital, built in a time of confident hope, was crumbling before their eyes due to a lack of investment. Margrit knew that one of the reasons that Kojo came home nightly to inhale deeply on a joint and sip a large tumbler of whisky was to forget the patients he couldn't help, the ones he had lied to about their prognoses, those he knew he could save if they only had the basic drugs available in the West. It was killing him slowly, she knew that, and it angered her on his behalf, knowing full well that it was the callous corruption of those in power that was leeching the country and its people of the right to basic healthcare.

In the many years she had been in Ghana, Margrit thought she had seen it all. Undeniably, too much to ever be very disappointed or surprised. Not many of the aspirations of independence had materialised, none of the dreams of the young professionals, like Kojo, who had returned in the sixties had come to fruition. Instead, life had been hard, consistently, depressingly so. She knew that it was unlikely that another coup would provide the answers, and yet they couldn't go on like this, with corrupt government after corrupt government, and what seemed a total lack of vision and leadership. She was an optimist by nature, and although living here challenged that on every level, she couldn't ever completely give up hope. She couldn't help but welcome any change that just *maybe* might bring the transformation the country needed, even though she knew that what was really required was an army of men like Kojo. Hardworking, dedicated, unselfish, committed. Wasn't that too much to ask of an average man? Because Kojo wasn't average. Nowhere in Germany, where Kojo had trained and where he would be eminently rewarded and recognised for his effort and skills, were any of his colleagues paid by their patients in hens or fresh eggs or cases of beer. And sometimes she wondered whether if they had had children to support, school fees to pay, lives to nurture, he would have been able to stick to his principles so steadfastly? Would procreation not have made him more acquisitive, more self-seeking? And didn't she facilitate his ability to remain pure by being self-sufficient, growing what she could, making her own clothes, not bleating on about going to Germany on holiday?

No, she knew another coup wouldn't make a jot of difference, not unless there was a sudden and magnificent change in the system, which made dishonesty unnecessary and wages adequate. A utopia where goodness was able to thrive without risk of strangulation by the strong, far-reaching tentacles of corruption and nepotism, without the ever present conflicting need to fend for oneself by any means whatsoever.

'Ach, *Schatz*, they are lucky to have you . . .' she said.

Kojo opened a sleepy eye and smiled.

'. . . and so am I.'

'You are.'

'I am serious, Kojo. I thank God every day for you.'

'Good.' He laughed. 'Me too, you know that. Not many wives would give their husband a regular pedicure.'

She thought about the foreign women she knew in Accra. Apart from Eva and Alfred, she didn't know anyone who was as contented as she and Kojo, and after nearly thirty-five years of marriage too. She often wondered what their secret was, wished she knew how much was pure luck, how much simply due to the fact that they were well-suited.

On reflection, she really hadn't even given her decision to marry Kojo much thought. It had seemed right, so she had agreed. Were they suited? She didn't know. They had had their fair share of ups and downs over the years. Maybe not having children had helped. When she met him at the university in Berlin, she had been instantly attracted to him; he was nothing like the other men she knew. She had been with a boyfriend at the time, someone she had thought she might marry, but she ended it after the first time she met Kojo. And their attraction for each other was mutual, that much she knew.

He was different in other ways too from any of the men she had known. Quiet, and peaceful. Never like those men who like to show off, to be thought of as the wittiest or cleverest in a room, with their wife or girlfriend gazing up at them. Margrit always wondered how those men didn't realise that their woman was the only person whose smile was genuine, that everyone else in the room thought the man was making a buffoon of himself. It still intrigued her when she came across this type, a bit like Vincent actually, and she knew that they instinctively disliked her. Her feelings for Vincent ran deeper than mere dislike. He made her skin crawl, in fact. She wasn't taken in by his suave exterior, the hand-cut suits from England, the polished brogues, his sharp accent and gift of the gab. Nor did she like the fact that Alfred was apparently doing business with him. Alfred was a good man, with the capability to remain so, but he was also weak and possibly a little overly impressed with Vincent, who was ten years older and incredibly successful. She could see that he was in awe of Vincent's Oxford law degree and that he could easily be influenced by him, and she also knew that Vincent would have no problem using Alfred, then spitting him out when he was done. Kojo had told her some years back about how a former business partner of Vincent's had been killed in a dreadful yet bizarre car accident. The car was new, the road was clear, the driver highly qualified, and no other vehicle had been involved. None of it had made sense at the time, and Kojo said that people believed Vincent had had a hand in it, either with the help of a fetish or more directly. She had laughed. It had seemed unlikely to the pragmatic Margrit that he could have had anything to do with the freak accident, but nevertheless she had seen him in a different light since.

She shivered despite the heat and focused on rubbing Kojo's feet. She thought again of their marriage. Even their interests were different; Kojo liked to read, she liked to garden. She liked animals, he preferred people. She liked to eat, he liked to cook. They balanced each other out all the time, and they did things that meant they were together, could chitter-chatter when they wished, but each was doing what they wanted.

Her parents had also adored him, maybe that made a difference too? They had visited twice before they died. They thought him wonderful, they told him so, and he treated them with the astonishing respect she had since come to see was a cultural trait; the ability to respect an older person for that reason alone. Her mother had whispered, 'This must be what it is like to be a princess', and Margrit had agreed.

She smiled now thinking how he had filled her life with magnificent peace and joy. The kind of happiness she had once thought was simplistic and unchallenging. But he didn't believe that a fulfilling life, a productive life, had to be hard or harsh, littered with goal-setting and ambitious achievement. He lived for his work, often practising outside his own speciality of paediatrics as was needed, and despite the frustrations of having to send children with curable conditions away to die because he didn't have the equipment or medicine to treat them. 'As long as I am doing what I can, I must focus on that, not on what I cannot do, what I would *like* to do. That would be like driving while staring in the rear-view mirror.'

Kojo despised covetousness in all guises, and this, according to Margrit, was the secret of his joy. He never wanted more, the next thing, the next day or week. He savoured what was before him for now. 'No one knows tomorrow,' he said often, quoting a popular slogan painted on the backs of *mammy* lorries.

Oh yes, Margrit knew she was lucky. 'Blessed,' Kojo would say, 'there is, after all no such thing as luck.' She rubbed the upper part of his foot now, his ankle, his calf, and he moaned contentedly.

Later they spent an hour weeding the vegetable plot where

yams and cassava grew. Kojo checked their banana and plantain trees, and looked to see whether any pawpaws were ripe enough to be picked. Margrit fed the puppies while Kojo washed Jimmy the dog, named after the American president that his wife so admired. She made some more dog food, using up the rest of the dried fish and *kenkey*, which she would store in the freezer. If the balls of fermented maize were nutritious enough for her and Kojo, they must be so for the dogs too. She mixed in a raw egg for Jimmy and coaxed her to eat as much as possible. Jimmy still hadn't recovered her strength after giving birth, which worried Margrit who was lavishing a lot more attention on her. 'You love her more than you love me', Kojo accused her often with a smile.

Tonight, after Eva's party, they would sit here as they always did at the end of the day surrounded by mosquito coils, Kojo smoking and swirling his whisky, Margrit sipping tea made from leaves from the lemon bush that grew near the kitchen door. They would reflect with inward pleasure on the peace and harmony that formed their life, and they would glow with the strength that togetherness brought.

Chapter Five

Funny, the things you can get used to, Eva thought as she washed her hair. How could she ever again take it for granted that water would flow when you turned on the tap!

Hadn't she arrived in this country with many wonderful expectations exuberantly provided by the man she loved, inspired by his vivacity and excitement, only to find something rather different to all the ideas and images that had been planted in her mind?

Alfred had been as delighted as a bride to be returning to his beloved homeland after too long in Britain. And whatever doubts Eva might possibly have had about West Africa had already been dispelled by her handsome, clever husband. He had spoken about his home with a longing that had seeped through Eva, making her keen to experience the place that made him tingle from the memories alone. On a bitter spring morning, when winter had already dragged for too long, he described the warmth of a tropical sun, 'strong enough to warm you to the bones'. He told her how the sea breeze along the long coast on which they would live could 'lift your soul with the salt-rich, moist air that smells of fresh fish. No smog and no traffic,' he had declared, 'and no ghastly underground to go scurrying through like nocturnal mammals.' Alfred preferred the top of a double-decker bus from where he could see the shape of the city he had grown used to, and refused to use the tube unless he had to make an extremely long journey. Then he would remain still and silent, unable to think about anything other than getting to the other end and back above ground once more. 'Thank God!' he'd say, visibly relieved, whenever they re-emerged into daylight after travelling from one end of London to the other.

He had described the life they would have. Maids to look after the children and do the cooking and the cleaning, anything she didn't want to do herself, he told her. Eva had imagined her maid would be a bustling woman in a white apron swirling a duster about, and had been apprehensive that she might meet the standards of such a person. 'And you will never have to cook if you don't want to. My mother loves to cook for me.'

Her face stretched in smiles and laughter as she watched his twinkling eyes describe his beloved homeland; the house he wanted to build for them, with every luxury they could afford. He told her he had just the piece of land in mind. He told her that he could guarantee that she wouldn't regret coming to Africa with him. 'You will love it there, babe', he told her over and again, and she believed him. Why wouldn't she? She knew she would love it in Siberia or in the Sahara as long as she was with him and she could feel the protective warmth of his love about her.

When they had those chats about going home, as even she began to call it, and he became animated and excited, she found that she had to touch him, to hold his hand and feel his tendons move as he spoke. She had to reach over to kiss him and tell him how much she loved him. 'Even if it were a hellhole,' she said once, 'I would still come with you, because I love you so much.' He had looked taken aback at her choice of word. For a moment they stared at each other and then they roared with laughter and embraced hurriedly.

Yes, he had neglected to tell her that many homes in the country's capital were not yet connected to the water mains or to the electricity grid, or that, more specifically, the guest suite in his uncle's house, in which they were going to stay for their first few months in Accra, hadn't been connected to either. Somehow he made it sound like an adventure, and Eva, with no real concept of what it would mean to live in a place where the temperature never dipped below twenty-seven degrees Celsius and where the humidity was persistently high, had happily trusted him.

When she prepared to step off the plane that first night, it was with equal measures of trepidation and excitement. Her tummy was a ball of nerves, but she felt as excited as a child on Christmas morning. Finally, she would see the place that had formed her lovely husband, she would meet his dear mother, they would begin their new life, make their home, and their first baby would be born.

When she walked through the open door of the plane, she was almost thrown backward by the wall of thick heat that engulfed her so fiercely that her skin erupted in goose bumps. The baby kicked the side of her belly vigorously. Did it feel the heat too, or was it reacting to her excitement? It was just as Alfred had said, she thought, as she felt the heat thaw away the deep cold left behind by a long English winter.

The air was hot and still and the airport building, long and low in the distance, was poorly lit with yellow lights. The first two letters in the large sign, K and O, were not working, and for a long while afterwards Eva didn't still know the airport was called Kotoka International Airport. The sky was inky black, and stars twinkled gently. She held on to the rail of the mobile steps with sweaty palms, and walked down on to African soil as spasms spread over her stomach. Soon her nostrils had filled with hot, unfamiliar scents. Well, she said to herself, this is it. And suddenly it all felt rather too final, alarmingly and surprisingly so, in fact.

In the arrivals hall, Alfred was grinning beneath the fluorescent bulbs. He had taken off his jacket and opened his shirt. He had beads of sweat all over his forehead, which he kept patting with his handkerchief. The room wasn't air-conditioned, and not enough air came through the small aluminium windows near the low ceiling. Eva felt her body temperature start to rocket. Her dizziness increased. Her skin erupted in cold sweat as her body battled the heat. She sat on the immobile conveyer belt and tried to keep the sick feeling at bay. Her skin was clammy, her face pale. Alfred crouched down and blew air on to her forehead and chest trying in vain to cool her down.

Eventually she recovered and smiled wanly at Alfred, who was stroking her forehead. Soon after, their luggage was thrown from a trolley on to a pile on the terrazzo floor because neither of the conveyer belts was working.

When they walked out into the hot night air, Eva looked about in half-dazed wonderment at the size of the crowd that had arrived to meet them. There seemed to be twenty or so people all trying to get close enough to Alfred to pat him on the back or shake his hand. There was a lot of cheery shouting and someone was singing. Eva felt another wave of dizziness. She grabbed Alfred's hand tight, but she could feel him being pulled away from her deep into the sea of unfamiliar faces and voices. She staggered and someone with a kind face smiled at her and took her arm. 'Please don't fall,' he said. 'Please, I am the driver, and you are very welcome to our country, madam.' She tried to smile back. He led her through the throng and towards steps that led down to a large car park.

Reunited with Alfred in the back of a rusty Peugeot with plastic seat covers, they were driven to his uncle's house. Once beyond the immediate area around the airport, the street lighting was inadequate and Eva could see very little. Some of the houses they drove past had lone light bulbs glaring from walls or gates, casting ashen shadows on whitewashed walls and shrubbery.

There were few cars, but those that passed them tooted horns regularly and loudly, and the driver of their car used his horn often too, tooting pedestrians out of his way, warning an oncoming car that had strayed on to his side of the road. At a busy road intersection, they passed rows and rows of tables and stalls where people were selling all manner of exotic and indistinguishable things by the light of smoking oil lamps.

Alfred didn't appear to realise that his descriptions bore no resemblance to the place in which their plane landed, the landscape through which they were being driven, this exotic place that she was going to have to learn to call home. She had expected Accra to be more developed, she had expected to see bigger shops, European-style housing, more tree-lined avenues. She had imagined something quite different from the sprawling shanty town she was being swept through. Conflicting emotions stirred in her as she thought about their one-way fares, her parents' goodbye. Her mind was muddled, besieged by so many new sensations and the sudden awareness of overwhelming unfamiliarity. Desperate to conquer her puzzlement, she smiled at everything Alfred pointed out to her, his face beaming with pride at his country, while she desperately tried to hold on to the sense of adventure that she'd had while planning this trip. She moved closer to him in the back seat of the car that was taking them to his uncle's house where they would stay until they could find a place of their own, and he put his arm over her shoulder, drew her even closer and kissed the top of her head.

As they approached their destination, the streets became narrow, and Eva saw deep rain gutters on either side of the roads. The housing became a lot more humble, shabby almost, without walls or gates or trees. The buildings were low and close together, covered in iron sheets. Eva took gulps of the cooler air that passed through the open windows. She could taste coal braziers, foreign food, the sea, heat.

By the time they got to Alfred's uncle's house, she was

sweltering, her dress stuck to the back of her legs, her hair clung to her neck in damp clumps. Her cheeks were red and warm, and she was light-headed, desperate for a shower and her bed. But there were even more people waiting for them, including Alfred's mother Gladys, who embraced her and then sat and watched her wordlessly.

For the next few hours, Eva fought waves of tiredness and struggled to suppress yawns. She couldn't disguise her shock when bottles of beer were opened and schnapps was poured, first on the ground, then into small glasses and passed around. Everyone started to tuck into bowls of steaming rice and chicken that appeared from the kitchen. She shuffled about on her seat, uncomfortably. It was close to midnight; she had been travelling all day, first by bus then tube then aeroplane, and she wanted her bed. She whispered to Alfred and he smiled and encouraged her to stay a little longer. Later, he explained to her that it would have been unforgivably rude to curtail the party when his family had been waiting all these years to have him back home, and after the effort they had made to welcome her too.

She knew then that whatever expectations she had of her new life would bear little resemblance to the reality. Frankly, she hadn't known *what* to expect. It wasn't as if she had been outside the UK before, what yardstick did she have to measure a foreign land by, let alone one this far from home.

She had read what she could find about Ghana, mostly light historic and political texts which described the sub-Saharan country as an underdeveloped tropical land ridden with malaria, but filled with 'the friendliest people one can hope to meet on the African continent.' Alfred dismissed the negative aspects. 'Ghana has only been independent for twelve years, and these things take time,' he said.

There was going to be nothing subtle about this country. She knew immediately that it would be impossible to be indifferent to it, and momentarily, even then, she knew that she would struggle to even like it.

When later that night it rained, it wasn't a gentle, nourishing drizzle, but a torrential, eroding downpour which drowned the sound of crickets in the dark yard around the house and brought swarms of rain flies that crawled wingless and aimless on the veranda floor. As the rain died down, Eva huddled up to her sleeping husband's relaxed body beneath their mosquito net. Outside, large frogs croaked and what she presumed were the large, glossy, brown cockroaches she had seen earlier, scuttled about on the concrete floor beneath their bed. She listened to rainwater drip from the roof and remembered the very beginning of the journey that had brought her here.

Far from her sleepy hometown in Norfolk, Eva felt wonderfully free in London, unaware until now that she hadn't been so back at home. It was the sixties thing that gripped her imagination and fascinated her; the freedom with which the girls she met went about with boys, the way they smoked and drank with voracity. How they pinned up their dyed blonde hair and lined their eyes with thick black, pulled their skirts high and their necklines low. Her favourite pastime became the watching of people. What wonderful times she had observing them, becoming more and more tempted to step into the thick of it herself.

It was on her birthday that she bought herself an orange mini dress in a boutique on the King's Road that played loud music. Then, goaded by her new college friends, and inspired by Twiggy, she cut off her hair. As soon as the first long, blonde tresses had gone, she shut her eyes, lamenting her decision. When she opened them, the hairdresser beamed at her over her shoulder and the other girls clucked about her 'amazing big eyes' and her 'incredible cheekbones'. She stared at her new hairdo, wide mouthed and stunned. As her confidence grew, she admired her new look tentatively, turning her head this way and that, and then, still a little inhibited, went back out into the damp London evening feeling much more authentic. She realised that for once it was she that was turning heads, attracting the admiration of strangers, and she noticed a lilt in her step.

She had been invited to a party by a couple of girls on her course. She didn't want to go, wanted to stay in and read a book, go to sleep, but they insisted. When they arrived, there was a handful of people gathered in the basement kitchen drinking beer and smoking cigarettes. A joint passed from mouth to mouth, eventually reaching Eva. She took it, dragged on it as if it was something she did every Saturday night, tried to look comfortable, cleared her throat and then moved away so that it wouldn't come back to her. Music was thudding loudly from the floor above and she went back upstairs to explore. The party had sprawled into several rooms, and she wandered about, squeezing past people who lined the walls in the large hallway. In one of the rooms a girl who had come with her group had settled into a fumbling, moaning embrace on a sofa with one of the boys.

She saw his long legs first, clad in drainpipe trousers, his pointed, laced-up black shoes. He was tall and looked older than the others, or maybe it was just that he was dressed quite nattily compared to them. He was laughing loudly at something one of the men with him had said. They were arguing about the merits of a controversial new building. She watched his eyes scan the room and then settle on hers. He winked at her languorously and smiled as though overjoyed. And when he smiled his pronounced cheekbones stretched upwards to display startlingly white teeth and a deep dimple on the left side of his face, and his eyes almost shut, but still they twinkled sharply through his lashes and remained fixed on hers. Eva took a step back and stifled her admiration. Why are they called blacks, she wondered, hoping the absurd question wasn't revealing itself somehow in her hesitant smile. This man had a sculpted oval face that was not black, but lustrous brown, and silken, like the finest chocolate.

She smiled back, and then coyly averted her gaze; she had never been winked at like this before. But she longed to watch him, and wished she could do so unseen. She could hear him arguing his point with the voice of someone used to being listened to. She dared to look again and found he was watching her while he spoke to his friends. Although she was a little unnerved by his stare, strong and determined from across the room, she looked back, drawn and electrified by it. He seemed to like that, and he winked again. And then, it was as if everything else just slowly drifted away. Later that night, she tried to remember who he had been talking to, who she had been talking to, but all she could remember was him there, looking at her, his smile for her alone, the dimple on one side of his long face, the high defined cheekbones, the chiselled, slightly protruding mouth, which she could tell would be soft and fleshy and unyielding at the same time. I would like to kiss him, she thought, blushing instantly. He started making his way across the crowded room. She turned away startled. She had to steady herself somehow. She held her bottle to her lips and turned to concentrate on what her friend was saying.

'You have the most beautiful eyes. But I couldn't quite see what colour they are from all the way over there,' he said, brushing her ear with his mouth as he spoke. Her friend touched her arm lightly and walked away.

His breath was warm and sweet with beer. He had his hands in his trouser pockets and he stood far enough from her, but she felt every hair on her body stiffen by his closeness. She looked up into his face.

'I thought so,' he said softly. 'Like pale denim my favourite blue.'

She laughed, totally disarmed, enjoying the sensation of being so closely scrutinised.

And then he kissed her. Just like that, his mouth was on her cheek, light and tender. And once more she fought the desire to put her arms around his neck and encourage him further.

Someone whistled and the spell was broken. She pulled back, feeling diffident. They were surrounded by people and she didn't even know his name.

'I'm sorry . . . I couldn't resist,' he said. 'I'm Alfred. And, you are having the oddest effect on me.'

She laughed.

'Right, I'll do this properly.' He held out a hand. 'I am Alfred Laryea, and you are incredibly beautiful.'

'No, I am not,' she replied without hesitation.

'You are. You are very beautiful, and it is a crime that you don't know it. Your eyes are striking. And so big. And you are not wearing much make-up like the girls all do these days. And your hair is lovely. Sexy and feline and yet so delicate.'

'You are embarrassing me now,' said Eva blushing. 'I'm Eva. Eva Granger.'

'Well, Eva Granger, it's a real pleasure to meet you.'

She chuckled. 'You are funny,' she said and then immediately wished she could come up with something a little less banal, but he seemed not to mind.

He asked her question after question. When had she come to London and why? Did she miss home? What was she going to do when she went back home? About her parents. He listened to every reply without taking his eyes off her. Did she like Chinese food or Indian food best? She admitted she hadn't ever tried either. He shook his head. 'We shall need to change that.'

She couldn't understand why he was interested in what she had to say, but each answer provoked another question or comment to show that he had been listening, that he understood, and he seemed to want to know everything about her. He drank it all in, as much and as quickly as she could give it to him, and yet he wanted more. He touched her frequently. A light finger on her hand, a brush of her shoulder.

Time passed quickly. The party started to thin out. Eva's jaw was aching from talking so much and laughing too. He stroked her cheek and said, 'I can't tell you how glad I am that I came to this vile party.'

He offered to walk her home. After their intimate beginning, Eva found it odd that he walked almost painstakingly beside her, their coats brushing occasionally. When she stood on the pavement next to the steps that lead to her front door with her keys in her hand, she paused and turned to face him. He looked serious. He was frowning and seemed to be contemplating something complicated.

'I have enjoyed our walk and our chat,' she said. She was about to turn and leave, thinking she had mistaken his interest, the kiss.

He held her face in his hands, kissed her, and then he nuzzled her neck and moaned. 'The problem is that I don't just want to kiss you.' He pulled away quickly, smiled in his disarming manner. 'Sleep tight and sweet dreams, Eva Granger. *Adieu!*' He turned and walked away leaving Eva feeling oddly disappointed and empty, as if the evening had ended too soon after all.

She watched him saunter down the road, his tall form and determined shoulders fading into the shadows. She wished then that she had had the brazenness to hold on to him.

Nevertheless, she smiled a lot to herself over the next few days. She imagined what he was like, tried to remember every detail, and then realised he hadn't divulged much about himself at all. She wondered whether he had simply been chivalrous and kind, and hoped that he had meant what he had said. But a man as beautiful as he is, she reminded herself, must have the pick of London. Maybe he had simply amused himself with her. It was plausible that he had several girlfriends, all glamorous and interesting, who comfortably ate Chinese and Indian and Japanese too.

On Thursday, when Eva returned home, her landlord Mrs Glasser called out from the living room that there had been a letter for her. She took it and looked at the unfamiliar scrawl. It was addressed to her all right, and she opened it with growing curiosity. 'Happy Birthday' it said on the front over a watercolour of a vase filled with pink roses. She opened it, perplexed, and read the beautiful, slanting ink scroll: *'Because you must have had a birthday in the last year and I wasn't there to kiss you. I was wondering whether you would care to join me for an Indian this Saturday night? I could pick you up at seven?'* She must have made an odd noise, because Mrs Glasser called out, 'Everything all right I hope.'

'Yes, thank you.' Eva said and went up the stairs two at a time, slowing down as she walked past the boy's room so she wouldn't wake him. She flung open her wardrobe and began immediately to tackle the troubling question of what she could wear on Saturday night 'for an Indian'. She couldn't wear her orange dress again and quickly decided that the only thing in her wardrobe that might not look out of place next to Alfred was the only other item she had bought in London. It was an elegant sky-blue dress that had cut-away sleeves and a loose round neck. It skimmed her body and ended mid-thigh with a lace trim.

She struggled to fall asleep that night and the next. She listened instead to the muffled sound of Mr and Mrs Glasser arguing again about what school they would send Daniel to. Mrs Glasser wanted him to go to a day school, come home every day, so she could keep an eye on what he ate, when he bathed and slept, how he grew. But Mr Glasser wanted to send him off to an exclusive boarding school, give him a lift up the societal ladder, a shove that would push him up higher than Mr Glasser had reached even though he ran a thriving construction company. 'You don't understand what it is like, to always feel as if you are on the outside looking in at the party, unable to join, separated by an invisible, highly effective partition,' Mr Glasser said. Through the thin floor Eva agreed with Mrs Glasser. It seemed quite cruel to send a seven-year-old boy to a boarding school far from home. Especially such an affectionate child, gentle and sweet, small and wheezy. Not at all possessing a strong constitution. How would he survive away from his mother? Eva had only been away from home a few months and although she wasn't pining for her parents, she did occasionally miss the comforting smell of home cooking, the kindness that passed without request from parent to child, that had allowed her to thrive unaware of how much she needed them. And she was an adult, poor Daniel was a child. Years and years away from any semblance of independence. But she had heard Mr Glasser's response: 'It will be character building, make him a man.' What kind of character, Eva wondered. What was wrong with allowing it to build itself up naturally, bit by bit? Let him take steady, slow steps from childhood at his own pace. And why on earth did he need to become a man so soon? She didn't understand. But she sensed that Mrs Glasser, with her sniffling voice and floral dresses, would not win this debate in the long run.

She was ready on Saturday night when Alfred came. She knew it wasn't obvious, but it had taken her most of the day to get ready. She had washed her hair and blow dried it, then filed her nails and painted them a pearly beige colour, painting her toes too, even though they would remain hidden in her shoes. Finally, she put on make-up, careful not to let it show. Even as she sat ready to go, she wondered whether to change into a different outfit. She waited for a few seconds after he rang the bell, then opened the door and practically walked into him. 'Have a nice time,' Mr and Mrs Glasser called out behind her.

It was still there, the sense that they had known each other for a while, the ache for physical closeness. When he kissed her on the cheek, smelling of lemons and limes, and coconut too, she thought, her cheek tingled where his mouth had been. There was a taxi waiting for them and when they were sitting in the back, he gave the driver instructions, calling him 'mate'. He adjusted himself to face her and asked her how her week had been. 'Fine,' said Eva. Her memory had misguided her, she thought. She had forgotten how slick his eyebrows were, how shiny his skin, and how striking his smile. When he smiled, the dimpled side of his face definitely lifted higher, making him look cheeky, transforming his eyes into sparklingly slants. His lips were full and perfectly drawn, his chin was quite square. 'I have never been in a black cab before,' she said to distract herself.

He tilted his head and smiled at her, 'A night of firsts then?' His thigh was brushing hers.

Eva blushed and turned to look out the window so that he wouldn't notice her skin redden. Her first journey in a London taxi, her first Indian meal, her first date with a black man... She was nervous and excited at the same time. She wanted to touch him, to hold his hand like a real couple, like two people who had longed to see each other. But he seemed reserved, and didn't seem to want or need any bodily contact beyond their formal kiss. He was sitting in his corner of the taxi, albeit gazing at her so that she felt she was being quite rude by looking out of the window from time to time to hide her nerves. She rubbed her hands together on her lap.

He reached over and placed a hand over hers. 'Relax,' he said and when her hands had stopped fidgeting, he didn't move his hand away, he rubbed the top of her hand with his thumb. 'You'll like this place. It's a gem,' he said.

She smiled. 'Thank you for the card you sent. It made me smile, the "Happy Birthday" on the front especially. Very original.'

'Oh good. And you look lovely tonight. That colour...' his voice trailed off and he smiled at her.

Eva imagined he was disappointed. She had seen that look before on her mother's face. The one that implied that more effort might have been made, that the best had not been achieved with her meagre assets. She thought maybe his memory had let him down too; now he could see quite clearly that of all the girls available to him in London, perhaps he had picked the wrong one.

The taxi slowed and he looked out of his window. She loved how effortlessly he spoke to the driver. She would have been awkward and apologetic, but he was assertive of himself and his right to be driven wherever he wanted. He paid and held open the door for her. She reached for the door handle as she stepped out, brushing his hand as she did so.

When they were seated in the restaurant, he asked her what she liked, chicken or fish or lamb or beef. She told him she didn't mind. He asked her whether she liked very spicy food, and she said she didn't know. He asked her if she preferred red or white wine, or maybe a beer, and she said she would have what he was having.

'Shall I order for us both then, will you trust me?'

She ate things that challenged her inactive taste buds. Things with unfamiliar names, like *pakora* and *bhaji*, coconut infused lamb, cardamom and coriander chicken, rice with pink and green bits in it. And they drank cool beer and talked. As the evening passed, Eva began to ask Alfred about himself, and freely he told her about his family in Ghana in West Africa. How he was the first in the family to be sent to school in England, that he had won a scholarship to a boarding school in Dorset and had been here since he was sixteen. He had a large family back in Accra, a 'beloved mother' and a deceased father, two brothers and two sisters, and innumerable cousins. 'The Laryeas are as plenty as the stars,' he told her, accentuating his African accent and making her laugh. 'It has been liberating being here so far from them all, away from obligations and responsibilities. I have even warned my mother not to give out my address in case distant relatives start to descend on me and want to share my digs. But I must say, I am ready to go home now. I have to finish this year and then I am off.'

'Oh.' Eva sipped her beer.

He held out a forkful of the spicy curry that he had warned her against. 'This one is not for first-timers, but you could try a teeny bit.' She leaned towards him to take it trustingly, without taking her eyes off his. He watched amused as she swallowed and then quickly reached for more beer to quench the flames.

'How can you eat that? It hurts!'

He laughed at her, his eyes disappeared into his face, and licked his lower lip slowly, leaving her with an overpowering desire to grab his hand and ask him to take her home, to his home, and keep her there all night. She put her cutlery down and drank the rest of her beer. Where on earth had these thoughts and longings come from? She was staggered by them, and the power that he seemed to be exuding; there was a connection so powerful, so full of a life of its own that it was rather frightening.

'I didn't overdo it did I?' he asked.

'No,' she was touched by his caring and wondered what he would do if he knew her thoughts. Would he pay the bill in a hurry, would he embrace her outside on the threshold of the restaurant, impatient and unable to wait until they were alone? Or would he continue to sit, maintaining the dignity that she was already beginning to associate with him, even though he was aroused by the idea that she wanted him so fiercely? She swallowed and looked around to divert her thoughts; how had she not noticed the multicoloured, ferociously patterned carpets, the glossy red walls, the guitar-based Spanish music which tingled in the background, clashing with the setting, the crooked wall lights, their near-empty plates smeared with hardening ghee.

'Reminds me of Ghana. This is the closest that I can get to home cooking, unless I go to visit my aunt in Hendon. She always has a fridge full of my favourite food.'

'So you will go back next year?' she hoped she had misunderstood him.

'By the grace of God.'

She had never heard anyone use that phrase before and was surprised that such an obviously worldly man thought of something greater than himself.

'Maybe I'll take you with me.'

She took a gulp of air and looked up at him bashfully, but he had turned around and was summoning the waiter to ask for some more of the cucumber sauce. He had an odd sense of humour, she thought.

When he dropped her off she wanted to fling her arms about him and keep him there. He held her with one hand firmly pressing on a spot just under her ribs, just above her belly button. She trembled and he pulled away.

'I want to see you again,' he said. 'If you like, we could go to the cinema next weekend?'

'Next weekend?' she asked, impatient that she had to wait a whole week to see him again.

'We could do something else instead?'

'No, I'd love to go.'

She slept fitfully for the rest of the week. She relived the way he had touched her, the way he had stroked her face as he said good night with another kiss.

And so they began a habit of seeing each other at the weekends. Going for long walks through Hyde Park or Regent's Park or sometimes along the river, then supper or the cinema, and once the theatre, where they saw the Thirty-Nine Steps. Then one weekend, he took her to a cosy Jewish delicatessen he knew where they ate the most decadent cream cakes she had ever seen. 'Friends of mine are having a party tonight,' he said, pouring her another cup of hot Earl Grey tea. 'We could go if you like?'

They didn't stay long at the party. It was crowded, loud and smoky. Alfred was distracted, seemed absent-minded. He kept touching her, stroking her hands, her shoulders, her neck, her hair. Then he grabbed her and suggested they leave. Go to his flat. She bit her lip, afraid, exhilarated. He noticed and said they didn't have to, they could stay. He dropped his hand to her waist, allowed it to lower and linger on the curve below. She took it in hers and held it. His long, strong fingers intertwined with hers; she thrived on the contrast between their hands, their skin; hers translucent and fragile, his dark and soft. She shook her head. 'I want to,' she said, aware of how desire had filled the space between them. She pulled him to her, kissed his lips, soft but firm and insistent.

Once there, he stroked her skin with the tips of his long fingers, barely touching her yet sending thrilling bolts down through her core to her feet. 'I have wanted to do this from the first time that I saw you,' he said.

'Then why did you wait?'

'I needed to know. You are . . . you haven't done this before, I can tell. And I wanted to know whether this odd effect you have on me would pass.'

'And did it?'

'What do you think?' he asked. He pulled her back, wrapped his arms around her, raised her on to her toes, cradled her head in his hand, kissed her. She let him envelop her, and felt as if she might swoon dramatically, but she was determined to remain as alert as possible, to savour everything so that her memory would not be able to rob her later of what had happened. She liked the tropical scent of his hair oil, the lingering whiff of aftershave. His closely shaved cheeks were taut and pampered soft. She clung to him to show him as best as she could, using every part of her, how much she wanted him, in no doubt whatsoever that it was love that had stirred her this deeply. She slid her hands over his wide back; she knew she would never let him go.

In the end, she wasn't sure how best to let out some of the emotions that were colliding and coursing through her. And then when he propped himself up on his elbows and scrutinised her lovingly, his deep warm eyes scouring her face, she smiled blearily. Tenderly, with fingers soft as a feather, he wiped away a stray tear from her cheek.

Once he unleashed it, Alfred's passion astounded her. He wrote her urgent notes: 'I must see you today.' Must? She hadn't realised such compulsion was possible in relation to her. 'You kept me awake last night.' How, she wondered smiling at the thoughts that flooded her mind. She bubbled with excitement at the thought of seeing him. Simply couldn't believe that he felt these amazing things for her. She agonised over how to keep his sharp brain interested, his beautiful hands busy.

Then, as if to ensure they didn't have to keep up the intensity of their weekend-long lovemaking and their frequent love letters, they had a quarrel. It was their first, and, as Eva knew, winding herself up all over again whenever she remembered it over the following weeks and months, it could quite easily have been their last.

They went to a pub close to where Eva lived on their way to the cinema.

Alfred had been reticent about going in. 'I am not sure about this place,' he said. 'I haven't ever been in there.' He hesitated at the door.

'I have been here lots of times with my friends. It's nice.'

He scrunched his lips. 'Evie, I don't know . . .' He hesitated. 'But if you really are that keen . . . but don't be surprised if we have to leave.'

'What are you talking about, don't be silly,' she said, pulling him in.

At the bar they waited an inordinate amount of time before they were served. 'We were here before them, and them,' Eva said, beginning to get impatient.

'Listen, mate,' said Alfred eventually, stepping forward. He had been standing slightly behind Eva, wanting her to order the drinks, it was her local after all, and he hadn't wanted to intervene unnecessarily. 'If you don't want to serve me, just say so and I'll go elsewhere.'

'Ah, I didn't see you,' said the publican without smiling. Then he served them without looking at Alfred.

'He is usually so friendly,' said Eva. She led him to a table in the corner where they could canoodle in peace. She stretched her legs and rubbed his under the table.

'You really are rather naïve,' he said shaking his head.

'What do you mean?'

'Oh forget it,' Alfred said, sounding irritated and not looking his usual self.

'So tell me,' said Eva leaning forward, keen to jolt their evening forward out of this gloominess that seemed intent on settling about them. 'Did I keep you up all night again?'

'Not really,' he replied abruptly.

She felt indignant. Smoke, theirs and the rest of the pub's, swirled before their eyes, through the fibres of their clothes.

'Then you can't possibly feel like I feel. Maybe I need to get myself a new young black lover,' she said, lowering her head and looking at him mournfully.

His features had darkened. 'I can't believe you just said that.'

She laughed. 'Oh don't be silly, Alfred, I was just joking.'

'Well, I'm not laughing. And if that is the kind of thing you find funny, there is no point us being together. I am not some plaything!' He stood up, picked up his coat, which was slung over a chair, and his keys off the table.

'Where are you going?' Eva felt a sickening sensation. She tried to grab his hand but he moved it out of her reach. She wanted him to sit down again, to appreciate that it was all a misunderstanding. 'Please don't go.'

'And don't ever call me silly,' he said. The expression on his face was one she had not seen before. He walked off leaving her sitting there with her shandy untouched, his pint still brimming.

'I was joking, Alfred,' she called after him, standing to her feet and pushing the table back impatiently to free herself from the bench she had been sitting on, spilling their drinks all over the polished table. She watched as he walked towards the door, barging into a man who refused to step aside to let him pass.

'Bloody monkeys, and they don't know how to treat a woman neither. Don't learn that where they come from,' the man said.

Eva felt her eyes prick. She didn't know if it was because Alfred had walked out or because of the remark. She scowled at the man, praying that Alfred hadn't heard him, yet for a moment torn between wanting to chase after him and stopping to give the man an education, to correct his view of the world. She stumbled out of the pub and started after Alfred. She was used to the stares, the odd question which she mostly ignored because it stemmed from ignorance: 'What are you doing with a blacky?' The observation: 'You really could do so much better, you know.' Or the curiosity of ditsy girls: 'So is it true? You know . . . you know?' 'You know what?' She would retort angrily. Stupid girls! Didn't deserve a response, yet so hard to ignore. She shouted for him and imagined she saw his step falter a little. Her heart was thumping in time with her steps. He had slowed down but she seemed no closer to him. She had to reach him to tell him how sorry she was, to try and erase the insensitive words she had spoken, to let him see how she instantly regretted offending him. Couldn't he see that she loved him? Yes, she did love him! She loved him, for who he was, not the colour of his skin. How on earth could she have been so thoughtless? How indeed? And why? She was driving this wonderful man away. She began to run, imagining that if she didn't catch him soon, she might never see him again.

When she caught up with him, he stood and let her hold his hands. She told him how sorry she was. He held her in silence for a while, then he said, 'I didn't think it was like you. I thought maybe we don't fit after all.'

She kissed him and felt his damp cheek. 'We do fit.'

'Maybe,' he said, waving his hand about. 'But not here, not in London.'

She pulled back and said, 'I love you.' Never before had her heart stuttered in this way, making her wonder whether it might pop with all this ardour, too much to keep holding onto. 'I really do,' she said to Alfred, wanting to make sure that he had heard her, that he understood her.

He looked at her fixedly. He remained silent, and when Eva

had given up hope that she might hear the obvious response to her declaration, he spoke in a gruff voice, 'Come home with me then, and help me make my life out there.'

'What?' The cold air was ringing in her ears, her nose was dribbling. 'What did you say?'

'I asked . . . marry me, Eva?'

She kissed him so hard her stomach knotted and her arms tired from reaching up so high. She couldn't bear the thought of ever being apart from this man again; she had known for a while that she would follow him wherever he went. Of course she would marry him. She held him tight. And move to Ghana. She looked into his eyes, saw the moistness; was it the cold? Yes, she would! He kissed her again. Even if it meant she couldn't come back home. She kissed him back. But hopefully it wouldn't come to that. But part of her already knew.

Love, passion, madness, whatever you wanted to call it, Eva now knew that it couldn't be parcelled in a neat box and presented with operating instructions. It came silently, and she knew it could go silently too. In between, it caused havoc with emotions, with diet and sleep. With plans and intentions. With family and home.

Just look how far she had come on the back of it. All the way to Africa for heaven's sake! There was no accounting for love. And there was no point dwelling on the past; it had happened and couldn't be changed. And she wasn't convinced she *would* change it. Modify a few things here and there perhaps. She smiled, grateful she didn't have a crystal ball. Who would embark on the journey of marriage or children if they could see what lay ahead? Wasn't the enthusiasm and optimism of youth essential for procreation, necessary to keep life endlessly ongoing? Wouldn't it be tempting, safer, in fact, to bind oneself to one's bed and wait for death to come swooping in if one could see what pain could come hand in hand with joy? How after all, failure wasn't always avoidable? No, she wouldn't have missed, not for the world, the wonderful things her life had brought her, or the journey on which it had taken her. To Ghana. Besides, she didn't believe any longer that the miracle of love and wonder came without some painfulness and turmoil and that brand of compromise that required so much self-sacrifice. Oh how fruitless, how exhausting, to conjecture and imagine things differently from the way they are!

Chapter Six

Gladys was sprawled on one of the armchairs while her maid Akua braided her hair, pulling and tugging it into place. Abigail sat on the floor reading her latest Nancy Drew mystery. On the coffee table there was a tub of Vaseline with a comb sticking in it, and Eva anticipated yet another ring of grease. Next to the pot lay rolled up strands of Gladys' unnaturally black hair. Eva watched as Akua took the comb to prepare a new square of hair. She combed a dollop of Vaseline into the hair and spread some on to the scalp around the hair before beginning to plait it.

With her hair pulled back from her face in tight braids, her lineless face still plump, Gladys appeared much younger than she was. She was shaving her eyebrows with a blade, but she laid the hand mirror she was holding on her lap when she saw Eva. 'I am also trying hard here,' she chuckled, 'keeping up with the younger generation is no mean feat, you know. And you know, this is what Abi's hair needs. Not this style you allow her to walk about with.'

'I like her curls. And I don't like the grease.'

'But look at how dull her hair is. You won't let me braid it, straighten it, oil it, in fact, nothing at all. I have to say that this afro style, not even combed, is not nice at all. It looks so untidy, a mess. Imagine if she has lice, will you even know?'

'She doesn't have lice! And besides, I always wanted curls like that,' Eva said. 'I think they are gorgeous,' she looked lovingly at her daughter who seemed oblivious to the discussion. 'When Abigail is older she can do what she likes with her hair.'

'Ah, you too!' Gladys looked at Abigail. 'She would look so pretty with her scalp properly oiled and her hair in neat, shiny cornrows.' She tutted and shook her head in bewilderment. 'And the ears too. It is time, you know. We must pierce them soon. She is about ten, isn't it, full-speed on the way to full-blown development! Do you want to wait until she has hips and breasts before you let her look like a girl?'

'Please can I? Say yes, Mummy. I *want* earrings,' said Abi suddenly enlivened by the conversation. 'Pleeease. Auntie Gee says I can have lots of different coloured studs.'

Gladys clapped her hands and grinned. 'Aha. Someone in this house can talk sense.'

'When Abigail is older she can decide what she wants, but where *I* come from, it isn't appropriate to pierce children's ears.'

'But we are not there? We are *here*, and over here . . .'

'We aren't going to get anywhere with this today,' said Eva, smiling resolutely. She called out for Faustina.

'I told her to start with the chickens.'

Eva scrunched her face. 'I thought you said Akua would do it. There are other things that I need Faustina to do.'

'Don't worry, we are operating on African time,' she said, looking at Eva with a little disdain. She was laughing, but her eyes were unyielding.

'Yes, I know. I don't think I will ever get used to it,' said Eva as she walked towards the kitchen. 'Neither will my friends; they will show up on time.'

'Don't worry, one day you will adjust,' called Gladys after her. 'In this life, we are all called to get used to different, different things.'

86

'Abi, come and watch the slaughter that is about to take place in our garden,' Eva said, and Abigail followed her.

'You see,' Gladys said to her maid. 'Some people think that having a white daughter-in-law is a nice thing. Never wish for something that you don't know.'

'Please yes, Auntie Gee,' said Akua.

It was the best way to think of Eva. It was the only way to describe her to anyone who would listen, as the 'white daughter-in-law who has married my son.' It paved the way for what was to follow and enabled the hearer to brush aside all the usual expectations of a daughter-in-law. It allowed the listener to refrain from too harsh a judgement and at the same time gave a host of explanations before they were required. For instance, as to why Eva didn't alter her plans when Gladys came to visit, sometimes asking Gladys to leave her son's house within a very short while of her arrival because Eva wanted to go and drink tea with her friends. It would not have occurred to a Ga daughter-in-law to be so rude. At the very least, she would take her mother-in-law with her, but Eva had never offered. A Ga girl would have understood the effort and expense that goes into making a visit like this. And what about the inability to offer her something proper to eat after the mother-in-law has made her way across town in an uncomfortable journey of public transport in the searing heat while bearing the favourite foods of her favourite son? Toast, a sandwich? Is that what they did back in her country? That was a snack, not a proper meal, not even enough for a child. This morning, she had to ask for her own egg! And what of the regular absence of any attempts to drive the tired, ageing mother-in-law home after her visits, but instead allowing her to brace the hot sun once more? She wouldn't have to ask for a lift from a good Ga woman. The offer of a comfortable homeward journey would guaranteed be thrust upon her. She would have to decline with mock modesty once, twice, and then eventually say, 'OK then,' pleased that she had raised her son well enough to marry a woman who understood the respect that was due to his mother. If necessary a Ga daughter would have forced the old and failing mother-in-law into the car and driven her home. Naturally, Gladys would expect no lesser treatment to be afforded to Eva's parents by her son when eventually they came to visit. Like every normal mother, she had been concerned about the possibilities of her son marrying out of their tribe, perhaps falling for a Fanti, an Ashanti or even an Ewe with all of their weird ways and rituals! In retrospect that would have been a smoother set of circumstances for Gladys to manoeuvre. As far as she could see, there was no tribe in this entire country that didn't espouse the need for deference to one's elders.

'Ah ah, as for these Europeans! Anyways, Akua, later you will put some cream in the children's hair, okay? But don't let their mother see you.'

'Please, yes Auntie Gee.'

Didn't Alfred notice? Of course he did. She had pointed it out umpteen times to him, and he still did nothing, as if this was normal behaviour, as if it was right for his child to be seen with this unruly hair at school, at church, at anywhere. Gladys couldn't understand it.

'They leave me no choice.'

'Please, yes.'

'After all, I am their grandmother. And if I am not the one to fulfil my responsibilities, then who will?'

'Auntie Gee, in fact, it's true!'

'Hey! Who asked you something, you this stupid girl? Do the hair well and stop talking.'

'Please yes, Auntie Gee.' Akua smiled. She pulled the braid a little tighter, determined that this would be the best hairdo she had ever done for Auntie Gee. She would make Auntie Gee proud of her; she wouldn't allow her to think it had been a bad idea to bring her along for the celebrations.

Gladys held her forehead, which buzzed from the twinge of the tight new braids and the overly burdensome responsibility of being the mother-in-law of this out-of-the-ordinary-girl Eva. Sometimes, how she wished she had someone to share in the responsibility of keeping this cross-cultural marriage ticking over.

Alfred was on the veranda outside the kitchen with Simon. He had been looking out the bedroom window when his mother arrived and had watched the hullabaloo of the taxi being stripped off its cargo. He looked over at Eva a little sheepishly as she walked towards him. She hated the mess and chaos, but freshly slaughtered chickens reminded him of his childhood. He salivated, remembering how often after a day like this, they could look forward to nightfall and balls of warm *kenkey* and pepper sauce bought from the roadside, to eat with freshly fried gizzards. Crunching through the fried skin into the firm, bouncy texture of the green-tinted, muscular meat.

'There is something about blood-letting that garners interest and enthusiasm across the world,' he said, smiling at Eva.

She turned her mouth downwards in distaste and positioned herself between Abigail and Simon, just as Faustina tightened her hold on the first bird, which was under her arm, and with one quick jerky movement wrung its neck. Eva groaned, covering her mouth with her hand.

Faustina pushed a sharp knife into the chicken's beak, made a deep gash, tipped it upside down and drained the blood into a bucket. Her dress was sprayed with blood, beads of perspiration had gathered on her head and her hands were covered with wet feathers.

'Give me a dead, clean chicken instead any day,' whispered Eva to her husband. She looked at her children watching the slaughter with interest. Abigail flinching from time to time, Simon covering his face with his small hands to hide the worst, all of them grimacing when Faustina twisted their necks, tight and quick as if she was wringing clothes, wrinkling their noses when the blood spurted into the pan.

Alfred started to tell the children about how he had had to kill chickens when he was a child. 'I haven't done it for years, of course, but Auntie Gee taught me how to do lots of things. She wanted me to be independent. I learned to cook, to clean, to wash and iron my clothes without fuss, and to kill and gut a chicken without a whiff of nausea.'

There was some truth in his siblings' taunt that he was a mummy's boy and was far too skilled at womanly tasks. But he had liked his mother's company when he was growing up; she didn't criticise him and very little he did failed to amuse her. As he grew he realised he had taken it for granted, that comforting pleasure of for ever being in the presence of someone who enjoyed having him with her, who lit up because he was near. He had no need now to slay chickens or wash clothes, nor in fact to chat to his mother, a fact that brought a little nudge of shame, but he hoped she understood that he was no longer the carefree schoolboy that he had been in those days. He was a man of standing, with business deals to do, important people to socialise with and a family of his own to raise.

'The hardest thing was catching the damn things because Auntie Gee likes to treat them to one last meal and a final fly about before they die'. He realised that his hands were moving with his memories, wringing the neck of an imaginary bird.

'When I was young and silly like you,' he said, pinching Abigail's ear, 'my cousins and I would let the dead chickens jerk around the yard expending the last of their nerves.' He chuckled to himself.

'How wicked, Daddy,' said Abigail, shocked.

He looked at Eva, grinning, but she shook her head, looking horrified. 'I think Mummy is very cross that I have arranged this mass killing in her garden. I am going to have to think of something nice to make it up to her later.'

'You are going to have to try very hard indeed, Mr Laryea.'

He looked away faster than he ought to have, and continued his story. 'Another time, we wanted to see what would happen if we cut a chicken's throat before it was dead and let it loose. The poor bird ran around and around, blood spurting out of its neck.'

'Enough,' said Eva sternly. 'You'll put them off, and I don't have the energy to deal with a couple of vegetarians.'

'What is a vegetareen?' asked Simon.

'Someone who doesn't eat dead things,' said Abi.

'We don't have vegetarians in Ghana,' said Alfred, 'so don't go getting any funny ideas.'

'What happened next?' asked Simon.

'I got into big trouble with Auntie Gee.' The chicken had seemed to squawk silently, unable to make a sound. Blood sprayed on to the white walls of the yard, on to the washing that was floating on the line, and on to his baby cousin's face when the headless chicken staggered by too close, causing her to cry out. Alfred and his cousins had held their sides and reeled uncontrollably with laughter while the poor chicken kept tottering on and on. 'She screeched when she saw what we had done. And then she slapped each of us a few times. We caught it and killed it as quickly as possible. I had never seen her that angry before.'

Simon and Abigail were dumbfounded.

'I know, you can't imagine Auntie Gee angry, but trust me, it is not something you want to see. "God's creatures are here to nourish us, not to amuse us," she told us. We had the worst punishment she could think of. First of all, we didn't have any of the fried chicken, then we had to wash the walls of the house and paint them, we had to do all the washing for a month, which included the baby's soiled nappies.'

'Yuck,' said Abi. 'How disgusting.'

'Eew,' said Simon, grimacing. 'Pooey.'

'Well, I know what to do the next time you two misbehave.' He laughed. 'And then, when my stepfather got home that evening, he lashed each of us with his cane until welts grew large and soft on our backs and bottoms, making sleep uncomfortable for many days.' The children's eyes were saucer-wide. 'I never crossed her again. And I never again drained the blood from a chicken without first killing it; after that I allowed the blood to drip neatly into a bowl or a bucket.'

The children watched Faustina and Solomon with respectful silence. They were plucking feathers from the limp chickens. They rummaged in the warm, soft insides like children searching in a lucky dip bag to remove the innards.

Faustina squeaked when she found an egg in one of the chickens. All formed and ready to pop out, the shell not quite hardened. 'Madam, do you want this one?' she asked with an expression that suggested Eva would not.

'You have it,' Eva said, unable to imagine consuming something so premature, and Faustina's face lit up. 'Everything is behind schedule,' she said to herself, looking around at the yard which was covered in chicken shit and small white feathers; the smell was pungent. 'I suppose I'd better iron my clothes myself. There is no chance of Faustina being able to do it.'

Alfred put his arm around Eva's waist, pulled her to him. She looked at him distracted by the distasteful scene before them. He nodded and then made as if to say something. She could guess what, the same instruction she had heard umpteen times already, 'don't worry'. A favourite phrase of the people she dwelled amongst. A few roads away was the 'don't worry' chop bar, and Eva often wondered what the clientele were not to worry about. The cost of the food? The source of the meat? Perhaps the flies that would plague them as they ate? Or maybe it was nothing to do with the food. Maybe it was simply life they were not to worry about. Eat and be merry, is that what it meant? It was a popular phrase painted on the backs of mammy lorries, either those two words on their own, or else embellished further, such as the one she had seen recently which said, 'don't worry for tomorrow may never come', alas true. Then there was the one she had seen just days ago which was now her favourite because it turned the whole concept on its head: 'don't worry me'. Just remembering it now made her smile. It had made her laugh out loud then, and the driver Solomon too had laughed, saying 'It is he who is worrying us, look at his lorry about to fall over.' And he was right, the *mammy* lorry was occupying the middle of the road, loping precariously to one side, threatening to spill its heavy load of passengers and cargo into the side ditch.

Relax, Eva told herself as she left them and went back upstairs and started to iron her cream linen dress. Relax, she instructed herself, and don't worry.

Her relationship with Gladys could be rather bumpy at times; Eva often didn't understand her or her motivations, but she had learned to keep their dealings to a minimum, that way she felt she could retain control of her family and do things her own way.

The morning after they arrived in Accra, Eva woke to find that Gladys was on the veranda waiting for them to wake up. Eva emerged sticky from their room. Gladys greeted her warmly and told her to sit in one of the chairs on the veranda. Eva smiled, hesitantly, and looked around. It had been dark when they arrived, and now she saw that in the middle of the yard was a large mango tree dripping with sweet-smelling fruit. The yard was paved with concrete and a young boy was sweeping away the leaves that had been shed by the tree. A low wall surrounded the yard. There were several large white flowerpots dotted around, in which dead rose plants withered. A couple of tiny scabby cats came meowing up to her and Eva bent forward to pick one up, but Gladys shouted and raised her hands to stop Eva.

'These ones are not like English cats, you must not touch them. They are mostly contaminated.'

Eva looked at the cats and thought they just looked underfed but she didn't say anything. Then Gladys stamped her feet on the floor to scare them away, startling Eva.

It was hot on the veranda. Sweat dripped down Eva's neck and back. She blew hot air up her nose and face and longed to go and have a shower, but Gladys said, 'I am here to get to know you.'

Eva tried not to laugh. What an odd thing to say, she thought.

But Gladys continued, 'Tell me about your mother, your father, your family. Alfred informed me that he did the right thing and asked for your hand in the correct fashion according to your customs? Which is a good thing because of course I did raise him properly, but you never know when you are not around to supervise your children whether they forget to do the right thing.'

Eva nodded. 'He did see my father, but he didn't exactly ask . . .'

'You see, I raised him well. And do you have many cousins?'

'I don't really know them, my parents kept themselves to themselves.'

'You don't know them? How terrible. What is that about? Here you will find that Alfred has a lot of cousins. You will find that family is the most important thing to us. And of course, my dear, I am thrilled that you have come to Ghana to have my first grandchild. Isn't my son thoughtful? I am so grateful to him for considering my wishes like this.'

Eva was puzzled. What was keeping Alfred? She had a lot of questions for him. What other facts had he misrepresented to his mother?

'We shall have a large outdooring and christening for the baby. I can do all the cooking and baking. I am a good cook, you see. And I hope it will be a girl. For your sakes. A girl is for forever. But a boy, well, he grows and takes a wife and then depending on the wife, well your position can be usurped forever.' She smiled at Eva. 'But I know that has not happened in the case of Alfred. I can see that he has made a good choice.'

'Thanks.'

'And with a girl you can have fun. Ears to pierce, hair to plait . . .'

'Oh, I don't know about earrings.' She was finding it difficult to concentrate, her skin felt clammy and she was perspiring. There seemed to be insufficient air in the compound and she felt as though she was being suffocated.

'Don't worry about that now. First we have to see what you are carrying, no?'

Eva faked a smile to hide her irritation. She had an increasingly uncomfortable feeling that she was going to have to fight a bit to retain control of all aspects of her life. She could see that without a firm hand this woman would interfere where she wasn't wanted.

'Anyways,' Gladys leaned forward and dropped her voice a bit. 'It is my duty to give you a few tips about being good wife. I am sure that your mother has already talked to you, but you see you are in Ghana now, and things are different here. Firstly, you must not stop trying to look beautiful for him, and our men don't like forceful women who have something to say about everything and who want to always be in charge.'

'Well, Alfred values my opinion . . .'

'Yes,' Gladys nodded thoughtfully. 'For now. Anyways, as I was saying, you will find that my son is a very good catch and there will be many women who are not deterred by the fact that he has a wife already. As long as they can see that he can look after any baby he fathers, they will follow him like bees follow honey . . . you look confused. I am only telling you this so that nothing will take you by surprise. In fact, most of our menfolk find it difficult to be satisfied by one woman alone. They think they are entitled to have variety in that department. So, if in case you should find out that Alfred has strayed one day, do not consider yourself particularly misfortunate.'

Eva couldn't contain her mirth any longer and she burst out laughing.

'Do you think I am funny? Okay, laugh then.'

'No, no you are not funny, it's just that I can't quite believe this . . . Alfred would never, well . . . he knows I wouldn't stand for it. There'd be no second chance if he was stupid enough to cheat on me . . .'

'Okay. Anyway, if you have any questions, any needs whatsoever, you must come to me.'

'Thank you,' said Eva. Her laughter had subsided when she'd seen that Gladys didn't look in the least bit amused. She couldn't wait to talk to Alfred and find out what this was all about.

'Oh, there's nothing to thank me for. You are my daughter now, and I want to be satisfied that you are happy. We don't want you to have any reasons for going back home. We want you to be very, very comfortable here indeed.'

The unfamiliarity was shocking initially. Eva felt crushed by the indescribable strangeness all around her. The vastness that separated her from home, physically and emotionally, was overwhelming, and she cried often, in secret. She was careful to rearrange her face and her hair before Alfred saw her, so that he wouldn't realise that she was wrestling with the choice she had made. She dreamed of hearing her mother's voice, seeing her parents again. They seemed so very far away, so unavailable, that she ached.

Alfred remained oblivious to her melancholy, which surprised her, but then he was over the moon to be home, cheerful while he set about the business of acquiring a piece of land, setting up his practice, meeting up with old buddies, visiting family.

How impossible it is to accurately describe a place one loves if one has never seen it through the eyes of a foreigner, Eva thought time and again as she marvelled at how different Accra was from anything she had imagined. And yet, in spite of the many mysterious differences, Eva felt she had adjusted well to her life here. She had done more than survive; Africa hadn't got her down, hadn't made her cower or lose herself. She was thriving in a manner of speaking. And it was due in no small part to her good friends whose support and understanding was essential to dealing with the frustrations and the loneliness.

Yes, it had seemed the right thing to do when she got here, to push the past away and concentrate on the future. But still, if she caught a whiff of cloves, or cinnamon, or melting brown sugar, and she had the time to close her eyes and think, she could dream up many of the smells of her mother's kitchen. She pictured roasted chicory, strong coffee and fresh apple pie, simmering rhubarb and cloves, sizzling pork belly with lemon and thyme; smells and sounds that had once upon a time welcomed her home. And today, that absent love, those absent grandparents, stood up and thumped away in her chest, rousing a yearning in her heart, a heavy desolateness that weighed her down and threatened to drown her. As she always did, she thought of her three children and comforted herself with the thought that they didn't miss something they had never had, that they lived fully loved lives, and that no matter what, she would never, ever voluntarily withdraw her love for them.

Everyone was gathered on the veranda outside the living room looking up at something. Eva went outside and she too saw the banner hanging over the front door. It shimmered in the sunlight, the pink and gold foil fluttering so that she had to concentrate to read what was scrolled on it; '*WELL DONE TO ALFRED AND EVA ON THE OCCAZION OF 10 YEARS WEDLOCK!*' It had been fixed in several places with brown sticky tape. 'My goodness!' She clasped her hand over her mouth, not knowing what to think.

'My contribution to you,' said Auntie Gee coming up behind her. 'I don't believe in celebrating things quietly as you know, my dear.'

'No . . . no, you don't. Well, I don't know what to say. The colours, the size . . . it is indisputably loud and clear.' She noticed that all her potted plants had been moved safely out of the way, and were now bunched in a group in the corner of the veranda.

'I've enjoyed being wed-*locked* to you, my love,' said Alfred, laughing.

'I'm glad you think it's funny,' Eva replied, smiling in spite of herself. 'Help me put the flowerpots back, please.'

'Of course, my love. So long as you let me show you just how much I've enjoyed the whole padlocked thing later,' he said, chuckling like a boy.

Gladys mumbled something to Alfred in Ga and Eva left them, heading for the kitchen, anxious to see how ready things were there.

Faustina and Akua had changed into their Sunday cloth and hidden their untidy hair behind ironed scarves. Faustina had bound Joseph to her back so he would go to sleep. 'If he sleeps now, later he won't be tired when we need him.'

The kitchen reeked of smoky groundnut oil and chicken, but Eva looked around in amazement, astounded at the level of readiness that had been attained in her absence. There were platters of fried chicken, plantain and fish covered with dishcloths, large earthenware dishes of *jolof* rice, plain rice, stew, and dishes of vegetables. The floor had been mopped and the surfaces around the food sparkled. The sink was clean and empty. Trays with shiny glasses, piles of crockery and cutlery gleamed. Eva put her hands to her face and gasped involuntarily.

'I really am impressed Faustina.'

'Madam, but why? Am I not always telling you to trust me? I am very capable of many things. And today, as I gave you my solemn pledge this morning, I will not let you down at all.'

'Yes, Faustina, you *are* capable. Tell Solomon to please go and help Architect move the pots on the veranda.' She went into the storeroom at the back of the kitchen just to check that everything there was in equal order.

Gladys came bustling in. She had tied a scarf around her head to protect her newly braided hair from lingering food smells. 'Okey dokey Fausti! Are we ready to go? Some guests are here. I think they came in a big bus, all at once. They will be asking for some of my proper food in no time at all.' When she saw Eva she exclaimed, 'What are you doing here? Go and greet your guests. Your friend has come. The Russian one, Yelena, no? You should go and sit with her.' She watched and waited for Eva to leave.

In the living room, Alfred had put on Bob Marley and the Wailers and was crouching down by his stereo sorting through his cassettes to find some to play later. Eva stopped beside him and placed her hand on the nape of his neck. She could feel his calm seep into her. 'I need a drink,' she said. 'Bloody hell, if I wasn't in such a good mood today, I'd want to kill your mother.'

He was engrossed in his music and didn't seem to have noticed her, but as Eva was drawing her hand away, he reached out and grabbed it, pressed his lips to the soft inside of her wrist.

'Will you open a bottle of the Mateus Rosé? It should be cold enough by now.'

He released her. 'Give me a moment,' he said, as he continued to sort through his music looking for something.

Eva walked out into her garden with a ready smile. A group of guests had gathered in the garden; a small sea of people in vivid colours wearing stiff, expensive cloth, head-ties, shiny stilettos and all their jewellery. A few children sat quietly next to their parents, their polished faces bemused as they watched Abigail chase Simon and a group of others about the garden, all of them screeching and laughing. An angelic looking girl sat as still as a statue in a layered burgundy polyester dress, white lacy stockings and polished shoes, quietly watching the trays of food that were being passed around. A couple of young boys wearing black suits and bow ties were playing with Lego, pretending to shoot each other.

Suddenly, Simon careered into her. He had decided by way of a last minute detour that she was 'home'. 'You nearly winded me,' she said, 'please go and run about in the back garden, not here. And take the other children with you.'

Eva loved the way everyone made such an effort to look beautiful, and all together the picture was lovely to behold, especially against the background of her shady garden. There were a few faces she didn't recognise and she couldn't remember if she had ever met them before, but she had learned from the past, when with honesty she had enquired: 'Have we met?' or 'Sorry, remind me how you are related to Alfred?' and had had to listen to endless reminders of the exact day and place they had met or the nature of the relationships so convoluted yet vague. At times, she wondered how she would cope in old age if she was already incapable of remembering people and faces.

Faustina came quickly carrying a platter in each hand, one with savoury *achomo* and the other with ground nuts. Akua held a tray heavy with sweating bottles of beer, Coca-Cola and Muscatella. They began serving a small group of women who were sitting in the shade in front of the veranda. Their shiny cheeks and mauve and red lips shimmered beneath a thin layer of perspiration. They dabbed their brows, carefully avoiding eyebrows which were pencil-lined and thin. All of them wore a lot of gold jewellery. Eva went up to them and greeted Mrs Akiwumi whom she recognised, a teacher who had known Alfred's stepfather.

'Eva! Well done oh!' she said. She was wearing a billowing floral dress with bell-shaped sleeves that covered her elbows. Her hair was tied behind a tight scarf because she hadn't had the time to get her hair done. Some grey frizz poked out around her temples, the only real sign of her advancing years. That and her large, wobbly body. 'Eva you have done so well, may God continue to bless you like this.' When she smiled, her face moved about softly, like unbaked chocolate cake. 'A two-in-one party, what a good idea is that!'

Eva was about to ask her what she meant, but Mrs Akiwumi continued, 'You know Eugenia, my doctor-daughter?'

Eva smiled at a thin woman who sat beside Mrs Akiwumi with her knees pressed together and her hands firmly clasping a shiny purple clutch bag. She was wearing a tight pink crimplene suit with matching shoes, and a necklace and bracelet of large red plastic beads. Two red beads had been pinned into her ears.

'Hello Eugenia.' Eva wanted to ask what kind of doctor she was, but she thought they might be insulted that she couldn't remember. 'How is work these days?'

'Well, we do our best, but it is hard. Our current campaign of family planning and hygiene is not doing well at all. It is very difficult in our culture, as you know, to tell a woman to limit herself to two children when she is expecting them to look after her in old age, and the chances are that one of them will succumb to some childhood illness. And you must have seen our latest cleanliness slogans along the road side? *Clean hands = Long life!* and *Faeces can kill, use a latrine.*

Eva nodded.

'Too much family planning too is not good,' said Mrs Akiwumi. Why you are still waiting to bring forth is also a mystery to me. Do you want to wait until I am too old to bath a baby before you give me a grandchild? Eva, I keep telling her, just have one and give it to me to look after and then she can go back to her work, work, work. But does she listen? Ah!'

'Ma, please. You know I don't want to be like all those women having children without fathers . . .'

'No child is without a father. You are the doctor, don't you know that? This is a modern idea that a father should be sitting side by side with the mother at all times, it is not necessary, you know? What matters is that *you* must have children. *You* must fulfil your God-given duty. Look at Eva here. Three! Ah-ah! Anyway I am tired of talking. One day you will see. But take it from me, "had I known never comes at first". Eva, it's okay, we are wasting your time, you go and see your guests.' She shooed

101

Eva off with her hand and pointed her chin in the direction of the big tree in the lawn where Yelena sat. 'Your friends are waiting for you. And all of them are mothers isn't it?' She tutted again and then set her face in a piteous expression to demonstrate her sorrowful state.

Eva tried to give Eugenia a conspiratorial smile, but she was looking straight ahead, her lips pursed. She wandered about greeting the guests. All everyone seemed to talking about was inflation, the budget, the state of the economy, the lack of hope and the need for change. They spoke, not in angry, passionate voices as Eva thought might be appropriate, but mostly in sombre and resigned tones.

The sun had slipped beyond the hottest point of the day but it was still high and burning through the dust-laden air. White handkerchiefs, pressed for the occasion, regularly wiped brows and faces, the creases in arms and necks. Eva smiled and greeted as she systematically and steadily worked her way towards Yelena and Dahlia, who sat under the golden rain tree. When she got there, she hugged her dear friends. It was Yelena who had introduced all this hugging. She thought shaking hands was too formal, that more physical contact was necessary between good friends; and she didn't simply pay lip-service either, she held tightly, squeezed fiercely, with strength that always astounded Eva. It often made her wonder where it all came from, as Yelena was tiny, albeit buxom and curvy.

'Thank you for coming. You could be lying on the beach by now.'

'And miss association duty?' exclaimed Yelena.

'Not for the world,' agreed Dahlia.

'And I appreciate it, believe me,' said Eva.

Over the years, they had attended each other's family weddings, christenings, outdoorings and funerals, presenting a strong united front in the midst of their extended Ghanaian families, a term which in itself carried an unfamiliar meaning; the endless half-siblings and cousins, uncles and aunts that weren't really so. Eva had given up trying to understand the real links between Alfred and his many cousins when it became clear to her that they themselves didn't know how that relationship had come to be, and when she tired of bearing the wounded looks if she asked, 'How *are* you related again?'

As Margrit had said, 'we don't have our families here, we must stick together, we mustn't let our guard down! We have to make it clear that we are not each on our own and helpless, that we too have our club, our own association.'

'A wives' association,' Dahlia had said, laughing.

'For foreign wives,' Eva had added.

'And that includes you too Yelena, you know that if you were a Ghanaian, you would be considered his wife as you are the mother of his children. Never mind that he doesn't think so.'

So they always participated enthusiastically in each other's ceremonies, standing stoically side by side. How they endeavoured to understand something of the convoluted traditions, to laugh and applaud when appropriate. And none of them would have thrived like this without the support of their friendships which sustained, encouraged and supported them, filling the gaping hole left by far away families and friends.

There was another thing that they had in common. None of their parents had so far had the right combination of means, health and desire to make the journey to Africa to visit their daughters, to see for themselves the conditions in which they were trying to forge lives. The parents communicated by occasional letter their ideas of what life in Africa was like. Their impression was a collage of scant information from their daughters, heavily supplemented by news reports of starvation, floods, coups, wars and apartheid. Nothing their daughters could communicate from here in a letter could possibly displace the prevailing images of Africa portrayed by the world's media. Eva reluctantly acknowledged that if she was sitting in her parents' cosy living room with cleanliness and order all around her and *she* saw a picture of her street with the rubbish strewn here and there, the gutter clogged with scum, women cooking and selling food next to it while their naked toddlers played in the dirt around them, she too would be left with an unfavourable image of Africa. Such palpable poverty, such total ignorance of hygiene and cleanliness would upset and overwhelm her. It was actually no wonder that these bleak images were the most newsworthy. But those images didn't carry the sound of laughter that she heard around her day in and day out, loud and uncontrolled, the sound of true happiness, a sound that would have caught Eva unaware if she had heard it back home. And somehow the cameras and journalists always missed the grins, cheeky, wide and confident, displaying rows and rows of big, corn-white teeth. Nor would there be interest in the warmth of real friendships. Friends who shared burdens, eased disappointment and disillusionment, and rejoiced in good fortune. Friends like these. When Eva had told them about this lunch, she had known before they answered that they would come.

'I was beginning to think we might have to cancel, what with all the rumours of a coup attempt this week,' said Eva. Between them, they had lived through several coups and coup attempts.

'Vincent is certain there will be another coup in the very near future . . .'

'How does he know?' asked Yelena.

Dahlia shrugged. 'I don't ask any more, but I think he knows people who know.'

They looked fed up and felt it too.

'It explains the emptying shelves. It will make life even harder again,' said Eva, resigned.

'He wants to get a gun,' said Dahlia. 'And I can think of nothing more terrifying.'

'No! You should talk him out of it,' said Eva. 'I think that's an awful idea . . . it would terrify me to have one in the house.'

'Oh, I'd *love* to have one,' said Yelena. 'It would make me feel safer.'

'There is no need! None of us is ever likely to be targeted by whoever takes over.'

'Well, you never know, that's Vincent's point. It can be all rather random. Anyway,' Dahlia said, with a jollier voice, 'let's talk about nice things. Your garden looks great.'

Eva could see that she had been biting the skin around her nails again.

'It is a paradise by anyone's expectations, a little Eden,' added Yelena. 'Everything looks lovely. Ah, you really have done well today. Cheers,' she said holding up her glass. 'This rosé is delicious too.'

'I do have some vodka left. I have hidden it so Alfred and his friends don't find it. And I might need rather a lot of it if my mother-in-law is to leave this house alive tonight. She is driving me mad!'

'What has she done now?' asked Yelena.

'Oh just the usual. Moaning about the children's hair, wanting Abi to have pierced ears. Generally trying to take over.'

'At least Alfred supports you,' said Dahlia.

'Yes, he does,' said Eva. 'I don't give him much choice, but yes, I am lucky, he is a good man.'

'And I would love to have some of your problems,' said Yelena.

'How did your visit to Wisdom go?' asked Eva.

Yelena shrugged. 'It's always the same. Empty undertakings which he does not live up to: how he is going to come and visit, pay for this and that, take them here and there. But I have decided enough is enough. I think I am going to do what Margrit keeps suggesting and approach his relatives directly, ask them to officially accept the boys as part of their family, maybe have an outdooring for them, some sort of ceremony . . .'

'What a fantastic idea,' said Eva. 'I think that is a great plan. I'll come with you if you want?'

'Will you? Please. I might need some help.'

'Of course I'll be there. We'll all go, won't we Dahlia? And Alfred will do what he can too.' She watched him mingle amongst the guests in the garden. He was wearing her favourite baby-blue linen shirt which hung loosely over khaki trousers, and suede loafers without socks. He would have powdered his feet before slipping them into his shoes, taking care not to let any powder show, and he smelled of his new aftershave. This was how she best liked him dressed. He looked incredibly youthful, hardly any different to when they first met; over the years, his body had remained lithe, like that of a well-developed adolescent. In the past year or so, a few grey strands had appeared around his temples, almost overnight. But how handsome he was, she thought. He sought her out from the other side of the lawn. He had always been able to communicate so effectively across a room of people and she felt the urge to go and touch him, to smell his cleanly shaven skin.

Vincent walked over to them just then. He clasped Eva a little too tightly for her liking, leaving her cheeks imprinted with his cologne so that every time she turned her head for the rest of the afternoon she got a waft of musky sweetness. She had spent years trying to like him, first for Dahlia, and now for Alfred. She knew their business association could mean good things; Vincent had introduced Alfred to some construction baron or other and as far as she could make out, Alfred was likely to make a lot of money, but she had given up trying to understand exactly what Alfred was doing with him because she only became more befuddled the more details he gave her. Something about Vincent just refused to sit well with her. What he did and where he did it seemed incongruous. He was a lawyer for goodness' sake, so what was he doing in construction? And besides, he made her uncomfortable and she dreaded his company; it made her feel unsophisticated and distinctly vulnerable. What was it Dahlia had said when Eva had initially expressed excitement that their husbands were working on a project together? 'As long as Alfred knows what he's getting into . . .'

Vincent nodded at Yelena curtly as he scanned the garden, allowing his eyes to linger over some of the other guests. She dared to glare at him while he was looking away, her lips pursed behind her glass in anger, but as soon as he turned his head she instantly looked down to the grass and felt relief when he sauntered off. Dahlia muttered something about needing the loo and left them.

'Poor Dahlia,' said Eva, watching her go. She had admired Dahlia from the first time they met. She was beautiful in spite of her slightly lopsided face and wide mouth. She was tall and fine-boned with creamy-chocolate skin and straightened black hair, and she had the big, strong teeth that Eva had hoped her children would inherit along with their African blood.

'I saw him at *Ruby's* last week,' whispered Yelena. 'Dancing away with one young thing after another.' She mumbled in Russian something that sounded violent and excruciating. 'He pretended he didn't know me of course, and I ignored him too.'

When Dahlia came back out, her smile was wider. She looked a little fresher. She had put on more make-up, more perfume. She picked up her full glass of wine and drained it in one go.

'How are things with Vincent, Dahlia?' Eva asked, searching her friend's face for the truth.

'Oh, the usual nonsense at home, is all.'

'What has he done this time?'

Dahlia shook her head. 'Not now, please.'

'Why not? Now is as good a time as any.'

'You really don't look fine to me,' said Yelena.

Dahlia leaned forward slightly and said in a whisper, 'I think I'm going to ask him for a divorce.' She touched her face, rubbed it, and left her fingers to linger.

'Really?' said Yelena.

Eva sat back, seeking the solidity of her chair.

'I can't take any more.' Dahlia held her glass up and Eva refilled it.

'My goodness, what are you going to do?'

Dahlia shrugged. 'I've tried to reason with him, see if we can come to some understanding. Find a way to go forward. I pleaded with him for the children. Told him to think how much damage it is causing them to live in endless strife, with his indiscreet philandering . . .'

'So why now? What has changed?' asked Eva.

Dahlia pushed her shoulders down, lifted her head. 'Last week . . . it was the children really . . . Cyril . . . poor child.' She stopped, gulped air, tried to hold off the feeling of drowning. 'He went into our bedroom – isn't that some joke, *our* bedroom – when was the last time that *I* shared *that* room? . . . and there for all to see was his father with some girl . . .'

Yelena and Eva looked shocked.

'Oh, he tried to play it down when he saw my face. Told me he rushed out, that perhaps he was mistaken, that he thinks he was seeing things that were still a part of his sleep.'

Eva adjusted the cushion behind her and tried to think of something to say but she couldn't.

'I think he's serious about this one, and he blames me. Says it's my fault. I have never known him that angry,' she said, looking blank. 'I'm worried he'll kick me out.'

'He can't do that! It's your home too,' said Yelena.

She had emptied her glass again. 'All because I begged him to keep his dalliances out of our house. Funny how you can keep lowering your standards until in the end you are bartering to be treated badly out of sight of your maid.' She laughed loudly and falsely.

'What a bastard!'

Yelena winced. 'Eva, you are talking about Dahlia's husband . . .'

'Well he is. And she has to accept him for what he is. Nothing is going to change if we keep making excuses for his behaviour.' She pursed her lips. 'So what *are* you going to do?'

'Maybe I should leave altogether, go home . . . back to London. See if I can get away, while I can.'

'He'll never let you go,' said Yelena softly. 'Not with them, surely?'

'But I can't leave them behind . . .' She sat back in her chair. For a while, no one said anything. She rubbed her cheek again. 'Well, now you know. And I am so sorry to talk about my messed up life on Joseph's day.'

'Don't be ridiculous, that's what friends are for,' said Eva.

'Thank you.' Dahlia patted her face, straightened her hair and held up her empty glass. 'But I don't want to talk about it any more. I want to enjoy the rest of the afternoon.' She beamed, and the stab of pain made her clench her jaw and wince a little, but her friends didn't notice.

'Will you be all right?' asked Yelena, forcing Dahlia to look into her eyes.

'Yes.' She smiled again. 'I just need time to think, to make a plan. But no more talk of this. Promise me. Let's enjoy the afternoon.' And she felt her public mask slip firmly back into place.

Margrit arrived then and joined them under the shade of the tree. She looked radiant and fresh. She beamed as she told them that Jimmy was doing well, and that her puppies were all flourishing. Abigail and some of the other children came running up when they saw that Margrit had arrived. 'No animals today,' she said laughing, and they went back to their games momentarily dejected. 'Cyril and Jasmine look as smart as ever,' she said to Dahlia who nodded. He wore a tie, she a fancy, frilly dress, and both of them pristine white socks. 'Don't they ever get messy?' Dahlia didn't respond. They are too clean and tidy for real children, Margrit thought, looking at them walking carefully behind their friends. Something isn't right there, never has been, and

109

their politeness, their smiles, their pretty clothes only heightened her suspicions.

Their conversation turned to the uncomfortable mood that seemed all pervasive and they talked about whether they were ready for another stretch of curfews and further food shortages. They compared food stashes and medical supplies, and reminded each other to store up petrol in tanks, water in gallons, and to hoard anything else that might suddenly become harder to obtain.

Gladys sauntered out to them '*Afishapa* to you all. Look at how you are all dressed so nicely.' She hugged each of the women. 'Yelena, the twins have grown so big! I saw them in the kitchen and I was shocked. Have you taken them to meet their family yet?'

'You have a good memory, Auntie Gee. Not yet, I think I will do it after Christmas. But I have started taking them to visit their father regularly, even though he does not really like it.'

Auntie Gee laughed. 'It will be his wife who does not like it. Well done for you anyway. A child should know his father, no matter what. Well done, Yelena.' She sat heavily.

'He knows that I am not happy that they live here and don't know much about their history, don't know their relatives. He should teach them his language at least, shouldn't he?'

'Yes, I don't know why these men who have married foreign women don't like to teach their children our traditions. Look even at my own son Alfred. Will he speak Ga to his children? No. He has left it to me to teach them various, various things.'

'I have asked him several times to introduce me to his mother, for the boys' sake, but he always says tomorrow.'

'No, no, no,' said Gladys, leaning forward. 'He sounds like a slapdash father, a man who has neglected his duties. You must persevere.'

'Yelena is too kind to him,' Eva explained.

'I have been telling her to insist,' said Margrit.

110

'I am going to go and see them after Christmas. I don't even know if they know about me, or the twins . . .'

'Yes! You must go there, they must do their duty. If you were from here your family would have taken you there by now. Anyway, the family will by all means embrace the twins; twins are special in our society. What did you say is the name of the father?'

'Tekyi. Wisdom'

'Ah. Is he an Akan?'

'I think they are from Winneba.'

'But we can go there . . .'

They all looked blankly at Gladys.

'All of us,' she said, gesturing inclusively. 'I can be like your mother, Eva and Dahlia and Margaret can be like your sisters, even we can take Alfred as your brother. We can be your family. We will ask them to perform a naming ceremony, by hook or by crook.'

'What a great idea, Auntie Gee.'

'I am always brimming with ideas as you know, Eva. I don't like my brain to be idle and useless. I don't want to be ageing unnecessarily before my time. It is a bad habit to be thinking of nothing. Take it from me. Yelena, you can take me to where they live so that we can inform them of our plans, and notify them that we are coming for them to do the right thing. We will all go, the more the merrier. We shall present a force to be reckoned with; a battalion of a family. After Christmas we will go, okay?'

'That would be wonderful,' Yelena said softly. 'I hope they agree.'

'Of course they will. Children are revered, cherished, celebrated, no matter what format they come in. That is one great thing about Ghanaians, they understand the value of a life,' said Margrit.

'Margaret is right. A child is a child after all. A blessing in any which circumstances.' Eva wondered why her mother-in-law was looking at her oddly.

Auntie Gee continued, 'Yelena, you don't worry, they will by all means be overjoyed. You see, it is only because you are a foreigner that they wanted him to have children with a Ghanaian woman too. In our culture the man's name and his children are of utmost importance. They are afraid that if any of you leave, their grand-children will be taken to far away unknown countries, far from us, far from their family and their inheritance. We do not understand that a foreigner will stay in our country for ever. After all doesn't everyone want to go home? You will never meet a Ghanaian any-where in this world who will not say he is going home one day. That is why most of those backward, less modern-thinking rela-tives want their sons to father children with Ghanaian women, to keep the name on this soil, in case the half-foreign ones follow their mothers, or go on their own to their mother's hometown.'

Yelena nodded.

'It is good that you respect our way of doing things. Very good. You see Eva here won't even let me pierce Abi's ears?' Before Eva could say anything, she continued, 'Anyway, how is your salon doing? When I have some money I will come so that you do my hair for me nicely, okay?'

'Don't insult me, Auntie Gee, *you* don't need to pay me. Aren't you like a mother to me? Come anytime you want, I will style it and make you look twenty again. We could even find you a new husband.' Yelena winked at her.

Auntie Gee chortled and her whole body shook. 'You are so funny. What do I want a man for at my age? I don't need someone to come and start telling me what to do, do I?'

'They are not all like that.'

'Well the good ones like Alfred are few and far between. As for me, I had mine. When my husband Ignatius died, I accepted that my time of marriage was good and over. But we can find one for you. Not a good-for-nothing-useless-type who doesn't look after his children. Don't worry, I will be on the look out?' She walked off giggling.

*

Not long after, Faustina came hurrying up to them. She had beads of perspiration on her head, around her nose and above her lip. Eva longed to tell her to wipe them away but she held back.

'Madam, please it's time to come. The priest is ready.'

'What?' She looked around for Alfred, but she couldn't spot him.

'Madam, please come now, now.'

'This is exciting,' said Yelena. 'Sounds like a surprise.'

Eva followed tentatively. 'I don't want any more surprises.'

'Just do whatever it is with a smile,' said Margrit.

When they got closer to the veranda, Eva saw Alfred deep in conversation with Vincent. He looked troubled as he listened to Vincent who was gesturing aggressively, pointing his finger at Alfred as he spoke, and Eva wondered what on earth was the matter.

Auntie Gee was holding Joseph who was wearing an outfit that Eva had never seen before. Well, it looked rather like something that Simon had worn for his baptism . . . 'No! What on earth is going on here?' she exclaimed.

The priest looked up and smiled. 'Ah, Eva, good you are here. We were waiting for you.'

'Did you know about this?' she whispered to Alfred.

He shook his head. 'Not until a few minutes ago. I couldn't say no . . .'

'Of course you could have!'

'Alfred knows the value of performing all his duties, isn't it Alfred?' said Auntie Gee, staring at him.

He shrugged, and looked away. Eva asked him what he had been talking to Vincent about, and he replied, saying it was nothing. He smiled at her but she was sceptical and was about to pursue her query when Gladys began to speak.

'Reverend Sackey kindly agreed to perform an interim baptism for my grandson this afternoon,' said Gladys loudly to the guests. 'And my dearly beloved son Alfred agreed that this was a good time to do it.' She whispered to Eva, 'It won't take long, then at least it will be done, just in case.'

Alfred put an arm around Eva and she shrugged and fidgeted until he removed it. He glanced at her. 'Sorry, love. She means well.'

Thankfully, it didn't take long. A quick prayer, a dab of water and Joseph was baptised.

'For now,' said Reverend Sackey.

The guests clapped, and Gladys looked euphoric. She made the sign of the cross, pinched Joseph's cheeks and said, 'Now I can sleep well again.'

Yelena handed Eva a full glass of wine. 'You must need this. Your mother-in-law really is quite something.'

'Determined,' said Dahlia. 'They all are.'

'She means well, for you and your family,' said Margrit.

'Well, sometimes I envy you that you don't have one to deal with,' said Eva.

'Maybe, maybe,' said Margrit.

'Madam, please the food is ready for your guests,' said Faustina.

'You knew about this, didn't you?' said Eva. 'You are supposed to be *my* maid and yet you act like a traitor.'

'Oh madam, please,' said Faustina smiling. 'You know how Auntie Gee is. Anyway, please, I am not a traitor.'

'Lunch is ready,' said Eva, turning to her guests.

Faustina had laid out the food on the long table in the dining room. Platters piled high with the fragrant orange *jolof* rice, bowls of fried chicken and plantain, and a deep pot filled with thick, oily groundnut stew, with peppers and chicken swimming in it. There were rice balls, pepper gravy, and *gari-foto* with chunks of tuna and boiled eggs. And here and there, Eva's earthenware vases filled with freshly cut purple and white bougainvillea flowers. Eva looked over at Faustina who hovered ready to help anyone. She was beaming, eyebrows lifted in eager anticipation of due recognition and praise, and Eva smiled back.

*

Eva sat back in her chair. Her empty plate lay on her lap. She felt a deep contentedness. 'Here's to us,' she said lifting her glass towards her friends. Today had gone very well, and she was filled with a peace and joy that she had learned she couldn't take for granted. She looked at Dahlia, gazed into her eyes and blinked hard, wishing her fortitude and wisdom too. She inhaled the sweet jasmine that trailed through a grille attached to the side of the house, which was just beginning to bloom, and whispered private thanks to her own god for the good things in her life.

Later their conversation was cut short when Auntie Gee called out to the guests. They heard the word 'cake' and everyone started to move back towards the veranda.

'Cakes?' asked Eva. 'What cakes? I didn't make any cake.'

'Let's go and see,' said Yelena. 'Your mother-in-law seems full of surprises.'

'My goodness,' said Eva when she saw the cakes. There was a huge light pink one covered in small and large purple roses which had pointed hard-looking green petals. The colours looked harsh and synthetic. In the centre of the cake was scrolled in neat silver icing: '*Alfred and Eva - Wed 10 Years - May God Bless U*'. Next to their 'anniversary cake' was an even larger, rectangular blue cake, which simply said, Joseph in purple icing, and beneath it was a large cross. There were purple angels and blue teddy bears stuck all over it.

Eva shook her head disbelieving. 'You had this planned all along,' she said to Auntie Gee.

'Oh, I wanted to be prepared. You know, just in case.'

'She lies, your mother,' Eva whispered to Alfred. 'I am so glad that you didn't inherit that from her.' He didn't laugh, and moments later he walked off briskly towards the stereo, which he had put on the veranda.

Suddenly a piano intro began very loudly. Majestic trumpets joined in. Alfred clicked his fingers to the beat and sashayed towards her, his lean hips moving seductively. His eyes were locked into hers. In those few moments, the guests all turned to watch as Alfred started to sing about a girl he knew and how he knew how much he loved her.

Eva grinned like a girl and bit her lip. Her eyes filled. How long had it taken him to learn the lyrics of their favourite Ray Charles song so perfectly, she wondered?

He continued to sing boldly, coming towards her. He winked lazily, and her heart leapt.

He reached her, took her hands in his, rubbed her fingers, started to twirl her. He pressed her to him, and they moved together in perfect harmony, stepping and swaying to the music. The guests clapped and danced around them. 'I love you,' he whispered, and they might have been alone.

When the song finished, Alfred released her, but held on to her hand. He turned to their guests, smiling radiantly. 'Ladies and gentlemen, may I have your attention for a little longer please.' Eva looked at him quizzically. 'I want to tell you some-thing,' he began. The guests shuffled in their seats to watch him expectantly. 'Many, many years ago, I was blessed to meet a wonderful girl in London.' People hooted and clapped. 'And I was wise enough to entice her to leave her home to come with me to Ghana and be my wife. Never in my wildest dreams did I imagine just what a good decision that would turn out to be. Now, we have three children,' he said. 'And Evie, today I want to thank you for each of them. And before our friends and family, I want to tell you how proud I am of you. You adjusted well to our life here, and I know it hasn't always been easy.' He put his arms around her and kissed her on the lips. Eva could feel the blood rise to her head. She smelt his aftershave. 'I love you so much,' he whispered, brushing her ear with his lips. He turned to their guests, 'Ladies and gentlemen, please rise and toast my wonderful wife.' He raised his glass high and said, 'To Eva.'

The guests toasted Eva, then clapped and cheered. There was

a chorus of 'Congratulations!' and Eva felt her eyes moisten. She put her arm around Alfred's waist and squeezed.

'And,' continued Alfred, when the guests had quietened down, 'of course, you mustn't forget that it is a wise man who can acknowledge the brilliance of his wife.' Everyone laughed and Alfred raised his hand and pointed his forefinger. 'On a serious note, however, I didn't want this day to pass without putting my money where my mouth is, so to speak.' Eva looked at him. Of course she should have known he was up to something. His face was shining like a child's. She should have guessed. He turned back towards the driveway and gestured to Solomon, who opened the gate. A shiny sky-blue Mercedes rolled off the street and on to the driveway. 'Alfred!' exclaimed Eva.

'Am I forgiven now?' He took her hand, squeezed it gently, and led her to the driveway. She had her free hand over her mouth to hide her amazement. The car had tan leather seats and a sunroof. 'It isn't quite new, but nearly, and I had it sprayed specially.'

It was her favourite colour. 'Thank you, Alfred,' she said, cuddling up to him. She was overwhelmed yet a little embarrassed by this public gesture of his love. She couldn't help wondering how much it had cost him. And she would never tell him, but she would much rather have had plane tickets for a little holiday back home.

'Eh, you are lucky oh!' said someone standing next to Eva stroking the car.

'350 SEL,' said another guest. 'Very excellent model, Alfred.'

'Very nice,' said Vincent, looking directly at Alfred with raised eyebrows. 'Very nice indeed . . .'

'In fact, you are blessed,' said someone, 'Mercedes is the best.'

All the doors of the car had been opened and there were people inspecting the seats, the doors, the dials, the boot. Windows were opened and closed, doors too, for all to hear the satisfying clunk of a rust-free car. The children clambered in and bounced on the well-sprung seats laughing.

'You can hear it, Made in Germany,' said one of Alfred's uncles, opening and slamming the door repeatedly. 'Not Japanese for the masses. This is real quality, you listen,' he said to the people around him.

'Do you want to take it for a spin?' asked Alfred.

'Oh no,' said Eva, 'not now. Can I do it later? I am bound to crash it if I take it out with everyone watching me.'

Alfred looked a little disappointed, but quickly rallied and said, 'You are most likely right. And look, they are serving the cake.' He clapped his hands and said sternly, 'Hey people, please out of the car! I didn't ship it all the way from Germany for you riff-raff to spoil it on the first day!' He shooed everyone out, rolled up the windows, locked the doors and put the key in his pocket. 'Solomon, don't let the children play near it,' he said as he walked back to the garden.

Eva sat with her friends eating cake. It had taken her a while to calm down. This was indeed the most amazing gesture anyone had ever made to her and she still felt overwhelmed. Remember how you feel today, she told herself over and over. Remember this joy and contentment, she whispered to herself. Bottle it in your heart and drink from it when things are less exciting, when life seems grey and pointless, and troubles appear to grow infinite about you. Memorise this! Never forget how wonderful it is to feel like this, she thought, and yet another fresh wave of contentment swept through her as she imagined the scene later tonight when she would be alone with Alfred.

Chapter Seven

Eva was making coffee for the remaining guests in the kitchen. She measured out her precious ground coffee into the percolator, savouring the smell. Margrit had brought her a couple of packs of coffee from a visit to Abidjan in the Ivory Coast a year ago, which she kept in the freezer and used only on special occasions. It was a lovely treat; a marvellous change from the Nescafé instant she drank every morning. She heard a noise she didn't like, tilted her head, furrowed her brow in concentration. Had she heard right? After a brief intermission, the chatter in the garden resumed. Thank goodness, she had imagined it. She noticed that her heart was beating faster; such a swift reaction, as if on permanent standby in anticipation of something dreadful.

Then she heard more of the distinctive cracks. Gunfire. This time closer, harder to ignore and accompanied by commotion outside. She paused momentarily, ceasing the flow of scalding water into the pot. Why had she had to travel all the way to Africa to learn the sound a gun makes? To learn the many things she didn't think she'd ever need to know. Bloody hell! The first time she'd heard a gun, a few years ago, she had mistakenly thought it was a firework or a car backfiring particularly loudly. But today she knew she had heard gunshots, lots of them. So Vincent had been right after all. More uncertainty, more upheaval.

Outside in the garden, she could hear guests talking loudly; anxious voices arguing. Someone was shouting. She heard the gate; she listened for Alfred's voice. She heard a misplaced, hearty laugh, a sound she could cling to for a while, keep the other abysmal sounds at bay. A moment later, Faustina came running into the house. She rushed in, letting the mosquito door bang shut behind her.

Eva had never seen her move that fast. 'Don't slam the door!'

'Madam, we are having a coup! Please, don't mind the door. They are firing bullets.' She spoke loudly, contorting her face as though she were recounting the death of a loved one. She held her head delicately as she did when her short hair had been recently pulled into new tight cornrows that snaked from the front to the back of her head. 'What are we going to do?'

'Well, we don't yet know.' She did know, but in the face of such histrionics it was impossible for her to suppress her need to rationalise everything.

'Madam, you go and hear what they are saying.'

Eva reached for the radio and switched it on, but all that played through the country's only channel was the telling military dirge. Things were clearly still in the interim phase, and bland music would play on a loop until whoever was trying to take over the country either conquered or was conquered. Until the leader, new or old, could get to the radio and declare victory, this music would play and the country would drown in rumours. Eva imagined a band of disaffected soldiers leaving their barracks, creeping towards Broadcasting House intent on taking over the country, with a tape of their preferred music in the back pocket of their leader. Or maybe there was a shelf in the studio labelled 'coup music'? But that would be too organised for the Ghana Broadcasting Corporation. Ridiculous anywhere else but here!

The mystery remained. This kind of music was never ever played on the radio in times of peace.

'You see now, I told you,' said Faustina, pulling the skin below her right eye down with her forefinger to emphasise that Eva must see. Eva was impressed anew by how Faustina's flawless blue-black skin contrasted with the deep red of her inner flesh. Remove the veneer of her skin, and the inner parts of this, surely the blackest woman in the world, would be indistinguishable from mine, she mused. She put the pot of coffee on the tray that Faustina had prepared earlier and picked the tray up.

'But why did the soldiers not wait for next week, when I will be safe in my village?' said Faustina in a cracked voice. 'Now how will I get there with soldiers roaming the streets asking for money will and nil? I will have to hide my money in my panties, madam.'

'Faustina, please,' she said sighing. 'Wonderful, just what we need!'

Guests were leaving, ending the party abruptly. Eva put down the tray of coffee and walked to Alfred through a tangle of rumours: 'this has been planned for a while'; 'there will be no mercy for the corrupt ex-leaders'; 'these guys are very organised – do you know they are financed by out-of-town money?'; 'this will finally bring the change the country needs'. How the hell did they know, she wondered.

'Another bloody coup, can you believe it?' said Alfred.

'I think you'll find that this is welcome news to many,' said Vincent. 'Trust me, this time we will get the right people.'

'How do you know?' asked Alfred.

'I know people, things,' said Vincent looking at Alfred. 'Come on Dahlia,' he said in a louder voice. 'And I recommend that everyone goes home as quickly as possible.'

'But they usually wait for nightfall,' moaned Eva. 'Why now?' She didn't want her party to be over yet, she didn't want her guests to have to go home. She realised she was being childishly selfish as it could well be dangerous out there.

Dahlia and Vincent left. They lived in the Airport residential area to the north-east of Accra, where most of the expats lived in large modern, square houses, surrounded by big gardens and big cars. Their neighbourhood never had water shortages, but was often targeted by soldiers and armed robbers alike. Besides, to get home, they would have to cross the ring road, pass the Police Headquarters close to Broadcasting House, key sites to anyone trying to take over power.

In Kaneshie, where Yelena lived, to the north west, it seemed that at all times of day or night people gathered on street corners to chat and flirt, to sell and buy. It was a safe neighbourhood at a time like this, but nevertheless Eva wouldn't expect her to risk coming across a band of unruly soldiers when she was alone with the boys. She told her to get going quickly.

'Perhaps we can give you a lift, Auntie Gee?'

'Thanks, Yelena,' said Eva. 'Adabraka is on your way, I suppose.'

Auntie Gee shook her head. 'Oh, I am not ready yet. I will go later.'

'But you need to get home safely. How will you get back?'

'Don't worry about me, Eva. Didn't I make it here on my own this morning?' She chuckled as though she had said something funny. 'Anyway, I will drink a coffee first. But you go, Yelena. And come and visit again soon. After all, are you not like family?'

Margrit and Kojo, who lived five minutes down the road, were happy to stay for a coffee. 'It usually takes them a few days to get to us,' he said. 'The advantage of living in an unostentatious part of town!'

The garden had emptied in moments. Most of the guests had departed hurriedly, calling goodbyes over their shoulders. Eva looked around at the debris of the party. Used napkins, dirty crockery, chairs and tables scattered here and there. Suddenly the music seemed too loud, the mess too great.

Simon and Abigail ran past her sucking lollipops. 'Who gave you those?'

'Auntie Gee,' they shouted without pausing.

'Haven't you had enough sweet things today? They'll rot your teeth. And don't run with them in your mouths!' she shouted, but they didn't seem to hear.

Later, Eva sat on Abi's bed and combed through her wet, black hair clumped like rats' tails, now washed clean of the grease that Akua had put in earlier, while Abigail sat on the floor reading her book with her wiry, moist body cloaked in a towel. Eva could hear Faustina singing to Simon and Joseph in the bath. After a while, the singing ceased and Faustina told Simon her favourite stories about her childhood in the village in the Volta Region. She described her mud hut with a thatched roof, in a compound that sat between a river that was prone to flooding and a cluster of hills that was filled with wildlife that Simon had never seen. 'We have bush rats, wild pigs, snakes. But no elephants, no lions, no giraffes,' she claimed. 'Those animals that your storybooks tell you live in Africa don't live near my village.'

There was something going on out there. Eva had lived through two coups already and, speculation aside, she knew what the gunshots, along with the absence of the usual endless talk on the radio, meant.

She normally preferred the BBC World Service, where they spoke softly, with a calm and demureness that was absent from the GBC. If the reception was poor, she listened to the Voice of America, but she didn't enjoy it as much as the World Service. The Americans spoke slowly in their irritating twang, reaching out with sugary kindness to the great uneducated masses that existed somewhere beyond the borders of their powerful country. Patronising listeners for whom English wasn't their mother tongue. The World Service on the other hand spoke to its innumerable overseas listeners with the same grace as the BBC used at home. No dumbing down as if the listeners in Africa needed every little nuance about life in the West to be explained at a tedious pace. Worst of all was the GBC, where music was disrupted constantly by the presenters' banal chatter. They loved to talk, the Ghanaians, there was no getting around that one. They loved the sound of their own voices. Just take Gladys, or Faustina. Or even Alfred. Give them half a chance, and off they went with some yarn or other that could last for the best part of an hour, spinning colour and shapes into their story, drawing their listener in deeper and deeper.

'Mummy, has there really been another coup?'

'What is a coup?' asked Simon, walking in wrapped in a towel.

'A change of government . . .'

'By soldiers, with guns?' asked Abigail. 'Does it mean there will be more killings like the last time?'

Eva shook her head. Simon looked apprehensive.

'Oh, I don't imagine that will happen, no.' But there always were; she knew it to be an inevitable fact. It irritated Alfred that she clung to a childish inclination to ignore bad things that made her uncomfortable, allowing herself to hold on to her own pleasant fantasy if it so suited her, even if all around her was evidence to the contrary.

'Will we have a new government? Will there be more things to buy in the shops? Maybe Ghana can finally become like England then.'

Eva chuckled a little. 'Who knows, yes, Ghana might become like England, although that wouldn't necessarily be a good thing. Ghana is fine just as it is, well, sort of. I mean, there are many good things about Ghana.'

Abigail shrugged. She looked distracted and agitated. During the last coup, she had heard umpteen frightening stories at school, which she had recounted daily to Eva. Tales of innocent men and women being tortured by soldiers. There had been accounts of decapitations, finger nails being pulled out, homes burned, people disappearing. She had been comfortable reassuring them that the stories were untrue since she had no evidence of such atrocities herself, and she couldn't fathom such behaviour. Ghanaians are nothing else if not kind, she told them; they are not barbaric. How could she make her children understand that although Ghanaians might not be the most adventurous or industrious, and that though they might be unruly, they were generally peace-loving, jovial, kind, not blood-thirsty? She told her children that the stories were the product of scaremongering and to put them out of their heads for good. To remember that children make things up. And adults too, for that matter. Sometimes, she consoled herself, the truth simply needed to be shaped to match the audience.

But Eva had had to work hard to undo the violent imaginings these stories had produced in her children's minds. Why did they have to live through this kind of upheaval again? She had hoped they had been too young to remember the last coup, too young to have been for ever affected by the macabre headlines, but now this. Would it all happen again?

She remembered how after the last leaders had been executed by firing squad, she had found Abigail examining the final grainy black-and-white image of the hooded men in the newspaper. Eva had been incensed that someone had carelessly left it lying on the veranda.

Abigail's face had remained knitted with incredulity for the rest of the day. With seemingly regular intervals, she asked another question that had slowly formed in her young mind. *Mummy, why were the men killed? What did they do that was so bad? What about Daddy? Do you think that they could come and take him? Do you think someone we know might be killed also? Do they have firing squads in England, Mummy?*

'No. No!' Holding her delicate daughter, she had had no idea what else to say. Her tight arms disguised her own unease as she rocked Abigail, but the damage was done, and there had followed nightmares and months of bedwetting for Abi.

Eva had said silent prayers of thanks that Alfred didn't have a government job, that they weren't Lebanese or Syrian, and that they didn't have any reason to be on any hit list. But how the questions had plagued her, and with them the horror that her child might be permanently scarred. She had to deal with the terrifying knowledge that she didn't know how to allay fears caused by the careless actions of armed men. Why *would* someone take a photograph of this? To prove how the men had died? To send a message to the people? And which of the lined up soldiers had pulled the deadly trigger? What had gone through their minds? And at what point did they reconcile themselves to the act in which they were about to participate, the men who had given the orders, those who had carried them out? Was it afterwards over a joint or a cup of *akpeteshi*? And what about the men who had never imagined their short lives would end like this, what on earth had they thought, felt in those final minutes? The tight blindfolds, being lead or shoved along on their final journey, the rope cutting into their wrists. And the conversation?

Tonight, she did the only thing she could, she put her arms around her children and hugged them long and hard. The warm tingling feel-good feeling she got whenever she held them spread through her; she could sympathise with their lack of understanding.

'We are safe here. Daddy and I are here, we'll keep you safe. No one is going to go out, and no one is going to come in. And who would be silly enough to climb over our wall?' She felt the tension leave Abigail's thin body and hoped Alfred was right.

She knew the routine by now. If there was a coup taking place, then the uprising would have started at the main barracks. Tales had spread after previous uprisings about how most of the soldiers fled at the first sign of trouble, making these coups d'état rather straightforward. With any luck the soldiers would never actually be called upon to defend the country from anything serious, she thought. After the barracks, from whence the rumours would fly ahead of them, the new leaders would make their way to

Broadcasting House to secure the airwaves. The music on the radio was the only guide as to what was happening out there.

When they were ready, whoever was doing the shooting would proclaim themselves. Until then, Eva and the rest of the country could wait and wonder, while terror and imagination ran wild across town.

Eva went downstairs in her silk nightdress, a gift from Alfred years ago. Oyster coloured, it skimmed her frame and made her feel special. Her skin was damp and fresh, the tips of her hair wet and cooling.

She could hear Gladys and Alfred talking softly outside where dark shadows had descended over everything. She walked toward the veranda, switched the light on, and instantly their chat changed, became cheerier and a little louder.

'Anyway, as I said, no more delays.' Gladys said in English, ending her conversation with Alfred.

'What delays?' asked Eva.

'Oh, nothing Eva. Anyway I was waiting for you,' said Gladys, sounding worn out.

'I thought you had gone,' said Eva.

'No, I couldn't leave just like that? But I am ready to go now. I am waiting for Alfred to give me a lift.'

'Is it safe?' She looked at Gladys, whose recently thinned, kohl-lined eyebrows were sagging sleepily. Eva turned to Alfred for support but he seemed distracted.

'People are still moving about; there has been no curfew proclamation yet. It's not far, I'll be fine using the back roads.'

'What a pity, Solomon would have driven you but he's gone to bed himself now . . . why don't we get a taxi for you?'

'Okay then,' said Gladys. 'If you insist, so be it.'

'No, Auntie Gee,' said Alfred rising. 'No. I said I'd give you a lift home, and I will. It's the least we can do after all your hard work.'

'I won't be long, love,' Alfred said quietly. 'Why don't you go up and wait for me?'

'Okay then,' said Gladys rising to her feet. 'I am ever ready.' She was smiling and shuffling towards Alfred's car.

'Sorry,' Alfred whispered to Eva. He stroked her face. 'I can't let her take a taxi.' He covered her mouth with his, held her for a moment.

'Are we going?' Gladys interjected.

'I won't be long, Evie. Wait for me,' Alfred said letting her loose. 'Don't fall asleep.'

'Wake me up if I do,' she said.

'Are you not ready?' asked Auntie Gee impatiently.

Eva let go of Alfred. 'Good bye, Auntie Gee. And thank you.'

'You too did well today oh!' Gladys said.

'Yes . . . yes.' Eva turned and went towards the house. 'Promise, Alfred.'

He turned and winked at her.

Eva heard Gladys ask him something in Ga. She patted her skin, dampening again already so soon after her shower. As she had in the beginning, she still longed to fling open the doors, allow the night air in, the hot out. But mosquito bites, swollen and itchy, and malaria, were much more disagreeable than humid, sticky skin.

As she walked towards the car, Gladys counted. It had been a good twelve hours earlier that she'd first arrived here, and several before then that she had arisen from her small bed to start cooking for the anniversary party. And the baptism! She smiled happily. Her determination and patience always paid off. She climbed in, pulled her cloth in with her and moved her body out of the way as Alfred slammed shut the door. It was hard, but she tried her best not to create unnecessary problems by dwelling on the small things, raising them to an unnecessarily high significance. After all Eva was a foreigner, still unaware of their rules, of what offends and what doesn't. Even though she had been living here for many, many years, she had a home somewhere else, somewhere far away. She had a mother and a father and who knew what other relatives. Heaven forbid if she decided to return to them with her children. What would Gladys do? Where would that leave her, she who was, after all, forever thinking of ways to get closer to her grandchildren, to teach them their language, their customs?

As they drove out into the street, she shifted to look at Alfred and told him that she was prepared to sort things out herself if he wasted any more time. 'The time is now,' she said forcefully. She told him that he had to take the necessary steps *now* to ensure that this boat of marital life was not rocked and toppled over, tossing them all into a sea of untold difficulties. He had been delaying for more than a year now, and while she could understand his trepidation, quite frankly, Gladys was not prepared to tolerate any more of his flimsy, cowardly excuses.

Chapter Eight

Dahlia's face was strained from the smile that she had kept in place for most of the afternoon. She lowered her hand. Her face stung. Unconsciously, she put her hand to her chest to still something. She could taste the relief of returning solitude. Slowly and steadily, drained from the effort she had expended, she made her way back to her room. She didn't bother to reply to the maid when she said, 'Madam, please what am I cooking for dinner?' She pulled along the banister, heaving herself up the stairs. She ignored Cyril calling to her and prayed that Vincent wouldn't summon her. When she got to her bedroom, she shut the door, turned the key and leaned against it. She had made it, she thought as she crept towards her bed. She lay and drew her knees up. She could feel the knots in her shoulders, the stiff cramp that travelled all the way down her back, tight from holding on to everything she felt. She swallowed the lump that had grown in her throat. It had been harder than she had imagined.

And now, she could give in to the overwhelming desire that had plagued her all day. To be home. To see her parents. To be in their lounge with the swirling multi-coloured carpets, the faint whiff of gas from the fire, her father dunking a McVitie's chocolate digestive in his cup of tea.

She hadn't seen her parents for many years. Twelve long years. Not long after her father uttered his disdainful words, she and Vincent had left London to begin their journey to a new life in Ghana. Sometimes the urge to speak to her father was unbelievably fierce. An unutterable desire to hold his hand in a way she never had, to look him in the eye like they did in movies, and to have a frank, honest chat with him. But what would she tell him? Would he know what questions to ask? Or would he know all he needed to just by looking at her? Without her needing to say anything? The way he had known if she was telling a lie when she was little? And would she reply by way of diversion that Africa was acceptable? That he might even like it, after some adjustments, mind. Depending on his expectations, that is. She didn't know what his expectations of Africa were these days, as correspondence with their terraced house on Ashby Crescent had rather dried up.

Sometimes she cried as the deafening growl of the weekly BA flight to London shook the windows, flying so close that if anything ever did go wrong, the plane's wheels would surely scrape off their sweltering concrete roof as effortlessly as her son scooped the frosting off the cakes she made. She often imagined herself seated in the air-conditioned comfort of the homeward-bound jet. Air hostesses with familiar accents would serve extravagant, icy refreshments as coolly as if they were handing out tap water. Their faces would be kind, with a sympathy born out of having seen exactly what the passengers were fleeing: the harsh, harried life of a third-world country. The countdown to London would begin; seven short hours till landing, perhaps in fog and dark drizzle, or a crisp, clear blue sky and sparkling dew, or perhaps on a chirpy, sprouting spring morning. Any version would do for a tattered, homesick soul.

She had written often initially, but then as her life became harder to describe, she wrote less and less. Correspondence with home, her past life, exacerbated her sense of shame, and now she often limited her writing to the space in a card at Christmas or a birthday.

Invariably, her parent's letters contained lists of her siblings' achievements. Darren's job and bigger mortgage, Rose's wonderful children who played the violin and cello. Without fail, her mother ended with the same directive: *write to us*.

When she did write, Dahlia told them nothing about herself, other than she was 'very well'. She embellished stories of her children's development and achievements, keen to show that here too there was progress, even if it appeared that things were stagnant and in decline. It was easier to deflect their focus, moreover, she was convinced that Vincent scanned her mail for evidence of treachery; whenever he handed her letters from the post office box she could see signs of disdain in his face, irritation that she still occasionally corresponded with home.

But in her own small way, she tried to balance out the stories they were likely to hear about Africa. Rarely uplifting, factually accurate reports of floods, droughts, famines, epidemics, military unrest, apartheid, or terrorism were not wholly representative of life here. What did they see on British television these days? She couldn't imagine that there might be interest back home for Ghana in the midst of the many other newsworthy stories of poor, hungry, suffering Africa.

The television seemed to feature quite heavily in her parent's lives, according to the letters. Comedy, in particular. As her mother wrote, 'Your father likes to laugh. It is easier to forget gloomy things when you laugh.' Was that an admonishment for her moaning? Had she moaned, she wondered, as she tried to recount her last letter. Once, she had sent them a reel of film to develop since it was impossible to have it done well here, and so expensive. She had been careful that each shot should matter; snapping the house from its best angle, her lush garden overflowing with flowering shrubs, her beautiful children in new clothes on their way to a party. When she got the photographs back, her mother had written a stern reminder that they were not rolling in cash, assuring her that it cost a lot of money to develop photographs in London too. 'You seem to have a nice life over there, can't you afford to develop your own pictures?' She had then added that it was a pity she lived too far away for them to get to know their grandchildren.

But still, how she would love to see her parents. Motherhood had brought fresh respect for them, healthy appreciation of their concern about her marriage. She might ask her father whether he had altered his perception of her choice. She might tell him that he had been so very right, just not in the way he had imagined all those years ago.

He had viewed her decision to marry an African, and the ensuing departure to his country, the recently independent Ghana, with hostility. 'Where, Guyana?' he had asked, mystified. 'No, Ghana, West Africa,' Dahlia had said smiling, waiting for understanding to flutter across their faces and illuminate their smiles. It didn't. 'Hasty' and 'imprudent' were two words he had used. There had been others, but the years had erased them from her memory. Those two had been burned into the back of her mind, from where they flashed up regularly to taunt, to question, to challenge her to dispute their accuracy.

After incomprehension came alienation. And of course, he had been sad. She had seen it in his eyes, and in the way he ignored her whenever she went to visit them afterwards. Her mother remained the same as she had always been: kind, keen to feed everyone who came through her door, but slightly aloof. Dahlia realised now that her mother was too busy dealing with her own disenchantment to take on more suffering for the potential mistakes of her daughter.

In the beginning, how easy it had been to smile at his ignorance, reject his concerns. Anything to keep her faith, to help her continue to live out her irreversible choice. She had wished she could hold his hand and show him the beauty of Africa; the place, after all, from where they had forcibly emigrated lifetimes ago, and therefore the land to which they should feel a natural connection.

The first driver she had had in Accra used to say regularly: 'But madam, no one knows tomorrow.' She repeated this to herself often. He was right. No one could have predicted the outcome of her marriage to Vincent; a man as civilised and sophisticated as he appeared to be. But the calamitous marriage couldn't be blamed on the country. Her husband's undertaking to love, honour and respect would have been no more watertight if they were living in England. Or would it? She would never know.

Things had completely fallen apart when Vincent's mother came to stay. They had barely settled in their new house when Ma Akos, as she was known to all, arrived from Kumasi. Looking back, it was clear to Dahlia that he had summoned her. She was a quiet, small woman, with a humourless face and little knowledge of English. Within hours, Dahlia felt like she was the visitor in her house. It was clear that Vincent and his mother had an unusually strong bond, and it made Dahlia feel like the outsider in the relationship. She had never heard him talk to anyone so respectfully, so gently.

One day during the first week, Ma Akos spent the morning making a light soup with smoked fish and large green and red peppers, teaching Dahlia how to chop onions perfectly, how to peel whole red tomatoes, and how to wait until the soup bubbled with a little oil on the surface from the fish before removing the onions and tomatoes and peppers to pulp them into a smooth paste in the mortar. She showed her what good smoked fish should look like, speaking carefully in Twi mixed with English. It seemed it took them all morning and part of the afternoon to prepare the soup, and when Dahlia refused to taste it because she was a vegetarian, Ma Akos was astonished and continued to mutter bitterly to herself for the remainder of the day.

Dahlia was relieved that evening when she heard the toot of Vincent's car to indicate that he was home.

'Go and greet your husband properly. Go and get his bag from him,' said Ma Akos.

Dahlia had perked up a little from her bored loll on the sofa, and was looking forward to having someone to chat to. She was taken aback by her mother-in-law's order.

'Go,' said Ma Akos again, making a shoving gesture and pointing towards the gate. She was holding the baby possessively, as she had been all afternoon. She nodded urgently towards the gate where Vincent's driver was still tooting impatiently for the watchman.

Dahlia stumbled off reluctantly and reached the car just as it pulled to a stop on the gravelled drive. The watchman opened the door for Vincent. He smiled at Dahlia and handed her his briefcase. She folded her arms and said, 'What, are you too tired to carry your own bag?' She wanted him to laugh out loud, to put a halt to the strangeness around her, but he didn't.

He walked off ahead of her into the house, leaving her puzzled. She strode in after him and prepared to launch into an account of how boring her day had been.

'Vincent?' she called, lovingly, sensing from his body language that she would have to wait to express her irritation.

He was in the doorway, greeting his mother. He held both her hands in his and nodded politely at her. They chatted softly, and as Dahlia caught up with them, she resolved to resume her Twi lessons. She had pleaded with Vincent countless times not to speak Twi like this in front of her because it made her feel left out. But he took no notice of her. She hated having all this unintelligible chatter in her own home; it left her feeling exposed. To what, she didn't know, but she knew it highlighted her isolation and her foreignness.

'Hello Jasmine, coo coo,' Vincent said, pinching her cheeks, while Dahlia stood by watching.

His mother said something in Twi and she and Vincent laughed.

Dahlia tutted. 'It is very rude of you to speak a language that I don't understand. I really shouldn't have to tolerate such rudeness in my own home.'

'Could you please put my bag in my study?' Vincent said.

She stopped in her tracks, turned and glowered at him. 'You can shove your bloody bag.'

'Ah ah!' said Ma Akos. She covered her mouth horrified, and slowly, mournfully almost, shook her head at Dahlia and walked off to the kitchen.

Vincent looked hard at her and Dahlia felt a sudden lack of confidence. She swallowed and found her resolve, 'Listen, just because your mother is here, you can't treat me like I'm your servant. I'm your wife, for heaven's sake.'

'Yes, I see. Come with me a moment. I want to show you something,' he said, holding out his hand.

She smiled, relieved. Her shoulders relaxed as she took his hand and went with him up the stairs to their bedroom. She gripped tight, taking all the reassurance from him that she could get. A silly misunderstanding this, the effect of having his meddling mother here. 'I can't tell you how glad I am that you are home. I have been so bored. I have had to cook all day, can you believe it? Me, the baked bean queen! And she wants to teach me to make *fufu* next,' she laughed and thought Vincent did too.

'And she carried poor Jasmine all day long. Poor darling didn't have a chance to play with her favourite toys or have a proper cuddle with me. Do you have any idea when she is leaving? It's just that she hasn't said and she has been here a few days already.' They had reached their bedroom. Vincent kicked the door shut and Dahlia continued, 'Don't you think it might be a good idea to ask her? I have this odd feeling that she is planning on staying too long, heaven forbid.'

Vincent let go of her hand, turned and slapped her hard across her mouth with the back of his hand. Unprepared, Dahlia was thrown against the corner of the door.

Her ears buzzed, words floated in her head in unformed sentences, her face throbbed. She put her hand to her mouth and saw that she was bleeding. She started to whimper, too shocked to do anything else.

'Don't ever disrespect me in public. And don't witter on about my mother with such insolent disregard ever again. She is your senior and as such you will respect her. Am I making myself clear?'

Dahlia lowered her head while he spoke not wanting to look at him, and later, when she replayed this scene to herself over and over and over again, she realised he had mistaken her loathing for acquiescence.

'Now, that really didn't need to happen. Let's take care it doesn't happen again, shall we?' he spoke kindly.

She lifted her eyes and stared at him seeking some understanding. 'Vincent?'

'Come on, let's clean your face up.' He held out a hand to help her.

Despite her revulsion, she took his hand. She stood stupefied while she tried to scramble clear thoughts together.

'Oh, look, you cut your lip,' he said gently. 'Here, let me see.' He rubbed at her mouth. She flinched. 'I didn't mean to hurt you. Luckily it's only a little cut, nothing much to worry about.' He smiled, and started undoing his tie. 'I am starving, what did you say you had been cooking?'

Dahlia was speechless, but Vincent didn't seem to mind. She didn't know if she was more indignant about the fact that he had hit her or because he didn't seem to think it was out of the ordinary. She opened her mouth and faltered. She was desperate to say something, as if she knew that time was of the essence, but she could form no viable sentence. She had to be in shock. When it passed, she would of course be able to think clearly, express herself suitably. First, however, she had to come to terms with the fact that he had hit her. She closed her wordless mouth.

'I am pleased that my mother has begun teaching you how to cook my favourite foods. Allow her to show you how, and you will make an excellent wife, and me an exceedingly contented man.' He came up and kissed her cheek, 'Friends again?'

She pulled back, waiting to see him try to hug her, beg for forgiveness, to be shown his desolation, but none of that came. She stumbled into the bathroom, slammed the door and retched. When she splashed cold water on her face, she stared dumbfounded at her reflection. Her lip hadn't swelled, thankfully. Instinctively, the knowledge crystallised: no one must ever find out about this. Never, she thought vehemently. It must be as if this had never happened. And suddenly the weight of this responsibility crushed into her and her feet felt too small and too shaky to hold her up. She sat on the toilet and stared at the terrazzo floor, the different shapes of jagged stone, black, brown and white, that had been polished smoothly into the wide expanse of beige concrete.

She was determined to ensure it never happened again. She was positive she could prevent it. After all, wasn't she driven, disciplined, successful in all other areas in her life? She could behave in the right way, say the right things, be the right wife, and keep this unspeakable side of her husband at bay. He needed her to, because, after all, he would be just as ruined as she if this happened again, if anyone found out.

She worked hard to learn everything that Ma Akos wanted to teach her. As the days passed and things reverted to normal, she believed that something to do with her mother-in-law's presence had caused Vincent's odd behaviour. She learned to keep quiet when she was around, to smile and nod politely, and to busy herself as much as possible outside the house. She took to being delayed on shopping trips, to running out of petrol, suddenly remembering the birthday of a friend, or a library book that had to be returned. She was often caught in traffic or in the scrum of a road accident, anything to buy herself time to pop in on friends, to go and sit on the beach by herself, to stroll aimlessly through the market.

Vincent helped by not mentioning it again. In the weeks that followed, he paid particular attention to her, told her a few times how much he loved her, how partial he was to her smile, how everything was going to be just fine. Then one evening he brought home a pair of gold pendant earrings, which he explained he had had made especially for her. 'I thought they would suit you, and they do,' he said smiling like a shy schoolboy. She shook her head coyly, this way and that, and felt them jangle against her cheeks.

By the time Ma Akos left several weeks later, Dahlia had started eating meat again and she could make all of Vincent's favourite foods. She had also learned to greet him at the gate and to carry his briefcase into the house even though there were usually two maids, a driver, a watchman and a gardener about who could quite easily have performed this task. She kept a mask of courteous indifference on her face in response to Ma Akos' approval. She also had his dinner waiting, his favourites only. He didn't like adventures with food, trying new things, or learning new tastes. Often he would call from the office in the middle of the afternoon and make a request for *fufu* and chicken soup, or *kontomire* and yam, which was without fail not what Dahlia had prepared. She got used to having to send the maid with the driver to get the ingredients and quickly prepare the dish as carefully as possible. She learned to keep supplies of dried and smoked fish and peppers in the freezer to cope with these emergencies. The dishes took ages to prepare well, they had to simmer for hours for the flavour of the chicken or fish or goat or snails or whatever it was to emerge.

'You must count your blessings,' Ma Akos had said to her in that first week. 'Ashanti men like to eat *fufu* every day, but

Vincent has been in London so he is different.' Dahlia had stared at her blankly. They had tried to teach her how to make *fufu*, but she had been determined not to learn. She kept getting it wrong, so that in the end, they had relented and let the maid pound the yam and cassava with the five-foot pestle, flipping it with moistened fingers until it became a sticky pulp. From that she formed two perfectly smooth oval lumps of *fufu*, which she placed in a covered Pyrex dish at the head of the table to await Vincent. He ate it with his fingers, dipping small pieces into the soup first and swallowing them whole. Dahlia, however, had still not learned not to chew her *fufu*, which offended Ma Akos and irritated Vincent, so they stopped eating it at the same table.

As soon as Ma Akos left, Dahlia had set about trying to reclaim her home and family. She went swimming with her friends and told the maid to make the *kontomire* that Vincent had said he wanted. She lied to him when he got back home, said she had been ill and that was why she had asked the maid to cook it. He didn't eat much of it; he sulked and told her that he could tell someone else had cooked the food, that there was no love in it. Once Dahlia would have been flattered, but that night, she noted with resignation that her feelings and her needs were a growing pile of irrelevancies as far as Vincent was concerned.

She looked up into the mirror now, turned her head this way and that to inspect her face. She was certain that no one had seen the bruise through her make-up at Eva's party. Besides, they wouldn't for a moment imagine where it came from. Even she struggled to believe it sometimes. Wasn't that why she was still here after all these years?

Two days ago, she had confronted Vincent about the latest woman, asking him what his intentions were and begging him to think about their marriage, their children, pleading with him to at least be a little more discreet. To end their discussion, he had punched her in the face so hard she thought she'd lost a tooth, and lying on the floor of their bedroom, he had kicked her in the ribs and called her names she had since been working on erasing from her memory. It was in many ways the worst attack, coming as it did after a harmonious lull in their relationship; it had been several months since the previous incident. She had found it particularly galling because the children were in the next room. They must have heard it all. She had remained in her bedroom nursing her bruised soul, her battered cheek, keeping away from her children in case she contaminated them with the vileness of it all, out of sight of the pitying servants and hoping her complexion would return to normal. If it had not been for Eva's party, she would have remained secluded in her room for a while longer.

Somehow it was harder to understand why she had never been able to satisfy him, why he needed to go elsewhere, than it was to blame herself for the beatings. It was much easier to identify the stupid things she did to provoke him to anger, to see why he lashed out, to accept that she should have seen it coming. And impossible not to swear to herself after each incident, that next time, next time she would act differently, she would prevent it.

She could see how ridiculous and pitiful her situation was. She who had once been an advocate for women, who had wanted to study law not to become rich, but to help women fight the injustices of the legal system that in her opinion was heavily weighted in favour of men. And here she was, demeaned, humiliated, crushed by a man who couldn't care less about the agony he was causing, and then, on top of it all, she had to hide the fact from her servants. Hadn't she always been vociferous about the denigration of the black man believing that he must rise up out of the situation the white man kept him in? And here she was a black woman – for she refused to use the colour variations she had been raised with, milky brown, fine-fine brown, not real black; she was black, and proud – disturbingly comfortable with black servants running after her, washing her underwear, changing her sheets, pretending that they didn't notice the extra make-up, that they didn't hear his screaming fits or the breakages. It would be easier if it was more predictable, if there was some recognisable pattern that might help her to take preventative action.

For too long she had been resigned to the violent state of her life. Before she had hoped that around the corner was a better day, a better time. She had hoped, willed him to get this anger out of his system, tried to improve her behaviour to please him, expected that he would eventually settle down for the sake of the children. But instead things had got progressively worse, and eventually she had been pulled into a deep hole, one which it was becoming harder and harder to climb out of.

She wiped her face and pulled her hair back into a bun. She wondered whether all this would have happened if she had kept her afro and her silver bangles. She had traded in her identity for what she thought he wanted: straight hair, discreet gold earrings, lipstick and plucked eyebrows. Given far too much of her soul. Offered more and more as he had taken less and less, until in the end when he had fully turned his back on her she was empty and spent, a self-doubting shadow of her true self.

And now, these unruly stirrings of resentment and rebellion. Wouldn't it be easier to accept the way things were for now if she could imagine some time in the future when things might be different? What choices did she really have? How could she fight? She had asked herself these questions countless times and no matter the answers, she was satisfied only for a while and then the questioning would begin again. Is there a way out? Is there something I can do? Should I be doing something different? She couldn't help wondering whether it was because they were here in his country, she a visitor, an alien, that she put up with the way he treated her. If she were the one with the upper hand in the immigration and nationality stakes, would she have packed up and left him the first time he cheated on her? She hadn't been afraid of him to start with; she had threatened to leave countless times and he mocked her, questioned where exactly she would go, and reminded her that no one would want her, that no one would believe her.

She thought about Jasmine, who was struggling to blossom under this cloud of worry. She thought of her raw fingers and felt the hard knot of anger within her grow a little more. Then it split, and more of the bitterness it contained seeped through her. She was going to have to do something. Her life wasn't going to change by itself.

Quite by accident she had paid attention when her mother said, 'Always keep some money to yourself that no one else knows about.' She had left her savings account intact in London. It had never really come up in conversation with Vincent; he had assumed she was as poor as her parents. He didn't realise that she had had three jobs and saved every penny she could. She had walked instead of taking the bus, never eaten in the students' union, and only ever had one drink in the pub. She was an expert at stringency even then, and by the time she had given up her degree course and made the journey to Accra, she had a useful sum in the bank, which she left to grow where it was.

She would have to overcome the shame of going back home and find the strength to deal with her mother's reproach, her father's 'I told you so'. She had to believe that they would see past her mistake and help her on to her feet.

If only she could make Vincent see that it was for the best if he let them go, then he could have what he wanted, the freedom to live however he wished.

She would talk to him tonight, try and lay out their options unsentimentally. He had seemed in a good mood at the party.

He was combing his hair, whistling. The room reeked of fresh-ness, shampoo and aftershave. He greeted her cheerily and she felt her shoulders tighten. She faltered for a moment while Vincent looked at her expectantly.

'Vincent, I want a divorce,' she said quickly, before she could change her mind. As soon as she had uttered the words, she felt stupid. She felt her skin prickle all over her.

He laughed rudely and shrugged his shoulders. 'Who do you think will have you? Do you think anyone else will provide as well as I do? As I have? I would advocate that you think some more about your decision. Don't act rashly.' He continued to stare at himself in the mirror. 'But go if you want. No one is keeping you here against your will.'

How could he be so flippant about a marriage, their marriage, about the children? She stood behind him and looked at their image in the mirror. Side by side they made a fine duo. The picture was perfect. If only the substance could be resurrected. Vincent halted his grooming momentarily and flicked his eyes towards the reflection of hers. 'I should be the one getting rid of you, you ungrateful creature. Sometimes I don't know why I keep you here.'

'What do you want from me, Vincent? Surely you don't expect me to continue to live like this, with the shame of your infidelity constantly hanging over me? You have to be fair!' She could hear the desperation that had crept into her voice.

'Well, I am not the one talking of leaving,' he said. 'I don't understand what you want. Women like you are never satisfied. You always want more. And if I gave you more, you'd want even more than that. You have a nice house, a car, a driver, money. Do I ever ask you what you are doing with all the money I give you? Do I ask where you go, what you do with your time all day long?'

'That isn't what this is about. This is about you and me, our marriage,' said Dahlia.

'You have so much more than my mother ever had . . .'

'What on earth does this have to do with your mother?'

'I owe her everything.'

She wanted to say that it was wrong that he adored his mother more than anyone else alive, but she didn't. She could see the discussion was pointless. Maybe if she left him to think about what

144

she had said, her decision, now that it had been elevated to that status, maybe he would come to his senses and they would be able to talk properly. Vincent was examining his tie, straightening a silk handkerchief in his breast pocket.

Dahlia wondered how this had happened to their passion. She had always been a little in awe of him. He was exceptionally clever and, right from the start, had been one of the few men to make her stumble over herself. He wasn't ageing particularly well; he had a balding head, a large forehead, and, increasingly, a paunch. The only reason he was attractive to women now had to be his power or his brains, and given what she had gleaned about the women he spent time with, it was unlikely to be the latter. She knew she was being generous calling them 'women' when they were simply girls, but she hated that term, which she reserved exclusively for female children. It was just another form of sexism that kept women in their place; refer to a woman as a girl, and she might act like one too.

She went back to her room and sat on her bed. Maybe it was all a lottery, pick a name out of the hat, marry the man and then cross your fingers and see. There had to be more though. She had to find out what, because, even if it was too late for her, she would at least be able to protect Jasmine from this same misery. Why was it that in matters of the heart, she abandoned her intellect so completely? She put her head in her hands and tried to think through the fog of emotions.

The door to her room opened suddenly and Vincent walked in. He stood very close to her, intimidating her without even trying, and said softly, 'I want you to understand that you may leave whenever you want. But you leave as you came. Empty handed.'

She swallowed as his words ignited the familiar uneasiness in her. She clasped her hands together for comfort. 'What do you mean?' she asked, as panic swelled her throat.

'My children. They stay in this house.'

'You can't mean that.'

145

'Listen to me. I could put you on a plane, send you back to your pathetic parents any time I want. The daughter of immigrants, of a tube driver, for God's sake! They should still be counting their lucky stars that you married so well.'

She opened her mouth to say something, but no words came.

Vincent nodded as if her silence indicated her understanding. He pointed at her and said, 'And if you try anything stupid, rest assured that I will not sleep until I find you.' He glared at her for a moment and then walked out.

Dahlia tried to steady her nerves. Why had she thought she would be able to go? The mere idea terrified her now. She would have to abandon their home and the country, and even then she knew he would find her, he would hunt her down and then what? She could visualise her lifeless body, Vincent playing the final act with impressive sombreness. There was no way he would allow her to go quietly. Hadn't be boasted often that he had never in his life let a grudge go unsettled?

It felt as if a large load had been placed on her and was crushing her lungs, forcing air out when she needed it desperately. She concentrated on taking in short and fast breaths. She put her head in her hands and tried to blot out the sensation that the walls and ceilings were collapsing in on her, that she was somehow drowning, being sucked down by a power she didn't have the energy or will to endure.

Chapter Nine

Downstairs, the house was still shrouded in the hush of early morning. The living room was musty; Eva drew the curtains and opened the louvers. In the kitchen, she put a saucepan on to boil some water. In her bare feet, she could feel crumbs and bits of dirt on the floor. She opened the door and walked out into the garden. If Alfred could see her, he would tell her to put shoes on, but she enjoyed feeling the grass, the life beneath. She whispered a quiet thank you to God for her haven; not believing didn't mean she couldn't petition or praise. Just because Alfred and his family had always attended church, been raised not to question an inherited belief, didn't give them a monopoly on God's time.

Zachariah glanced at her, nodding a silent greeting, and then quietly continued sweeping the yard. Eva appreciated his stillness as she paced in the murky calm, enjoying the dampness of the night-rested greenery.

She walked the length of the garden towards the row of casuarinas trees that bordered their land. Tall, willowy branches drooped downward, shedding their needles in the dryness. She heard Zachariah whistling. She turned to see him pull a packet of Rothmans from his trouser pocket and open it. She watched him put a cigarette between his lips and strike a match. He stepped back and admired his work briefly as he puffed on his cigarette. Any contentment or dissatisfaction was tucked behind his bloodshot eyes. All there was to know was in his slow, gentle hands and his straight shoulders, his firm brow and silent lips.

'You can stay here today, if you want . . .?'

'No, madam, is okay.'

Eva wasn't surprised that he was not fazed by a few soldiers on the streets. She hoped he would get to his day job safely. He had a face that didn't offend, clothes that didn't shout out to be noticed, and he was thin and aged and wore local shoes. All in all, not a picture of hidden wealth, stolen money, fraudulent misappropriation of the country's gold. He would spend the day there gardening, more physical labour, yet more cola nuts to keep him stimulated.

He returned each night, rolled out his mat towards Mecca and prayed before he positioned himself for the night on his low, hard chair, shaped rather like a wooden deckchair at the side of the house, facing the front gate. He was supposed to stay up all night and protect the Laryea family from the evils of night-time Accra, but Eva knew he slept, he was human after all. Yet over the years, she had become accustomed to having a night watchman, someone who sat sleeping between her family and the undefined hazards out there. It enabled her to sleep in her air-conditioned bedroom in the quiet knowledge that there was someone who would alert them to anything sinister before it engulfed them.

Occasionally Zachariah would be drawn into a conversation with Solomon or with a passer-by or the driver of a visitor, but more usually, he sat quietly on his chair with his prayer beads in his hand and his eyes closed, humming to himself. Eva had often wondered what his life was really like. What was home like for him? She wondered how he was able to conduct a normal life in between this endless working. She had always admired him, but hadn't been able to bear thinking too much about the details of his existence, they were too uncomfortable, too painful.

And yet something made him different from others, more enterprising, something kept him going on this treadmill that was his life of work, sleep, work, earning just enough to get up and do it all over again.

Faustina arrived hurriedly to start her usual morning cleaning, allowing the door to slam shut behind her.

'Please don't slam the door.'

'Madam, please don't mind the door. Do you know I have risked my life by coming here? In fact madam, there are many maids in my situation who could not venture outside their quarters in such a time of grave danger,' she continued sounding winded. 'And, in fact, I cannot clean the windows today.'

'Why?'

'Madam, who is to say that a stray bullet won't come flying through the air and penetrate my neck or even my heart leaving me dead, my poor children motherless, without a home?'

'Don't be ridiculous! There are no stray bullets hovering above the house waiting for you.'

'Eh madam, in fact, this is not a joking matter at all . . .'

'It wouldn't occur to me to joke,' muttered Eva.

'. . . yesterday do you know what they did? They have demolished Makola market and slayed most of the market sellers for hoarding goods and raising prices . . .'

Eva sighed and poured some Ideal milk into her coffee.

'In fact, these kind of people may not rest until they have killed us by force. They want blood, yours, mine, anybody's, they don't mind which one.'

How exhausting it must be to be so fearful, thought Eva. Heaven knows what it is that happens to them as children, what they are taught at school to make them all so scared. They are like startled sheep, one runs off in one direction and the others follow without question. Even with Alfred, for all his erudition, the list of things he was anxious about was tiresomely long and it had grown with the birth of each of their children. In the beginning Eva had laughed at his absurd worries thinking he was joking, but as she began to realise he wasn't, she had learned to say nothing, sometimes having to bite her lip hard. And she had learned that she had to do the things he forbade when he wasn't around to see her flouting his rules.

'Alright then, don't clean the windows,' she said tiredly, walking into the living room with her coffee.

At the window, she stretched her neck to look through the leaves and branches that grew near the gate, over the top of it, through the holes in it, keen to get some sense of what was happening out on the street. The louvers that Faustina was refusing to clean were covered in a light film of Harmattan dust, but it was the mosquito net, which covered the windows, that distracted her. It was grimy, blackened with trapped dirt. Why hadn't she noticed it before today? Noticed the way less and less light could enter the house? She looked curiously at the shadows around the room, cross, as though they had crept up on her in spite of her relentless cleaning.

Along with the netting, burglar-proof metal patterns covered all the window openings, still able, when she forgot to look right through it all, to make Eva feel caged in her own home. She made a note to tell Zachariah to wash down the mosquito nets.

She peered beyond all her barriers to what she could see of the street, where there was nothing to see. A freshly tarmacked road, edged with dull red sand, and further edged with rain gutters that she couldn't smell from here. Even if Faustina's information was wrong or embellished, clearly the coup had been a success. The usual footfall was absent; the sounds of life stilled. By now the bread seller should be passing, her freshly baked buns snug under white net fabric balanced on a round wooden platter on her head. There should be children on their way to school via errands to the market or carrying buckets of water to their parents, and toots from impatient taxi drivers alerting lazy pedestrians of possible collision. There were no slouching, scraping sandals slowly, lifelessly, making their way to work. No unnecessary outings until the coast was clear, until the danger had passed, until . . . until what?

And poor, poor Dahlia. Trapped at home with a man who didn't want her any more. Eva couldn't imagine what she was going through. She went to the phone and dialled, but all she got was an engaged tone, which could mean anything in this blasted country, she thought angrily. She hoped her friend was all right, wished she lived closer so she could check in on her.

But the country seemed to have come to a stop once again, and Eva knew it would remain in this unhurried, ambiguous but tense state for a while, and that all attention-seeking behaviour would be shelved. Everyone would avoid courting the consideration of excited, newly empowered, hashish-assured, untamed, directionless, yet well-armed, uniformed men.

The idea that another lot of military-clad men, the third in eight years, could make differences that the previous lot had failed to was beyond Eva. As far as she could see, none of them had taken this poor country and its long-suffering people any further forward in terms of development. If anything, the people had been brought to their knees, trampled on when progress marched past them. And to think that just over twenty years ago they had walked boldly, independently away from Great Britain. What a shame, a waste even. Her friends agreed with her. They debated it often, the way this country rich in minerals and other wonderful things could be so cripplingly poor. They had their opinions as to why no government seemed to be able to get it right. 'Because of the way they think,' said Yelena. 'Because of their lack of initiative,' thought Dahlia. 'It is complicated, but basically it is education that is needed,' was Margrit's view. If she stopped to think it through, it was patently obvious to Eva what was wrong. In addition to a lack of incentive, the people suffered from poor organisational skills, little motivation, and a lack of pride in their personal surroundings. Things essential for any sort of progress. 'Progress as defined by the West,' her husband would retort irritably when she complained about his countrymen. 'Well, what other kind of progress is there?' she had responded. 'Don't you want Ghana to advance and become a developed nation?'

She had lived through this before and knew that by now they were on their way. Pressing their uniforms perhaps, shining their boots, donning their terrifying attire. They would be greeted with inflated insincere respect. Everyone could be sure of only one thing. Today they were in charge. Tomorrow, it might be someone else. Tomorrow, imagine the impossible, there might be order, they might be commanded back to their barracks with opportunities for lording it over gone before they had been properly taken advantage of. Today was their chance. It was all they could be definite about. Live for today, for this moment. Enjoy it! Power is sweet!!! They might as well have those slogans emblazoned on the backs of their camouflage jumpsuits, scrawled in blood on their foreheads. Their actions would speak for themselves. The longer term was for their leaders to worry about.

She remembered again how proud Alfred had been when he told her about his country, how wonderful it was, how she wouldn't need to bring anything from Europe, no disposable nappies, no cosmetics, nothing, because everything she might ever need could be obtained there. She had believed him and arrived almost empty handed, only to spend weeks wondering whether they were in the right country, the one he had described in glowing phrases, painting a picture of golden sun, lush landscapes and burgeoning economic boom. She had had to discover for herself the humidity that sat glossy on painted walls, the dust that blew in on the wind, the mosquitoes which dictated that evenings, when the temperature rose because the breeze dropped, would only be spent outdoors by the foolish or poor.

She looked at the louvers lined with dust and wondered when Faustina would overcome her phobia of flying bullets, for how long the windows would remain too close to the frontline.

Chapter Ten

Yelena was on the floor of her tiny storeroom making a list of the things she needed for her home and the salon. She wouldn't go out today, wouldn't open the salon, but she would put the bonus hours to good use.

The room was stacked to the ceiling with provisions in rows with their labels neatly facing forward. Daily she opened the two heavy padlocks on the door to this room, to which she alone had keys, and checked for evidence of mice, cockroaches, anything that might endanger her stash. She also had two large chest freezers packed with food in the garage which were kept locked. She trusted her maid and treated Sarah well enough, but she didn't think it prudent to allow her to see the full extent of this supply.

Yelena didn't like bare shelves, the idea of not having enough, or running out, so she stored. She needed no further analysis of the situation. It had to be done, even if it meant dedicating an inordinate amount of time, money and energy to worrying and thinking about it. Besides, knowing she could provide for her boys, which she did without any support or help from their father, made the responsibility of raising them on her own a little less terrifying.

In the background, the radio music stopped suddenly. The rasping voice of a man calling himself Captain Afriye crackled out. He informed his countrymen that there had been a change of government, that under his leadership, the Ghana Liberation and Security Convention or GLSC for short, had taken over power in order to liberate Ghanaians from the corrupt and selfish rule of the previous government.

Yelena looked up. She felt a sinking sensation as she listened. His voice sounded ominously determined through the airwaves, bloodthirsty even.

She found herself thanking God that she wasn't there in that studio with him. Somehow the idea of death and terror seemed much more likely now she had heard his voice. She realised how paternal some of the previous men had sounded compared to this one.

Afriye reeled off the names of his faction hurriedly, in the way she imagined she would if someone was pointing a gun at her head. Her stomach tightened and she realised she had tensed her shoulders, holding them up by her ears. Would this lot go further? Would they wish to prove themselves different, more drastic? Would they wish to make history? She swallowed. Her mouth was dry. She would have to check they had everything they needed at home, avoid any unnecessary outings. Were her friends safe and sound? Did they have everything they needed? She prayed quickly for the safety of everyone she knew.

The radio continued. 'I urge you all, as patriotic nationals of this our great motherland, to help us restore our country to its position of greatness, to fashion a beacon for our great continent by doing your part. Desist from acting in an uncontrolled manner. Desist from hoarding goods and foodstuffs. Such actions will be considered anti-patriotic, an offence punishable under military law. And with immediate effect all citizens must observe a curfew between the hours of 6 p.m. and 6 a.m., i.e. the hours of darkness, but apart from that I urge civilians to go about their legal business freely. Let us rebuild our nation into a country we can be proud to love. Thank you and goodbye.' There was a scuffle in the studio, she heard a chair scraping, and muffled voices. Someone flicked a button and then nothing but the crackle of disharmonious radio waves. Moments passed and then the military music started up again.

Even if she knew what *her* part was, Yelena couldn't imagine being able to do anything about it. Looking after her children, getting on with life, was sufficiently time consuming. She was trying her hardest to create something of a Christmas spirit now, in spite of the fact that there would be nothing that she associated with Christmas here. She could go on and on about the things she hadn't had time to wonder about when she boarded the flight to come here. But why would she have thought about such mundane things? She was freshly in love then, and when you are in love isn't it impossible to see the gaps there will be in your life once the chinks have widened enough? Well, no one could accuse her of not trying or doing her part.

The more she thought about it, the more troubled she felt at the prospect of another round of curfews, more power cuts, yet more shortages of everything. She began a mental tally of the things she was low on: sugar, milk, and anything for the freezer. All of it was so much harder on her own. At times like this, she too would have liked a husband to moan about. She thought about what Dahlia had told them yesterday. She would have made that Vincent into sausages by now if he was her husband! She would phone her friend later, check that she was fine.

She had written a long list of things, crossed them out, then written them again. Flour, but she had quite a bit, and several bags of home-made bread buns in the freezer. Sugar. She had at least six cartons in the freezer where they were safe from ants, and a couple of large plastic boxes filled with granulated sugar too. On and on she went, rice, eggs, powdered milk, tea, coffee, Milo. Anything in a tin, anything useful for the salon, any cleaning materials. She put her pen down. There was no point. She really did have enough of everything. Enough to last her six months, frankly. She put her list down to rest for a moment. She looked about her and then picked up the piece of paper again and wrote: *Anything*. She would buy anything she could afford that was edible, freezable, storeable. One could never have too much, no? And especially what with this new coup. At least they were relatively safe here in Kaneshie, a nondescript suburb of middle to poor housing. No one very rich lived here, or if they did, they hid their wealth. It wasn't like the Airport district or the other neighbourhoods where the expats lived, Cantonments, Labone or Ridge, where the roads were quiet and leafy and the houses big and wide. There were always tales of chilling incidents from those areas at times of unrest. Armed robberies, murders, kidnappings. If she could, she would buy a gun, that was what she would buy. Something reliable to protect herself and her boys properly from any hooligans that might ever dare to stray out this far. She had various weapons dotted about her house which might look quite innocuous to the uninitiated eye, a hammer near the front door, mosquito spray on a shelf by the back door and a rolling pin on the window sill in the kitchen. Underneath her bed was her prize possession, which she put in her bed each night, a large, old cricket bat she had got from an English diplomat who was returning home. He had been baffled that she didn't want the balls or the stumps to go with it, but eventually had shrugged and given it to her for free. He'd done so with a distinct look of concern for her, and it didn't lessen when Yelena leaped up to hug him and kiss him on the lips, her eyes joyous and her smile beaming.

Please God, she whispered now, whatever happens, don't let there be too much bloodshed.

She went back into the kitchen to check on Jonas and Joel, who were at the little table doing the written Russian work she had set them. They could speak fluently because she refused to speak anything else with them, but their grammar and vocabulary was nevertheless limited and she wanted them to improve. Once a week they had a Fanti teacher, a young man Yelena had befriended who lived close by, who came to teach them their father's language. Naturally they hated it, but Yelena didn't entertain their opinion on this matter. 'One day you will thank me. I won't have you living in a country where you don't understand what the people are saying about you, to you, around you...'

When it looked like the twins were nearly done, she went to phone Eva to thank her for the party. They discussed the coup and she said that there were no signs of soldiers or any unrest in her part of town. She tried Dahlia, but Vincent answered the phone and said that she was unwell and in bed. Margrit's phone had never worked, but Yelena knew she would be fine, she always was.

With her work done and the boys playing quietly, she sat with a cup of lemon grass tea and wrote in her diary. It was a less a record of her life than a collection of her thoughts. She was driven, she knew, by a sense of her mortality, leaving her boys before they knew who she was and so it was to them that she addressed the entries. She had had another of those dreams, the one in which she was suddenly dead and her boys alone. She had vegetable juice for breakfast, ate as healthily as she could when her emotions were in check, and did an aerobics routine she had devised for herself each morning. She'd found a lump in one of her breasts a few years ago, and while it had not amounted to anything menacing she now checked them regularly.

But she wasn't one to take chances, she couldn't afford to be irresponsible. She was planning the boys' confirmation. She had been debating for a while whether they should be Catholics or Protestants, and in the end she had decided that they should take their father's religion and become Anglicans. Her family was neither and she would personally have liked the boys to be Catholics because she really liked the imagery and ritual, but anything that bound them a little tighter to their father's heritage would be a good thing. They would have three Godmothers each, Margrit, Eva and Dahlia had agreed already. Given that Margrit was an atheist, she had wondered at first if she might protest.

Today she wrote about what she hoped the visits to Wisdom would mean for them, *because I love you so much and you need a father*, she drew a smiley face at the end of the sentence. She wrote that she knew how ridiculous her hoarding obsession was, but that they would understand one day when they too were parents and realised that an astonishing thing happens when you bring a human being into the world and know that you would do anything to protect him. She scribbled a couple of pages of thoughts. She never reread what she had written. She shut the book and finished her tea.

Later she dusted the bookshelves in her living room, mopped the green linoleum floor, cleaned the louvers and plumped up the sofa. She had wanted to repaint the walls, she was bored of the peach colour and fancied something different, but now was not the time to be looking too affluent. Anyway, she was proud of how lovely she had made her little bungalow. But how excited she was about the prospect of owning her own home! She had succeeded in buying some land, and had already drawn up the design of her house. She wanted it to be elevated on stilts, like the old colonial houses, with shutters like Margrit's house, and plain square rooms like Eva's. Three bedrooms she would have, and a large central living room. It had been a long process this land purchase, and she hoped she was there now, having paid three lots of chiefs money for the same land. They had built a wall around the plot from breeze blocks and they were finally about to lay the foundation.

Then she cleaned out the salon with the help of the twins. It was due to be repainted, but that would also have to wait. They took every item down and Yelena wiped the shelves, mopped the floors, and scrubbed the walls with Vim. When all was clean and sorted, the boys rearranged the shelves beautifully and put the posters back up while Yelena made some more bread. It always helped, the kneading, the pulling, the smell of yeast. And warm bread, ideally with a bit of butter, well there was nothing more heavenly, nothing more grounding, no? Besides there was nothing else to do; the usual television broadcasts had been suspended, there was nowhere she wanted to go while things were in this unresolved phase, and the six o'clock curfew made the day particularly short.

Chapter Eleven

At the weekend Alfred Laryea usually lingered in his bed, but he had been sleeping poorly all week. This morning, he had stirred when Eva woke and watched her with quiet yearning as she looked out the window.

She hadn't changed in all the years. Her body had swelled with each baby, but then duly shrunk back, leaving barely any evidence. Her hair was shoulder-length now, and although she had taken to dyeing it occasionally, it still had the fragile, wisp-blonde quality he loved. She refused to cut it short, into the elf-like style she had had when they met, saying that she wouldn't be able to get away with it now, but she would. He loved that about her, her charming self-deprecation; she genuinely didn't know how alluring she was, which made her all the more so.

When she left, he stretched his long slim body on the crumpled sheets, and wishing for a little more sleep, made himself get up. He was sleeping poorly; too many thoughts woke him each night and circled exhaustingly, leaving him feeling only more confused and overwhelmed about the decisions he had to make.

Their bedroom was cocooned from the outside; the air-conditioner drowned out all external noise. Thick velvet curtains blocked what light managed to filter through the many trees that Eva had planted in the garden. Alfred had finally forbidden her a few years ago from planting any more trees; she had already succeeded in turning the place into a tropical forest, killing most of the grass, but he suspected that she deliberately ignored him. For one, she had paid no heed to his wish to have an English-style garden with defined, interesting borders and a healthy lawn, and instead had created this unkempt, overgrown greenness she needed to see everywhere. He had told her on many occasions to ask the gardener to tidy the garden, impose some structure and order, to paint the flowerpots white, and to lay new lawn and tend it better, but nothing changed. The last time he had raised the subject, she had replied exasperated, 'This isn't England, you realise. This is Africa. We don't have the rain for green grass. Since you have lived here longer than I have, I would imagine you know that!'

'Bloody hell,' Alfred exclaimed out loud, his thoughts returning to the worries that had stopped him sleeping. Why did he have to tell her? He could think of many reasons why he shouldn't. But he was cornered; his mother was right, Eva would find out sooner or later, the truth always came out, someone would say something. And if he wanted any chance of keeping her, his family, he had to be the one to tell her. Besides, he felt he would eventually lose his mind if he couldn't release this endless, tormenting guilt. Feeling winded, he leaned forward to rest on the window sill. Damn! She didn't even realise how far she had pushed him away during the last pregnancy. He exhaled loudly, now that was cowardly, he knew better than to find some way to blame her.

Damn Vincent too! Things had not gone smoothly with the project they were working on in Tema for a Canadian company. It had seemed straightforward when Vincent first approached him, it had kept him out late and overly preoccupied. In truth, he had been so flattered that Vincent wanted his involvement so much that he had overridden his instinctive reservations and ignored Eva's opinion. Besides, the generous backhander he received in dollars which secured his continued involvement had blockaded him in. And now, after confiding in Vincent, he realised he had never had any reason to trust him. Maybe it was paranoia, but Vincent would have no qualms about breaking up his marriage if it suited him.

Alfred knew he was one of the lucky few who, using his skills, was able to make a decent living, plus a bit more. Inflation had rocketed steadily over the past few years, and if he didn't blur the rules of integrity a little here and there, then he too wouldn't be able to make his earnings cover their living costs. But he was now ruing his choice of business partner, his decision to give into the lure of the money.

That he had been expected to bribe the officials at the planning office was not the issue. Vincent had intimated that they could all make a lot more money if they cut corners with the construction by using cheaper materials for the warehouse. Alfred was well aware that they would be compromising safety requirements by doing so, they had had a massive argument and Vincent had turned nasty. He had threatened to have Alfred reported to officials at the planning office who could have him struck off as a licensed architect. Alfred relented, avoided Vincent as much as he could, and remained perturbed about the consequences of the cuts they had made. Then a wall collapsed and trapped three of their workers. Two of them were dragged out dead, the third had his legs crushed so badly they had to be amputated. Then followed harrowing meetings with the wives and other relations of all three men, pleading with the big men to help them, compensate them somehow for the loss of their breadwinners. In the absence of national insurance schemes, any savings, they were destitute and despondent and their children faced a life of even deeper poverty. Alfred was racked with guilt. He wanted to do the right thing now and urged Vincent and the Canadian representative to pay off the families, to offer them an annuity that would help them, but Vincent had been adamant. He wanted Alfred to make the problem go away. Ever the lawyer, he argued that to pay out would be an acknowledgement of guilt and would unravel their entire deal. He insisted that they continue to deny any responsibility, that they should argue that the men had not been wearing their safety gear, which they had, and that they had been in a no-go zone, which they hadn't been. He had insisted that the families be made to see that it was no fault of the employers and told Alfred to offer them a little something as a sign of goodwill and to keep them quiet.

It was left to Alfred as the project manager to deliver the news to the families. He faced them feeling gutless. When he had offered them the equivalent of a paltry three months' salary per family, one of the wives looked at him and said in a still, small voice, 'You don't look like a person who is wicked. Be careful that what you have done to me, someone doesn't do to you, because I can see that you have a lot more to lose than me.' She had stood and walked out leaving Alfred despising himself in a way he hadn't imagined possible.

Vincent had patted him on the back, laughed with him and praised him for 'handling things so marvellously' and Alfred had felt even more cowardly, vaguely frightened of Vincent who seemed for ever connected to the right people, a little too unsafe.

Now Alfred couldn't sleep for seeing the faces of the grief-stricken women and the lifeless bodies, the damaged lives. Wouldn't it be easiest to go back to London now? That was one of the options that had plagued him again last night. Get away before everything is blown out into the open and comes crashing down. He had the distinct feeling of losing control of his otherwise carefully orchestrated world, losing everything he held dear, his family, his home, his business. Why the hell had he got involved with Vincent? Greed, he supposed.

But how would they make it back in the UK? He would have to start at the bottom again, hope to persuade someone to hire him. And how would they get on the property ladder or pay school fees? His children wouldn't go to state school. He would be miserable there, the sense of failure would haunt him, the knowledge that he had fled a situation he had brought on himself. And they would be too close to his in-laws for that whole issue not to be addressed in some way. He had never mentioned them again after the first time he met them. He had let that relationship slip into the recesses of his mind to lie dormant, knowing he would never again have to interact with them from this far. But it would be too much to expect the same of Eva. She would want to see them, to integrate them into her life, the children's lives. Living in London would be complicated and besides, damn it, he wanted to be here! This was his home, this was where he was a somebody, not another foreign man observed with frowns, scrutinised for errors, used to illustrate a stereotype. In his own country he didn't have to justify himself, apologise for being the man he was, continually check that he was blending in.

He rubbed his temples. The coup hadn't helped. Although it seemed to have been a smooth takeover, he had stayed home, not wanting to take any chances of leaving his family to fend for themselves. The news was bland, severely edited of course, but there were the usual rumours and everyone was getting on with doing what they needed before the curfew. Eva thought he was frustrated at not being able to get on with his projects and had commented on how he was moody and withdrawn and altogether not great company. The strain of lying was beginning to seep through, the frustration of having to pretend. It had taken his appetite and his concentration even.

How best to preserve and uphold their little unit? Weren't they a team, him and her? They had been, he thought. They would be able to work it out, they had to. They had faced other challenges and come through, hadn't they?

He put on a cassette from his vast collection of jazz recordings, turned the volume up to a deafening level and stepped into the bath. He scrubbed himself with his sponge till he was covered in soap suds. He put on the hand-held shower and let the water trickle down his back and his stomach taking the suds with it. It was here, in the safety of the soothing warm water that he allowed his shoulders to release their load and his face to drop, his tears to fall. He cried like a child, secure in the knowledge that if Eva walked in she wouldn't hear him above the sound of the music and the shower, and that even she wouldn't think it possible that the hoarse sounds that were spewing from the pit of him could be produced by a grown-up man. He clasped his hands and leant them on the tiled wall, bowing his head beneath them. It took him a fair amount of willpower to stay standing on his feet.

He stepped out of the bath and the water dripped off him, drenching the bathmat. He shaved, soaked his smooth skin in aftershave and put some coconut oil in his hair, giving it a sheen, and then combed through the softened curls. He stared at himself in the mirror and said out loud, 'Be a man I can be proud of.' His birth father had said those words to him on the eve of his journey to England all those years ago. He hadn't explained further what he meant, what kind of behaviour or achievement, other than the obvious, would make him proud. He had summoned Alfred to bid him farewell and issued him with a series of instructions that had sounded more like warnings to Alfred: Work Hard; Don't Let Me Down; Be of High Moral Standing; and then finally, almost like an afterthought, but clearly the dictat that encompassed all of the others: Be a Man I Can be Proud of. He sent Alfred off, non the wiser about how he could make his father proud, with nothing but a pat on the shoulder and a scrap of paper on which he had written the address of an old acquaintance who lived in London.

Alfred hadn't lived with his father, the one whose name he bore, for long. In fact, he had always considered his stepfather, Ignatius, to be his real father. He had been raised by his mother, who had never been married to his father, and he had lived with her and her family all his life until a year before he went to England. One day, not long after he was given a glowing report, stating that he had once again come top of his class in maths and science, his mother informed him that his father wanted him to go and live with him and his family. Without much delay, Alfred was packed up and moved into his father's big house to live amongst his many half-brothers and sisters with their piano, maids, and daily tutors for maths, English, French and Latin. He missed his mother and rarely saw his father. When he was summoned to see him, it was to be punished because he hadn't performed as well as he was expected to by one of the tutors, or because his standards had failed to improve at school, or because he had been caught with unpolished shoes or a shirt hanging out of his trousers. As often as he could, Alfred would stop at his mother's house on the way back from school for some food, which he much preferred to the food cooked by his father's maids. 'It is the same food, but it is the love that you can taste,' Auntie Gee would say, her entire body shivering with joy as she watched him wolf down bowl after bowl of her cooking. She listened to the tales of life in his father's house with interest, and clearly relished the fact that with all his money and privilege, they couldn't produce food as good as she did in her measly kitchen with constrained funds.

He got to know his father through accounts of his temper, his success and his power, which filtered down from his siblings and other relations who lived in the big house. They helped Alfred embroider the picture he was painting of his father, filling in the shadowy persona of the stranger. When Alfred found out that he had won a scholarship to a school in England he was pleased because he hoped that his father might be pleased. But his father's response, 'It is the least that I would expect given the privileges you have,' had left him disappointed. He resolved to work even harder and was more determined than ever to earn his father's praise.

'You have lived up until now without any congratulations from him and you haven't died. Don't forget that,' his mother said to him when he recounted his father's comment.

'You don't understand,' Alfred said. And fully aware before he spoke them of the sting in his words, he added, 'It is not as if you know much about education.'

All the way to England and for the first few cold months of his life in boarding school, his father's instructions plagued him. He wrote regular letters stating his achievements. He was in the soccer team, he was learning to swim, he was in the top 5 per cent in maths and science, and he was the captain of the cross-country team. He never received a response. Eventually, as the demands of school away from home, new food, an unfamiliar way of life and unpredictable, unfriendly weather took hold, he wrote less and less until he stopped altogether, surprised that no one seemed to notice. When he finally got a letter, it didn't contain the words he had once dreamed of, rather it informed him that his father had passed on to the next world. He sat on his bed and tried to picture his father's face, to see him in his mind's eye, to remember if he could the contours of his face, the lines around his eyes, aware that before too long it would be harder and harder to remember him clearly. But it was already difficult; the harder he tried to picture his father the murkier the image in his head became.

It was too far and too expensive for him to attend the funeral, so he decided to perform personal rites in the privacy of his college room. He wrote a long, final letter to his father, thanking him for acknowledging him, 'for there are many lesser men who would not have done so.' He thanked his father for helping him to have the opportunities that he did. His hand wavered as he wrote, his brow knotted from the strain of his honesty. 'I don't know what it means to be a man you can be proud of, but I have decided that I am not going to try to live up to that expectation, for I have come to see that you might be impossible to please. I cannot make it my life's work to try and achieve the unattainable. I don't know you well enough to judge you, and I have not lived long enough to be in a position to criticise you, but I do know that I don't want to be the kind of father that is feared or reviled by those who wish instead to love me.' He sat back and read the letter. He was surprised how little sorrow he felt as he tore up the letter and decided that he would apply to study architecture. He wouldn't become a doctor or a lawyer, which was what his father had wanted. Architecture seemed far enough removed from either field, and as far as he could figure out there were no architects in the family, no one to whom he would be compared and measured against for the rest of time.

It was only when he returned to Ghana, long after his father had died, that he began once more to wonder what his father would think of him, his wife, his choices, how well he had fared under the elusive life headings. And with each year that passed, he felt less self-assured about his early convictions, and he realised that he now viewed many of his father's choices with a great deal more kindness and understanding.

Ten years, he thought, smiling wryly. Who'd have thought it? He had had his fair share of worries, and had even on one occasion questioned the wisdom of his decision. There had been a couple of hysterical outbursts when they first arrived; once Eva had cried for days on end because one of the maids broke a vase that she had brought from England, an old birthday gift from her mother. And then out of the blue she had become paranoid when he chatted in Ga to his friends in front of her. Yes, they conversed and laughed in front of her, but not *about* her, about nothing much in fact, but she had asked them brusquely to speak in a language that she could understand. He had told her that there was no need to be so rude and she had scowled at him front of his friends and walked off muttering. 'Just teething problems', was how his mother had described their difficulties. He had tried to explain to Eva then that he was no longer on foreign soil, they were back in his country, where he had a reputation to build, where society was small and a name everything.

Could it be they had expended their quota? Wouldn't he find out soon? Looking over the past couple of years, he could see the bumps in the road. The baby, her exhaustion, his work. They had given each other less time, there had been less spontaneity, more friction, and he had became weary from the effort of it all, exhausted by the sense that no matter what he did, he was failing her, he was unable to protect her from some unnamed thing. After all, he couldn't change the country just for her, and it was that which sometimes seemed to be at the core of her frustration.

Eva itched and fidgeted uncomfortably in the stale, dull atmosphere. Another day stretched before her without potential. Each minute ticked away as if it had been doubled for good measure.

Over the past week, she had managed to speak to Yelena a few times, always after trying for hours, so she knew she and her boys were fine. She didn't worry about Margrit, who had after all, as she reminded them often, lived through the war and could cope with anything that Ghana threw her way. It was Dahlia she was worried about. Both she and Yelena had tried innumerable times and neither of them had been able to get through to her. How Eva wished she could see her, offer her some support, a hug, a chat. She imagined how alone her friend must be feeling and hoped that she knew that they were all thinking about her.

Outside, the dusty greenery was still in the breezeless heat; the roads quiet. It seemed that everyone in the vicinity was waiting to see what would happen. In the unusual tranquillity, birds chirruped incessantly. No need to extend their vocal chords in order to be heard today. The garden bulbuls and the grey-headed sparrows seemed startled by their amplified birdsong, questioning the quiescence. Even the birds have to work harder here, thought Eva, as she listened to their strident song.

She felt hemmed in. Aggravated by the audacity of the faceless soldiers and their leaders who had ransomed the nation.

There was usually nothing on television at this hour but she switched it on thinking that there might be some special program today. There was only a picture of the country's coat of arms, a shield held up by two eagles adorned with black stars, perched neatly on the words 'Freedom and Justice'. Ah, how she would like some of that now. Freedom! And maybe justice too. There was much injustice here, in her opinion. The lack of freedom, the lack of choice, the lack of water, from the ground and from the sky, and what about the lack of order, predictability, progress, cheese, strawberry jam . . . it was all rather inequitable. She pressed the off button hard in an attempt to stem this childish mood from swamping her, and before she could hear much more of the mournful music.

There was still no news on the local radio station, but the BBC news bulletin mentioned that the new military government in Ghana, West Africa, was denying rumours of widespread turmoil. It was never Germany, Western Europe, or New York, USA. Why did the British need to be informed where Ghana was? Hadn't they given it up a mere twenty years ago? Clearly it hadn't featured much in the nation's consciousness so they had already forgotten where it was. She could understand that Ghana might be a place some casual visitor might forget, someone returning to an easier way of life. But, as Alfred pointed out regularly, and she was able to concede this point, the British had owned this land, had happily harvested it of its riches, and now why didn't they care even a little for the welfare of the people? But how could they when they didn't even know where it was? All in all, perhaps it was a small blessing that they had mentioned Ghana at all. Eva wondered for how much longer this story would be of interest to the West and whether it had even registered with her parents. In any event, it wouldn't take much to knock it off the agenda. 'We are too far away to matter,' Alfred had reminded her in the past when she had wondered out loud whether her parents would be troubled if they had heard of the latest crises: the tsetse-fly plague that had wiped out herds of cattle, the endless drought that had brought the nation to the edge of famine, the outbreak of cholera that had killed horrendous numbers of babies and children, or the malaria epidemic that had wiped out those that cholera had only weakened. 'So long as our deaths and diseases are contained by our shores we are not a hazard to them, so why would they care?' he had said.

As the broadcaster droned on, Eva realised that she wasn't hearing what he said apart from the headlines that had little impact on her peace of mind and her way of life: problems with the IRA, something about Jimmy Carter, and a lot of excitement about the latest developments in space exploration. All so much more interesting to them, and completely irrelevant to us, thought Eva. So much for globalisation. Much better to stick with your own. See the world in terms of your own environs rather than through the telescopic, frustrating focus of some distant media.

Eva listened for a while to a discussion on the problems of dairy farming in Sub-Saharan Africa. Listened to the different accents of callers from Zimbabwe, Sierra Leone, Zambia. They didn't have the capability to make international phone calls from domestic lines in Ghana and Eva marvelled with a little jealousy at the additional advantage that these other Africans had. Not only Western food and good roads, but the ability to speak to Europe whenever they so wished. How amazing! The discussion ended and Eva swivelled the dial to find some music and shifted in her seat to air her sweaty legs. She looked longingly at the front door as if she could will a stronger, fresher breeze to come through. The radio reception was poor, perhaps even the airwaves were clogged with dust. Eventually she found a station playing Congolese music; ebullient, fluid guitar, snatches of French, a beat reminiscent of the rumba, which it was impossible not to tap to. It sounded good, even though the sound ebbed and flowed with the unsteady radio waves, and Eva was grateful to feel her mood lighten somewhat.

The baby woke from his nap and started to cry, and Faustina went to get him. He bounced on her hip blowing tiny bubbles with his mouth as she carried him down the stairs. Eva managed a smile and a gentle wave as Faustina took him into the kitchen to feed him.

The children spent the day loping around, their lithe bodies moulded over the armchairs, languid and emptied of vitality by boredom. Simon took off his T-shirt and lay still on the marble floor to cool his body. Joseph, who had just begun to crawl every-where at great speed, was rolling about in nothing but a terry nappy. Eva rarely dressed him in anything more in an attempt to keep him cool and stave off yet more of the prickly pink heat rash that ravaged his chubby body. All of them had spent their first months on this hard floor.

She could bear it no longer. She wanted to see what was going on out there for herself. She had managed to obey Alfred till now, but she felt too on edge. She walked around the house to the back gate, hitched her skirt into her pants and climbed up the leafy metal pattern in the central panel. She lifted her legs care-fully over the spikes at the top and lowered herself down on the other side.

The street was deserted. Eva walked down the quiet back roads in the direction of the main road. She felt apprehensive. She knew she was being foolhardy, but still she pushed along keen to make her escape worthwhile. Was this that latent sense of exploration and adventure that had brought her here in the first place? She rarely walked along the main road, but even from the comfort of her car, she could feel and smell the energy of it.

A few yards from the gate of the house, there was usually the woman who had a stall selling *yo ke gari*, a popular breakfast dish that Eva had only tried once, the overcooked black-eyed beans were served with *gari* and pepper sauce. The woman always looked tired and hungry. Tied to her back was a howling baby, several months old, who wanted to break free. The woman ignored the baby's cries as she worked. Eva had given up counting how many different babies the woman had had bound to her over the years. And she no longer wondered to what kind of home life the woman returned each morning, how much money she earned selling breakfast; the reality of this woman's life would be too incongruent for her to understand.

It was here in Ghana that Eva had first had to confront real neediness. And in time, she had had to decide that she couldn't afford to worry about each haggard, overworked mother, each child hawker that really ought to be in school. She still saw need, but she also saw an unwillingness to do anything about it. Wouldn't these people that she pitied do something to improve their lot if it bothered them as much as it bothered her? The *yo ke gari* seller didn't need to sit by a dirty, smelly gutter and she certainly didn't need to keep having babies. Now she saw more easily past the deprivation to the apathy and sloth which she thought lay beyond.

Today the street was quiet and empty. A few remaining old neem trees spread their shade over where the street vendors usually sat on the wide pavements. Periodically she had to step aside to avoid a gaping hole in the pavement where a large slab was missing and iron rods and the gutter below poked through menacingly.

She walked past the electrician's kiosk, a sky blue structure with the words: 'As Good as Knew' inscribed above the shutters.

The wooden structure was ramshackle. One of the legs was propped up on stones to balance it on the uneven sandy pavement. A large padlock secured the door, but one firm kick and the door would buckle. Behind the shutters, this kiosk was crammed from top to bottom with grimy old transistor radios, kettles, toasters and television sets that were stacked haphazardly, regeneration a seemingly debatable prospect. Had their owners forgotten them? Did the electrician keep them in the hope that he would be able to fix each one if only he could find the required spare part in another condemned machine, thereby guaranteeing a new lease of life to one of these otherwise unpromising gadgets? On shelves that lined the kiosk he had coils of wire, various tools, piles of browning papers and bits of equipment, dirty and rusting in old milk powder tins. Everything was kept, just in case.

She had sent the toaster here when it stopped working within weeks of Alfred buying it after Faustina had disobeyed the instructions for use. She was pleased, and a little surprised, that the electrician had been able to fix it, although a few days later the entire electric circuit in the house blew and there was a distinct smell of burning from the toaster.

She strolled past the spot where the tailor usually sat underneath a tree with his Singer machine whirring away, a tape measure around his neck, mending and adjusting items of clothing. He could look at the customer and with one quick appraisal, tell whether or not something was the right size, how many inches the dress needed to be taken in or let out. His trade was fuelled by the roaring second-hand clothing sales that went on in the market where containers full of clothes from the West arrived, yesteryear's fashions discarded. There was no tailor today; his benches were gone. He carried them home every night with his machine, but there was a sign hammered into the trunk of the tree that said, 'Speedy Modern Fashions', which was adorned with graphics of scissors and a pair of trousers.

And there should have been the man who sold a colourful display of plastic buckets and containers. The breakfast vendors, selling bread and Tom Brown porridge, tea and boiled eggs, or for those who wanted something heavier, rice, *gari*, beans and stew. Further along was the 'Don't mind your wife' chop bar, which seemed to be open twenty-four hours a day, but which today had its shutters firmly shut.

Eva stopped at the Syrian supermarket Quality First. She shopped here only occasionally; it was too expensive for her budget. Besides, the owner sat behind the tills and stared unabashedly at any female shoppers as if he believed that by entering into his shop they wanted to be ogled by an overweight man with greasy hair whose tight shirt had too many buttons undone. The steel shutters glinted ominously in the sunlight and the car park was empty of the large shiny trucks the owner and his sons usually parked here.

A young man poked his head out from the alleyway of the shop and took a step towards her. 'Madam, why are you walking around like this? It is very, very dangerous. They have killed a lot of people. They say that there are dead bodies all over Makola market. It is not safe, you know.'

'Oh, who says? Aren't those only rumours?'

'Please, it is not rumours. They are on the rampage. And you are very eye-catching. Please go home to your children.'

Her stomach had begun to churn. But the fact that he knew she was a mother made her smile. Was it the strain on her face? Or the knowledge that nothing else would keep a woman like her in his country?

'Please madam, this is not a smiling matter.'

'Fine! I'm going, don't panic.'

As she walked off, he called after her, 'Please, use the back roads.'

You see, she wanted to tell her children, you see how kind and caring they really are? They are not at all brutal or fierce. Look how this man who doesn't know me from anywhere is pleading with me to be safe and sensible. It was the appalling, unfounded rumours, which unfortunately never fully dissipated, that caused fright. Her spirits were oddly lifted. She looked about her and realised how quaint this street could be. The activity usually distracted from the bones of the architecture, mostly older houses from the colonial days with shuttered windows. They could do with some freshening up, the yards in front of them could be a little cleaner, the pavement and the gutter too. Less rubbish, less urine, a few more trees and flowering shrubs and it would be really pretty.

Chapter Twelve

Later that evening, after she had kissed the children good night, Eva came downstairs fresh from a shower and was surprised to find Vincent talking to Alfred on the veranda. They stopped talking as soon as they saw her, but Eva could tell that the tone of their conversation had been confrontational. Their appeared tense and hostile. Alfred glanced ever so surreptitiously towards the gate and when Eva looked over she saw two armed men next to Vincent's car.

'Vincent! Gosh, I've been trying to phone Dahlia . . . is she okay?'

'Eva, hello. Yes she's fine . . . shouldn't she be?'

'Oh good. I've been worried about you guys, but I see now that I needn't have been,' she glanced towards the armed guards waiting by a shiny Japanese four-wheeled truck.

Vincent grunted.

'I suppose they get you around safely during curfew?'

Both he and Alfred looked unfriendly. Vincent glanced at Alfred, a signal of sorts, and he said to Eva, 'We are having a private conversation, love. Why don't you go in, I'll only be a minute.'

*

Eva lay in bed reading a book, but couldn't concentrate. She was intrigued about Vincent's visit, by his new car and his armed companions. Dahlia had intimated that he might have connections to this new lot of leaders, hadn't she? An hour after she had left them, Alfred had come into their bedroom and gone straight into the shower. She could hear his prolonged bathing, and as she waited for him to emerge, she struggled impatiently, reading and rereading the same page of her novel. Eventually he came out, and stood in the middle of their bedroom. Droplets of water snaked down from his hair and on to his shoulders and back into the towel around his waist. She got up instinctively and walked towards him. He embraced her, held her close against his lean body.

'So Vincent is Mr Big Man now, eh? What was that all about?' She could smell his fresh skin, could feel his pulse on her cheek, his fingers on the back of her neck. He was playing with her hair as he always had, running his hand up her head, pushing her hair up with it.

'How I have missed you,' he said, sounding anguished.

She turned her face up to his and looked into the deep wells in his eyes. He quickly started kissing her ear, but in that moment, she had seen something she didn't quite recognise.

'Yes,' she whispered, aware that she was tensing up.

He nuzzled her and kissed her cheek.

'Is everything alright?'

He didn't reply. He slipped the straps of her nightdress over her shoulders, let his towel drop. He tightened his grip on her and she was staggered by the strength of his passion. She heard him moan; a tormented sound.

She pulled back, aware that something was not right. She was surprised to see that his face was wet. 'Alfred?' Someone is dead, she thought immediately. Who? Dahlia? Or one of her parents? Someone else? Was he ill? She held the tops of his arms and tried to get him to look at her. 'What is it?' she asked, afraid to know.

And then it was as if her question released him and his body quavered as he started to weep. He let go of her, dropped his hands to his side, his whole body wilting and drooping like a scorched sapling.

'What is it Alfred?' She had seen him like this once. When his favourite cousin had died leaving three young children and a bewildered widower behind, Alfred had retreated to the privacy of the bathroom to mourn. On one occasion she had even heard him punch the tiled wall with his fist and had winced on his behalf. That night she had wanted to stroke his head, to kiss his cheek, but he had pushed her away and she had lain beside him in an immobilising cloud of her own.

'Eva . . .' his voice was coarse.

An unfamiliar quiver darted through her. 'Alfred, what on earth is it?'

He flopped on to the bed with his arms draped over his thighs to hide his nakedness.

She sat beside him but was too frightened to touch him. 'What is the matter?'

'I have let you down . . .'

'No! No, don't be silly! Of course you haven't.' He shook his head slowly.

Full of foreboding, she whispered, 'What do you mean?'

'You don't understand. I . . . in the worst way possible.' He took a gulp and looked at her, shaking his head as if to dispel the words he must speak, the plaguing thoughts he had to utter.

'What have you done?' She pulled back. Her mind ran ahead of her, giving her an inkling of what to expect, but her heart refused it. She wouldn't abandon her faith in him so easily.

'I . . . you pushed me away. I . . .'

'When?'

'With Joseph, when . . .'

'When I was just pregnant? Well? I was exhausted, and miserable . . .'

'I didn't mean to . . .'

180

She was becoming impatient with him for drawing out this scene, for making her the one to pull out of him the information that he clearly wanted to share with her. 'Could you please tell me what is bothering you?'

'I had ... I ... oh Evie.' He turned to look at her now, unclasped his hands and moved as if to touch her, but she moved back instinctively, protectively. She was trying hard to stay calm, inside everything raged wildly.

'I had an affair, an unforgivable affair . . .'

Something sharp seemed to pierce through her abdomen. She shook. And yet she had a peculiar desire to laugh out loud. She chuckled, stifled a sob. Stood up and stumbled to the other side of the room.

'Evie, it didn't mean anything. I love you. I was lost. It was a mistake.'

She was trying hard to focus on him, the words. She kept blinking, trying to see through the odd haze that had suddenly clouded everything.

'It didn't mean anything . . .'

This is what happens in films and books. And to other people. Not to me, us, she thought to herself.

'I wanted you to know . . .'

'Why?' Her voice was hoarse, far away and unfamiliar.

'I don't know, I suppose I had to.' He was pleading with his eyes. 'I had to tell you, the lie was crushing me.'

'My God! And I always thought you were better than this, a good man, not like all the others . . .'

'I know you did, I've let you down . . .'

'Who is it?'

'No one. I saw her once or twice that's all. It was . . .'

'Who is it?' She hadn't really wanted to know, but this question would keep others at bay.

'Why do you want to know? I only needed you to know so that we could start again . . .'

'Start again?'

He continued to speak as if he hadn't heard her. 'I realised I made a mistake. I tried to end it . . .'

'End it? So it was clearly more than "once or twice" then?'

'There is a child . . .'

'What?' she whispered huskily. She felt tremulous, her arms folded in front of her like a shield, but the words pierced through. She felt under attack.

Now that he had said the worst, he seemed determined to continue to unburden himself. 'A boy. About one now I suppose . . .'

Eva put her hands in front of her mouth to stifle herself.

'I have nothing to do with them. I made a mistake, Eva. It is you and the children that I want. You are everything to me.'

Her legs felt hollow and she lowered herself onto the edge of their bed, staring straight ahead of her. His tears were irritating her now. Bizarrely she could almost visualise the child, and the image was insolent. Small and chubby sausage-like arms, a grin slowly populating itself with teeth, a child toddling his way into his second year, another boy for Alfred, brought into this world not long after her Joseph had arrived. A twin of sorts. She felt trampled and wheezed, struggling for air. Through the sound of blood crashing through her ears, she could hear Alfred say, 'I'm sorry' over and over again. The words floated about blankly filling the empty space between them, unable to penetrate the thick sentiments now wrapping themselves tight around her, long, strong bands of emotions that were too varied and erratic for her to process adequately. An underlying ache was spreading through her, numbing her. She banged her head against the wall desperate to feel something, to keep herself alert.

She opened her eyes. He was looking at her, his face crumpled. She stood slowly, holding on to the wall for support, and walked towards the door.

'Evie, please . . .'

'I need to be alone.'

She stumbled down the stairs.

It was hot. All the windows were shut, the curtains drawn. There was a little moonlight that made its way through the various barriers to cast shadows in the room. Eva fumbled through the shadows, past the coffee table and the sofa and fell into an armchair.

She wanted to feel nothing and concentrated on that. She wanted her mind to drift off into a place of quiet away from the devastating revelation, to a place where this hadn't happened, where it wasn't true. But even as she tried to shake off the circular questions and the unexpected feeling of bereavement before any of it could drown her any further, her mother's aged words sliced through the silence of the stifling room: 'You will live to regret it. They are different from us, it cannot work. It is hard enough if you stick to your own. And then you'll want to come running home when it goes wrong. But you won't be able to. Your father won't have it, you know . . . you have made your choice.'

Over the years after her mother had first uttered those words, they had continued to echo from time to time. They had angered her when she heard them; then they had disturbed her. Yet, even now, in the midst of this mayhem, it was clear to her that it didn't make sense to bemoan her choices. It would be like trying to relive the previous moment, only just past, but gone for ever. And besides, how could she feel sorry about the children? Sacrilegious, the mere thought. And what about the faithful and loving and passionate marriage that, until a few moments ago, had been all hers?

The heaviness became heavier. The news solidified into a new reality, a variation of the truth she had believed to be her life, and the pain it brought was deep and raw. Living tissue wrenched from living bone, things that had been joined for ever forcibly parted. She placed her hand on her breast as though she might be able to soothe the burning, and yet it ripped further through her, shifting everything she had known to be real and safe. And wonderful. Her faith, their future, their past. In a moment, it had all been torn up, shredded into a million fragments, then flung into the air like confetti.

She opened her mouth and released an agonising cry from the pit of her stomach that alarmed even her ears and notified the rest of her being that something had shifted.

She would never have imagined this possible. She could never have seen this coming, been prepared for this, although she had lived in this country long enough to understand that the rules pertaining to matters of fidelity and trust between married partners were rather more fluid here than back home. She had seen Alfred look at other women over the years. Caught him flirting, had occasional misgivings. But she had never distrusted him enough, never believed it possible, not with the way he loved her, adored her.

Soon she found herself wondering what the woman looked like. What she had that had attracted Alfred, whether she was witty or funny, beautiful or beguiling, or just simply conniving. And then she felt the first waves of anger. For Alfred. And for this pitiful country, where nothing had been easy. Yes, there had been joy and laughter and privilege in a manner of speaking, but also immense frustration and irritation. Sun that was too hot, humidity that was too high, rain that was too hard, shops that were too empty, people that were . . . oh she could go on about them and then she might never stop. Yes, it had been hard, but it had felt worth it. And now?

Was the immediate and instinctive desire to go home so strong because she knew she couldn't? Given the option, would she want to pack up tomorrow and go back to her parents hoping to be welcomed like the prodigal son; feted, mothered, soothed. Yes! How she longed to crawl into her bed and daydream silly dreams of her teenage years, while in the kitchen her mother made leek and potato soup followed by apple crumble.

She lay motionless trying to stop the thoughts. She could hear a buzzing in her head. She wanted to stifle the hammering in her heart, and yet it remained. She wrung her hands until they stung and she thought the skin might tear. Her mind was heavy and spinning with the unknown. She tried to lengthen her breaths: in and out, in and then out, until she felt calmer. Shock flooded her, freezing the blood that coursed through her veins until she felt numb, tranquil, nothing moving, as though asleep, her breathing barely there.

Yet she remained keenly here, aware of the darkened room, the moonlit shadows of figurines on her shelves, the furniture, the outlines of trees in the garden, the quiet of a tropical night filled with insects, the chatter on the streets, dogs howling at the full moon.

Chapter Thirteen

Dahlia sat splayed on the floor of her bedroom. She held the phone in one hand. She couldn't do it. She couldn't tell any of her friends; she simply didn't have the strength to. She would do what she always did, cope on her own, hibernate until she was strong enough to go back out and resume the starring role in her life.

Besides, she thought she had heard him approach her door a moment ago as she was halfway through dialling Eva's number, she was sure she had heard footsteps or a voice, but after she had hung up, kept still and quiet for a while, she realised it was her imagination, equally trampled and jumbled. He wasn't here, he'd left this morning. She looked at the phone. She couldn't tell them, but how she wanted to; how she wanted someone else to know.

She had been awake all night, had watched time go by until finally she could call someone, hopeful that in sharing her plans she would feel further mustered, renewed by her decisions, and now, at the appropriate moment, she had lost her strength. Maybe she *was* pathetic. Maybe he was right.

Her hand shook violently now as she stared at the receiver,

hearing the dial tone droning patiently in the background. Somehow she couldn't make herself call Eva again.

Resigned, she lifted her legs and tried pulling her knees towards her, but the movement was excruciating. She crawled up on to her bed slowly and huddled under her sheet, careful to arrange her limbs in the least uncomfortable position. She shut her eyes, and the image of Jasmine's terrorised eyes, and Cyril's gaping mouth pleading, danced before her in bright, garish colours, heightened by her lack of sleep, enhanced further by her own memory.

Now she was in an abyss, deep and black, without much light or hope of escape. She knew that any flight would have to be planned and executed in the next few days before energy failed her and the hole closed over the top of her head, sealing her in for-ever.

She stared straight at the white walls before her. How had they slept, she wondered? How had her babies slept after last night? Had they had nightmares? Had they wanted her? She didn't know because he had locked her door. 'For your own safety . . .' His words echoed dreadfully now.

She shook them away and tried once more to figure out where she had gone wrong, when the evening had started to disintegrate.

It was lunchtime. She was eating with the children as she always did. Jasmine's favourite dish of rice with black-eyed beans cooked in coconut milk, and some roast chicken. When they heard the car at the gate, all three of them stiffened a little. He was far too early. Dahlia smiled to encourage the children.

'How are you, Vincent? We weren't expecting you this early.' She stood up. 'Would you like to join us? Shall I get you a plate?'

He smiled, surveyed them happily, it seemed, and nodded affirmatively. Then he wrinkled his nose. 'But what are you eating?'

'Rice and beans,' said Cyril happily.

Vincent turned and stared coldly at Dahlia. 'You know I can't even bear the scent of coconut milk, yet you think to serve me this for my lunch? You think this is appropriate?'

'Of course . . .' Dahlia shook her head, as though trying to awaken her brain. 'I'll get you something else . . .'

'Do you not understand me when I say I don't like the smell of coconut milk?' His voice was rising now. 'Do you expect me to sit here holding my nose?'

All three of them laughed. Only a little. Maybe that was it; maybe that was when things took the turn. They shouldn't have laughed. But it was hard, even in the face of dire consequences to always remember to do the right thing. The right thing. Oh she *had* tried. She never stopped trying, but the right thing seemed to shift and change all the time, or maybe she just couldn't keep up. Maybe she was stupid, as Vincent said time and again. Too thick and slow, too backward, useless . . .

'Please come into my study, I want to talk to you.'

Dahlia's shoulders dropped. He liked the study because it was insulated, away from the kitchen and the maid, away from the boys' quarters and the houseboy and the driver. She looked at him imploringly. 'Please, not now. Let me finish with the children.'

He walked off, ignoring her.

'Daddy, please!' Jasmine.

'This isn't fair!' Cyril.

Vincent turned to see something he didn't like. Perhaps an expression of admiration on Dahlia's face, perhaps confirmation of the defiance he had heard in their voices, or maybe, for the first time, he saw clearly that they were a team united against him.

'All three of you, please.'

'No! Vincent, leave them out of this.'

'Now!' His voice bellowed and all three of them shook.

The study had wood panelled walls and a large Persian rug. It was lined with books. The curtains were heavy velvet, like the ones in the living room, but there were no windows. There was always a studious hush in here that Dahlia imagined could be lovely.

Vincent pocketed the key to the door, and turned on the air-conditioner. It hummed to life, blasting out cool air, and Dahlia realised she was perspiring, her hands twitched with nerves. The three of them stood in front of the desk. Vincent rummaged on it looking absentmindedly for a few moments at some papers.

'Vincent, for goodness' sake, leave the children out of this. Whatever grudge you have against me is personal to me.'

'You see children, there is something you need to know about your mother . . .'

'Vincent, please . . .'

'Shut up!'

She was desperately trying to make eye contact with him, wanting to persuade him out of his bad temper, but he stared at the children.

'She is a wicked woman, out to destroy our family . . .'

'I am so sorry. I made a mistake. A silly mistake. Forgive me, please. Come on Vincent?'

There was a brief lull, then Dahlia heard Jasmine snivel. Cyril was nibbling his finger, his infant desire to suck his thumb fierce, but fear of his father's reproach for doing so was stronger.

'She was a no body when I met her, she comes from nothing, and she will go back to nothing if she doesn't stop this constant disrespecting of me.' He came around the desk and stood in front of Dahlia. 'And I won't tolerate disrespect,' he whispered, shoving her backwards hard.

She would wonder later why she had always felt protected by the children's presence. Taken completely off guard, she fell roughly on to a side table, which broke with her weight. She tried to scrabble to her feet. The children rushed to help, but Vincent told them to leave her alone. He walked over and stood straddling her so she lay trapped on the floor.

189

'What do you think, Jasmine, do you want to end up like her? Useless? A fool? Do you?'

Jasmine snivelled.

'Answer me!'

'No . . . no.'

'And you, Cyril. Do you see what foolishness does? Do you want to be a fool too?'

'No.'

'Good.' Vincent stepped over her, took a couple of steps away. Dahlia tried to get up, looked at the children to give them strength. She didn't see the kick coming, and when the tip of his polished brogue hit her just above her hip, in the soft of her buttock, she folded over and moaned quietly. She couldn't scream out, not in front of her children.

They started to sob.

'What are you doing? Don't waste your tears. Tell her, tell her to stop being a fool.' There was another kick, further up, and then another in a leg, one in a thigh. Each vicious, punctuated with a name: fool, slag, bitch . . .

'Vincent, please . . .' Her hands cradled her head protectively. She felt something wet land on her hand and spray on to her hands and face. She looked. Saliva. 'You *spat* at me?' It was clear to her that the voice she heard wasn't hers. It wasn't Dahlia Blake speaking. It was someone else, some*thing* else, a thing worthy of being spat at by another human being.

He stood between the children, a hand on each shoulder protectively. 'Tell her, Jasmine.'

The sound, the worst thing that Dahlia had ever heard, was more excruciating than the throbbing in her body, more debasing that the spit on her hand. With her mouth hanging open, aware she must appear tragic and pathetic, she listened to her daughter's voice, broken and desperate, pleading with her: '*please just do what daddy says, please stop . . . please just stop being . . .* and her father egging her on, '*say it, tell her, maybe you can get some sense into her thick*

190

head'. And Jasmine, after a long awkward moment, with her eyes closed: '*Mummy, please stop being a fool* . . .' and then her daughter snivelling, and Dahlia's heart tearing open.

'Cyril?'

'Mummy, stop being a fool.' His voice, cool and unemotional like his father's.

'Good boy!'

Dahlia felt the stab of an icicle. She started to tremble. Was this it, then? Was this graduation day for them? Or the beginning? She started to retch, hoisted herself up with one hand, keeping the other over her mouth, determined she wouldn't vomit in here, not in front of them.

The children were silent. Dahlia stood. Observed them all for a moment. Saw the horror in Jasmine's face, saw Cyril biting his lip painfully, then his mouth opening and closing as if he would make a sound if he knew it would help. She hobbled out of the room angrily. Never had she been this ashamed. She knew then that if she had the strength, if she had the tools, she could kill him there and then. She had always understood the defence of a battered wife accused of murder, but had never been able to fully empathise. Now she could see clearly that everyone has their own breaking point.

A fool. The word had felt like a fresh punch in the stomach, winding her completely, hurling her back on to the ground once more. But she couldn't sink without a trace. She wouldn't let him do that to her, to the children. She would have to go before her mind completely ceased to function; over the past few hours she had watched it fragmenting. She had to keep herself strong, she had to get through this and out the other side. She would go. If not now, very soon, then never, at least not in any fit state to live, that much she could see clearly.

Chapter Fourteen

The knocking woke Eva. She pulled the sheet under her chin and stared at the door. She couldn't face them.

'Mummy?' It was Abi. The door handle depressed slowly, and Eva could almost see Abi's furrowed brow of concentration as she lowered the sticking handle down and tried to push open the door. The door and the entire frame rattled a little. The door didn't open.

Eva had taken no chances last night. When eventually she had stood, feeling deadened and leaving a sweat patch on the arm chair, she had come into the guest bedroom and locked the door. Then she had lain awake listening to the dwindling chatter out on the street, heard the plaintive howling of distant dogs. It was still pitch black when cockerels began to crow. Wearily she thought, possibly the worst night of my life is drawing to a close. She slept fitfully and dreamlessly.

'Mummy! Let us in.' Abigail sounded scared.

My little worrier, Eva thought. So like her bloody father, seeing danger everywhere. Grown-up and sensible before her time.

Her arms should long to wrap themselves around these warm, loving creatures, the only things that made sense now. But she couldn't go out there, where He was. She didn't want to, not today. Independent of her resolution, it seemed her body couldn't move. Her limbs felt lifeless, as if all her response sinews had been severed. Simon had joined Abi and they called her name again and again, louder and louder, until childish impatience peaked in fear.

Nothing.

And even as their diminished voices, deflated of confidence, continued to plead timidly, she felt the strong pull of what seemed like drug-induced sleep drag her deep into a darkness that offered solace and the promise of a restored soul.

'Mummy!' The sound coming through the keyhole shattered Eva's slumber. She blinked, confused, and tightened her fingers around the cover. How could she have dozed off?

'Mummy, Simon wants you . . . Simon, stop crying!' Abi's voice vibrated with the effort of trying to get through the locked door.

No. She wouldn't face them this morning.

'Why aren't you talking to us?' Abigail too sounded tearful as she rattled the door in anger.

'Mum . . . *mee*,' wailed Simon, clearly liberated by his sister's demonstration of true emotion.

Someone kicked the door.

'Don't cry like a baby,' said Abigail. Eva heard her sniffing, heard the tremor in her voice.

Suddenly they let go of the handle and it pinged back up; the door moved a little.

'Daddy, is Mummy dead?'

So, he was out there. Why did she feel afraid, she wondered, irritated. She listened to him comforting the children, guiding them away from the door. She heard him say loudly, to her, 'Mummy isn't feeling very well. She has a bad headache and needs a little more quiet and rest. I'm sure she will be better later this afternoon.'

'Damn you!' she said, rolling on to her side and closing her stinging eyes. She wouldn't think now. Yes, she did have a bad head, and a sore heart. Damn him! She refused to think about anything. Let him imagine that she would be up and about again, that their life might pick up where they had last laughed together, loved together.

This too shall pass, she whispered to herself. When she imagined her tears had been cried dry, she sat up. She looked at the empty bed. Would she become accustomed to not seeing Alfred beside her? His sheet flung off in sleep, one hand shielding his eyes. His perfect torso. Just days ago it had been inconceivable that a time might come when they would not wish to sleep intertwined in each other. It made her feel sick to think that he had lain like that next to someone else. Why had he done it? Again she felt a stream of tears build, and she willed her mind to turn away from the dismal questions. There was no way back, only through. They were going to have to finish this journey one way or another, heart-wrenching grief and all.

She had to stop the thoughts. She tried to dream instead. She visualised London. She could smell fresh toasted teacakes and proper tea. She could see the grey, rain-laden skies, she could smell the freshly cut sun-baked grass in Regent's Park, the damp wooden floor of the number 14 bus as it trundled her down the Fulham Road, tangy chips wrapped in grease and vinegar-sodden paper.

Eva could tell it was approaching midday when she opened her eyes. The house had the hush of a hot day. Outside, movement was heavy and monotonous, the sounds tired and slow, evaporating in the heat of the hazy brightness. She must have dozed off, exhausted by the tireless, circular thoughts that had been plaguing her.

Last night's events had erased the parameters she thought made up her life, and now she felt formless, unfastened. She had wrestled all night with her instincts, trying to configure a perspective that made sense. And she had decided she wouldn't analyse, wouldn't argue, would stop telling herself that by pressing pause on this life while she took stock would make her a bad parent. She wondered whether she had scarred her children by her behaviour this morning, ignoring them like that when they were needy. The thought hovered in her mind like an exotic bird, she let it, watched it dispassionately, curiously almost, wondering how long before it flitted off, only vaguely fascinated as to where it might drift, seeing as she would give it no room in her crowded mind.

But why had he spoiled things? What part had she played in this? When had this happened? When she was pregnant with Joseph, feeling sick and fat and tired? Or after, when she was breastfeeding, tired, down. She turned over and stared at the other wall, as if that might help resolve the torment. But it remained. What was she like? Had there been others? How many? And what did he feel for this one? And yes, she could hear Gladys' voice loud and clear, 'that is how they are, it doesn't mean anything. After all you are the wife . . .' She had heard it all before years and years ago. When as a young and perhaps slightly possessive wife, she had become overly jealous of a woman who had showed interest in her husband. Gosh, she couldn't even remember the details now, who she had been and where they had met, but she could remember the fuss she had created. She had had a tantrum and thrown fragile things, and Alfred had sent for his mother to talk some sense into her. And that was the sum of her sense; he is entitled to act insensitively because he is a man. At least that was how Eva had interpreted the facile and banal advice her mother-in-law had given her. Well to hell with them all. She wasn't built to put up with this kind of behaviour. If there was something special in the diet of a Ghanaian bride, some gene that they were born with that made them compliant, well she didn't have it. And even in her befuddled state, she couldn't believe that was true. Few of the Ghanaian women she knew were really like that, no matter how much they smiled and nodded, no matter how docile and submissive they appeared. They had simply mastered the art of pretending to be submissive, when in fact they were feisty and ballsy and full of get up and go. She wouldn't be fobbed off with any of Gladys' advice this time. Oh, but she would love to hear how Gladys would explain this away, and wouldn't she just soon enough? The woman couldn't keep any of her opinions to herself, no matter how ridiculous they were.

She got up charged by the fuming thoughts swirling around her head, heavy and misty, making her heart race. Tired of feeling down, she opened the door carefully and crept towards their bedroom. She could hear Alfred's voice downstairs, the children too. Anger reared up in her. She would find it, she thought. But what did it look like? And where would it be, she wondered? How the hell was she to know? She shook her head vehemently. This angry debate was hardly going to help, was it? How did she know what a clue looked like? She had missed them all, hadn't she? Because there must have been some . . . some *sign* that her marriage was unravelling, that her husband was straying . . .

She could no longer see clearly. The room swam before her. She wiped her face ferociously, angry with these wretched tears, then sniffed and looked about her. A lump caught in her throat, wet and thick. Her pulse, still rapid, like that of a hunted animal, her shoulders hunched ready for fight. She looked around the room. She had strewn the floor with Alfred's belongings. Like a person possessed, she realised now that she was calming down, she had torn through his belongings, his shirts, suits, underwear; she had turned everything upside-down and inside-out looking. She had never doubted him, never seen them before, but now she could see the clues she should have noticed. The new aftershave, new shirts, a receipt for something she didn't recognise, a book she had never seen. Why hadn't she noticed these signs before? But what would that have mattered? Would she have been able to prevent this? She felt light headed, suddenly exhausted. She sat on the bed, fell flat on to her back. She turned on to her side, hugged herself into the foetal position and wept until her head thudded. But it hadn't been her responsibility alone, this marriage, had it? It wasn't only up to her? Everything seemed to slow down, and she found herself drifting off, backwards, and as she fought the circling thoughts, she realised she was grieving not only what was now lost, gone for ever, including her expected future, she was also mourning her past, her youth, the years she had given Alfred, the trust, the devotion. Her parents. How she had loved her father. Look how much she had given up! And now, it was as if someone had pulled the plug and she was watching, powerless, as everything she had held dear drained away.

She began to feel immobilising waves of anger and remorse. She grabbed a pillow and shoved it under her head. Her body was rigid. Enough of this blubbering, she thought. Enough! She wouldn't. She couldn't.

And from the deepest depths of her being came an unexpected and overwhelming craving to be held by Alfred. A raw yearning to confide in him, the one person who knew her best and who had loved her the hardest; to share with him this monstrous, and terrifying uncertainty. He who, with ease, would have made her feel better. But how could she? How could he possibly comfort her after he had caused this? How could he make it better?

The strength of her sobs shocked her. From the pieces of her splintered mind came a desire so fierce it made her gasp: she wanted to go home, to crawl under the blankets around her bed, to hear the deafening silence of the Norfolk countryside at night, to taste again the carefree slumber of her youth, to be woken gently by intermittent wafts of baking bread and fresh coffee.

Ten years on, and still how crisp the details! The last time she went home, the sky had been azure blue and cloudless. Blossoms had given way to budding fruit; apples and pears and cherries that would be jammed and pureed later in the year. Tight roses bloomed everywhere, filling the hazy air with delicate, intimate scents. Eva took a lungful of air, felt her chest rise with the effort. She was heady from it all.

She stopped walking; they had reached the top of the street. She let her hand fall from Alfred's and turned to him. 'Smell . . . listen!' Overhead a small plane droned. Wasps buzzed out of sight. A lawnmower rattled along somewhere filling the air with the smell of fresh grass. 'This was the best bit of my childhood; we could play for hours and hours out here.' She opened her eyes and looked for his reaction. He was gazing down at her, grinning. Then his face grew serious, he put his hands on her waist and pulled her tight against him. 'What an effect you have on me Mrs Laryea.' She pushed him away, laughing. 'Alfred! Not here, behave yourself!'

'Why?' He released her reluctantly, biting his lip. 'Come on then, let's get this over and done with so that I can get back to continuing our honeymoon,' he said putting his arm around her shoulder.

'You distracted me. You're always doing that,' she said. 'You didn't even hear what I said.' She stuck out her lower lip in a mock sulk.

'I always listen to what you say. And more to the point, I take you very seriously, my little love.'

She looked up at him. He was wearing a tweed jacket, a blue shirt undone to reveal the first hairs on his torso. She was always thrilled to walk beside him, proud to be his. But now, she snuggled into him, willing the closeness to ease away her discomfort, the turmoil in her stomach, nerves, excitement; she was treading into the unknown, and yet she knew it all, everything was familiar.

She paused at the small path that led to her parents' front door, where a red geranium stood as always. She smiled nervously. 'Well, here we are Alfred. This is where I grew up.'

He dropped his hand to her waist. She took it in hers and held it. His long, strong fingers intertwined with hers; she thrived on the contrast between their hands, their skin; hers translucent and fragile, his dark and soft.

He looked around while she scanned his face. She knew he hadn't given much thought to what to expect, and in all probability was not surprised or impressed or disappointed. Or nervous. She took a gulp of air, smoothed her skirt, pulled down her blouse, adjusted her hairband and reached out to ring the bell. Alfred grabbed her hand away and leaned to kiss her. She turned to admonish him, and he took his chance and kissed her again.

'Not here,' she murmured, pulling away from his soft lips. 'And what's made you this insatiable today?' she asked giggling.

'You, Mrs Laryea. You have this weird effect on me,' he said against her ear.

'They might see us,' she said, struggling to ignore the currents his fingers sent down her back.

'So?'

'Enough!' She took hold of his roaming hands. 'You will just have to wait until later,' she said as she leant out of the way of another kiss.

'You are a spoilsport, Mrs Laryea.' He pressed the bell while Eva once more prepared her appearance, then he leaned against the door post and winked at her lazily.

Then her mother opened the door. She smiled a smile that only those who knew her well could read. She held out her arms and embraced Eva somewhat awkwardly. Eva gripped her, seeking familiarity and comfort in her hairspray, the Chanel perfume she had always worn, the old face powder.

It had been a while since she had last seen her parents, when they had last seen their girl. When she stepped back, Eva thought she saw tears gather in her mother's eyes for what had already gone. Alfred stood by watching them with folded arms, grinning. Eva introduced them. Helen vacillated for a moment and then put out her hand. Alfred took it, stepped into the gap, pulled Helen towards him and kissed her firmly on the cheek. Eva noted her discomfort. 'I see where Eva gets her good looks from,' he said. Helen put a hand up to her face, stroked her cheek absent-mindedly, smiled a little more broadly and then moved back to let them in.

As they walked into the kitchen, Alfred pinched Eva's bottom and she reached out for his hand. He took it and wound it behind her, keeping her near, making her safe.

He kept talking, admiring the house, the decor, the photos of Eva that hung in the hallway, laughing at how serious she had looked as a teenager. But his voice was far away, odd and out of place in here. Not the kind she had ever dreamed of while she had lived in this house. It was as if she was being pulled into a time warp; the smell of wax on the parquet floor, the cooking, the hush. Nowhere in London was this quiet. With the door closed, and the windows too, came the deafening silence that Eva associated with this house, when the only noise she had heard at night was the sound of her thoughts. The house felt smaller than she remembered, different. She faltered. She hadn't expected to feel this way. She tightened her grip on Alfred and pulled herself back to the here and now, looked up at him, smiled.

Eva's father was in the kitchen filling a flask with hot water. He was wearing a jumper she remembered – green, orange and brown stripes snaked across him in varying thicknesses – a pair of old cor-duroy trousers, and brown brogues. His hair was a little overgrown, and a lot greyer than when Eva had seen him last. He seemed to examine her, his eyes cheerless and searching. After what felt like an eternity, he put down the kettle and patted her shoulders. He squeezed them briefly then hesitated as if con-templating a proper hug. He seemed to be trying to remember something too. Or perhaps he was trying to commit this moment to his deepest memory, an image that might be easier than the reality, than what he was being made to confront. Is that what we are all doing, Eva wondered.

'Dad, this is Alfred.' She stepped to the side so that he could greet her father properly. Jack didn't step forward, didn't smile more or less.

Alfred nodded politely, and smiling fully, reached out to shake hands. Jack turned and started refilling the kettle.

Eva looked at Alfred to apologise, but he was still smiling. In that instant, he seemed to grow taller, his shoulders pushed back and broader in his jacket.

'I owe both of you a debt that I could never seek to repay,' he said. 'Your daughter is a wonderful, wonderful woman.'

Eva noticed how Jack looked Alfred up and down quickly, like someone who had given his word that he wouldn't. Then they sat side by side at the table in the kitchen amidst the comforting aromas of stewing rhubarb and fresh cake. Opposite them, in their customary places, her parents sat, uncomfortable in their own home. Eva tried once more to shrug off the odd sense that she was a stranger here, that by bringing Alfred to meet her parents, to see where she grew up, she too had taken on the guise of visitor. She looked around, tried to make herself feel at home, as if she belonged, but there seemed to be a thick wall of invisible glass between them.

Once or twice when he thought no one was looking, Eva saw the barely disguised shock in her father's eyes. The skin around his eyes was twitching and Eva, feeling less and less composed, couldn't help imagining what he was thinking: my daughter has chosen this man, has done unspeakable things with him . . .

She turned to face Alfred. The sun caught the side of his face, his smooth skin the colour of a polished chestnut, his teeth glinted. His hands were relaxed on the table, strong hands that looked manicured, but were naturally so. He was leaning in to listen to something Helen was saying. If he was feigning interest, it didn't show. He nodded encouragingly, his face pleasant, his pronounced cheekbones lifted further in a smile. Eva was filled with a strong, gushing emotion that seemed ready to choke her. She swallowed, tried to concentrate on what they were saying, but couldn't. She moved her leg closer so that her thigh touched Alfred's and immediately he reached under the table and put his hand on her leg, just above her knee. He pressed a little, not pausing for a moment in his conversation. She felt a tremor. He stroked her leg, and pulled back her skirt with his fingers. He rubbed the softness of her inner thigh with his index finger, applied warm pressure to her skin, and unable to hold back any longer, Eva allowed a moan to escape her lips.

Everyone looked at her, Alfred too, with his best quizzical expression, his perfect eyebrows raised. 'Did you say something Evie?'

He looked at her with the unashamed desire that so disarmed her, and she forgot for an instant about her own discomfort, about her parents, the kitchen, their news. She twiddled her shiny wedding band and chuckled.

Her mother's expression was serious, disapproving almost, reminding her of when she had misbehaved at mealtimes. She could feel her father's disappointment. He looked sour. Alfred put his arm around her and pulled her towards him. Eva noticed her parents stiffen, and realised she was waiting to hear a reproach. She felt a sudden urge to get up and go out of the room, to her old bedroom maybe – which had been a refuge in the past – but she couldn't. It was her father's study now, they had told her in a letter. And she knew she wasn't free to go wandering about as though she still lived here, still belonged. They hadn't said as much, but she could tell, and she didn't want to ask. Besides, she didn't want to leave her husband alone with them in case they broke their silence unspeakably.

'Eva is right about you being a fabulous cook, this is delicious cake,' said Alfred, taking another bite. Crumbs dribbled off his chin on to the plate. 'Absolutely delicious!' He finished the piece, wiped his face and looked round the table at them all. He drank some tea and then said, 'I couldn't have another sliver could I? This honeymoon thing is making me ravenous.'

Eva watched as he reached for the knife and cut himself a piece. She glanced at her parents. Her father was staring at the cake, her mother was watching Alfred, her mouth set hard to hide her embarrassment. Eva took another piece of cake herself to deflect their attention a little. It was her favourite, chocolate and orange, one of her mother's best, but it was dry and hard in her mouth and hard to swallow. She sipped more tea to ease it down and yet it scratched her throat.

Alfred stroked a lock of delicate blond hair that had strayed to the side of her face and tucked it behind her ear. 'She hasn't told you, has she?'

Her parents looked at her.

'I . . .' she started. She looked at Alfred. His brown eyes big and unflustered. 'Well, I'm . . .' she shrugged and smiled, hoping they could see her joy, that it might somehow be sufficient for them.

Her mother was looking at her with poorly masked incomprehension, as though she might break down, her father scowled at the table as if he had been served a particularly distasteful dish.

Alfred had been watching her patiently while she tried to get the words out. 'We are having a baby!' he blurted, his face lighting up even more, his perfect teeth suddenly whiter, his handsome face glowing. Eva remembered how excited he had been when she told him. She had worried he might think it had happened too soon, but he was elated, and it was inconceivable to him that her parents might not be pleased to hear that they were to become grandparents. Where he came from life was sacred, to be celebrated at all costs, especially, as he told her, where the child was being brought into a union with mother and father so easily identifiable.

Helen spluttered, but kept her teacup up to her lips like an inadequate shield from the news she had just received, coughing a little to clear the tea from her airways.

'It is exciting, isn't it? I cannot wait to tell my mother. Eva didn't know how you would take the news but I knew you would be overjoyed. What parent wouldn't be? Isn't that what I said Eva? I only wish we'd had time to get a bottle of something festive.'

Eva was impressed that he could carry on comfortably in spite of her parent's obvious discomfort; it was as if his ease was only serving to exacerbate their unease.

Jack flinched and moved as if he wanted to say something, but Alfred continued to talk and talk. She felt such pride in him. It was irrefutable; they had to see it? They must see how he loved her, how she loved him. It was in every adoring, longing look, and although she alone knew what he was thinking, what he wanted to do, what he would do when they were on their own later, they too must sense it? Suddenly she longed to be away from here with him, to reinforce their union, their love. And she wanted to escape this awkwardness, which she had never before felt around her parents.

She said that they had to leave. She wanted to end the pain, the dejection she couldn't make sense of. She felt hemmed in and wanted to step out, back into their life, leave before all the memories of her childhood, tranquil and playful, became too spoiled to be of value.

Alfred stood up and said, 'May I use your lavatory first?' There was an awkward space in time in which no one moved or responded to him. 'You do have one, don't you? Even here in deepest Norfolk, you must do,' he said, grinning like a mischievous child. 'It is in Africa that the existence of basic conveniences can be a little hit and miss, but not here,' he laughed uproariously. He had opened the kitchen door and looked out into the hallway at the other doors that lead off it, then he turned and looked expectantly at them. For a moment, Eva imagined that he would go and find it himself, wandering through the house, opening all the doors. The one that lead into the living room reserved for important visits and Sunday meals, or her parents' bedroom into which she had never been allowed without permission, or her own childhood bedroom. Suddenly, as if they had all had the same thought, Eva and her parents moved at once and gestured towards the bathroom door.

As soon as Alfred was out of earshot, her father narrowed his eyes and said with his lips barely moving, 'How dare you?'

'Dad . . .?'

'How dare you bring a filthy nigger to this house?' He was leaning forward, straining with the effort of keeping his voice down, his hatred contained. His fists were balls on the dining table. 'And don't even *think* about bringing any of your darkie children here.'

She gasped.

'No daughter of mine would do this . . .'

'What are you saying?' Eva was staggered by the hatred in his eyes.

'I only agreed to let you come here today because your mother wanted to see you one last time . . .'

She looked at her mother who turned away, making it impossible for Eva to see whether she shared her father's sentiments. She wished she wanted to reach out and hold their hands. But wouldn't they recoil at her touch, and she at theirs? And what did he mean by 'one last time?' Her throat tightened, she felt choked. *Alfred is clever and funny and kind. He loves me beyond my own imagination and will look after me till death . . . he has given me his vow.* But how could she assure them that it would be fine, if they really couldn't see for themselves?

'You are nothing . . . nothing to me,' he hissed.

Eva lowered her head and put her hands over her ears to still the sound, just as she had as a child when she wanted to protect her soul from some unpleasant noise. Her mouth filled with bile and she knew she would be sick if she let herself.

'I no longer have a daughter.' He pushed the table and stood with his back to them, staring into the garden.

She felt her strength drain away. Her sight was blurred by tears that she didn't want to let fall here. She stared at them, one then the other, and back again. Her father, having spoken his mind, refused to look at her. His jaw remained clenched and she could see he was waiting for the end of this objectionable episode, unsure how much longer he could contain his anger. Her mother looked distraught and as distressed as Eva felt. So why didn't she speak up? Say something, Eva willed her as she stared at her, into her. But Helen shook her head almost imperceptibly, shrugged her shoulders slightly, said nothing.

When she saw movement in the hallway, Eva quickly wiped her eyes and stood up. She could hold on to her nerve for a few minutes longer. She tried to think about the rest of the day. They would watch a movie maybe, they would have a beer in the sunshine out there, he would hold her, love her, again and again and again.

'Well, thank you,' Alfred said, grinning, and in his closeness, Eva felt a flutter of relief. Fierce pride surged through her. She held onto his well-developed forearm tightly for a moment.

At the door, her mother kissed her without seeing her and Eva put a hand on her own churning, flat stomach.

She stayed close to Alfred, touched him again, rubbed his back, laying down a challenge to her father, daring him to acknowledge the unit they were, stronger and more defined after the past hour.

He wouldn't look at her. He ignored Alfred's outstretched hand and simply nodded at them, said nothing, his lips drawn into a thin, tight line which Eva knew suppressed wicked thoughts. And displeasure.

She couldn't wait to get out into the fresh air. The house felt stale and claustrophobic now. She tugged at Alfred. Tears of anger pricked at her eyes; she should have known better, she shouldn't have brought him here, exposed him to this. She wondered whether he would have come so willingly, whether he would have been so charming if he had known how her father felt. Would he have sat so politely in the presence of such loathing without feeling the need to counter it or defend himself from it? Without the need to flee from it?

A few steps down the path towards the gate, Eva turned to wave once more at her parents, but they had gone. The doorstep was bare, the door was shut. She stumbled and Alfred grabbed her hand and pulled her along. 'Come on, let's be off,' he said, walking fast.

They would come to accept him in time, she thought, trying to keep up with him. They had to. She whispered, 'I am so sorry, Alfred.'

'Hey, hey,' he said, stopping. He put his arms around her, lifted her off the ground and kissed her softly with a tenderness that made her tingle. He stroked her cheeks. For once he looked serious. 'My angel, my own precious angel. Don't worry about it. They were a little shocked, that's all. It was a lot for them to take in. The last time they saw you, you were their little girl. Now you are my wife, and pregnant too. They'll come around when they see our beautiful children.'

'They won't. They are angry with me.' She sobbed. 'I don't understand them. They don't like you Alfred . . . they can't.'

'What they think is of no consequence to me, and shouldn't be to you.' He grabbed her hand and walked on resolutely. 'Don't worry about them,' he said firmly. They continued in silence for a while, and then he said more softly, 'And don't ever think you need to apologise for them, do you understand me?'

She sniffed, wiped her face. She tightened her hold of his hand.

'It's you and me babe,' he said smiling at her. 'You and me.'

She looked up at him. He was back to normal, grinning cheekily, winking. He put his arm around her shoulder, cradled her to him and said, 'Just you and me babe. And it's going to be great.'

*

207

The children were asleep when Eva eventually came down. The power had been cut at some point in the afternoon and Faustina had left lit lanterns around the house, casting about a pale, gloomy light. There were burning candles on the coffee table which brightened the ambience a little.

Alfred was on the sofa sipping a whisky. He put down his newspaper as soon as he heard her coming down the stairs. 'How are you?' he asked kindly.

He got her a glass and poured her a drink. She stared ahead. She couldn't look at him. She didn't want to see his eyes, his lips. He put it on the table in front of her.

The air was static. Eva held her glass to her nose, so she wouldn't smell him by mistake. He would have to find his own way back. It was he who had flung their lives into this quiet, alarming pandemonium.

'I got a phone call from Mr Mensah, you know, he lives near my mother. Apparently she has been unwell, I'm going to go and see her tomorrow.'

Eva watched his candlelit shadow dance on the grey-white walls. She thought of the irony as they perspired in the heat of the tropical night, warmed further by the numerous tiny flames. The house sweltered amongst the glittering lights, unable to cope with the stifling heat; it had been designed to be air-conditioned, built in an age when such frequent power cuts had not been envisaged.

'These soldiers are cowards. They want to operate in the dark, which is why they have cut the power.'

The black smoke from the kerosene lamps was beginning to line her mouth.

'I wonder what on earth they think they are going to change this time.'

Eva longed to fling open the doors, the windows, to pull down the mosquito netting and allow the air to flow and cool their bodies and the concrete walls that entombed them, but the house would be invaded by mosquitoes.

'Maybe we could leave? Think about going back to London?'

She felt a flicker of surprise, but didn't have any desire to respond.

'Well . . . we need to do something. And . . .' he put his head in his hands. 'I just don't know what to do. I desperately want to go back to how we were. And we were good in London, weren't we?'

London, she thought, her head nodding away spontaneously as her mind tried to drift back. 'That was a long, long time ago. An entirely different life, in fact. That was before this, now we are in the after . . .'

'Please, Evie. I know I have made an unforgivable mistake, but I am desperate to make amends. I'll do anything to have your forgiveness, a chance to start again.'

She looked away, too tired to answer. He said something, but she had stopped listening. She gaped out into the ominous darkness outside. The lights on the veranda and the gate were usually on at this time, casting a soothing glow over the house and garden. There were no lights anywhere outside now, no noise from the neighbours' houses, no cars purring past, no chatter of passers-by, and no Zachariah. He hadn't come tonight, maybe because he thought it wiser to stay where he was after all. Yet Eva felt safe in their sturdy, concrete house. Untouchable almost. She was living with the unthinkable and so far it hadn't killed her. Worrying about it wouldn't have stopped it from happening, perhaps that's why it had happened. In any event, why fret about what the soldiers might or might not do? About what might or might not happen to the country? The future made no sense now anyhow.

'Eva?'

She blinked and turned to look at him.

'I was saying we need to get through Christmas somehow for the children . . . then . . . then I can leave? If that's what you want?'

She stared past his face at the wall.

'Have we got everything we need? We have no idea how long

things will be in turmoil for. We should make a list. And please don't go out. Mensah said the University of Legon campus is littered with dead bodies.'

She bristled without looking at him.

'Please take this seriously. Mind what you say in front of the servants. We can't trust anyone. Not even our friends . . . be careful what you say to Dahlia. I don't think Vincent is altogether trustworthy . . .'

She wanted him to shut up. But on he went, and she couldn't drown out his voice sufficiently with her thoughts alone; she wanted to stuff her fingers in her ears.

'Maybe we should hide some provisions in one of the bedrooms. Why don't we store some things in the wardrobe in the spare bedroom?'

'This isn't the second world war!'

'Well, even then it was those who prepared themselves at the first sign of trouble that got off most lightly. I'll make a list. It will help me to know what we need when I am out and about. I'll try and get to my mother tomorrow. She should be with us really, shouldn't she?'

Don't get any funny ideas, she thought.

'Can't we talk? Please?' He looked imploringly.

'I don't want to talk to you Alfred.'

'I know you are . . .'

'You have no idea . . . don't tell me what you know.' She was tremulous. She had been trying to stay in control. Now she was losing her composure, damn him!

He swallowed. 'Yes . . .'

'You have no idea what you have done!' she screamed suddenly, her whole body shaking. 'And stop being so bloody understanding. Your snivelling and grovelling is making me sick.' She turned away, but not before she had registered the fresh guilt in his face.

'I'm sorry . . .' he sighed.

They sat in silence and she looked around. She had been very happy here. She had made it into a home. She had loved this house into life, transformed it from a clean, modern project into a cosy retreat. She had used her flair for home-making to soften the lustrous side of Alfred's taste. Plain white curtains hung over every window. Denim blue and white linen cushions adorned the dark furniture, which was always polished and gleaming. The walls, which she whitewashed afresh each year, were covered with local arts and craft. Masks, made from cheap wood polished to look like rich ebony, fertility dolls and statues bashed to look old and authentic. She bought these pieces with money that she put aside each month.

Did lying come easily to everyone here? Her parents had instilled the need for honesty into her. No one she had known growing up thought it was right to steal things big or small, to tell lies, black or white, but living here, amongst these people, including her lying, cheating husband, who so easily massaged facts and reality into the various shapes that suited them, had rubbed away her trustfulness. Over time, she had learned not to believe a lot of what she was told. Not to believe the driver when he said he would be on time. Not to believe the maid when she said she had mopped the floor, not to believe the fruitier when she swore to Eva from the bottom of her heart that the pawpaw was fresh. They lied easily, and confronted, they fobbed her off with further lies. She had been determined that her children wouldn't think deception was the norm, that they would understand that lying to protect, lying to avoid offending, lying in order to advance or to help was still lying, and that lying was bad. Evil. Destructive. Just look what it had done to them, to their love. Look how everything was in tatters now.

'What is she like, anyway?' she asked.

'What?' He looked aghast.

'What does she look like? Is she thin, fat? Tall, short? Is she educated? Is she black? White?' She surprised herself. Did she really want to know? Actually, yes. But only in her quest to assure herself that it wasn't her fault. And yet she knew that the facts on their own would not be able to restore order, her marriage, her toppled confidence. Would not be able to dislodge the images that danced repetitively in her head; her Alfred with someone else, gazing, smiling, loving . . . 'Why?'

'Eva! Please . . . don't do this.'

'I need to understand why you did it. Why you went back for more.

He looked at her mournfully and shook his head.

'Well, where does she live?'

'Oh . . .' he waved his hands about vaguely.

'What is the child called?'

'Eva, please. What is the point?'

'What? What is it that you don't like? Is this too uncomfortable? I thought you said you wanted to talk?'

'About us, about what matters . . .'

'Us, you and me? Or all of us? All your children, including the poor baby bastard? And we can't leave out his mother, who will now for ever be a part of you. That wouldn't be fair. Don't you see? You widened the circle of our family, you brought them in . . .'

'Of course I see what I did,' he hollered. His face was contorted. His fists were scrunched. 'I made a bloody mistake!'

'Yes. And you can't get rid of him now, change your mind, pretend he doesn't exist. That would be a double mistake.' She shook her head, exhausted.

'Okay, I'll tell you!' His face was crinkled in agony.

'Oh, don't bother.'

'What *do* you want me to do, Eva?'

'I'd like you to leave. Move out so that I have space to think. I can't think with you here. You're in the way.'

'Eva, no. Please?'

'You asked what I want.'

'Think about the children . . .'

'Obviously you were able to forget about them when it suited you.'

'Please sleep on it. If you still feel this way, I'll leave . . . after Christmas? But running away from this isn't going to help, is it? I love you, Eva.'

'Oh, shut up!'

She closed her eyes and tried to shut out everything. She could smell his aftershave. How she'd like to confide in him, her best friend of all these years; to tell him how heartbroken she was, about the disorder in her mind, how vulnerable she felt, how unsure of herself. How all her self-confidence had melted away in an instant. How a man, this man, had let her down, broken her heart, and with that, torn a piece out of her, left her feeling incomplete, unable to imagine ever feeling whole again. How she had never imagined being able to feel such pain.

'I realise I don't have the right to ask you for anything, but . . . we are their parents, that's not going to change, whichever way we end up going.'

She said nothing, feeling a sudden claustrophobia. When it didn't pass, she stood up. Her head swam a little.

'Please don't go?'

'My head . . .' she said, misusing the truth. She glanced at him again. Had he even begun to understand what he'd done?

'I'll go, you stay here,' he said, getting up. At the foot of the stairs, he paused. 'Oh, Yelena called earlier, I told her you were unwell. She said she'd try again tomorrow, to remind you about coffee at Margrit's?'

He went up to bed slowly, his heavy tread on the stairs pulsing hypnotically in her blurry head.

It throbbed, her head, and her stomach ached. She pulled her knees up tightly and wrapped her arms about herself praying and hoping that this wave of nausea, this feeling of powerlessness, would pass quickly.

213

'It's all up in the air,' her mother used to say, which even as a child was a term that mystified Eva. Up in the air how? Balanced on some fine wire? Floating around? Where would *it* land and how? And then would *it* all break? This was exactly how she felt right now. Everything had been unanchored, ready to float off in any which direction. When would the shifting come to a stop? When would things settle again? Because only then could she begin to make sense of what had happened, what was still happening. She would concentrate on the now. She had to. Later she would think about easing these new creases from her heart and stemming the flow of pain. Then and only then might she begin to know what she felt, what she wanted, what to do.

And a wave of bottomless grief began to build as she contemplated another long night. How the hell would she get through it?

It had seemed the right thing to do when she got here, to push to the furthest parts of her memories, the life she had left behind. And in the distance, the memories of home were fading old sepia photographs left unprotected in this harsh climate, cracking and wrinkling, annotations on them melting away with time. But never had she entirely stopped longing to go home. To rekindle the relationship she had once had with her parents. No one had warned her that the longing to be parented would not fade away when she became a parent herself.

She wondered now what might have been if she had stayed in London. Or gone home? What if she had never gone to London and met Alfred? Would she have married the kind of man her parents had envisaged for her? And she had to admit she had no clear idea what such a man might look like, what he might do or what he might think, other than that he would be rather different from Alfred in every respect. Well, then what? Wouldn't she have spent the rest of her days resenting her parents for making her give up the love of her life?

But now that their prediction had come to pass, now that her marriage was in tatters, couldn't she simply give up, accept defeat, pack up and go? Would she be welcome? They had told her no. And over the years, in letters, her mother had confirmed this. She never said so, but Eva knew that her father considered her dead. She could not go back there. Besides she couldn't afford the air fare. And how would she provide for herself?

Why had she believed with such conviction in a country she had never visited before, been this willing to cut her ties with her homeland, not bothered to think about a career? How had she been able to rely fully on a man capable of deceiving her like this, so completely and magnificently?

Chapter Fifteen

Eva opened her eyes. Outside it was not fully day. The alcohol she had drunk last night had ensured sleep, albeit restless. Her head hurt, her neck was stiff. For her first waking moments her mind was blank; then steadily, fragments of her new reality flowed through her thoughts until her mind was deluged. Her eyes began to well up and her heart clamped as dread settled around her like an already familiar blanket. She rolled over on to her side. A tear slid over the bridge of her nose, into her other eye.

The bleakness was crushing. She hadn't woken to find order restored; she never would. There was no hope. The past had vanished, and with it what she thought was her life, her future. There was no more clarity this morning than there had been yesterday, only the same anguish and despondency.

But today, thank heavens, she was meeting Yelena and Dahlia for coffee at Margrit's house for the first time since the coup, and she was looking forward to being able to talk to them. She knew now that she had never really understood what Dahlia was going through. Maybe it is impossible to understand this kind of distress without first-hand experience. Would they think it was her fault that her husband had had an affair? Wasn't it something to do

216

with her that had made him go looking for something else? Isn't that what everyone would think? Is that how Dahlia felt?

Over breakfast, she held her cup of coffee tight and sent her thoughts off into the distance. Periodically she stretched her face this way and that, widening her eyes to stop them from welling up.

She couldn't drown out the children's voices. They grated and whined through her thoughts. They seemed to have picked up on the fact that she was unusually inattentive; they fidgeted and bickered, the baby whinged, his moaning getting louder and louder until the collective din sounded in her head like a nail being scraped on a blackboard. She didn't feel ready to cope with them. Their neediness, their very existence was irritating her. If only she could have a few days without them she might be able to see a way through this, make some sort of plan, instead of being further drained by their wants. They represented her life with Alfred; their complete and in many ways, perfect life. And yet, out there somewhere was a brother of theirs that indicated a rather different truth. When would they meet him? Would they like him? She looked at the baby who sat in his highchair where Faustina had put him after she had fed and changed him. He had given up trying to get her attention and was chewing on his fist. She noticed with faintly detached dismay that he had tears on his cheek. Absentmindedly, she handed him a crust of bread and tried to smile. Would he know his other brother, be friends with him one day? She wondered what his name was, whether he looked like Alfred. What future lay before him, how different would it be from her children's? She realised she was weeping again.

Simon tried to reach for a pot of jam. He wavered, distracted by her tears, and knocked over his mug of Milo.

'I have just about had enough of you children!' Eva cried out, the words chafing her throat. 'When will you learn to sit still, to

217

ask for something to be passed to you? How many times do I have to say the same thing?' She banged the table with her fists. Simon cowered at this unfamiliar display of temper. She saw him nibble his lower lip, she heard the baby start to wail, and still she continued, 'When will you learn? Or will you disappoint me your whole lives? Just like your bloody father...!'

Abigail bit her lip, watched with growing distress and then she too started to cry silently.

'Faustina!' Eva hollered, pushing her chair back. Somehow the tablecloth had managed to get caught up in her chair and it pulled sharply, jerking everything on the table. Abigail's over-full mug slopped its contents everywhere, the milk jug toppled over. 'Bloody hell!' cried Eva.

Faustina appeared, wiping her hands on her apron. 'Oh madam? What's the matter?'

'It's a bloody mess...'

'It's okay, madam, I will clean up okay?'

Eva turned away from them, brushed her wet face furiously. She walked into the living room and slumped on the sofa. She glanced at the table to see the baby raise his arms to Faustina who unbuckled him from the highchair. Simon gawped at her, seeking forgiveness, longing to be reassured that she still loved him, wishing for a cuddle. But Abigail looked wronged. She was eating her toast, chewing slowly, turning the same mouthful of dry crust around and around in her mouth.

Eva stood, ran up the stairs and stumbled into Alfred. Had he been standing there listening? Spying? He looked dejected, searched her face for some explanation or sign. He reached for her hand and tried to clasp it in his, but she wrestled free with vicious strength.

'Don't touch me,' she spat at him and half-ran, half-walked towards the spare room, her heart pounding away, her head spinning. She shut the door behind her quickly, and sat leaning against it. She hugged her knees. Was she going mad? What kind of monster was she? They needed her, and yet right now she felt she would gladly never see them again. Wouldn't they all be better off without her?

'Eva?'

She jerked in surprise and moved her head from the keyhole.

'Please Eva, we need to talk.'

She could hear the desperation in his voice, she knew the way his eyes would be filled with passion, she knew how wide and strong his arms would be, how safe she might feel . . . who might have known that the one person she would most need, most long for, was the very one who had willingly caused this pain, deserted her, leaving her life upended? Was that why she didn't want to face him?

She hadn't imagined it possible that she could long for him as much as she did, that her arms would yearn to hold him, all her senses craving him. Her eyes stung, her tongue was stuck to the roof of her mouth.

'I am so sorry, Evie. I would undo this mess if I could,' he whispered.

'Go away.'

'I won't . . . I can't. I love you.'

The indescribable weight on her chest grew heavier. When would it stop, this dizzying, out of control feeling that she hadn't stopped falling?

'It meant nothing, Evie. Nothing . . .'

Sharp pains pierced her. There was no sign that this unimaginable ache would subside, that this immense anguish that had engulfed her without warning would ever pass. Would the debilitating blows that seemed to be pummelling her ever cease? If she didn't do something, this would overwhelm her, drown her, kill her even.

She got up, had a shower, scraped her hair into a bun, pulled on a dress, not bothering to put on any make-up, and jumped into her car. She sank against the cool leather seat and gripped the big steering wheel, pulling it hard as if she might dislocate it some-how. She stared ahead. How stupid she had been to think this thing was a love gift. She put the key in the ignition, dropped her head on to the wheel. He had even had it sprayed her favourite colour especially. Her head relaxed and the horn went off, startling her.

She sat up and pulled the lever to adjust the seat a little roughly. She could imagine Alfred wincing. She twisted the rear-view mirror a little too firmly. How far would she have to go before it snapped, she wondered.

Solomon hurried over to the door. He had been waiting patiently by the gate for her to leave. 'Madam, is okay. That's how it is the first time. But you go slow, slow, you will be okay.'

She ignored him, turned the key, over-revved the engine, taking pleasure in its pain.

'Eh madam, you will spoil it, oh!' pleaded Solomon, tapping the door.

Eva released the clutch and juddered out the drive. On the road she accelerated and sped off. The wind blew through the open windows and through her hair, whipping it around her face.

It looked as if the majority of shops and businesses had reopened and people were out and about carrying on as normal, as Afriye had instructed. He had also ordered all children to return to school on Monday for the last few days of term.

Eva stopped at Quality First out of curiosity, because the shut-ters were still firmly drawn, the car park empty.

The kind watchman who had warned her to go home the other day was sitting on the doorstep of the shop.

'Eh! Madam, you again?'

'Why is the shop not open?'

'Madam, you haven't heard?'

'What?'

'They say the owner has been shot for profiteering. They dragged him from his bed and shot him there and then.'

'My God! What is happening to everyone? Who told you?'

'Madam, please I am the watchman. Of course I know.'

'Is he dead?'

'Of that I am not sure.'

'But why?'

'Because they are stealing from us. They cheat us in their shops.' He spoke softly, with far less passion than previously, when he had warned her about the soldiers. Why didn't it ring true? Was she too numbed to feel any real anxiety? Could it be that in just two days she had become completely hardened, incapable of taking in any more bad news so that even this horrific report simply bounced off her like rain on concrete?

'So why are you still here?'

'Even if he is dead I need my pay. His son has to pay me.'

They were widely despised, the Syrians and Lebanese, for their seemingly effortless success in the face of so much poverty and need. After previous coups, they had always disappeared for a while, but then resurfaced, creeping back out unharmed and re-establishing themselves with the same apparent ease. Will everyone deemed to have too much wealth be despised, she mused, and who will determine what is too much? What will be the measure, she wondered. A car? A maid? Enough to spare?

'I suppose it is easy to be jealous of someone who is successful,' she said.

'Jealousy does not come into it, madam. The money he pays me to be here from morning to night cannot even pay for my children to go to school. I have to drive a taxi to make the ends meet. Is that correct?'

'No, no. But does he deserve to die?'

'He deserves it, madam. They sell things at inflated costs, they squeeze us dry and take advantage of us. Have they forgotten that they are guests in our country?'

221

His words and sentiments sat at odds with his appearance, his kind face, which showed neither anger nor suffering, his clothes, clean and neat. As she drove off, he waved her off with a smile.

She realised her skin was covered in goose bumps; the watchman's views, delivered with such calm, had shocked her. She wasn't particularly worried about what had or hadn't happened to Mr Quality First; she didn't have any more room in her heart. Didn't that make her equally callous? Beneath a thin veneer of civility and sophistication, she thought to herself, are we basically all just self-interested? Capable of anything, including murder, or at least of not being sufficiently perturbed by murder, when our own safety is at risk? She felt another icy wave of dread sweep over her skin.

Margrit's home was a small bungalow with oversized windows and folding shutters, painted in flamboyant colours, which she changed regularly. These days the building was lime green, the shutters dazzling yellow. 'Haven't you seen pictures of Caribbean houses? They don't go in for all this bland nonsense,' she explained. 'We are in the tropics, a chance, no question, to be bold and beautiful, nah?'

Eva walked through the pink iron gate. She had to push away several branches of overgrown foliage as she made her way up the short path of stepping stones to the house.

Margrit rushed out to greet her with arms wide open. Something in her gesture reminded Eva of her mother, and how as a child, her hugs could make anything feel a bit better; how her tight squeezes, a whiff of perfume and hairspray had the wondrous capacity to lessen any pain. Eva felt a fist thud against her ribs.

'What is it?' asked Margrit. Then, again and again, in a soothing voice, she said, 'It's all right.' She held Eva tight. 'What's happened?'

'He's been having an affair . . .'

'Ach . . . no . . . not Alfred too? Oh Eva . . .'

They sat and Eva noticed her hands were shaky. And as she told Margrit everything, she realised her heart was coming apart again, piece by piece.

'A child?' said Margrit, sadly.

Eva nodded.

'I am surprised, although I should know better than to be so.' She tutted and shook her head. 'Ach, I am so angry with him, I just have to say that.'

Eva steadied herself and dabbed at her eyes. 'I'm sorry I . . .'

'Do not apologise to me, for heaven's sake!'

Eva shook her head. 'I thought I had finished with this crying. This has taken me aback, that's all.'

'You will mourn for a while, unfortunately, that's how it is. What else do you feel?'

Eva shrugged. 'Numb, a lot of the time now. And so bloody homesick. I wish I could go home.'

Margrit nodded with understanding. 'And the children?'

'Perplexed.'

'You are too, I am sure. But they don't know why, hopefully?'

'No, no. But they can see that we are not talking, that I am upset about something.'

'Yes, yes. Look, come with me, let's make some tea.'

The house was sparsely decorated. Everything was plain and old, but somehow stylish. The kitchen was thoroughly un-modernised, with a concrete floor and purple cupboards. On one wall, Margrit had painted a mural of a green and purple bougainvillea so that it seemed to grow from behind the stove, branching out over everything as it clambered towards the ceiling.

Margrit shooed away the cats that were lying in front of the cupboard so she could get mugs out. Eva could hear the chickens in the bathroom; Margrit used it as their coop so their eggs couldn't be stolen. Eva had learned to time her visits so she wouldn't need the loo, which was perpetually covered in chicken muck and feathers.

Margrit handed her the tea. Eva took the mug of lemon grass tea and smelt it. She saw a hair floating in there, and knew she wouldn't be able to touch it.

Back on the colourful veranda, Margrit sat back in her old wicker and started feeding one of the puppies. 'It won't take long. He is quick, this one.'

A large copper leaf shrub grew at the far end of the veranda, with long furry tendrils like monkeys' tails dangling over the railing. Underneath it, Jimmy lay feeding her other offspring. A cat licked itself clean on one of the chairs and another arched its back as it scraped along Margrit's leg. The air stank of animals. Eva wondered if Margrit had the water to give the dogs a proper wash. Just down the road from where Eva lived, the water pressure was much worse here. Very often, when Eva had water, Margrit didn't. On numerous occasions, Eva had invited her and Kojo to come and have a shower in her house. Margrit seemed never to be overwhelmed though, never flustered, always coping.

As Margrit put the dog back next to its mother and dusted her hands on her lap, Yelena arrived, calling out to them through the thicket as she made her way up the garden path.

'Thank God *you* are here Eva, I thought everyone might be sick. Dahlia is unwell . . .' she looked questioningly when she saw Eva's face. Then, as Margrit updated Yelena, Eva listened quietly to what should have been someone else's story. Even now, she thought it would be fairer if they were talking about someone else, not *her* Alfred. But why should she be immune to this? Wasn't that the same as saying, *I am better than this, more superior than this kind of pain . . .*? Would it really be better if someone else was suffering instead?

'Ah, my darling, not Alfred! I am so very sorry . . .'

'Yes,' said Eva. 'I wish I knew what to do. The only thing I know I want to do, I can't. I want to go . . . home.' The word dragged everything inside her, and racked her chest, which had tightened again. She tried to calm herself, and yet knew she had to fight for air.

'Take your time! Breath slowly. In . . . out. There, there, it's okay now,' Yelena said, cradling her. 'Here, sip your tea.'

'But couldn't you go home for a visit, though? Don't you think they would understand? You're their only child after all,' said Margrit softly. 'Maybe after all these years, after all this time . . . they would be glad to see you?'

'No. I can't. They've made it clear that they don't want to see me again, at least my father doesn't. Besides, Alfred has behaved exactly as they expected him to, after all, I married a savage.'

'Well, then you can't go,' said Margrit. 'But before you make any other decisions you have to give yourself time. You will feel better again, but you first have to go through all the emotions, like a cycle on a washing machine. It is going to take you time, *Schatz*, time.'

Eva felt a wave of nausea swell in her, making her feel sick. Talking about it with her friends made it more real and horrific. She realised she had been secretly hoping that they would have answers. 'I can't think straight. I don't think I can get through this. It feels as if my world has exploded. I don't know which way is up any more . . .'

'You don't want to leave him for good though, do you?' asked Margrit.

'Shouldn't I?' Her voice was rough from the effort of sharing.

'Well, I don't think so, since he says he's sorry, but it isn't my marriage. Anyway, there will be time enough to decide what you want later.'

'The thought of leaving is . . . is terrifying, yet I am not sure if I can go on living with him. Whether I can put up with a compromised version of what we had.'

'Yes, well it is too soon to be considering such huge questions. When you feel more like yourself, you'll know what you want. Even if it seems unthinkable now,' said Margrit. 'Concentrate on one day at a time, on feeling stronger in yourself. You will feel better soon. Nothing lasts forever, even sorrow like this.'

'I don't know what I feel, what I feel for him, yet the moment before he told me, I knew I loved him, that I adored him . . .'

'Well, you are angry and down,' said Yelena.

'So sad.' Her shoulders fell.

'Of course.'

'I feel unhinged . . . and afraid. Terrified in fact. And so very disappointed.'

Margrit and Yelena nodded and made encouraging noises.

'I feel vulnerable. Lonely, I miss him . . . I wish I could turn back the clock so it hadn't happened . . .'

'Oh, I know,' Yelena whispered putting her arms around Eva. 'It is natural. You don't have a heart of stone. It would be odd if you were smiling and saying to Alfred, never mind, let's pretend this didn't happen. Something died. How you thought your marriage was, is not really so. You have to give yourself time to accept the shock of it, and you have to mourn it. Imagine what it would say of your marriage, if you didn't feel dreadful. And there is no need to try and be brave. We must treat your heartbreak with due respect and patience. If you break a leg, we won't expect you to dance the next day will we?'

'And the shame! I thought my marriage was perfect, well, you know what I mean, and now I feel like a stupid fool, it makes me livid; I want to break things, to hit him . . . and I could kill him.' She looked at her friends, her anger reflected in their eyes. 'I want to hurt him, to make him suffer.'

'I know exactly,' said Yelena.

'He says it meant nothing . . .'

Yelena hugged Eva. 'Ah, they do, the good ones at least, some don't bother saying anything, trying to justify it, no apology. Alfred means it. He is a decent man.' She swallowed. 'It doesn't make what has happened acceptable, but it does keep alive a hope for the future.'

'That is what you want, what we all want, isn't it? The possibility of things being somehow all right again? Not necessarily perfect, but tolerable, maybe even fairly good,' said Margrit.

'And he loves you, he says he does, no? And you only have to look at him to realise he adores you . . .' said Yelena.

'Then why did he do this to us?'

'He's a man, he's human. We all have our weaknesses . . . it was a moment of madness perhaps? Maybe she pursued him, they do you know. He would be a good catch. Besides, he is a good man . . . yes.' Yelena raised her hand to still Eva. 'You might not wish to hear it right now, but trust me, he is. You have to remember this is his first mistake.'

'Gosh, is this the Alfred Laryea fan club?' said Eva smiling for the first time in a while.

'We don't want you to make a rash decision. He is not the first man to cheat on his wife, and he won't be the last,' said Margrit. 'I mean, no offence to Dahlia, but this isn't Vincent we are talking about.'

For the hundredth time, Eva wondered why Dahlia put up with Vincent's philandering when it hurt this badly. Had she given him one more chance after the first time? How long had it taken for him to use it up? And how many more chances had she given? How many chances sufficed? And yet she could already see that her choices weren't clear cut. She would struggle to set up home separately in this country without a lot of money, where housing was so unavailable. And if she left the country she would be leaving her home, her friends, her hopes and dreams, her entire life behind.

'He didn't have to confess to you,' said Yelena. 'You have to admit that is pretty decent.'

Eva tutted.

'And he could have left you for her.'

She sat back in her chair and sighed.

'Yelena is right. He *is* a good man. But you have to see that for yourself. I am not condoning his behaviour for one moment, but the way I see it, you really only have two choices: take him as he is or leave him.' Margrit rubbed Eva's hand. 'Don't for a moment think that I don't think this is appalling, absolutely so.'

'We could have been like you and Kojo, a perfect love affair, adoring each other to the end . . .'

'This is not my story, Eva, this is yours. The only thing I know, after my many years of marriage is that your only hope is to leave the problem behind you. Only if you are ready to accept his apology and really forgive will you have a future with Alfred. And I would say that that might be the most optimistic future you have. But you would need to move on and not keep bringing it up, keep looking for signs, for evidence that he is at it again . . .'

'How can I though? How can I trust him again?'

'Time, time. Then in exactly the same way you trusted him in the beginning. You had no way of being absolutely certain that he meant it when he made his vows to you. You have no way of proving that he was faithful to you back then, do you? All you had was his word. Yes, he has broken that now, but does that mean he is not capable of making and keeping another promise?'

Eva sighed. 'I wish I could wake up and find I was dreaming.'

'Dear darling Eva,' said Yelena putting her arms back around her.

'He was my best friend! It will never be the same again . . .'

'No, it won't,' said Margrit, 'but that doesn't mean it can't be as good, or even better. You can move forward.'

'I've asked him to move out. I need time and space.'

'Eva, is that really what you want? The woman, whoever she is, might make a move for him. He is vulnerable, he feels bad. In time, he might turn first to whoever makes him feel better.'

'You think I should run after him, sweep this under the carpet . . .'

'Not at all. But he needs to know that he will be eventually forgiven.'

'I hate him. I thought he was better than this . . .'

'Everyone makes mistakes,' said Margrit. 'It's your decision, we can only say what we think.'

Eva sighed, thinking how overwhelming and unbearable the weight of taking decisions and assuming responsibility was. She was exhausted by the effort of sharing her heartache.

'What you need is to go home and sleep. And don't make any decisions, not for a long, long time. You need to sleep and eat well . . . I know that sounds silly at a time like this, but you need to be strong, your emotions are taking a battering, keep your body well,' said Margrit, getting up. 'I'll get you something to help.'

Eva nodded. Her eyes welled up again, with gratitude this time, appreciation for her good friends, her own Ghanaian family. She had been wondering, now that she understood Dahlia's life a little more, whether she had been a good friend to her, whether she had ever really been there for her, truly empathised?

Margrit handed her a brown envelope. 'Valium. I always have some of these in the house. They will stop the pain, help you sleep.'

Eva nodded.

'And we are with you. You are not going to have to deal with this by yourself, *ya Schatz*?'

'Yes, I know. Thank you. I'm so blessed to have you . . .'

The children were playing outside and Faustina was lying on a mat under the shade of a huge tree with the baby. She was staring at the sky through the leafy branches of the mango tree when she heard the familiar noise. Not one she had ever heard so close by, not one she ever hoped to hear again. It was loud and sharp. Later she would tell Eva, 'Madam, I knew it wasn't a firework, it was too loud. And only one bang too. Just like that.'

Behind the high white wall, she could hear running feet, tooting horns, cars screeching to a halt. All of them, Faustina, Solomon, the children, felt the pull of the excitement out there.

229

Afraid of what was happening, they dropped everything and ran to peer out through the circular hollows woven into the centre of the big metal gate. People rushed past the house. Simon and Abigail craned their necks and saw a crowd gathering at the corner of the house where there was a junction. There were jumbled exclamations in vernacular and pidgin. Solomon shouted 'They have killed someone!' He opened the gate and went out to see. Faustina grabbed Abigail by the shoulder when she tried to follow. 'Don't go outside! Madam said I must not let you go outside.' But Abigail wrestled free from Faustina and ran after Solomon. He looked at her and smiled.

'Aren't you afraid?' she said, following them.

Simon and Abigail looked like adventurers walking towards the agitated gathering.

Everyone was talking and shouting at the same time. A boy in tattered clothing stared at them in their white trainers, looked at each item of clothing they were wearing. When his eyes reached their faces, he laughed and said, 'the *obronies* have come to see.'

It was as if his grin gave them the courage to plough through the crowd that was about three people deep. They parted willingly, and those that had already been to the centre made room for them. Simon stumbled across a foot and an old lady reached to steady him. 'Be careful you don't fall?' she said, smiling kindly.

When they reached the inner ring, Simon clung to Abigail. There was a hush. Faustina saw the man lying on the ground, who looked as if he was pretending to be dead. He was well-dressed, his shirt neatly tucked into his trousers, which were beige and clean, and he was wearing old black trainers without socks. His arms lay straight alongside his torso, his legs straight also, his feet touching. He could well have been standing to attention when he fell back stiff, solid. Amongst the droplets of sweat glistening on his forehead, directly above his nose, was a little hole the size of the back end of a Bic pen, a depression really, rather than a hole, where there was a little dark moisture. It looked like the honey madam sometimes bought. Sticky, dark, too sweet, and tasting of flowers.

It felt as if they had been standing there for several minutes, but it must have been only a few seconds when Faustina shouted at the children, 'Don't look! Don't. Let's go back. Now! Turn around, this isn't good. Let's go. No, don't look at him.' But they were staring quizzically at the dead man, his eyes widened with terror. How long had they looked, how much had their minds recorded to play back later? Eventually, Abigail yanked her brother and marched him back.

Simon sniffled.

'Don't be a cry-baby,' Abigail said cruelly as they approached the house.

'I am not a cry-baby,' he said, pulling free from her hold. 'And anyway I am not crying. You were the one who wanted to leave and run to Mummy.'

'Well, it is rude to stare, even if the person you are staring at is dead, and you *were* staring,' she said, pulling a face at him.

'You wait till your mother comes back,' said Faustina. 'I will tell her. Do you want me to lose my job? If I lose my job how will I feed my children? You bad, bad children.'

'We are not bad,' said Abigail angrily.

'You are not too old for me to smack you, you know?'

'If you hit me I will tell my father and he will sack you,' said Simon, stepping out of Faustina's reach.

'Tell him if you like. Do you think I am scared of you? I will still smack you if I want. Why did you go and look at the dead man? With his spirit still there looking for somewhere to go?'

They walked in silence the rest of the way.

When they got home, Abigail ran to the toilet and reached it just in time. When she was washing her hands, she heard something outside the window and her legs turned soft. She grappled with the door handle, terrified, and ran to join the others looking anxiously behind her.

231

'Did you see his ghost?' asked Faustina, laughing.

'It is not funny,' shouted Abigail.

'There have been ghosts here forever and ever amen! But now we have an angry spirit loitering near our beds. It is not good for us that the man has died before his time outside our house. I will tell madam she has to call someone to come and pray.'

'He had sweat all over his face from running fast,' said Abigail.

'I saw where the bullet went into his head,' sniffed Simon.

'Oh, don't cry,' said Faustina, patting Abigail on the back. 'Come, come,' she said gathering her into her lap. 'You are not too old for me to carry you. You too Simon, come.' With both of them on her lap, she sang, 'Don't cry, don't cry, it will be all right,' swaying them a little from side to side.

Eva was furious when she found out that her children had witnessed such horror. What was turning these people into murderous savages?

In the past, she had seen and heard the terror of thieves as they were chased down the street begging for leniency and forgiveness. Whenever a thief was caught, he was beaten until some respected member of the community or the victim stepped in to plead. Eva often wondered how desperate these thieves could be to chance the ferocious temper of the community at large. It was common, a risk of the trade, but she didn't know that thieves were ever actually killed for stealing.

And how on earth could she erase what they had seen? To behold a dead person must be bad enough, but someone who not five minutes before had been pulsing with life and now lay dead. By force too . . . how gruesome! A violent, untimely death was shocking to hear about, to contemplate, how much more so to witness. What kind of impact will this have on them, she asked herself over and again. She decided the best thing might be to play it down, try and brush it away. The less talk of dead men the better. No further gory details would be elaborated and shared,

232

only to be stored deeper in their memories from where they could emerge to cause further damage later. She told the children to fill their thoughts with nice things: chocolate, ice cream, birthday parties, the beach. There was little she could think of offering them as a distraction. There was nothing on TV and even if they were open, the cinemas only featured Kung Fu films these days. She had loved going to the cinema when they had first arrived; open air auditoria where the crowd cheered and commented the whole way through. Over the years she had been living here, there was less and less pleasant about the place.

That night, Abigail pleaded with Eva to let her sleep in her room.

'I am not going to bed yet.' Eva hugged her and whispered, 'What are you afraid of exactly?'

'When I close my eyes I can see him. I can't make his face go away. I can see him with lots of blood everywhere. And his eyes are open and his arms and legs are bent and tangled. He looks uncomfortable. But why weren't his eyes closed, Mummy? And I don't think there was any blood. Why do you think that there was so little blood, Mummy?'

'I don't know Abi. Please, don't think about it.'

'Wouldn't he have shut his eyes when he saw the gun?'

'Try not to think about it any more.'

'But I can't help it. I keep wondering what it was like for him. And where he is now.' She shook violently as she recounted the myriad scary stories Faustina had told them over time about ghosts and spirits and dead ancestors, about how they roam the earth when they are lost or looking for revenge, how mighty they are, and how tonight there was possibly one at their front door.

Eva put her arms around her daughter and said, 'There is no need to be afraid of him. He is dead, he can't harm you, no matter what Faustina says. He wouldn't have hurt you when he was alive, how could he now? He didn't even know you.'

'But Mummy, Faustina said . . .'

'I don't really want to hear any more of what Faustina has to say on this matter. But you know what, maybe she could sleep in your bedroom with you. How about that?' Abigail looked comforted, and Eva felt relieved that they were making progress.

When she told Faustina to sleep with the children, Eva detected an element of joyous relief. Clearly, no one wanted to sleep alone tonight.

So Abigail and Simon crammed into Abigail's bed so each of them would feel the warmth of another kindly soul all night. 'We are like sardines,' said Simon giggling.

Joseph lay in his cot in the corner, and Faustina lay on her rattan mat on the floor wrapped in a cardigan and socks to fend off the cold from the air-conditioner.

'If you childrens misbehave in the night, you will see what I will do. Some of us have work to do tomorrow.'

Eva said good night and turned off the light.

When the chitter-chatter died down and the dark grew familiar, Faustina suggested they should pray some more. To the rhythm of the sleeping breaths of her brothers, Abigail and Faustina prayed for the dead man's family. Then they prayed for everyone in the house by name, and for all of their relatives too. Again and again Faustina prayed, droning on and on until Abigail couldn't keep up and her eyes grew heavy with sleep.

Eva sat sipping at a tumbler of brandy, becoming increasingly irritated. As he walked down the stairs, she steeled herself to face him. He smiled and came towards her. She shook her head, her hand lifted involuntarily, and he stopped in his tracks. She could smell soap on his skin, she could imagine how warm he would be. She longed to hold him. Then another wave of anger made her quiver.

Hundreds of unanswered questions floated freely about her mind. For one, she had always imagined that she would know if he cheated on her, that his sleeping might be disturbed in some way, perhaps by guilty tossing and turning, but she couldn't remember a time when his deep, loud snores had ceased to reverberate around their air-conditioned room.

'Why did I need to know?'

After a long silence he replied. 'Eva, I only told you because the lying was killing me.' He sounded resigned, which annoyed her. 'Perhaps I shouldn't have said anything. I didn't know what to do, the lie was destroying something in us anyway . . .'

'Not the lie, Alfred, what you did. And why did you do it? Why did you have to cheat, to ruin everything?'

'But it doesn't need to be ruined, can't you see that? Please be reasonable.'

'Reasonable! Don't you tell *me* to be reasonable. It wasn't me who did this! You have acted the prize bastard. You cheated! You lied! What else have you lied about? How am I going to be able to trust you again? Can't you see that you broke something precious, something fragile? How do we get back to where we were? Don't you see it's impossible?'

'No. I don't. I mean, I do, but aren't we are strong enough? Surely you can . . . we can . . . if we really want to, we can rebuild our marriage, put this behind us, move forward.'

'Oh, go to hell! Today our children saw a man shot dead outside our house.' It had to be his fault, somehow every ghastly thing from now on had to be down to him.

'What?' He put his drink down on the coffee table hard.

'A man was shot outside this afternoon. The children went to look, apparently. While I was out.'

'Why the hell were they outside on the street? I thought I asked for the gate to be kept locked?'

'Well it wasn't. And I now have two petrified children up there asking all sorts of difficult questions. This bloody country!'

'I did tell you . . . Eva, you have to keep the gate locked at all times. And please stay home as much as possible. I am going to put Solomon on duty twenty-four hours a day. No one is to spend more time than is necessary outside. Do you understand?' His voice had risen. 'Eva . . .?'

'Flexing husbandly muscles doesn't suit you,' she said bitterly.

'You will obey me on this. It is a matter of life and death, and I refute the idea that your coffee mornings are more important . . .'

She flung her glass at him with all her might. He ducked and it flew over his head and into the wall behind him, shattering and showering sparkly fragments everywhere. 'You're just like the rest of them, a bloody tyrant. Don't think you can start telling me what to do!'

'You could have hurt me,' he said in a quiet, shocked voice.

'Good.' She stood up and walked off. She wanted to run outside, out the gate, up the street and just keep on going.

Chapter Sixteen

On the first night that they moved into this house, Alfred had held Eva in his arms and told her that his greatest dream had come true. He had always wanted his own family, his own house, and here he had both. 'I have lived all my life with too many relatives, too many people. And now, it's just you, me and our children. Perfect. I used to dream about this.' She had looked at him adoringly as he reminded her that he had spent years in London dependent on family members. And hadn't their first months in Accra been spent in his uncle's house? 'It is a recipe for disaster to live with relatives. You will see that I am not a typical Ghanaian in that way, granting endless invitations of hospitality and accommodation. You won't have to put up with my relations living with us ad infinitum, my dearest,' he had told her, kissing the nape of her neck.

Eva, filled with the confidence of youthful love, believed that together they would be able to overcome any difficulty that might jeopardise their blissful union. Besides, how hard could it be to cope with a visit of indeterminate length from an awkward relative? Since then, however, she had witnessed the difficulties some of her friends had experienced by having relatives living with them. Dahlia seemed to forever have some relative of Vincent's staying with them, and the strain it caused had made Eva glad for the assurance Alfred had given her all those years ago. She never imagined that he might one day change his mind.

Eva had just sat down to have lunch with the children and she was ravenous from days of not eating properly. She had made her preferred comfort food: a roasted chicken, rice, tomato gravy and salad. She hadn't laid a place for Alfred, but he had joined them, sat in his usual place, joking with the children, doing his utmost to keep the mood light while Eva studiously ignored him.

The gate bell rang and Eva looked up, surprised. 'I am not expecting any visitors.' It didn't occur to her to look at Alfred for a clue as to whether or not he was expecting anyone. This was, after all, the first meal they had shared since his revelation.

The bell rang again.

Eva looked at her family one by one, warning them not to move. She continued to serve up rice and gravy, determined not to be distracted, but the bell rang again, this time long and insistently.

'Oh!' said Alfred, as if he had suddenly recalled. 'It might be my mother.' He stood up and walked to the front door.

'Just what we need! Great! Perfect, in fact . . .'

'She's my mother, Eva . . . we have more than enough food, don't we?' He walked out of the door towards the gate.

Eva watched him with her spoon in midair. She had a compelling urge to throw it at the door, flinging grains of rice everywhere. She looked at the children, who were observing her carefully with hesitant smiles. She put the spoon down and walked into the kitchen where she grabbed her knees, bent her head and let out a silent howl.

She heard the children greeting Auntie Gee, and her large, hearty laugh. She heard them giggle in turn as she embraced them and tickled them sharply in their ribs. Eva stood up, shook her head so that her hair tousled itself back into place and walked into the dining room.

'Oh Eva,' Auntie Gee said, coming towards her with outstretched arms. '*Afishapa*, Merry Xmas to you too.' Her embrace was strong and Eva could smell warm, floral talcum powder. 'I was even lucky that I got a taxi today. There are not many on the roads you know, but I told Alfred not to bother to come and pick me up. After all, I know how busy you are always.'

Eva looked quizzically at Gladys' maid, who was walking past the house carrying a large, bulging bag on her head. 'What is she carrying to my boys' quarters?'

Alfred and Gladys turned.

'Ah, she too brought her things.'

'Let's open a bottle,' said Alfred, making for the kitchen.

'What things?'

'Oh, just this and that; her daily requirements.'

'Hang on. I don't understand. *What* is she taking to the boys' quarters? Alfred!'

'Ah, here come mine,' said Gladys, beaming.

A man was heaving two large suitcases, filled to bursting, towards the front door.

'What is this? Alfred, what the hell is going on?' Eva's voice had risen now. She looked at her husband willing him to explain, say something, anything to bring a little more sense to the situation.

'Driver, put those ones here. Careful now, I have valuable belongings in there.'

He dropped them by the door and muttered, 'You have to pay me extra, the bags are too heavy ah-ah!'

'Please! Don't drop them so hard.'

'Alfred?'

'Only three left.'

'*Three* more bags?'

239

'My mother is coming to live with us for a while.'

'Sorry?' Eva glared at Alfred with folded arms. He was hovering by the kitchen door, refusing to make eye contact with her.

The baby started to bawl.

'Oh *kaafo*, don't cry, Joseph. Grandma is here now.' Gladys waddled off to the dining table, picked him up and jiggled him around, singing.

The man lugged the rest of the cases to the front door and stood panting. 'Auntie, what is in your bags? Gold?' He laughed and winked at the children who had got down from the table and were jumping about, excited.

'Where is Auntie Gee going to sleep if Mummy is sleeping in the spare room?' asked Abi.

'Well, I thought you and Simon could double up again for a while.'

Eva walked over to Alfred. 'How dare you? Without even asking me . . .'

'I felt bad leaving her on her own out there,' said Alfred in a whisper.

'Alfred, please pay the driver. I don't have any change. Is everything in order? Oh, are you discussing me? Don't worry Eva, I won't be any trouble, okay? As for me, I am flexible, I can fit in anywhere . . .'

'I'm sorry. I think there has been a misunderstanding,' said Eva, shaking her head. 'Alfred didn't tell me you were coming.' She could feel the heat of blood in her cheeks.

'Oh, then it is a kind of surprise, isn't it? A Happy Xmas Surprise! Anyway, I am going to change the baby, he is too wet. Abi, get the nappy for me please.'

'This isn't really happening,' said Eva.

Alfred paid the driver.

'I could kill you,' Eva whispered.

'Oh no, don't say that,' said Gladys. 'That kind of thing is not funny you know. For the words of our mouths bind us . . .'

Eva tutted, marvelling afresh at how wonderful her mother-in-law's hearing could be.

'Eva, what did you cook? I am starving hungry. And you will see how I can cook for you now that I am here. And anything else, you just say the word and I can do it.'

'I'll get us a drink. We could all do with a drink. Auntie Gee, you don't need to change the baby now, sit down and let's eat.'

'Nothing is too much for my grandson,' said Gladys, who had laid Joseph on the floor and removed his nappy. He kicked his freed fat legs happily and chewed his knuckles.

Shaking with rage, Eva followed Alfred into the kitchen. 'How could you? I don't need or want your mother living with us. And her maid! Why the hell do you think this suits me? And since when do I not have a say around here any more?'

'Please lower your voice, Eva.' He was rummaging in the cutlery drawer with his back to her and didn't turn around. 'You are the thoughtful one in this marriage. I thought you'd understand. I couldn't leave her there while it is so precarious out there. It won't be for long.'

'Don't tell me to lower my voice,' she hissed. 'And don't think because she is here you won't have to move out.'

'No . . . of course. Yes.'

'You could at least have asked me first! How the hell do you think it makes me feel to see her arriving here like this with so many bags?'

'She is my mother . . .'

'And what about her other relations? Why can't they have her? How dare you?' screeched Eva.

'She lives in one damp room in a compound with a latrine. We have four toilets and four showers.'

'That has never bothered you before!'

'I got a message that she had been ill with a fever. Besides, she is vulnerable. I couldn't leave her at the mercy of any ruffian who might wish to take advantage of her.'

'Don't be ridiculous. Your mother is more able to cope than anyone I know. She is hardly vulnerable. And you've always said in the past that Adabraka is a safe area, no one with any real money lives there any more.'

He flapped his hands in defeat. 'We have the space. And we could do with the company, Eva.' He looked at her, compelled her to look back into the deep wells in his eyes. 'We need something . . .' He shrugged.

'And you think that inviting your mother to live with us will help?'

He glanced furtively at the door. 'Yes. I hope it will . . .'

'Gosh you're stupid! She meddles. She tells me what to do. And she'd better not expect me to wait on her hand and foot . . .' She shook her head and hissed, 'Bloody, bloody marvellous!'

They stood in silence for a while. Alfred looking imploringly at her, muttering periodically how sorry he was. 'About this. About everything, Evie . . .'

'Where is the man I married? I don't think I know you any more. How could you do this to me? After everything else? After how you've let me down already?'

He looked at her and shook his head. 'I don't deserve your forgiveness, but that is what I want, more than anything else in this world. You . . .'

'Don't start, Alfred!'

'Let's talk properly then. There is still an 'us' isn't there?'

'You've broken us!'

He put a bottle of Frascati on the table and leaned on it for support. 'I don't know what to do,' he whispered. 'For God's sake, please . . . I'll do anything . . . help me. Can't you . . . can't you forgive me?'

Eva looked at him and felt something rip a little further inside. The sensation was so intensely real, she could feel blood pouring out from some wound deep in her. She stood rigid. How could *she* help *him*? She didn't know what to do. And who would help her?

She shook her head, she felt defeated and tired. 'How long have you invited her for?'

'I don't know.' He turned away, composed himself. 'Who knows how long these armed hooligans will be roaming the streets?' He grabbed three glasses and walked towards the dining room, pausing at the door. He looked at her but she looked away, unwilling to say anything more. He pushed open the door and headed into the dining room. 'Come children, the food is getting cold, let's eat,' he said cheerfully as he poured the wine. He looked at his mother. 'Let's drink to our health and happiness.'

'And family,' said Gladys, lifting her glass to Eva who had come back in. 'In the end, that's all that matters.' She took a sip and screwed up her face. 'It is too bitter. Have you got some cola? I will mix it to make it taste nice.'

Alfred got up to get a bottle of Coca-Cola.

'Can we have some too?' asked Abigail.

Eva shook her head. 'It's bad for your teeth.'

'Please . . .' said Simon.

'Oh, but it is Christmas time! Eva, let them have it.' Gladys clapped her hands. 'We are going to have so many good times. You wait and see!'

The children laughed.

Gladys chortled, her shoulders wobbling gently as mirth visibly bubbled through her. 'Finally I can teach my grandchildren to speak Ga! And all of our customs if I am here from morning to night.' Joseph sat on her lap. She was feeding him rice with her fingers and in his other hand he held a chicken leg, waving it about victoriously.

'I prefer him to sit in his highchair to eat.'

'Oh, he is okay here. Look at how he is happy. Isn't it Joseph?' He grinned on cue, scrunching his face so that his eyes disappeared and he flaunted all eight of his teeth.

Eva put a forkful of cold rice and chicken into her mouth. She felt besieged by all she had had to cope with over the past few days, and now she had Gladys here too. She ate mechanically, swallowing barely chewed food.

After lunch, Auntie Gee sat with her feet on the coffee table. Her toenails were painted in shimmering purple, and were too long. Eva's eyes felt heavy; two and a half glasses of wine and the heat made her drowsy. Joseph lay on a mat on the floor fast asleep, his legs flopped open and his arms flung above his head. Simon and Abigail were climbing trees at the back of the house; every now and then, one of them squealed or laughed. Alfred was telling his mother something in Ga, and she was giggling louder and louder.

Eva became irate listening to them; the comfort and intimacy of their banter made her feel as if she was the outsider. 'So, has your son told you what he has been getting up to recently?'

'Eva, don't.'

'Well, I think your mother should know, don't you?'

'Know what?'

'Alfred?' Eva stared at him. It was in that moment she realised how deep her anger really was. It was vast, like a black bottomless ocean. With all of the same might. Try as she might, she couldn't see past what he had done, couldn't imagine how she could ever trust him again. And looking at him was like looking at the badly scarred face of a loved one for the first time; she couldn't decipher the man she'd known and it terrified her.

If she had had the opportunity, if she had been back home in England for instance, on her own ground, with options at her disposal, she would at least have moved out of the house, moved in with her parents or a friend, options unavailable to her in this city.

She looked at him now, realising that she had been paralysed by the inability to think straight; she didn't know how they would ever get back on the right track, in which case where did that leave them? She had refused to talk about it because too many of her thoughts would come tumbling out: Where could she go?

244

What would they do? Did she want to leave him? A divorce? The word cooled her blood somewhat whenever she thought about it, embroidered as it was in her mind with heavy obscurity.

And did she need to know whether or not there had been others? Or whether there would be others? Now that he had crossed that line, wouldn't it be easy for him to do it again? What would stop him? And could she accept that? Would she be able to forgive this once and never again? Or would forgiving once mean doing so over and over, lowering her standards now and forever more?

And there was the child, whose being clouded over all her thoughts. Whenever she was ploughing through the mess of queries, making progress of sorts, the child dragged her back down, trapped her in the maze of unanswerable questions.

Maybe if she had been able to satisfy her overriding desire to be alone and away from him, the anger might not have grown in this way, like some out-of-control cancer. After days of refusing to vent her feelings and her thoughts, she now felt ready to burst with rage. She wanted to hit him, pummel him until he too hurt. And then there was that part of her that wished he could hold her and reverse the past months, erase his indiscretion. But she might as well wish for the moon. She hated feeling so vulnerable, so afraid, so alone, so desperate to go home, in fact.

She swallowed and stared at him. 'Alfred has lost his tongue, Auntie Gee, but what I think you should know, what he should tell you, is that he has had a child with another woman.' Eva was torn between wanting to keep staring at Alfred's broken face and needing to see how Gladys would react.

Gladys had pursed her lips and looked glumly at Eva. 'Ah, yes.'

'He has produced another grandchild for you. A bastard.'

'Oh Eva, please we don't use that word . . .'

'I am sorry, but do you understand what I am trying to tell you? He has been unfaithful, cheated on me.'

'Yes, yes.'

245

'And is that all you can say? Do you think this is acceptable?'

'They came to tell me . . .'

'You knew . . .?' Eva blushed. Her hands shook and she clasped them together to steady herself.

'Wait, Eva, let me explain.'

'Auntie Gee, I didn't know . . .'

'Alfred, please shut up,' said Auntie Gee without looking at him.

'How could you? I thought you wanted us to be friends?'

'We are not friends, Eva! I am your mother-in-law. We are stronger than friends. But you see, it is normal in our culture. The child also has a family. They too have to know who the father is. They came to me to acknowledge the child, what was I to do? After all, he is my grandchild too.'

'But, how did you know that she . . . his mother . . . you know her?'

'Oh no. It is the extended family that brought him. Not the mother. She is not welcomed in my house of course, but I know what my children are up to. This family also lives close to me, and they too know what their children are up to.'

'I feel so stupid. Who else knew my husband was sleeping around . . .?'

'I wasn't sleeping around, Eva.'

'Why should I believe you? You lied to me. How many times did you come back from her bed to ours and hold me, touch me, smile in the morning as if nothing had changed . . .? You bastard!'

'Oh Eva, please,' said Gladys. 'This is my child, he is not a bastard. I don't like to hear that word. A fool maybe, yes, but please, control yourself.'

'Me control myself?'

'Listen to me, Eva. That woman is of no consequence. It is the child only that I care about because he too is a Laryea, whether or not we like it. And it is not his fault so let us not divert our attention from what is going on here.'

'I have tried to tell her that the woman means nothing to me, but Eva won't listen.'

'Alfred, shut up,' said Auntie Gee.

'I thought you were different. I thought you believed in marriage. You are educated and sophisticated . . . I had you on a bloody pedestal. *My* Alfred would never do *that*, I said.'

'I know. I let you down.'

'Anyway, please, we are being diverted from our focus. Listen to me Eva, you are still the mistress of this house. It is a position for you to keep. Or, if you want, to give up. As for Alfred, over my dead body will I allow him to maltreat you . . .'

'I would never maltreat Eva. I love her. I have never . . .'

'Alfred, shut up. This is not going well for you.'

'Can you *please* stop telling me to shut up! For God's sake.'

'So now you want to call on the name of God!'

'I made a mistake . . . a grave mistake, I accept, and one which I will have to live with forever. For that I must be treated like a child in my own house?'

'In fact, at this moment, we are not discussing what you think or don't think. But a house with strife is a divided house,' said Auntie Gee firmly. 'Weak and susceptible to attack. There has to be reconciliation. So we are going to do it now.' She clapped her hands to emphasise her determination.

Eva looked at Alfred, but he appeared equally surprised.

'The floor is open,' said Auntie Gee.

Alfred raised his hands and dropped them heavily. 'I don't know what else you expect me to say. I have said everything I know to say. It seems to makes no difference whatsoever.'

'Please, that is not the attitude I was hoping for today. Eva, anything to say?'

She shook her head.

'I am warning you both!'

Eva kept her eyes on her glass so that she didn't have to look at either of them.

'Eva, can't we discuss this on our own? Please? We have always managed before when things were tricky. Why won't you let me make it up to you?'

'How?' Eva said, surprising herself with the vehemence in her voice. 'My children have another brother. Tell me, how should I inform them of that? And when do I do it? Or will you? When do we take him in and make him part of this family? Or should we wait until he comes to introduce himself of his own accord? I am sorry but I don't have the script for this. He is part of you . . . and part of my children.' Her voice had dropped to a whisper. 'How dare you be indignant? How dare you draw attention to *your* feelings? How *dare* you.'

'I'm so ashamed,' his voiced had cracked and leaked its confidence. It tugged oddly at a remote part of Eva's consciousness. 'But haven't I been a good husband? Because I tried to be . . .' He swallowed and Eva looked at him. His eyes had filled up. She was astonished by how young he looked, stripped as he was of his self-confidence. A far cry from the first time she saw him, big, strong, poised. But how striking he still was, how beautiful his face.

She didn't respond.

'I provided in every way I could. You pulled away when you were expecting Joseph. I really needed you then. I was lost, I floundered . . . and yes, I erred. But I always have and always will provide for you and the children . . . *our* children.'

Yes, he had provided. Materially speaking, their marriage had been very successful. Alfred had built a big house for them; a house that was bigger than she had ever imagined living in, not that she had ever imagined living in a house in Africa. She was lucky, and she knew it. Some foreign wives lived for years with relatives or in rented accommodation at the whim of landlords upping the rent as often as they liked, or evacuating them with little notice because a cousin needed the house.

Oh, but if Eva really wanted to, she could tell Alfred now about

248

all that was wrong with her life. And she could go on for hours. There was much wrong with it, including him. She could tell him about how sometimes the endless difficulties of living here overwhelmed her, how she blamed the people, their beliefs, in fact the whole continent. How she was frustrated that he didn't acknowledge how hard it had been for her, how hard it still was. She could tell him how fortunate it was for him that she was not one to complain unnecessarily; in general she realised that it was a pointless pursuit. The only way to continue making some sort of success of this marriage, this life, was to keep adapting, keep coping with whatever it and this country threw at her.

She had tried to make this place her home; after all where else could she go with her three children and no money? And she could tell him that since his dreadful revelation, Norfolk had been calling her back more than ever. *Come home, come home.* She could hear it deep in her consciousness all day long. She had been having the most sensual dreams about it, she could smell the wet autumn leaves, overripe apples and coffee. She could see her bedroom with the musty, hard mattress, the starched white bed sheets, the itchy brown blanket, the old rug, and the dried flowers she had picked as a child on a walk in the woods that hung on her wardrobe. She had started dreaming of her childhood again, and she hadn't for years.

She was proud that she had survived for so long here without having a mental breakdown, without turning to alcohol, without going home once, without going anywhere at all in fact. And yes, she could remind him how a few years ago, Alfred had agreed to take her to Lomé on a little holiday. They were going to stay in a Western hotel, eat French food, lounge by a clean pool. And then he had had to cancel it, and she had been upset for days. She listened to the tales of others who regularly went back home to Europe and those who went to Abidjan and Lomé, and even as far away as Botswana, but with less interest in the details, now that she believed she would not experience the things they described.

They might as well have been describing a visit to the moon, for all she cared. She no longer longed to go and see if what they all said was true. That there are parts of Africa where the roads have no potholes, where the shops are stocked with plenty of foreign goods, fruit jams, Swiss chocolate, cheese, delicacies she couldn't recall the taste of, that there were places in Africa where water shortages and military governments were unheard of. She had thought it better to manage her expectations and avoid disappointment, to enjoy what her life could deliver with sureness rather than to dream about unlikely happenings. After all, she knew many other foreign women who did not have the comforts she had. Yes, he had provided. But, she had expected rather more . . .

'Alfred, try again. Remember, if at first you don't succeed . . .' said Auntie Gee.

He walked over to her and said something in Ga. She stood up and shuffled off singing: *'Praise the Lord who reigns above and keeps his court below; praise the holy God of love and all his greatness show . . .'*

The two of them sat in silence for a while. The clock ticked rhythmically. In the sky, a military helicopter droned past.

'Eva?' She turned to look at him. He was standing by the window with his hands in his trouser pockets. He was watching her in a way that unnerved her a little, his face distant and unfriendly. 'I am telling you once more that I am sorry. I don't know what else to do.'

She looked away, already feeling the mounting pressure to formulate a response. *Why did you do it then?*

'I have done everything I can think of, said all I can. You already know that I would undo what I did if I could. I told you because I thought not telling you would destroy me, us. Believe me when I say I would undo it if I could. All I want is you, my family, as we were . . . I see that perhaps I want too much.' He walked to the door, paused and turned around. 'Do you want a divorce?'

She was winded by his directness.

'Do you want to go home? Because you can, I'll pay for you to go.' He held up open arms. 'Go, for God's sake, if that's what you want, because we can't go on like this, in this hellish limbo . . . and . . . take the children . . . if you want to.' He shrugged as if they were debating something mundane. He stared at her. 'Because I can assure you that neither of us deserves to continue living like this.' His voice broke and he quickly turned and walked out. His lithe body taller, his shoulders square beneath the loose shirt, as if he had shaken off the pain as best as he could, learned to walk comfortably with the hobbles.

Eva found Auntie Gee making *achomo* in the kitchen. 'I am going out.'

Gladys smiled at her. 'Yes, that is good. Now that I am here, you can go and see your friends as much as you like. We can leave this for today. I am here now. We will sort this out for sure. Don't worry about this matter, or the children. Everything will be okay, okay?'

Later Gladys looked at Alfred fiercely. 'Divorce? Are you a fool?'

'Auntie Gee . . .'

'Listen here. Your marriage is in a dire position. If you are not careful, things will end completely. When disaster starts it usually gets worse and worse until all things are out of control.'

'But . . .'

She lifted a hand to silence him. 'I am here for your benefit. You leave it to me. We shall take one day at a time. We will sort this mess out. But you,' she said, pointing her finger at him, 'you must be on your best behaviour day after day, do you follow me? Do you want her to go back to UK and take her children with her?' Gladys sniffed. 'What would I do then? And you too? We have to tread carefully.'

Alfred groaned. 'If I had married a Ghanaian woman, she would have forgiven me by now . . .'

'Well, as I always say, "had I known never comes at first". And besides, a good wife comes around but once in a lifetime, you know. Eva is a good woman, a very high-quality wife in fact, and you need to make every effort to restore your marriage. We must leave no stone unturned.'

'She is making it impossible.'

'Ah! Are you feeling sorry for yourself, you this boy?'

'She won't even talk.'

'But she talked just now. Didn't you hear what she said? She is angry. It is normal. If she was not bothered about this marriage do you think she would be angry like this?'

Alfred sat and shook his head in silence.

'You don't worry, my son. I am on your side as I am on Eva's side too. We will sort it out. I will sort it out. We will get things back on track as soon as possible. Over my dead body will I sit back and allow things to completely fall apart and let her take my grandchildren back to UK.'

Chapter Seventeen

At *Yelena's*, Eva found her friend finishing off a blow-dry for a young Scandinavian-looking woman. Even on a Sunday, Yelena opened the salon for a few hours and she had clearly been busy. On the red linoleum floor, there was a pile of fluffy hair. Cat Stevens played on the stereo.

Yelena waved and gestured to a seat. 'Just give me a moment.'

All the chairs were upholstered in mock black leather, and several had gashes and rips which Yelena had mended with sticky tape. Eva sat and fluttered through aged, curled magazines, but the goings-on in the salon were much more interesting, and distracted her. She loved coming here and already she felt a boost.

Yelena had converted her living room into a salon a few years ago. On one side of the room were four chairs in a row facing a wall of mirrors. On the opposite side of the room, there was a sink in the corner for washing hair. Above the sink were shelves crammed with shampoos, conditioners and hair colours. Most of the rest of the wall space was covered with pages that had been pulled out from hair magazines. Eva couldn't imagine that anyone ever came in here and requested one of the hairdos exemplified on the wall. Unrealistic punk shapes, trendy boy cuts, and styles with long glossy curls tumbling here and there, creations involving false hair. One poster was of a beautiful black girl with wet jerry curls and pink glossy lips, parted a little to reveal a hint of teeth. Is that what she looks like? Pretty, seductive, young? She turned away.

Next to the sink were a couple of red swivel chairs where a woman was having her nails painted by a girl on a stool. There was a trolley next to her which was filled with dazzling nail colours, nail polish remover, pumice stones, nail files and other instruments. The girl rummaged in the trolley for ages each time she wanted another implement or bottle.

Besides Yelena, who did all the hair-cutting, there were three assistants who washed hair and performed manicures and pedicures. All of them had arrived with little experience. 'I prefer it that way. Otherwise you are paying to undo their bad habits,' said Yelena. It was extraordinary that they got so much done in this small space. Yelena had to keep moving this way and that if one of her assistants wanted to get past, but it didn't bother her. Expertly, she brushed the woman's hair into a puffed-up bob with the help of a fair amount of hairspray. 'You look like an American movie star now,' she said to the woman as she admired her handiwork. 'Your husband will love it.' She took payment from the woman, smiled sweetly as a generous tip was handed over and said, 'You really didn't have to, so kind.' As soon as the client had gone, she turned and hugged Eva. 'What a lovely surprise.'

'I had to get out of the house for a while. Alfred's mother moved in this morning, apparently indefinitely.'

'Oh no!' Yelena tutted. 'Well, you know you must do everything in your power to make her stay uncomfortable. Don't let her think it is a nice place to be. Or she might stay for ever.'

Eva groaned. 'I know she will take over my kitchen, cook from the crack of dawn. I don't know why she needs to make so much food. Even my coffee will be tasting of palm oil soon.'

They laughed.

'It is what they do. Women here of that age, they cook. What else is there for them to do?'

'And they go to funerals.'

They laughed again and Yelena continued, 'You need to think deviously, I know you can do it. Put aside your honest nature and think like someone desperate, figure out a way to make her leave. Come with me,' she said, taking hold of Eva and pulling her towards a sink. 'I will wash your hair and blow-dry it while we talk.' She poured a pail of water over her head and started to wash her hair, massaging Eva's head with firm rhythmic strokes. 'Too much tension is bad. You need to relax a little.'

Later, Eva watched as Yelena forced the plug on the hairdryer into a three-hole socket using a pencil in place of the third pin. As she fiddled with the plug and socket trying to get the hairdryer to work Eva turned to stare in the mirror. Her face was drawn and pale, her eyes tired; she looked away.

'Here we are,' said Yelena triumphantly.

'I didn't think you'd be busy.'

'It has been quiet all week, but today has been good. So, how are things, apart from his mother.'

Eva swallowed. 'He offered me a divorce . . .'

'No! No! Eva, you don't want that, do you?'

'I honestly don't know what I want . . . well, I do. I'd like to rewind the clock . . .'

But she knew she didn't want a divorce. She couldn't go home, and couldn't imagine setting up home on her own in the UK without the support of her parents, not with three children and no real qualifications. And how could she afford to live here on her own? Where would she work, and where would she live? Oh, and how the declaration *for better or worse* rang loud. Far louder than it had on the day, challenging her now, when then the words had been merely lovely and romantic and hypothetical.

'Good! It is so hard on your own, Eva. Not as straightforward as you might think.'

Eva nodded, she knew she didn't really understand what Yelena's life was like.

'Ah, these men! We fall in love with them, follow them to this . . . this place . . . and then they go and change,' Yelena said, stroking Eva's cheeks.

'Yes. And enough about me. How are you? Have you thought any more about the boys' outdooring?'

'Well, I'm going to see his mother straight after Christmas. I have made up my mind.'

'Will you tell Wisdom?'

'No. What is the point? I don't think he will support me, even if I involve him. I suppose I am hoping that even if they don't agree to the outdooring, well maybe at the very least the boys can develop a relationship with their grandmother and all of their Ghanaian family. At times like this, the lack of family seems so much more severe.'

'Doesn't it? And, that's why I came today. I want you and the boys to spend Christmas with us. You shouldn't be on your own with them again. This year I am not going to accept your usual "no" for an answer. Say you'll come? And bring your things so you can stay the night. Or two.'

Yelena's face burst with a smile. 'Eva, I'd very much love to. Somehow this year, I can't face it by myself.'

'Good. And Auntie Gee can help you deal with Wisdom's family. You know she'd love nothing better.'

Eva felt something loosen in her. She smiled some more. Funny that forgetting about herself for just one moment, reaching out to someone else in spite of her pain, could bring such wonderful release.

'Have you heard from Dahlia?'

Yelena looked puzzled. 'No. No. I was hoping you had?'

Eva shook her head. 'I've tried to call since she didn't show up at Margrit's, but her phone must be out of order, all I got was the engaged tone.'

'Maybe we should check in on her. Why don't we go together? I can leave the girls in charge here for a while.'

Dahlia's garden looked immaculate in a most effortless manner. The driveway was lined with stunning colourful roses growing in large flowerpots which had been freshly whitewashed. The shaved lawn was green and thick, even in this drought, and Eva could see that someone had swept up fallen leaves from beneath the sprawling almond tree that grew near the house. The soil around the bedding plants was a healthy black and had been recently tilled. Dahlia didn't garden herself. But as Vincent insisted that the outside of the house was pristinely presented at all times he hired a team of gardeners to keep it so. In spite of her and Zachariah's valiant efforts, Eva's garden never looked this tidy, this lush and extravagant, and she looked on admiringly.

Eva knew they had to have the water on all night to keep it like this, an idea she couldn't get comfortable with. She simply wouldn't be able to justify all that water, even for her beloved garden, especially when there was hardly enough as it was. She knew she would never be able to consent to such extravagance, even if they had fewer water shortages, like in this part of Accra, where buckets and drums of water were rarely needed. It was the legacy of her upbringing, the never-waste-never-squander mentality of her parents from which she hadn't fully escaped. She had to admit that perhaps it couldn't matter to her enough that her grass was brown and waning green in equal parts.

Eva and Yelena had been waiting for half an hour and still no Dahlia. The maid told them that Vincent had gone to Kumasi for Christmas and the children were out with their cousins. Yelena fidgeted in her seat, twirled the glass of water the maid had brought her and looked about once more, puffing hard. The veranda was covered in large earthenware pots filled with trailing green plants, small palms and shrubs. Flowering lilies, jasmine and ivy trailed overhead on a pergola. It was quiet here, tucked away like this. No noise from the streets, the cars, the house, only the occasional chirp of a lone bird. The white wicker chairs had been repainted recently, she noticed, and while the large, lumpy scarlet cushions Dahlia had made years ago had faded, they still looked pretty.

Yelena went to the back door and called out for the maid. 'Did you tell madam that we are here?' she asked.

'Please yes. Please she is coming.'

'Dahlia?' Yelena called out into the hushed house.

'Please madam, she is up steps. She cannot hear you, but she is coming. You can go and sit.'

Yelena looked fleetingly at the maid, but continued to stand at the threshold of the living room. Eva sauntered up to join her.

'She is on her way, apparently.'

'It is so unlike her to keep anyone waiting.' She turned to the maid who was stirring a pot on the stove. 'Was she asleep?'

'Please yes,' said the maid.

They never came into the house unless it was raining; they always sat outside in the garden, which Dahlia seemed to prefer. The living room was dark and cramped, despite the space and the white walls. The furniture was grotesque, heavy carved black armchairs and sofas that Vincent had brought down from Kumasi one weekend, much to Dahlia's embarrassment. They were large pieces, each a little like a throne, upholstered in colourful patterned fabric, with pink and red hibiscus flowers. On the floor there was a lime green and brown rug and on the bookcases that ran along the length of the living room, large bound books that looked like they trapped too much dust, and piles of vinyl records. The coffee table in the middle of the room was vast, with elaborately carved legs and a glass top, and on it there was an ornate empty vase.

Eva turned when she heard footsteps. Dahlia walked towards them carrying a tray of tea. She was wearing a lot of make-up and had styled her hair differently so that instead of her usual neat ponytail, it was parted and some combed down the left side of her face and curled under her chin. She wore a scarf around her neck. Her eyes were glassy, their lids heavy and swollen.

'My God Dahlia, you look terrible,' said Yelena. 'What happened to you?'

'I used the wrong shampoo and my face swelled up. I have an appointment to see the doctor . . .' She turned to go back inside. 'I'll just get the milk.'

Eva frowned and looked at Yelena, who was shaking her head in disbelief.

Dahlia returned smiling. 'So, how are you ladies? Sorry I didn't make it to Margrit's. How is she?'

Eva stared into her friend's vacant eyes. 'Dahlia, how are you? We've been frantic.'

'I had malaria. And I'll be honest, I've been feeling very low . . . Christmastime and all that, but I feel much better now . . .' She did sound fine; her voice lilting but strong.

'Dahlia, are you sure . . .?' asked Eva.

Her face flickered.

'You can talk to us,' said Yelena. 'Is he still seeing that girl?'

'No change there. I just find this time of year difficult, I miss home . . .' A tear ran down her face and she wiped it away. 'But look at me being silly. Don't we all miss home?'

'Is that all?' whispered Eva kindly.

Dahlia winced, bit her lip and stared down into her hands which she started to wring. 'I have to go home,' she whispered, suddenly panting.

'Don't worry,' said Yelena, taking her wrists.

'I have to get out of here . . .' Her voice was heavy and solemn.

'What's happened? Are you all right? What is it?'

Dahlia choked on her words. 'I just have to get out . . . Vincent has . . . what if he takes the children . . . what if I never

259

see them again?' Absentmindedly, she pulled her fingers through her hair.

'What is that on your head?' asked Eva, leaning forward.

Dahlia lowered her hand, shook her hair into place. 'I bumped into my wardrobe the other night when we had no power. The batteries in my torch had run out and . . .'

Eva shook her head, slowly at first, then faster. 'Dahlia, what really happened to your face? It wasn't the shampoo was it? And at my lunch party . . . there was a mark here . . .' Eva touched her cheekbone. 'You were hiding something . . . you had on so much make-up.'

'Oh, you know how clumsy I can be . . .'

'It was a bruise . . . and there was a mark on your neck. You weren't yourself at all. If I hadn't been so wrapped up in myself . . . did he hit you?'

'Eva . . .' said Yelena.

But she saw it clearly. How, here and there, over the years Eva had known her, Dahlia had walked into more than her fair share of wardrobes and open doors, how she had tripped over too many toys and missed steps.

'No! Enough, Dahlia!'

Dahlia gasped. Her face dropped and she stared at them with a fear so raw.

'He hits you?' asked Yelena.

Eva felt a chill travel down her back. 'Is that what he does?' her voice thickened and caught in her throat.

'No. He gets angry, that's all. It's . . .'

'Dahlia, stop the lies! Listen to yourself for God's sake!'

'Darling, do you want to wait until he puts you in a coffin in front of your children?' said Yelena.

'I . . . he . . .' her face had drained of all colour. She looked like a corpse with her make-up shimmering in the heat. Her mouth fell open and her facade crumbled further.

'You can trust us.'

'He did that, didn't he?' said Eva, pointing at Dahlia's head.

Dahlia nodded weakly.

'And the mark on your cheek?'

She nodded again.

Yelena wrapped her arms around Dahlia and rocked her. 'How long has this been going on?' she whispered.

Dahlia made an odd sound, as she tried to stifle a moan.

'Since . . . the beginning?' said Yelena.

She nodded.

Yelena spewed incoherent Russian and kissed Dahlia's cheek over and over.

Dahlia lifted her hand to her neck and undid her scarf and they saw the dark marks around her neckline.

Eva covered her mouth, afraid that she would be sick. She tried to still her stomach. It seemed no one spoke or moved for a very long time. She felt her pain mingle with, and then disappear into, the vast unfathomable pain of her friend, who had once again put on a sterling effort to look beautiful and in control. She shook her head, wondering how often Dahlia had come amongst them like this, pretending, acting, lying. And then going back to . . . *that*?

'What about the children?' she whispered.

And then Dahlia crumbled even further. She looked wretched. Her face stamped with hopelessness. She dropped her head so she wouldn't have to confront their shocked faces any longer.

'No!' said Yelena appalled.

'No,' she whispered. 'No, he has never touched them . . . he . . . but they know . . .' She covered her face with her hands.

'They have seen? They have seen him do this to you?' Eva was shaking.

Yelena gripped Dahlia tighter.

'You have to leave. As soon as possible.'

'Without him finding out,' Yelena said, lowering her voice to a whisper, as if the trees around them might be able to relay the news to Vincent. 'You can't stay here!'

'But he'll find me wherever I go.'

'You have to go, before he goes too far and it's too late . . .' said Eva. 'We'll look after you, protect you.'

'How?'

'She is right,' said Yelena softly. 'We'd need to get Dahlia out of the country.'

'But we can't just leave you here. Not now; I won't do it . . .'

'Think, Eva. What we need is to put Dahlia on a plane. We can't keep her hidden from him until then. He mustn't suspect anything is different. Our priority has to be to get you properly out of his reach. As soon as possible.'

'He'll kill me if he finds out.'

'He can't! He wouldn't,' said Eva. She stared at Dahlia. How could she be so sure, when she was no longer sure about anything? 'Has he ever said anything . . .?'

'He must not find out,' said Yelena slowly, unwilling to continue that conversation. She looked at each of them in turn. 'We don't want to find out what he's capable of. Don't even tell Alfred. Not a soul must know.'

'He'd happily get me deported . . . what if I can't get back to see the kids?'

They sat silent. They had all heard the tale of the Austrian woman whose husband had encouraged her to go home and visit her parents without the children. When she wanted to return in time for Christmas, she found out that he had asked the authorities not to renew her visa, leaving her stuck in Salzburg without her children.

'BA usually has seats,' said Eva after a while. 'Although, who knows what the coup has done to their schedule.'

'Do you have money?' asked Yelena.

'I have some. I don't know if it will be enough, the prices keep going up.'

'We'll get the money,' said Eva.

'I can't take our passports without him finding out.' Dahlia started to breathe heavily. 'I used to keep them in the drawer in my desk, but he's moved them.'

'You listen to me,' said Eva. 'You have to stay calm. You need to find them. One of us will come and help you when we are ready.'

'I'll go to the travel agent on Monday first thing,' said Yelena.

'And we'll get you to the airport without Vincent finding out,' said Eva.

'Thank you girls,' said Dahlia. Her eyes welled up. 'I need a drink. I'll fetch us something.' She wiped her face feverishly as she went. She got a bottle of whisky and poured each of them some. They sipped at tumblers in silence, thoughts and questions, too ominous to voice, floating around them unspoken.

Walking away and leaving Dahlia that afternoon, in the dark, quiet house, was one of the hardest things Eva had ever done. She felt as though she had been flattened by something heavy, as if some profound load had been rolled over her again and again. Her heart bled for her friend, their dashed hopes and disappointments fused in devastating waves of despair. How often had they discussed their marriages? How often had they vowed to try that little bit harder to understand Ghanaian life, to negotiate the cultural maze that could leave them feeling disorientated afresh? Tried to bridge the world they had inhabited at home and the one they lived in now, where even the good men were drawn, from time to time, into an abyss of traditions, doing and saying things their wives couldn't comprehend?

She remembered their shared mistakes in the beginning as they had each adjusted to Accra, to the endless frustrations, the repeated misunderstandings, the shortages, the weather, the people, the food. And they had tried; how they had tried to fit in! They had helped each other to make sense of the senseless, laughed at the bizarre habits that no one took the time to explain to them, taught each other to smile more, moan less and to survive and thrive, despite the circumstances that could easily overwhelm them. And yet neither of them had had the courage to share the deepest darkest moments. Why was that, she thought now, her face streaming. What had stopped them from sharing?

Eva didn't want to go home. She wasn't ready to be a mother again, to deal with that selfish, incessant neediness of young children. She was heavy-hearted, and tormented by what she had heard. She felt tremendous guilt that she had never really noticed what Dahlia was going through. What kind of friend did that make her?

So, she continued down the road to Margrit's house in search of some insight, some comfort, in the midst of her confounding pain. Margrit was the wise one, the unconquerable one. *Made in Chermany*, she said laughing, whenever the others commented on her fortitude.

Eva banged on the gate as she pushed it open, and was instantly aware that all was not right. Something or someone was in pain, she could make out a guttural moan. She pushed through the foliage and walked towards the veranda where she saw Margrit sprawled on the floor, cradling her dog Jimmy. Both of them were moaning, and Margrit was rocking back and forth.

She looked up when she heard Eva approach. Eva was shocked to see Margrit's face swollen with angst. Margrit tried to smile in greeting, but it only made her expression more grotesque.

Margrit recounted what had happened. As she spoke, she noted numbly how the hoarse voice she heard, although hers, was totally unfamiliar.

'I got back from my swim at the pool and look what I found.' The house was in disarray. Burglars, she presumed. 'But as we have nothing valuable in the house, they simply wreaked destruction everywhere. They took all my chickens and the puppies, I assume to sell or eat,' she said blandly. She lowered her voice and continued as if she didn't want the dog to understand what came next. 'Poor Jimmy must have tried to fight them, and I think they bashed her with something hard, maybe a pipe or a bat? I think she has broken ribs, I am not certain, but she is wheezing.' She was stroking the dog, whose whimper was waning, blood gurgling through her nose.

'Shouldn't we take her to the vet?' asked Eva.

Margrit shook her head. 'There is nothing they can do for her. She will need to be put down.'

'Oh, I'm so sorry,' said Eva.

Margrit looked up at Eva, her eyes deadened. She continued to stroke Jimmy and rock her.

Her animals were everything to her. She loved them as some loved their children. To be fair, she didn't have children and therefore perhaps she shouldn't really make such a direct comparison, but she loved them as people with all of her heart and might, and isn't that how a parent loves her child? She remembered when Jimmy was a baby, how she used to leave the light on in the kitchen at night, the radio playing softly, so that Jimmy wouldn't worry, wouldn't wake up and yelp, just as any baby left alone for too long in the quiet, dark. Of course, if it had been up to her alone, she would have had Jimmy in her bed, but there Kojo drew the line. 'As for this, if you do it, I promise you that I will divorce you . . .' He said it smiling, but she knew from the way he spoke it with unflinching firmness, that on this matter, he wouldn't relent.

She had bottle-fed Jimmy when she hadn't been eating well, sat up with her when she gave birth, encouraging and assisting as much as she could. And how many hours had she spent grooming her, shampooing her, brushing her fur and trimming it occasionally? Jimmy rewarded her by following her about like a shadow. 'Go to your mummy,' Kojo would say to her, and it seemed that was how Jimmy regarded Margrit.

And now, she was murmuring into her ears, comforting her,

wishing she could take away the pain, calm her down, remove her distress. The barbarians, she thought with fresh anger.

'And my neighbours,' she said with vehemence. 'None of them did anything to stop it, to help? I mean it doesn't make sense that they would be able to just stand by and listen?'

Eva rubbed her back gently. The sound that Jimmy was making was excruciating, but it was getting weaker.

'Why didn't they do anything? They would have heard the dogs. They must have heard something.'

But they don't necessarily care, Eva thought. They think we don't fit in, don't belong. She realised that none of them had gone out of their way to make friends with their neighbours, mainly because they felt misunderstood and unwelcome. Over the years Margrit too had, it would seem, alienated herself from her neighbours through myriad cultural misunderstandings and expressed frustrations.

All of her friends, foreign spouses, had invariably offended their Ghanaian friends and relatives and neighbours with their blunt, you-need-my-opinion approach, which was generally interpreted as insulting. Heaven knew how many grudges her own neighbours had against her for telling them to clean their gutters or to stop beating their children. Yes, they smiled, they nodded, they appeared indifferent, but what right did she or any of her friends really have to tell them how to live, what to do? What right did they have to assume that they knew better, that their opinions were welcome or valid? But they had learned in time, all of them, and they tried harder to suppress their opinions, to smile and shut up. But was it too late? Was this the inevitable end result of the many mistakes they had made over the years?

She cried herself to sleep that night. And as her heart grieved, she yearned for Alfred; her friend, her confidant. She would have shared the whole of Dahlia's loathsome story with him tonight. He would have held her. He might have kissed away her pain. He would have bristled with anger at Vincent. He would have known what to say, what to do, how to help. She wished so desperately to be lying next to him, to be asleep in his shadow, their bodies turning this way and that, in tune even in sleep. They had been good together. Their marriage had been good. *He* was good, gosh, a saint, by Vincent's standards.

And her standards? What were they? And could they take the strain of bending a little more now, adjusting to the new reality of her marriage, she wondered? Surely they could. They would have to.

Chapter Eighteen

Eva sat reading the newspaper on the veranda to pass the time until she could speak to Yelena. Periodically she looked up at the garden, where Zachariah, who had come back unexpectedly this morning, had tidied and watered. She couldn't believe how nervous she felt about their plan. It was Christmas Eve in two days, and Vincent would be back at some point between Boxing Day and New Year. Ideally they could put Dahlia and the children on a flight before he got back from Kumasi, only Dahlia didn't know precisely when he would be back.

She tried to resist biting her fingernails, wishing for the umpteenth time that she could confide in Alfred. He had implied the other day that he didn't trust Vincent. Why, she wondered?

And if Gladys wasn't here with her bloody interfering, she would happily do some cleaning to pass the time, make her feel she was achieving something while she waited. According to her rota, she and Faustina should have been cleaning out the fridges and then the shelves in the larder with hot soapy water, but it was impossible with Gladys in the kitchen. 'Faustina and Akua can do it. That is what they are here for,' she said, whenever Eva tried to do any housework. Then in private she told Eva, 'You must remember who you are.'

It seemed that for the most part, Faustina was thriving with the independence, and enjoying having Akua to boss about. In fact, it seemed she was cleaning harder and more thoroughly than ever.

It was quiet, Alfred had taken the children to school on his way to the office, and Faustina had gone to the market to shop, taking Joseph with her. Eva tried to concentrate on her paper, but the words swam before her and she flicked through the pages lethargically.

She heard a rattle at the gate. She saw a man wearing an army cap looking through. Within seconds, more capped heads appeared. They started shouting for the gate to be opened and began shaking it violently. She started to feel afraid. Akua and Auntie Gee came hurrying from the kitchen. Zachariah and Solomon came from the boys' quarters, and Eva instructed them to open the gate. She could see even from here how frightened Solomon was, but Zachariah seemed as unfazed as ever.

The soldiers walked towards the veranda. Then a military truck stuttered on to the driveway and stopped; more men clambered out of it.

The men approached slowly, with paced gestures in the manner of the slow-witted. It was clear that for the past two weeks they had slept and lived in the dungarees they were wearing. Their hair was uncombed and had begun to form knotted locks.

The soldier leading the pack stopped by the tree where Eva's orchids grew. He stroked the thin and tall stem, the glossy leaves. He plucked the flower and put it behind his ear.

'Please don't pick my flowers. That is a rare orchid.' Eva glanced towards Zachariah, who nodded his head ever so slightly.

'Hey! Hey!' shouted several of the soldiers, moving quickly towards the women with their guns lifted.

'Eva, be quiet!' hissed Gladys.

Eva looked over at Gladys. She could see Gladys was afraid,

but she herself felt nothing. Only relief that the children were at school and that Faustina had Joseph. Strange perhaps, but this was her house after all, her garden, and a natural instinct to protect what was hers, her hard work, rose up fiercely in her. 'I don't want them picking my flowers,' she said defiantly.

'Mind how you talk to our sergeant, eh!' shouted one of them.

'Be very careful, my friend,' said another.

The others seemed to be waiting for their leader's reaction.

'Your flowers?' he asked, reaching for another flower, which he plucked.

'Oh, don't do that,' shouted Eva.

'Eva, quiet!'

The soldiers had gathered a few feet in front of the women. They lowered their guns into more comfortable positions, but the nozzles still pointed at them.

'Have you perhaps forgotten that you are a guest in our country? This is my land,' said the leader, stamping his boot on the pathway. 'Mine, not yours.' He pointed a finger at Eva. 'We can even ask you to return to your country if we want.'

'Please, we beg,' said Gladys. She had cupped one palm on top of the other in a suppliant gesture.

'Shut up!' he growled. Spit flew in an arc from his fleshy mouth.

Eva felt her stomach cramp involuntarily. Her hands were shaking. She felt a surge of anger. How dare they violate her sanctuary like this? The man stepped closer and Eva wrinkled her face in disgust; his rank body odour was overpowering.

She could see the hatred in their eyes. Anyone would think she was to blame for the state of their country. Well, it wasn't her bloody fault . . . she shook her head. But she knew Auntie Gee was right. Maybe if she could cooperate with them, give them what they wanted, they would leave quickly. The flowers would grow back after all. As annoying as it was, as reckless and violating as this idiot's behaviour had been, this was no time to lose perspective.

Perhaps she must remember their need to indulge in the fruit of their country, to throw their weight around in a way that was usually the sole domain of the ruling classes who had been educated abroad, in *abrochie*, a place these soldiers knew they would never see. She humbled her expression and the soldier's face relaxed too.

'What do you want? I mean, what can we do for you?' she asked nicely.

The man took a step closer. Never before had she seen such dark passion, such murderous resentment. If she lifted her hand or he his, they would touch. She could smell stale, unwashed body, rusty like dank metal. His hands were trembling and she imagined that he was using a fair amount of resolve to restrain them from striking her. The whites of his eyes were coloured, perhaps from drink and hashish, and his pupils were dilated. But the thoughts she could sense swarming his mind were not dulled by drugs. They were heightened and loosed by his intoxication, causing his lips to curl upwards in contempt.

'We are going to teach you a lesson. The lesson of respect for authority. Is this how you talk to people in your country?' He waved his hand as if indicating her country, some place far beneath him. 'No wonder there is so much licentiousness there. Why children can talk to their parents anyhow. We don't do that here.' He leaned towards Eva until his lips were a millimetre from hers and shouted, 'Here we have RESPECT!' He stared straight into her eyes with blind hostility, and Eva wondered briefly where it came from. She wiped spit off her face. Next to her Auntie Gee stood stiff like a stone statue, her chin raised defiantly. The man smiled suddenly, his large spaced-out teeth glinting. He raised his gun and without surrendering his gaze, he swept his free arm around and behind him. 'Pick all the flowers!'

'No!' said Eva. 'You can't do that. Why would you want to do that?'

'Eva, please,' Gladys whispered urgently.

Please what? Eva wanted to ask. Someone needed to stand up to all these bullies, they were going too far. Someone needed to shout out loud that it was time to end the pretence.

Gladys grabbed Eva by the arm. 'Leave them.'

Behind him, the soldiers were looting the garden of all colour. Gleaming crimson hibiscuses, radiant frangipani, purple and white bougainvillea, glorious yellow oleander were pulled randomly from branches and strewn on the ground. The men acted hurriedly, as if time-restricted, frenziedly pulling whole shrubs apart, leaving the garden looking as if it had been ravaged by some determined, devastating ailment.

Eva had never before felt threatened by another human in this country. By mosquitoes, disease, potholes, frustration even, yes, but not people. The Ghanaians she knew were, if nothing else, easygoing and full of good humour. Not bloodthirsty. And Vincent? She saw Dahlia's battered face. He was a live, educated monster. How did it make him feel when he smashed his fists into her beautiful, soft face? Did he hear the crack of bone? What about her pleas, the children's? Her blood boiled. What else had he done? How much agony had her friend really suffered at the hands of that brute?

She couldn't watch the violation of her sanctuary, her home, in silence. She felt her blood race. She felt her heart beating in time to their boots stomping over her lovely garden. The desecration was heartbreaking. Any terror she ought to feel was kept at bay by a fierce desire to stand up to them, to stop the bullying and intimidation, on behalf of herself and everyone else they bullied.

'You are behaving like . . . animals,' she said, unable to contain her words. 'That is why this country is in a continuing backward spiral.'

'You don't understand?' said the sergeant in a soft, menacing voice as he edged closer. 'Are you refusing to learn your lesson? Eh?'

'Please, don't mind her. She is foolish,' said Auntie Gee, pulling Eva towards the house.

'Let me go! What exactly am I to learn from such behaviour? That you have a gun and so you are more powerful than me? And for that you have destroyed my beautiful garden? Your mother should have taught you that . . .'

'Do not call my mother's name in vain!' he said, his shrill voice reverberating.

'Eh madam!' said one of soldiers shaking his head in disbelief.

'*Please* . . .' said another, his voice filled with desperate hope that she might soon find her senses.

Auntie Gee held on to Eva with both hands, her fingernails digging into Eva's arm, and ignored Eva's attempts to break free.

Eva thought they all looked more afraid than she felt. There was no point being reasonable with them after all. No one in this bloody country seemed to follow the rules of normal human behaviour. Would she ever understand them, they her? And now her frustration and her anger swelled further. 'Well, your teachers then,' she said. 'That would be a better use of your time and talents. Go and fix the school system. Stand with guns at the gate and ensure that the teachers come to work and teach the children, rather than just sending them on errands. And teach the children not to litter, not to urinate on the streets. Teach them to love their beautiful country, to plant nice trees so they can sit in the shade and admire the flowers. You are in power now, do something that gets you somewhere, that takes you and your fellow countrymen further along, not backwards . . .' She paused.

The man was gazing at her antagonistically. Behind him, his followers had dropped their mouths, incredulous at her audacity.

'And now what are you going to do, Mr Big Man?' She was shaking with rage. And there again was the awful bottomless desolation that she felt for Dahlia and Margrit and herself which was too all-consuming to leave any room for these idiots to affect her in the way that they wanted. She sat heavily on one of the chairs overwhelmed by an unexpected inappropriate desire to go to sleep. The same thing had happened when she had been in labour with Simon. She had desperately wanted to give in to a similar powerful wish to lie down and sleep a while, to come back to the ordeal later. The doctor had later explained to her that it wasn't such an uncommon reaction after all.

Auntie Gee interrupted her reverie brashly. 'Eva! But you too! *What* is wrong with you? Listen, Big Man, please, don't mind her. You can see she is talking nonsense.'

The leader gripped his gun, but he seemed taken aback that Eva was not terrified of him. 'Put her in the truck,' he said, swivelling on his heels and walking off. He stopped to urinate on the lawn before he climbed back into the truck.

'We are not going! Eva do you know what they do to women there?' She tugged Eva, tried to get her to stand up, but Eva had put her head in her hands and didn't cooperate. Auntie Gee had to bend down, which she found awkward, and she whispered, 'We need money. We must offer them a bribe. We are not going with them. They rape women there. And other terrible, terrible things.'

Eva didn't move. Had she expected to be dead by now? Had she lowered her head to receive his bullet? If he had any intention of shooting her, he would have done it by now, she thought. He probably didn't like blood. It was even plausible that he had never killed anyone in his life.

Auntie Gee let go of her and tottered over to the truck, folded her hands politely, smiled up at the leader and said in a soft voice, 'You can see that my son's wife is not well. And she is foolish too. She is a foreigner, as you can see. And she still hasn't learned our customs, in spite of all my efforts. You can see for yourselves how she is. Please forgive her. Forgive us both. Please let us know what we can do to apologise, to show you that we have learned our lesson.'

He ignored her and stared straight ahead while he waited for the others to get in.

Eva stood when the soldiers tried to pick her up. They bundled the women carefully into the back of the truck as if they were suddenly nervous about hurting them. Their bravado seemed to have dissolved without their leader goading them on.

Eva turned and saw that Akua and Solomon were peeking from the boys' quarters and that Zachariah was speaking to one of the soldiers in the front of the truck in a soft murmur, and she wondered what he was saying. 'We will be back soon,' she called. 'Pick the children up from school. They can have *palava* sauce for lunch. Ask them whether they want plantain or...'

The man in the front must have allowed Zachariah to come with them because suddenly he climbed into the back and sat opposite Eva, looking at her with his kind, calming face.

'Madam, please is okay,' he said.

'Yes, shut up!' hissed one of the other soldiers. 'Why won't you do what you are told? If you were to have cooperated with us, we might have talked to our sergeant, begged him to forgive your behaviour, but you won't stop all this talking! Ah! Why? Because of you I am not going to eat my *banku* this afternoon,' he said making a loud chewing noise with his mouth and hitting the side of his head to indicate her stupidity.

Eva imagined that this was not part of their plan, and that as the engine revved up to drive off into unchartered territory, they were a little unnerved by their passengers: a disobliging white woman and her gibbering relation. And the lack of direction from the front of the truck was evidently exacerbating their frustration; the sergeant was reading a copy of the *Graphic*, one booted leg up on the dashboard and one elbow jutting out of the window, much as if he was on an *akpeteshi* break.

Auntie Gee began to sing a hymn, slowly and mournfully.

One of the soldiers who had been quiet so far, poked Eva in the ribs with the nozzle of his gun. Eva looked at him. He had a kind face, not the face of an assassin. Wide and beautiful, with a flat nose and nice full lips. Youthful facial hairs were sprouting around his chin and over his top lip, beads of perspiration had gathered on his forehead. She smiled at him and shook her head in the manner of a disappointed mother.

'Do you know that insubordinate people have died?' he asked.

From the front, without turning around, the sergeant said, 'Don't mind her. She will learn her lesson. I was trying to help her, to be reasonable, and she insulted me. You leave her alone. She will see.'

'And you, where are you from?' asked Auntie Gee softly, looking at the soldier nearest to her.

Taken aback, the man answered politely.

'Ah, you are a Fanti. And you?' She went round the truck asking one by one and they answered meekly. 'I hope you are making your parents proud,' she said with nod of her head.

Eva needed the loo. And she would be damned if she didn't retain control of her bladder in front of these savages. 'Listen,' she said slowly. 'There has been a misunderstanding here. Where I come from, we don't pick other people's flowers.'

'Hmm!' said the man in the front in a hostile tone.

'I have not learnt all your rules yet, I suppose. I don't shake with my left hand . . .'

'Respect, you have not learned respect!' he spat.

'Yes, my husband says the same thing.'

'We are still working on her,' said Auntie Gee.

Eva detected a sliver of a smile on several of the soldiers' faces, which made it all the more easy for her to say her next words. 'I am sorry that I offended you.' She projected her voice towards the front of the truck.

Everyone looked expectantly towards the sergeant for some sign that he had heard her but there was silence.

'Offer them something,' whispered Auntie Gee, nudging Eva hard.

No way, mouthed Eva with determination. She wouldn't go that far.

'Please, my son's wife has apologised,' said Auntie Gee optimistically before Eva could undo her apology. 'We are sincerely sorry for wasting your time. We know that you have more important things to do. Perhaps if we return to the house we can find some further way of expressing our thankfulness to you for your kindness and patience.'

Eva looked out the window to distance herself from the grovelling.

The sergeant said something to the driver who pulled over on to the side of the road. He swivelled in his seat to look at Eva. 'You are very lucky that your relative is with you. Your days were numbered.'

The driver turned the truck around and they headed back to the house. The atmosphere in the truck changed immediately; the soldiers seemed jovial even. They eased their guns towards the dirty metal floor, they wiped sweat from their faces, they exchanged jokes and laughed.

As soon as the truck had pulled once more on to the Laryea's drive, and the soldiers had unhooked the back and helped the women out, Auntie Gee pulled and dragged Eva into the house, moving faster than Eva had ever seen her move, and with more determination too. 'Will you please kindly go and find some money now?' she said looking around furtively to see if the soldiers were following them. 'I will stay here, so they don't come into the house again. Who knows what additional schemes they might come up with?'

'Having problems?' asked the sergeant, walking towards the door.

'No!' said Auntie Gee as she shoved Eva.

Upstairs, Eva stood and looked at the phone for a moment. If this had been a movie, they would have come with her to make sure she didn't use it, but this was Ghana, they could take the chance that the lines were down. Besides, who would she be calling? Who would come to rescue her? They were acting lawfully after all.

She fought back frustration as she retrieved some of her secret stash of money. She took it downstairs and thrust the money at Auntie Gee, unwilling to give it over herself.

The sergeant took the wad and put it in his back pocket without looking at it. 'Learn your lesson.' He said, pointing a finger at Eva. He turned and walked out, pausing beside one of his men. He took the soldier's gun, cocked it and aimed at the far wall of the house and pulled the trigger, producing a crashing bang. His men yelped, cheered and hooted, and with renewed vigour, clambered back into the truck.

'Jesus!' said Auntie Gee. 'We could have been dead.'

'He is just showing off,' said Eva unflinchingly. 'Good riddance, though.'

The truck pulled out of the drive with the soldiers waving and grinning at them. Zachariah closed the gate and, without wasting any time, started to clean up the garden.

Eva walked towards the house calling for Solomon to lock the gate. She gripped on to the veranda railing for a moment to steady her shaky knees.

She poured Auntie Gee and herself a brandy, flopped into an armchair and sipped hers slowly. She was aware of a warm fire in her belly. She could feel every tension ease away, she stretched her feet on to the coffee table and pointed her toes, and as she listened to Auntie Gee recounting her version of events she began to laugh hysterically.

'Are you mad, you this Eva? I am shaking like a leaf and you are laughing? This is not a laughing matter. A close encounter with death! God Almighty, what is happening to this country?' She looked at the ceiling as though she was expecting God to answer her there and then.

Eva felt as if she had dislodged a large debilitating blockage from somewhere inside her and she began to weep. Her body pulsated with the fear that she ought to have felt earlier, as she realised how stupid she had been.

'It's okay, Eva,' said Auntie Gee.

But Eva couldn't stop; she sobbed until her mouth was dry and her heart stung.

'You are in shock now, I suppose, which is a good thing, because otherwise I would be accurate in saying that you are mad.'

They sat in silence sipping their drinks.

'Maybe we need to spill some blood here after all,' said Auntie Gee. 'Appease what needs to be appeased.'

Eva shook her head. 'What? How? You are not making any sense.'

'Yes. It could even be that woman, or her family. We may never know. Or the dead man, the one who was shot outside. I mean, why did he have to come die right outside on our doorstep? What is that nonsense all about?'

'He didn't die on our doorstep. And what does he have to do with anything?'

'If you look at the recent events, you will see that there is evil at play. Now we too have by a whisker escaped with our lives . . . or was it just a warning?'

Eva finished her drink and closed her stinging eyes.

'Yes, we need to spill some blood. I will call the priests to pray.'

'Priests? How many? And if you mean *juju*, Alfred doesn't like all that stuff.'

'Maybe because of you.'

Eva felt tremendously tired and drained. 'There is a whole other side to him that I don't know, isn't there?'

'No one knows another person completely well.'

'I thought I did,' Eva mumbled to herself.

'Oh you do. But we have to do something here. Yes! I cannot take any more chances with the precious lives of my precious grandchildren.'

'What exactly *do* they do anyway?'

'You leave it to me, you don't understand these things. I will sort it out. Make sure all necessary precautions are taken.'

'As long as it isn't anything scary. I don't want possessed people or headless chickens running around my garden frightening the children.'

Auntie Gee laughed a little. 'No. No. Don't worry.'

Solomon interrupted them to say they had had cleaned up the garden.

'You or Zachariah? And where were you when those soldiers were here?' asked Auntie Gee.

'Please madam, in the boys' quarters.'

'Shame on you! What would you do if you were now faced with two dead bodies? What? And you call yourself a man? Look at how Zachariah helped us, but you, you are nothing but a cowardly fellow!'

'Oh Auntie Gee, please am not a cowardly fellow. I was obeying instructions . . . it was the soldiers . . .'

She dismissed him with a flick of her hand. 'Get away from my face. I will tell Architect that you are useless. What would have happened if I had not been here?'

'Oh, I beg, Auntie Gee.' But she had turned her face from him to indicate her disgust and that the conversation was over.

Eva lay back, embracing the lovely drowsiness that was overcoming her.

Dusk was approaching, and outside there was a rush of activity as everyone hurried to get to where they needed to before six o'clock.

Abigail followed Eva around like a shadow not wanting the sun to set, not at all like the child she could normally depend on to be cheerful and easygoing. She was still thinking about the dead man and had started wetting her bed again.

Eva had tried to telephone Alfred, who should have been home by now, but the phone had been dead all day. She fiddled with the wires again in case they had come loose, which sometimes happened, pressed the button several times hoping to revive the dial tone, but nothing.

'Where is Daddy?' asked Simon, wide-eyed.

'Oh, don't worry, he will be here soon,' said Auntie Gee.

Abigail looked upset.

'Abi, he will be fine. Don't worry. Come with me to the kitchen. When I am displeased about things, when I have a feeling that all is not how I want it to be and I want to forget my fears, I cook.'

'I don't want to cook,' wailed Abi.

'No, we are not cooking proper food today, we can make toffee.'

Simon squealed and jumped about.

Eva walked in just as Gladys was pouring a heap of sugar into a saucepan. 'Please don't use all my sugar!'

'Don't worry, Eva. You go and rest a little. This won't take long and you can have your kitchen again.' She put the pan on a low flame, handed Abigail a wooden spoon and said, 'Stir. Don't stop until I tell you.' She sat on a chair. 'Abigail, Abigail. When are we going to pierce your ears?'

'Today?'

'But your mother says no.'

'We can surprise her. She won't mind once they are done.'

'Who knows, maybe you are right,' said Auntie Gee, winking. She was still angry with Eva. But now, she focused on the good things before her. Two beautiful grandchildren eagerly watching her make them toffee, and another on her back. She took every opportunity to tie Joseph to her back now, even though he was strictly beyond the age of needing to be tied like that. But he was warm and comfortable, and she liked the sounds he made when he was chattering away non-stop in a language that only he understood. What a miracle, she thought whenever she listened to him. One day this same stream of nonsense will turn into sense. Just like that, almost overnight, I will understand what he is trying to tell me.

'How is the sugar doing?' She moaned with the effort of getting up. She peered into the pot and told them to stir harder.

'Daddy said that you were there when Ghana became independent. Is that true?' asked Abigail.

'Ah yes.' She smiled. 'I can remember it as if it was yesterday.' And she could, if she tried hard enough, still feel the optimism she had felt deep in her about the future. When she looked around at the young people, swaggering about with smiles on their faces, running around trying to make money and be like the westerners, she realised that they too had optimism; it was simply of a different nature. Perhaps a cheery outlook is essential for youthful endeavour, one of the things that life gives you freely so that it can knead it out of you with age.

'It was a long time ago. I walked with thousands of others to the old polo ground. We were all hopeful and excited, gathered like merry schoolchildren. We were so over the moon to be watching the birth of our shiny new nation.'

'Did you see Nkrumah?'

'Yes, I did! I pushed my way through people, under smelly armpits and fat stomachs. You see, in those days, I was very slim-slender, not a roly-poly like I am today,' she said wiggling her bottom on the seat. The children laughed and Gladys felt a wave of warm happiness.

'What was he like?'

'He shouted a lot. And he was pouring with sweat. He kept pumping the air like this . . . and everyone chanted, *"Osagyefo, Osagyefo"*, which means, victorious leader. Do you know, when he told us that our beloved country was free for ever, I cried.' She tutted and added, 'I was young and a bit foolish. In those days I used to cry here there and everywhere, you know.'

But that night *had* been special. She still tingled when she thought how proud she had felt to be a citizen of such a new state. How thrilled she felt that she could, if she had somewhere to go, get a passport with the name of her own country on it, one chosen by the people, a name which meant something to them. Although she had to admit that the name Ghana had surprised her; she didn't understand why they had chosen the name of an ancient empire which hadn't even been located anywhere near the modern day country. But then, what did she know? At least it rang better than 'the Gold Coast', which she had always found so unimaginative, and a little patronising, as if the fact that there was gold in their ground was the only thing that mattered about their country.

And on that night, in the middle of the singing and dancing crowd, some intoxicated, others simply euphoric, Gladys had secretly wondered whether anyone else in attendance had any of the scepticisms that were pinching her mind? Did any of them wonder how this bunch of well-educated men would learn how to lead a country overnight? How they would know all the little ins and outs that exist behind the scenes of power? Could it be adequate to learn how to lead in the process of leading? How would they manage to keep the country on track? Sometimes, she barely managed to keep her household in order. Even a life of planning meals, shopping, cooking and cleaning sometimes failed to follow the kind of consistent pattern one might expect. There were always hiccups and mistakes, food burnt, ingredients forgotten. How much more was there to go wrong in running a country? She was glad, even with all the optimism of youth that she still had on her side in those days, that she didn't have to worry about the things that Nkrumah and the rest of the Big Six had to deal with.

'Hope is rejuvenating. It was a marvellous time indeed,' she said, shrugging off her memories to return the present.

It was time for the milk. She poured a little at a time and continued to stir until a sticky caramel formed in the pan. When it was thick, she removed the pan from the heat and used a wet spoon to form balls of caramel, which she rolled into long cylindrical shapes on a board. She placed the hardening toffee on to a plate.

'How many pieces each?' asked Simon.

'Two?' She laughed at their faces. 'Okay then, four. You should keep some for your friends.'

'Mummy doesn't like it if we have too many sweets,' said Abigail.

'Then don't tell her.'

The children sucked and chewed on the toffee.

'Do you like it? I can make it again.' She took Joseph off her back and sat him on her lap. She put a piece of the toffee in his mouth and let him suck on it. His face softened with pleasure as he became accustomed to the rich sweetness, and when she took the toffee away, he started to grizzle.

'All right, all right' she said, putting it back in his mouth.

When Eva saw Gladys feeding Joseph a piece of toffee, she said, 'You have undone in a moment all my hard work with this child. I don't want him to develop a sweet tooth!'

'He has already found it,' said Gladys laughing. 'We Laryeas all have one.'

'I still can't get through . . .'

'What if he doesn't come back,' asked Abi.

'Abi, don't worry,' said Auntie Gee. 'Come, bring your brush and I will do your hair for you. Two braids as you like it, okay? Eva, do you know, I have just remembered that Alfred said he would sleep at his office tonight maybe.' She winked. 'And children, it is nearly time for your dinner-surprise. I brought some nice red plantain and I have told Faustina to make *tatalé*.'

Simon exclaimed, 'Mummy never, ever makes us *tatalé*.'

'They can eat on the veranda for a change. Tell Faustina to light some mosquito coils.'

The sun disappeared and everything was shrouded in sudden darkness. Eva lit a candle and they sat around the table. The *tatalé* made a lovely change from bread and eggs or bread and margarine with Milo. Even Eva had some. Pulped ripe plantain, mixed with a whisked egg, some flour and red pepper, and then fried in palm oil, the plantain cakes were a delicious blend of sweet and spicy.

The children enjoyed the novelty of eating on the veranda with the smell of the mosquito coils and relaxed as Auntie Gee told them how their great-grandfather had been a chief, and had had four wives and thirty-two children.

'Woah!' said Simon.

'We must have thousands of cousins then,' said Abigail.

'Ah, yes, you do,' said Auntie Gee.

And Eva remembered the words her father had said to her when she had taken Alfred to meet them: '*Just like that you have gone and related us to hundreds of Africans . . .*'

She sloped off to try the phone again. She came back out looking uneasy and announced that it was bedtime. The children moaned, but Auntie Gee told them she had plenty more stories to tell them, and many nights in which to do it. 'But come here first, let us pray.' She made them stand in a circle holding hands and began to pray fervently and loudly for the children. She prayed for the protection of the Holy Spirit, and the presence of God Almighty. She rebuked 'demons, devils, abominations and evil premonitions and anything that might wish to unsettle the sleep of these golden angels tonight'.

Eva watched the children's faces as they prayed. Abigail serious and Simon smiling.

Eva and Gladys sat on the veranda in the hushed dark.

'Well done for making them feel safe again.'

'The power of prayer,' said Gladys. 'You should also pray. It will help you. And protect you at the same time.'

'I wonder where he is.'

'He will be okay. Don't worry about him.'

'But who is he with?'

'Oh, not another woman, that is for sure. He isn't a fool!'

'Ha!'

'You are precious to him Eva . . . to me too . . .'

'This isn't the way to go about things though, is it? Why stay out without telling me? He should have told me he was staying out. He had to know I would worry.'

'The phone is not working. I am sure that he forgot the time, that is all. You know what these men are like. But it is a very good sign that you are worried about him, isn't it? It is good for you to see that you care. It will help you to see things clearly for what they are. Okay Eva?'

Eva tutted. Conflicting emotions warred in her. Irritation at being told what to do, anger that Alfred thought it was appropriate to let her worry like this, annoyed that she even cared. And warm appreciation for this odd companionship.

'In addition, it is too late to do anything, and pointless to do any worrying.'

But Eva was worried. The euphoria she had felt dealing with the soldiers had long passed, and now she realised that with a different soldier she might actually be dead. And the house was too empty without Alfred, not right; she felt jumpy now.

'Let's have a drink,' she said. 'What would you like?'

'Do you have something sweet?'

Eva poured some Cinzano Bianco into two tumblers and splashed a little coke over Auntie Gee's. 'Here. Cheers to us.'

'Cheers, my dear!' said Gladys. 'This is what Ignatius and I used to do in the beginning.'

'What was he like?'

'Oh, Eva. He was wonderful. But I was married for too brief a period. In spite of being good wife.' She looked into the distance, mournful almost. 'I was obedient, I didn't stray from my duties or wander off with my dreams. I fulfilled every requirement of a wife, the kind that brings no shame to her husband's name.' She sighed heavily. 'Yet, I know that if I were to sit in front of my dead husband and detail my dutiful behaviour, my devoted sacrifices, he might raise his eyebrows in surprise. That is, assuming he listens properly to what I have to say in the first place. In fact, he might not have any recollection of the many things that are still listed in my mind despite the passing of time.'

Eva chuckled.

Gladys turned to look at her. 'That is how they all are. And there is no medal for being a good wife. I know that sometimes they misuse us. Or forget us, or neglect us. I know that sometimes you may think he does not appreciate you, but Eva, to have the love of a man who is good most of the time, well, that is a blessing indeed, you know? And now, it is time to move forwards Eva. If not, you will fall even lower.'

'Auntie Gee, please.'

'Let me finish. What you need to do is to write a good report about Alfred.'

'Sorry?'

'Write down all the good things about him. So that you stop focusing on the bad thing that he has done, which it has to be said, in our culture is not the worst thing a man can do, but . . . but I understand that in yours you have different standards.'

Eva made a disparaging noise and sipped her drink.

'I know that there are many things that you can include in your list. You must count your blessings. Firstly, he is present.'

'What?'

'Well, he is here. There are many fathers and husbands who are absent, but Alfred is present.'

'Secondly, he is hard working. Thirdly, he is trying his best. Don't forget his example was not good. An absent father with three different wives, even more, and many children all over the place. But Alfred here is trying his best. Fourthly, he has been honest and told you about this child. That is not an easy thing for a proud man to do. He took the risk that you would leave him. Frankly, he would be a shattered man if you go back to your country.'

'I don't know . . .'

'Eva try. Please try your best to forgive him and move on.'

How? Eva wanted to ask. Why? She couldn't figure out the answers herself. She could learn to live with a different reality, with the rage, maybe even deceit. But betrayal? Disappointment? How could she come to terms with that? Where would she ever find the strength to rebuild things after such disillusionment?

'Imagine someone telling you could never return to your home.'

'Oh, that would be easy for me. Here you have flushing toilets and bathtubs so I would not complain.' She laughed. 'But anyway, no one said you cannot go home? You can go for a visit?'

I can't, she wanted to shout out. I can't! She squeezed her eyes tight. 'Auntie Gee, I want to hear *your* story. I am bored of thinking and talking about mine. Tell me about your husband.'

'Yes, Ignatius,' she said in a dreamy voice. 'He was a good man. As is our Alfred . . . anyway, as you know, by the time Ignatius came along and asked for my hand in marriage Alfred was six, and to be honest with you, my family couldn't hold back their delight that someone would want their daughter with their grandson in tow. And when the time came, they requested only a modest gift on my behalf.'

'So, no cows, no gold?'

'No, no! Just some cloths and some gin for my father. But I was so excited. We moved into large rooms in Jamestown, in fact, not far from my family home. You know he was a maths teacher at Accra Academy?'

Eva nodded.

'It was a nice time. I used to sit in the courtyard cooking and sharing stories with the other women in the building. We took it in turns to watch each other's children so we could get on with our work. Shopping, cleaning. Then that man Ignatius bought me a little gas stove so I could cook indoors. He said he was concerned about the bacteria outside. I mean, what kind of nonsense is that? You see, some times education can tamper with a man's common sense. Anyway, I continued to cook outside, but I would turn the stove on and smear a little bit of rice and stew around it so he thought I had been using it.'

'I always knew you were devious!'

'Oh Eva, I am not. But you see, what would have been the point of explaining to a man who has never cooked a proper meal that it is easier to do so on a coal pot? Why prick his puffed-up pride because you don't like his stove? That is not devious. That is wisdom, knowing when to talk and when to be quiet. Anyway, it was most useful to all of us when we needed some hot water quickly to clean a baby's sticky eye, or to wash a wound, or when a sick child needed some soup.' She took a sip of her drink, and sat back with folded arms. 'Every morning, he brought me a cup of tea, with plenty of sugar and milk. He would smile at me and hold my hand. He would say our morning prayer out loud, then he would kiss me on the cheek and set off to work.'

'He clearly was a good man.'

'He was. Like Alfred you know. But then the foolish man had to go and die! So unexpectedly and suddenly too! He came home and ate his dinner as usual. That day I made *kontomire*, you call it *palava* sauce, which was his favourite, with yam and pepper sauce, which coincidentally is also Alfred's favourite. He ate well, licked his fingers, drank some beer and marked a pile of homework with his usual vigour. Then we retired to bed as normal. Oh Eva, for many days afterwards, weeks and years even, I went over those hours looking for a clue, something that I could have done differently that would have kept him alive. You know, he might even still be alive now. I would have someone to cook for every day, someone's clothes to mend. Someone to annoy me, you know how they are . . .' She sniffed. 'But the next morning he lay burning with a fever. His clothes were wet as if I had poured a bucket of water in the bed with him. Nothing whatsoever that I did could lower his temperature. The school doctor came and gave him quinine and paracetamol. Then he died, just like that. Before I had had the chance to appreciate the gravity of his illness or to contemplate that such a young, virile man could die and leave me. Just like that.'

'Auntie Gee, you must have been heartbroken. You've never told me all this, not like this anyway.'

'Ah, it was a long time ago.' She looked into the distance. 'The best days of my life. And anyway, looking back is too costly. All we have is the here and now.'

Age had taught her that not even the minute that is yet to come can be counted upon, how much the following day or year. And to be honest, it frightened her when she heard young people talk of the future and their plans as though they had some guarantee of how things would be, how time would favour them, if at all. It stupefied her that they thought they had all the time in the world to dilly-dally and waste. Her husband too had had big plans for himself, which had been unexpectedly curtailed when he was struck down in his prime.

Before they went up, she said, to Eva, 'Let us also pray before we go to bed.' She began loudly, calling on Jesus to be with them and protect them. 'Let us leave the lights on downstairs. And can you come with me to my room? It is too dark for me.'

Eva laughed, but then realised that she was serious and accompanied Gladys to her room. They switched on lights as they went. On her bedside table, along with the Bible open at Psalm 23: *The Lord is my shepherd*, was a crucifix, which Auntie Gee explained, 'Keeps evil at bay.'

Eva nodded sombrely. In the sallow glow of the electric bulb, she looked weighted down by the memories she had shared. Eva gave her a hug. 'I am just down the corridor if you need me.'

Chapter Nineteen

On Christmas Eve, Yelena made the third of her daily visits to the Akwaaba International Travel Agency. Mr Martey, one of the agents smiled at her when she arrived and then summoned her as soon he had finished with the woman he had been dealing with. 'Are these your children?' he asked looking to either side of Yelena where the boys stood. 'What fine boys.'

'Thank you, yes. What is the news today . . .'

'Today, dear Lady, I have finally got some good news for you as I promised.' He chuckled and then leaned forward and said in a soft voice, 'BA is putting on an additional flight to make up for the missed flights. It is possible they are going to divert the plane from Freetown to pick up some of our backlog passengers. If you follow me this way, we can organise it as you wish. You say that you don't mind the exact departure as long as it is as soon as possible, is that right? Well, then when we have the flight details we will prepare the tickets. One adult, two children, isn't it?'

Yelena followed him into the back office. There she handed over the money and secured a receipt made out on a scrap of lined paper with an indecipherable signature on it.

'Please don't forget that if you don't have a visa, we cannot let you board the plane.'

'That will not be a problem. It is not me that is travelling, it is my friend. She is British.'

'Righty-ho! That is fortunate. I hear the queues at the High Commission are very long indeed. Please can you write the names of the children who are travelling here and their date of birth?'

He looked at the piece of paper on which Yelena had written down the three names. 'Ejura-Wilson . . . any relation of the lawyer Ejura-Wilson?'

Yelena swallowed and thought fast. Blast this tiny city where everyone knew everyone else. She stared straight into his eyes, smiled and lied. 'No, but you know how it's like here, everyone is a little related, no?'

He chuckled and looked at the paper again. 'Ejura-Wilson. I see . . .'

Eva was on the veranda admiring the garden, which was beautiful again. Zachariah had quietly performed magic. He had cut back all the shrubs so it looked as if their defilement was a natural precursor to an intended trim.

She watched him light up another cigarette and felt a desire she hadn't in years.

'Is there any way . . . could I have a cigarette? Please? I will replace it of course . . .'

He held out the box, averted his eyes from hers and said nothing. It was his last cigarette. She hesitated, but he rattled the box to indicate that she should take it. He got the matches out and lit the cigarette. Eva sucked hard, as if her life depended on it. She felt instantly light-headed, amazed how easily she might slip back into the on-off habit she had abandoned when she met Alfred.

'Are you all right?'

He nodded, looking surprised, which upset her. Did she really come across as that uninterested in the lives around her?

'I mean do you need anything? You should stay here if you like, if you don't feel safe out there . . .'

'Thank you, madam,' he said. He nodded and went off to refill the watering can.

She watched him go, as stoic and calm as ever, and wondered whether he heard from his children, whether he longed to see them or hold them, whether he still thought of his wife and the other children. Perhaps not thinking about them, not talking about them, had killed the memory too. Was it always simply a matter of time?

He had told her all he ever would when he was brought for an interview by a friend who worked for someone Eva knew. He was from the Dagomba tribe, from a village near Tamale in the North. He had lost his wife in childbirth and two children to cerebrospinal meningitis. He had dropped off his two living children at a Catholic orphanage on his way to Accra. Then he had walked hundreds of miles to the coast, unable to afford the bus fare. He had felt that the honourable thing to do was to give all his worldly possessions to the orphanage as payment for them taking his children, so he had sold his small herd of cows, which as it happened had been depleted by tsetse-fly disease, and given all the proceeds to the nuns. What after all was he to do with a toddler and the baby that had killed its mother, children no one in the extended family wanted to look after? 'We have beliefs about a child that kills its mother on its way into the world, madam,' he had explained to Eva in a bland voice devoid of mourning. She squinted then widened her eyes in disbelief at various stages of his convoluted, sorrowful account. How could so much misfortune happen to one person, she had wondered dubiously at the time. But he had been thin and gaunt, and older looking than the forty years he claimed to be, and his sickly eyes gaping at her with a surprising honesty, forcing her to examine his pronounced cheekbones and high forehead, wildly patterned with scarification. And that was the most he had ever said to her.

Sometimes, she wished she could listen afresh to their conversation with the admiration she had subsequently come to have for him, drowning out the scepticism she had felt when she first heard what she believed to be yet another sob story. Yet another sympathy-seeking soul who believed that somehow because of the colour of her skin or the size of the wall around the house, she had a magic wand with which to soothe the bumps life had given him.

She finished the cigarette, stubbed it out carefully and looked at the stump. Her head swam, but she had enjoyed it. She pushed her shoulders back, lifted her head up and swivelled her jaws, which ached from all the grinding. Somehow they would all survive, they had to; they would get through this.

She was still lost in her thoughts when the gate bell rang and Auntie Gee rushed out looking excited. 'It must be the priest.'

'A priest? Why do we need a priest today?'

'I told you, because we are not taking any chances.'

He walked into the garden quietly. He was a small man, and slim, with a kind, clean-shaven face. When he smiled, his firm lips parted and Eva saw that several of his front teeth were missing. His hair was neat and his nails were cut. Somehow he didn't fit the image that Eva had of a *juju* man. This man didn't look mad or scary weird or other-worldly, no more so than a hippy, really. There was a young woman trailing behind him who had a muscular face that was drawn in thought, and who looked humourless, and a young boy who remained near the gate where he tethered a goat to one of the casuarina trees.

Auntie Gee greeted the priest with two hands and a sombre nod, and offered him a seat on the veranda. Faustina appeared with a tray with two glasses and a bottle of cold water and poured some into each glass, then she retreated to the corner of the garden near the kitchen from where she and Akua could follow the proceedings.

Auntie Gee spoke urgently in Ga, explaining to the priest what had been going on. In the background the goat bleated mournfully from time to time. The priest listened with patience, in the way that Eva admired of the faultlessly polite Ghanaians, nodding intently, never interjecting, while they waited for their turn to talk. Through it all, he and his companion appeared riveted, emphasising understanding and amazement at various points in the story.

When she had finished, Eva asked, 'So what are you going to do?'

'Yes,' said the man smiling.

'He doesn't speak to you,' said the woman. 'But he will pray now. There are spirits, bad ones, evil ones that have to be asked to leave here.'

'Ayee!' shouted Faustina clutching her head. 'Madam, I told you.'

'Hey! Who is talking to you?' shouted Gladys.

'Anyway, he will pray for you all, for the house, for the garden even, and for Auntie here,' the woman continued, gesturing at Gladys, who nodded with a satisfied look on her face.

'But who is he praying to?'

'To God of course, and to our local gods also, and the spirits of those who have gone already to the other side. All of them can help,' she said stretching the word 'all' for several moments, as if to endow them with additional powers.

'Interesting,' said Eva.

The man said something in Ga and Gladys nodded.

'We can start,' said the woman.

They turned to watch the man. He took a bottle of musty liquid from his assistant, unscrewed it and started to sprinkle it all over the grass and along the path in front of the house. He walked slowly up and down with his bare feet, pausing to grip the ground with each step. His eyes were partly shut and he nodded as he walked, talking to himself in low mumbles. His face became contorted, looking serious then incredulous, his eyebrows knitted in grimaces. After a long while, his features softened once more and he appeared calm again. He opened his eyes and stared straight ahead. He said something to Auntie Gee who was hovering at a safe distance from him and she wrapped her arms around herself.

'They have agreed to leave, but they want some blood first,' said the woman for Eva's benefit.

'What does that mean?'

'A sacrifice,' said Gladys.

'Who wants a sacrifice?'

'The spirits.'

'Right,' said Eva, trying hard not to smile. Auntie Gee stood in her flowing batik dress and headscarf, clutching her waist to steady herself from the disconcerting news. The priest had a calm look of wisdom and revelation, and his interpreter was suitably solemn. In the shadows of the kitchen veranda, Faustina and Akua stood, looking agitated.

'Do whatever you want, but please don't kill any human beings.'

'Oh no madam, not at all, we don't need a human sacrifice, the goat will do,' said the woman.

'Ah, the goat. Well, thank goodness for that,' said Eva. 'Will you be doing this today?'

'Oh, yes, yes. The sooner the better, such an urgent situation should not be left unattended. As a precaution, we brought something suitable. But the cost is extra of course.'

Eva nodded as if she understood. 'But I'd appreciate it if you could get it over and done with before my friends arrive,' she said, walking into the house to get changed. She had managed to speak to Dahlia yesterday, and was pleased to hear her sounding buoyant. Vincent's absence was incredibly well-timed. The four of them were gathering to try and finalise their plans; she crossed her fingers.

When she was ready, Eva got the remainder of her savings. She looked at the envelope. She had been hoping, dreaming, that one day, she would be able to go home. But realistically she knew that she never would. She bit her lip. Dahlia needed this so much more than Eva needed her hope. She had tried to not think about Dahlia being gone, only about her going, but she realised now how much she would miss her. Her legs were less steady as she went downstairs and hid the money high on a shelf for later.

On her way into the kitchen she saw the goat lying dead in the middle of the lawn and hurried outside. 'Good God! My grass!' Its throat had been cut and its long tongue hung loose from between its bared teeth. Blood had drained out of it on to the grass and soft innards peeped out of the deep wound. It must have defecated as it died because there was a fresh pile of droppings at its other end. Flies were beginning to hover over the warming blood, and there was the undeniable stench of goat meat.

Auntie Gee appeared oblivious to everyone but the priest to whom she was whispering over and over, 'Thank you.'

He too was quite unperturbed, beaming and looking happy with himself. He was talking to Auntie Gee softly, ignoring Eva, mumbling gently, almost as though he was commenting on how fine the grass looked, in fact. The young boy was bundling the goat in a large sheet of plastic, which he bound with string. He had called for a taxi, which had pulled into the driveway, and together with the driver, he carried the goat and put it into the boot of the car.

'Well, I have to say it looks as if all in all things went quite smoothly. No headless chickens, no painted naked men,' Eva said. 'Nevertheless, thank goodness it's over. Faustina, over to you now,' she said, pointing to the grass and the drops of blood that lead from the place of death all the way to where the car had stood.

'Madam, don't worry, I will do it right now. Akua, bring some water and clean the grass.' She too glowed. 'Today is a good day, you will see, today is a good, good day. Now we can sleep in peace again.'

'Eva. Good news! The spirits have been evacuated,' said Auntie Gee.

'Great! And I am having coffee here on this stretch of lawn with my friends in half an hour!'

'Or even madam, you can have tea in the living room with your friends . . .' said Faustina.

'Praise God,' said Auntie Gee, stumbling into the house looking delirious.

Eva shook her head to dispel the familiar turbulence that she felt far too often around her incongruous mother-in-law.

Yelena arrived at Wisdom's house in a smart baby pink polyester dress and white high-heeled slip on shoes, so that her children could wish their father a Happy Christmas. The twins were in smart collared shirts with their hair brushed smooth. Joel carried a bottle of whisky which Yelena had wrapped and Jonas a card, in which she had had to encourage them to write more than their names.

In the boot of her car was her sleepover bag, and somehow knowing that she would not be going home alone for a quiet Christmas put a lilt in her step.

After the usual stiff greetings, after Wisdom had asked the children the same questions, which they answered in the same polite way that made her proud, she uncrossed her legs and crossed them again. She leaned forward towards Wisdom and said, 'I am going to see your family next week to tell them that I want the boys to have a proper outdooring . . .'

'What are you talking about? Outdooring for who? They are grown now.'

'I know. But better late than never, yes?' She smiled. 'I want them to be accepted by your family, to feel part of the Tekyi family . . . I have already visited your mother.'

'My mother?'

'The twins' grandmother, yes. She told me she is very fortunate to have the boys.'

'But outdoorings are performed for babies, usually at eight days . . .'

'As I said, better late than never, don't you think? Or do you not think they are worth it?' She smiled at him alluringly.

The Wife walked in just then, followed by her maid who carried a tray with some drinks on it, and Yelena sat back surprised. Well, this is a first, she thought.

'As it is Christmas,' said the Wife, 'a little refreshments?' She pointed to a bowl of *achomo*, which the maid had put on the table in front of the boys. Then she sat down next to Wisdom while the maid opened a bottle of Sprite for each of the boys.

'So, I was just telling Wisdom that I visited his mother to discuss plans to have the boys outdoored. I will let you know in plenty of time where and when it will be, but it will be soon after the New Year, I hope.'

The Wife looked at Wisdom as if there was something that she expected him to say. Speechless, he shook his head.

'And, although at first I didn't care if you took part or not,' Yelena continued, looking at Wisdom, 'I am afraid that I am going to insist that you do your duty for them. I would like you to stand up and be their father, in public, in front of all your family and mine . . .'

'Your family is coming all the way here?' asked Wisdom, surprised.

'Isn't he already doing his duty?' said the Wife.

'Oh, not really,' said Yelena smiling. 'His mother agrees, in fact.'

'My mother?'

'Yes . . .'

'And you say that your family is here?'

'I have my own family here.'

He looked confounded.

Yes, thought Yelena, family does matter. Wouldn't he treat us all with more respect if my family was closer?

'Well, I don't really see the point. They have my name, they know that I am their father . . . these things are costly . . .'

'Is it his money that you want, because . . .'

'I don't want your money,' said Yelena. She felt her bosom heave. Not much further to go, she thought. She would go the whole way. She swallowed and then said the thing she had always thought she would never mention. 'You remember when I gave you all my savings in Kiev to bring to Ghana.'

The Wife turned to Wisdom sharply.

'You were going to use that money to help us get started here.' Yelena paused and looked around the house, knowing that some of her money had gone into this. 'I know it wasn't much, but it was all I had, Wisdom. So this, this you will do for me, for your sons . . . you will acknowledge them in the correct way. On this I will not take no for an answer. I know that deep down you are a good man, you can do this. It is for the twins; for Joel and Jonas, the boys that *you* named even before they were born.' She looked at the boys who were gazing at her. 'Yes, your father picked your lovely names, have I never told you?' Of course she never had. It hadn't come up, it had been too distasteful a memory; the afternoon they had lain side by side and he had rubbed her bare, distended belly in ever decreasing circles and pronounced his preferred boy names: *Jonas and Joel Tekyi*. She had smiled, delirious in that moment, unaware of the need to think beyond their happiness.

She stood up, took a boy by each hand, and walked out to the lovely sound of the Wife berating Wisdom for allowing that white woman to come in here and embarrass her like that.

'My husband a debtor? And to a woman too? What shame have you brought on me . . .!'

*

300

Dahlia looked lovely, her hair had clearly been just blow-dried, and her skin glowed, more than it usually did, with perfect make-up. The children stood beside her smiling demurely, and looking smarter than Eva's children ever did, faces powdered, hair neat, clothes unrumpled. No wonder we never suspected a thing, thought Eva, as she took in the perfect picture. How much you can hide behind this well-pressed presentation, she mused, as she glanced at the scarf that Dahlia still wore around her neck, tucked inside the collar of her white shirt. Yes, it was all too pristine.

Dahlia handed Eva a tray of cassava cake and warm peanut biscuits. 'I have to keep busy,' she said when Eva told her off for making so much effort.

When the children were out of earshot, Dahlia pulled out a carrier bag of clothes and handed it to Eva. Her face had changed in an instant and she looked less sure. 'I took what I could, what I thought no one would notice, bits and bobs, underwear and the like. I'm going to try and smuggle some more things out, I can't risk taking a suitcase.' She looked around furtively to make sure no one had seen her hand over the bag.

'Of course, I'll give you one of ours.' She stroked Dahlia's arm.

'I went to the tailor this morning to order some trousers and jackets for the kids; it will be cold in London. I have had to come up with the oddest excuses for wanting to measure them,' she said forcing a giggle. 'I just hope that I gave him the right measurements.'

Eva smiled. 'I haven't heard from Yelena, have you?'

'Dahlia shook her head. Not since yesterday. She was hoping she'd get the tickets today . . .'

'Let's keep our fingers crossed.'

'They are. Painfully so,' said Dahlia.

'Ah, here comes Margrit. I'll leave you to tell her about you and Vincent . . .?'

In the kitchen Eva paused for a moment and stared at the

beautiful platter of cake and biscuits, carefully covered with a pretty, embroidered napkin.

She shook her head angrily. And again it occurred to her, what if this was what Alfred's betrayal had taught her, to be really, truly compassionate, to be able to share a friend's pain, to simply listen, to hear. Without the need to give advice, or offer to make it better, to judge or correct. Could she be a better person for it?

She knew then that she couldn't go on like this. She didn't want to revisit her request for him to move out, but she had become comfortable holding off the decision-making, action-taking that talking about things would require. Remarkably, and wonderfully, in fact, Auntie Gee's presence had made everything more bearable; she had birthed life into the deadness that Eva had felt all around her from the moment Alfred confessed; made comfortable a space that she would otherwise have found suffocating.

At the door, she paused to watch Margrit cradle Dahlia's face. She was telling her something and Dahlia was nodding silently, taking in whatever it was, hopefully locking it deep, storing it for when she needed the strength of Margrit's usual wisdom. How many more times would Dahlia have to recount the reality of her life, how many more times would she see her hurt and shame reflected on the face of her listener? How long before the words were emptied of the power to evoke excruciating memories? She brushed her hair off her face and headed out.

'Margrit had to put her dog down,' said Dahlia stroking Margrit's arm.

'Isn't it just terrible? How are you feeling, my love?' asked Eva.

Margrit shook her head. 'I miss her so very terribly, she followed me wherever I went like a shadow, and she loved me more than anyone else. Eight years I had her.'

Eva poured tea and handed a cup to Margrit.

'Kojo gave her something in the end, we buried her in the garden. Now he has been ill ever since, fatigue I think . . .'

'You know they believe here that your pet can take your place

302

in death. We had a dog that suddenly became ill and then died when Vincent was very ill once, and our maid told me that it had had to die to take his place, strange isn't it?'

'Life here *is* strange. And what is this I hear about these dreadful soldiers coming here? You must have been terrified, what happened?' asked Margrit.

Eva described that morning once more. The men, their guns, the truck. How Auntie Gee had pleaded with her, with them. Their rank body odour, their dirty outfits. The hatred in their glare, as if she was to blame for the state of their country. The spitting, the antagonism. The urine on her lawn. The senseless destruction. She was beginning to feel the same anger rise up in her when Yelena arrived, smiling triumphantly.

She held up a bag of bread buns. 'Fresh from the oven. Well, they were fresh this morning!'

'How fabulous. You can't imagine how pleased we are to see you!'

'And . . .?' asked Margrit, eyes widened in anticipation.

'Boys, off you go and find the others and play till you drop.' She pulled a bottle of vodka out of her bag, lifted it into the air and said, 'Let's drink. We have the tickets!'

Eva jumped up and grabbed Yelena. 'Hooray! I'll get the glasses.' She ran inside past the children who were shocked to see so much joyous energy.

Dahlia beamed. A smile so wide and deep. Joy bubbled to life within her alongside fear, so much fear and immense unknown. How does elation feel, she wondered. Would she remember when it came? Would it come again?

'Here's to us. To surviving.' Eva took a long sip of her vodka and then handed the money over to Yelena. 'For the tickets. You keep your money Dahlia, something else might come up.' They looked at her, amazed, and she shrugged. 'I have been hoarding my housekeeping money for a while now . . .'

'But what were you going to use it for?'

'That doesn't matter. I want you to have it.'

'I'll repay you somehow,' said Dahlia.

'Don't think about that now.'

'Yelena just told me about Alfred,' said Dahlia. 'I'm so sorry, Eva.'

'Yes well, disappointing isn't it. I hate him for letting me down. I thought he was better than this . . . sorry Dahlia, I didn't mean it like that.'

'Don't worry. I thought the same thing once about my husband. It would be abnormal if you didn't feel that way. You question your choice, don't you? If I made such an error of judgement, what does that say about me? How stupid am I because I chose a cheating, lying bastard . . . right?'

'Oh, Dahlia, I am so sorry.'

'I've lived with those questions daily. A friend said to me once long ago, "you have to accept that you just picked a bad one".'

'No way!' said Yelena.

'Yes. She meant well I am sure, she thought she was being supportive, but how the words cut me like a knife. The truth is you can never fully understand a relationship from the outside. This is about you and Alfred, your past and your future, and in any event, things are never very black and white.'

'Yes . . .' Eva thought how in fact, when you are the midst of it all, everything looks rather grey, seems rather fluid and unclear.

'I know everyone wonders why I put up with him all these years, but I had to hang on to the fact that I did choose him. I am not ready to say that I made a complete mistake, I might never be . . . and deep in there somewhere is the man that I fell in love with and chose to have children with.'

'I can't imagine how you went home to him time and again,' said Margrit, still coming to terms with what she had heard.

'It's horrifying that you didn't think you could tell us.'

'The less I said, the less I believed it was true. It was as though there were two of me . . . I feel strong now because you know. I suppose I should have told you a long time ago.'

'But you couldn't. How could you?' said Yelena.

'Ach, when do you start to share something like that,' said Margrit.

'But now it's time to look ahead.'

'Are you sure you want to be alone tomorrow? It is Christmas after all,' said Eva.

'Yes . . . I know the children would like to come here, but I need the time to get myself completely ready. I don't know whether I'll have another opportunity, Vincent never tells me when he's coming back, but he doesn't travel on Christmas Day. I need to take advantage of the peace and quiet, to go through my things and make sure I take what really matters to me. And I need go through photographs, which I'm dreading most of all.'

'I'll come and help you with that,' said Margrit. 'That's not a job to do alone.'

'Please let's just all stay vigilant for the last few days,' said Yelena in a grave voice.

They all looked a little perplexed at her.

'Well, I just think we shouldn't lose focus. We can't afford to make any mistakes. Vincent mustn't find out,' she said. She had wanted to tell Dahlia about the man at Akwaaba International Travel Agency, but somehow she couldn't. Maybe she would tell Margrit later, but for now, she just couldn't bring herself to. 'This cake is delicious,' she said instead.

The banana cake Eva had made had risen magnificently and was golden brown, gooey and still warm, and rather delicious. She had put extra sugar and quite a bit of cinnamon and nutmeg in it to disguise the taste and smell of weevils in the flour.

'The best thing about baking here is that you never know how it is going to turn out. I never seem to have the same ingredients twice. One day there is no sugar, or no eggs or no milk. It is actually quite wonderful to be able to surprise yourself as you go along,' Eva said, and her friends agreed.

Then they chatted about what it would be like for Dahlia, arriving in London after all these years, how she would feel, what the children would think.

'What do you think the children will miss the most?' asked Margrit.

'The weather,' Eva thought.

'The food,' said Margrit.

'No, their friends, surely,' said Yelena.

'And their father, of course,' said Dahlia.

'Oh, but you mustn't think about that,' said Yelena.

'I'm going to miss you so much,' said Eva.

'I'm going to miss you all too, you have given me so much more strength than you could possibly imagine. And now . . . now I can actually dare to hope again, to dream again. And don't you worry, I'm taking memories, memories of the good times we've shared,' said Dahlia.

Then, as if they had been released from something, they laughed. And as they did the memories came flooding in. And how many there were. They marvelled at the things they had achieved, the things their children had done, victories over the extended family, the climate, the alien lifestyle. They reflected on the hours spent together in shady gardens, by the sea, the annual barbeque at the American Women's Association, the sponsored walks organised by the British Women's Association, the time they had tried aerobics classes and given up one by one because it seemed too much effort. Really, each of them could look back and see just how very far they had come, how much they had conquered, how proud they could be.

Christmas Day dawned hot and dry. Everyone woke tired and sticky from a sweaty night of fitful sleep. The power hadn't come back on until early this morning and the bedrooms had been almost unbearably hot without the air-conditioners. The fridge was struggling to regain its coolness. The lettuce and spring onions in the bottom drawer had wilted, the bottled water had dripped condensation wetting everything below.

Alfred had taken over in the kitchen and the house smelled of cooking bacon.

He had been furious when he returned home the day before and heard about the soldiers. And although Eva had thought it best to downplay the retelling, Gladys had gone into gory detail, stressing in particular, it seemed to her, the part about Eva's initial refusal to comply and hand over a bribe.

Eva had shrugged, suddenly brave again because he was home.

'Are you mad?' he had said. 'A few flowers can grow back tomorrow.' He clasped his hands. 'I don't know what I would do if anything happened to you or the children.'

'You weren't exactly here to protect us, were you . . .' she had said, aware how much that would hurt him. 'Anyway, I don't think they had any intention of hurting us. The only way to deal with a bully is to stand up to him.'

'Please think! These men are not rational. What if they come back? This should be a lesson to us all to keep that blasted gate locked. Solomon should tell anyone we don't know that we are not in.'

'Do you really think that Solomon or one little padlock will keep out a band of armed soldiers? Besides, I don't think they'll come back.'

'But why us? Why did they come here? I want to know whether you have offended someone important.' Auntie Gee asked. 'Such things are not simple coincidences, you know?'

Alfred knew. 'I suppose we stick out here. People get jealous.'

'Indeed you are a beacon of the good life. You know, jealousy leads to murder Eva.'

'Oh for goodness' sake, there is no need to overreact! If they want to come in, they will, I refuse to live like . . .'

307

'Enough Eva!' Auntie Gee had shouted, clapping her hands loudly to end the conversation. 'As for this one, you will listen to your husband. We cannot allow this unfortunate incident to take us backwards when we are starting to move forwards, albeit at a snail's pace.'

And this morning, everyone seemed ready to make breakfast a jubilant event. The children were boisterous and tucked in happily to the feast that Alfred had prepared; bacon, eggs and pancakes too, which they spread with pineapple jam and ate rolled up. The adults chattered and laughed loudly, comfortable in the carefree mood that seemed to have settled around them.

Faustina proudly paraded between the kitchen and the dining room bringing in more pancakes, more bacon, more tea and hot Milo while the family ate.

'Faustina, one more egg please,' Gladys said when Faustina came with the third batch of bacon. 'I have not eaten such nice eggs for a long, long time.'

'I have been thinking, maybe we should buy a rooster or two?' said Eva when Alfred joined them.

'Don't even think about it, Eva. I don't want any livestock. They will pick at all the grass and cover the place with chicken shit . . . sorry, chicken poo.' The children sniggered and he winked at them.

'Eva what a good idea! Fresh eggs daily from your own back-yard. But you need to get maybe a half dozen or so.' She grinned at Eva and licked some egg yolk that had dripped on to her fingers.

'I thought twelve?' said Eva. 'Maybe two dozen even, go the whole way?' She looked at Alfred and burst out laughing.

'Very funny,' he said.

Everyone joined Eva laughing at him, but Eva noticed the question in Abigail's eyes. Was this laughter here to stay, or would it disappear suddenly and be replaced by that other mood, the odd silence, the angry crying, the broken cups? Eva winked at her and was pleased to see her expression lighten up, her smile widen.

By late afternoon, when they had opened their presents and the children were happily admiring their new things, puzzles and some colouring pencils for the boys and books and a diary with a 3-D hologram on the front for Abigail, Eva and Yelena were feeling quite fuzzy and peaceful from sipping wine all day.

Auntie Gee came out with Alfred, Eva noticed that she was half-pushing half-pulling him and speaking in Ga. 'We are joining you,' she said, sitting in the chair nearest to Yelena so that Alfred had to sit close to Eva.

They chatted merrily for a while about this and that, homework and school reports, and reminisced about their own education. Then they talked about food supplies, the drought and the coup – how Afriye seemed to be in charge of his troops and how Accra had become soldier-ridden almost overnight. How they tooted their camouflaged trucks as they paraded on their way, heralding their arrival wherever they went to do whatever it was they did. And how what they did was retold in ripe, elaborate rumours, while the truth remained scarce and unverifiable.

'Why these hooligans think they can come and rule over us because they are carrying guns, with no respect for the rule of law makes my blood boil,' said Alfred.

'But who will stand up to them? I wouldn't want to die for my country, do you? It is not worth it. I don't understand those who say they will,' said Yelena.

'It doesn't help that facts are embellished, and rumours inflated, making everyone more disconcerted than they already are. And they play on our fear of God, of Satan, fear of our dead ancestors, and so on.'

'A good amount of fear is important,' said Auntie Gee.

'But everyone is too afraid, you are right, Alfred,' said Yelena. 'What was the point of asking the British to leave I wonder?'

said Auntie Gee. 'When they were here, I could buy Lipton tea whenever I wanted. Now look at us, we are like the walking wounded, stumbling around trying to feel our way in the dark.'

'Well, their time was up,' said Alfred.

'We have been on a steady decline since they went, have we not?'

'It doesn't help that these idiots seem determined to unravel things even more. Freedom of speech sits at the nucleus of the civilised world. How dare they tell us what we can and cannot listen to or watch?' Alfred said. Broadcasting had been heavily censored in order to 'protect the innocents of our dear country from all that Western filth,' as Afriye had recently announced in his address to the nation.

'They have a point, to a point,' said Auntie Gee. 'Some of those films are full of licentious behaviour, foul language, drinking, blasphemy. Even that James Bond is not ideally watchable by a good Christian.'

The phone rang loudly and Alfred went to answer it. He popped his head around the door and said 'For you love. It's Dahlia.' As he handed the phone to her, he whispered in her ear brushing her with his lips, 'She sounds awful.' Eva couldn't resist closing her eyes and inhaling the comforting smell of him. 'Happy Christmas, Dahlia darling,' Yelena hollered from the veranda.

'*Happy Christmas to you, Happy Christmas to you . . .*' Eva sang into the phone. From the veranda Auntie Gee and Yelena continued singing. When Alfred was out of earshot, she asked whether everything was okay.

'Yes, I just wanted to say thank you again. We've had the most lovely day here, me and the kids.'

Despite herself, Eva had started to fret. 'Thank heavens. Listen, if you change your mind you just come on over, right? We're always here for you.'

When she put the phone down, she stared for a moment into space. How brave she was, beautiful Dahlia. She hugged herself

310

and stood silently awhile, then she realised that Alfred was standing next to her, stroking her arm.

'What is it?'

'Nothing. I'm just feeling a little sentimental. It's the wine . . .' She turned to him and let him put his arms around her. He held her tight and pushed his face into her hair, remembering the scent of her.

'God, how I've missed you Evie.'

She pulled back suddenly aware of the embrace, so comfortable she'd paid no attention to it. 'I'm not ready for this, Alfred . . .'

'Please Evie, can't we just try?'

She looked away. She couldn't rush past her reservations into this.

'Say soon?'

I hope so, she thought. She wanted to, but there was something she had to do first, something that might help to clear her mind and answer her nagging thoughts, that might help to save them.

Chapter Twenty

'You are going to take me to see her.'

'Who?'

'You know exactly who. I'll get my keys.'

'But Eva, this is not a good idea, why do you want to go there? I can't take you there.'

'Yes, you will!'

Auntie Gee was dumbfounded. 'But Eva . . .?'

'I haven't asked you for anything since you have been here. You want to help me? Us? Well, then take me to see her now.'

Auntie Gee shook her head as though that might help her to make sense of the situation.

'Please?' asked Eva firmly.

They didn't talk on the way there. In the silence Eva studiously avoided thinking about what she would say, how she would feel.

Every once in a while, Eva glanced across at Gladys, but she sat with her hands clasped on her lap and her face pointing forwards, watching the road. They drove along the coast towards Tema, between Labadi on the left and the sea on their right. Past fishing boats resting on the sand, fishermen mending their nets underneath old coconut trees bent by the wind. Eva rolled her window down and let in gusts of salty air.

When Gladys told her to take a left turn, Eva felt her arms tense. She gripped the wheel harder and looked at the scenery. She didn't particularly want to remember where she was going.

They turned on to a small, quiet road. At the junction, a woman sold fat loaves of white, doughy bread, covered with a net curtain. Children played around her, pedestrians strolled past, men sat in the shade of a large tree eating mangoes. They could be anywhere in the middle of Accra. Didn't it almost always look the same anyway?

The house was surrounded by a low wall that had been painted the colour of honey a long time ago. Gladys pushed open the brown metal gate. Eva followed, wishing she hadn't come. Inside, the yard was neat. An old woman sat in the shade of the house while a young girl braided her hair. Here and there, a few chickens scratched about.

Eva saw a flicker of recognition cross the woman's face. The girl stopped what she was doing and stared with a mixture of amazement and something closer to awe.

There was a brief exchange in Ga between Gladys and the woman and Gladys gestured towards the house. 'I will wait for you here.' She reached for Eva's arm and said in a soft voice, 'Her name is Agnes.'

Eva lifted her chin up and swallowed her nerves. She knocked on the mosquito-screened door to what looked like the kitchen. It was dark but tidy. There was an aroma of something sour cooking. Beans. She saw the large, steaming pot on the stove.

A slim girl walked towards the door. She slouched her bare feet on the cement floor.

'Agnes?'

'Yes?'

'I am Mrs Laryea.' She pushed her sunglasses on to her head. 'Alfred's wife.'

The girl stopped, her hand dropped from the screen. She gaped slightly, but her expression remained the same, defiant and almost irritated.

In the moments that passed, Eva took in her features through the mesh, saving them for later when she might know what to do with them. Pretty. Young. Possibly not very educated. Not wealthy. How the hell had they met? She swallowed again.

'What do you want?'

'I don't want anything from you. I came to tell you that Alfred . . . my husband Alfred is not going to leave me, and I am not going anywhere. He is my husband.'

Nothing. Between them the air was still. The pot bubbled on the stove. Eva continued to stare at the woman. Through the protection of the mosquito screen, she searched her face for information to brood upon later.

'I am not going back to the UK. I am staying here. My children are Ghanaians. They too are staying here. We are a family. Do you understand me?'

Possibly in spite of herself, the girl nodded.

'Good. We are a family. I am sure you are nice person, but he made a mistake. Now leave him alone . . .'

Eva looked beyond the girl in the direction of a noise she recognised and loved; the wet gurgling, incoherent chatter of a toddler with much to say. Her heart lurched. She adjusted her sunglasses back onto her nose and watched the baby totter in with the strong, eager steps of a new walker, grinning victoriously with self-satisfaction. He was naked but for a terry nappy. His chubby arms stretched out towards his mother as he stumbled forwards. Eva's breath caught in her throat and formed a constricting bubble. Her mouth dropped open slightly, but she regained her composure quickly and tried to hide the fact that she felt utterly winded. Before her was a live copy of the aged black and white baby photograph of Alfred that Auntie Gee carried in her purse, presenting it proudly whenever she could, a darker version of what Simon had looked like as a baby.

The woman turned towards her child and Eva swivelled and marched towards the gate. She heard Auntie Gee puffing to keep up with her. She got in the car, which was steaming, gripped the wheel and pulled, lowering her head on to it. Gladys rapped at the window and Eva reached over to open the passenger door.

'Eva . . .' she said as she manoeuvred her weight into the seat.

'If I ever get even a whiff of something like this . . . a whiff of indiscretion, I will leave.'

'Yes.'

'He'd better understand that.'

'Yes.'

'And if that woman or that child ever crosses my threshold, comes even close to my house . . .' She looked at Auntie Gee with nearly closed eyes. 'If there is even a rumour of a rumour . . .'

'Yes, yes, I understand. You will go home.'

'I won't go through this again.'

'No. Of course not.'

She rolled down the window, started the engine, and put on the radio.

'Well done,' whispered Auntie Gee. 'In fact, I am most proud of you Eva.'

At home, Eva had a long shower. She used up both of the buckets that Faustina had carried up yesterday, which had cooled overnight. Her tired eyes felt soothed and her face less taut. She put on her favourite dress, a white linen A-line one with silver buttons down the front.

Downstairs, she poured a lot of brandy into a glass and topped it with a dash of Coke. She handed Auntie Gee a glass of Coke.

'I want you to make sure that he looks after the child.'

Auntie Gee spluttered her drink all over her dress.

'He must have an education too. Opportunities. It isn't his fault. You must see to it that that happens. But Alfred mustn't have any contact with them. I don't want the child coming and going. I will have to figure out what to tell my children in due course.'

Gladys nodded in awe. 'I didn't know you could be so wise. You have indeed excelled today and done a good thing. Oh, well done Eva!'

Eva laughed hollowly. But she felt unimaginably lighter. Everything seemed clearer already. Is that all it takes, she thought in wonderment. One decision? One teeny step in the right direction?

'Do you know, at first I was concerned when I heard that Alfred has married a white woman. All sorts of things bothered me. How you would find our ways, whether you would respect me even, whether you would go and take my grandchildren away . . .'

'Of course I respect you Auntie Gee. I don't always understand you though.'

'Anyway, I have to say, you have turned out to be okay.'

'And I am glad you think that.'

'There is only one thing that I still long for.'

Eva raised her eyebrows.

'I just want to pierce Abi's ears. You know that usually we do it at birth. Now she is growing up. We should do it quickly, before she is a woman.'

'I want her to be able to choose for herself.'

'Yes, but it is our culture, hers too.' Auntie Gee looked mournful. 'It is a shame for a girl. Maybe another time then, okay?'

'Oh, all right . . . since it means so much to you. Maybe you're right.'

'O amazing-grace-Eva! Wonderful! I will do it today, even. Hallelujah!'

Chapter Twenty-One

It was overcast. The blanket of high cloud seemed to have stilled the air. The sun was intense and glaring. Another sweltering, dry day.

'I just want to find one in which I know I was content,' Dahlia said. She and Margrit sat in her living room leafing through photographs in an old Gem biscuit box. Her hands shaking so the photos fluttered.

She was smiling in nearly every photograph. Her lips drawn wide, her eyes appearing to twinkle. In some she clutched a fat baby or had a child on her hip, and in others they were on her lap or clinging to her knee. There were snapshots of birthday parties, anniversaries, Christmases. There were big, fluffy white cakes, lots of children in frilly, lacy dresses, bow ties and long socks with buckled, shiny shoes. In some, Vincent smiled too, standing next to her, behind her, or with his arm around her. In others they were on their way to celebratory gatherings, weddings or christenings, in which Dahlia wore large stylish hats, her make-up immaculate, her smile prominent, her shoulders up and back. Her waist was tiny and firm in her fitted dresses, her shoes and bags matching. And always, the children, mini versions of their parents, dressed to perfection, in shorts with braces, ties and bow ties, dresses with fancy detailing, frills and ribbons, bouffant hair pulled and clipped to match; each image the flawless depiction of a happy family.

'They are all painful. I can only remember the wretchedness; the nasty comments or the wicked things he did . . . but it can't be that there aren't any lovely ones . . . it's not possible . . .' Her face was streaked, she sniffed hard again. Desperately, she lifted whole clumps of photos out of the box, taking less care than normal not to smudge them, not to bend them.

'Dahlia . . .' Margrit gripped her hand. 'It only seems that way now. Take a few, put them away and later, in a while to come, you'll think differently about them.'

'This was my life,' she said. 'This is what it amounts to. A pile of sad memories recorded for eternity, lest I dare to forget. How is that possible? I didn't realise it at the time . . . there must have been some good times. There must have . . . I was ecstatic to have my babies, to have this home, wasn't I? But look at them! Look at my eyes . . . why didn't I get out earlier?'

'Hindsight, Dahlia. It is never that simple.'

'Why did I let him rob me of all this time?' She threw the pictures into the box, sniffed and stood. 'Why did I put up with it? What for?' She had raised her voice, snot ran down on to her lip and she wiped her face with the back of her hand.

'What about the first pictures? In the very beginning? Surely there are some good memories?'

'I have gone all the way back to the start. I can see what my parents are thinking when I look at the wedding picture. I can see the disquiet in my mother's eyes. I can see that I am smiling too hard, that Vincent is . . . look,' she thrust the photograph at Margrit.

'Dahlia . . .'

'Anyone could see that he is a monster. Why didn't they tell me?'

'How would you have heard them? And besides, he changed . . . you can't blame yourself for how things turned out.'

'I don't want any of these.' Dahlia shoved the box away, her face marred with painful memories, lost hopes and dreams. The photographs had managed with painful incredible accuracy to document the tragedy that was her marriage.

'At least take some of the children. One day you will be glad you did.'

'I loved him . . .'

'Yes, I know.' Margrit put her arms around her friend. 'Believe me. One day, this too shall pass. Everything passes, nothing lasts forever. You have many happy years before you. It's up to you now . . . it won't be like this always. Now you will have the chance to make completely new memories with the children, joyous ones. There will be plenty of time for new photographs, things you want to remember. Believe me.'

'I loved this country, I wanted so much to make it my home.'

'Ah yes, I know, but you haven't got a choice my darling, not at the moment anyway.'

Dahlia was pacing about the room distracted, like a person overwhelmed by a museum collection. She stopped in front of some framed photographs, stroked the frame of their wedding photograph.

'What about other mementoes? You should take a few things. You are not coming back into this house . . .'

Dahlia picked up an ornate clock. 'A wedding present from my parents. They'd want me to have it, but he'll notice.' She shook her head. 'I can't wait to be on the plane, to just go.' She wanted to know how she felt, to really feel what she ought to feel, but she didn't dare. Not yet.

She turned and looked about the room as a whole, the furniture, the rugs on the floor, the curtains. She tried not to see the individual touches, her hand in the picture, the colourful paintings she had hung, the statue of a girl carved in ebony that she had

319

bought in her first year here, the cushion covers she had made, the embroidered seat-backs she had crocheted. She tried to bank the scent of her home. That was as much as she could take. Her heart tugged and tore, while Margrit rubbed her back and whispered vaguely comforting sounds.

Dahlia locked the study door behind them just in case. She had found the spare key in Vincent's bedside cabinet. In the room, she held on to the doorknob for longer than necessary unable to go any further. She could feel a fist clench her lungs and she tried hard to drown the sounds, but she could hear their voices, the words as clear as when they had uttered them. His mocking, theirs frightened, her pleas.

Her skin tingled with sweat. She heard Margrit murmur encouragement and she opened her eyes a little. Quite instinctively, they were drawn to the spot on the carpet where she had lain. She looked away, made herself focus. She tried to forget the shame and to feel only the resentment and fury that had come later.

She looked around. The curtains were drawn and the room was murky and warm. On the desk, the piles of paper seemed to have grown. The shelves were disorganised. In the corner of the room, next to an armchair on which a rumpled suit lay, there were several boxes of tinned and jarred food.

'How does he find anything in here?' whispered Margrit.

'I used to tidy it up for him myself, but now he doesn't let me.'

'You start on the shelves, I will look on the desk.'

'We need to do this together. Even though it looks a mess, he knows when anything has been moved. We have to make sure that we leave everything exactly as we find it.'

They searched painstakingly. Dahlia lifted one thing, Margrit looked beneath, and together they made sure they replaced the items in the same spot, at the same angle. It was exhausting, stifling. They hadn't dared put the air-conditioner on or open the windows in case any of the servants realised they were in there.

'I think I might faint,' said Margrit, dripping with sweat.

'Do you want to sit a while, have a rest?'

'No, we have to get this done. Let's keep going. This room makes me claustrophobic though, it gives me the creeps.' She blew air up her face, wiped her forehead with the hem of her dress and opened the bottom drawer. There was the usual pile of papers in disarray. She lifted them up and something heavy clunked on to the base of the drawer. Both women drew a sharp breath as they stared at the shiny pistol.

'I knew he would get one! What does he need a gun for?'

'Okay, let's stay calm.'

'I don't want a gun in my house, I told him, begged him . . .'

'Does he even know how to use one? He wouldn't ever use it, though, would he?'

'What, to kill me?' Dahlia let out a shrill peal of laughter. 'No, he'd use his bare hands . . .'

'Has he ever threatened?' asked Margrit in a whisper, trying to dislodge the image of the mangled car, the broken body of Vincent's former associate, an image she had never seen, a story she had never believed, but which now seemed all too real.

Dahlia looked at Margrit's frowning face and sobered up. 'No, no, he's never threatened to kill me, he wouldn't . . .' She shook her head. Had he? She squinted, trying to remember some of the things he had done over the years, some of the things he had said, implied. Would he have to say the words before she found out all he was capable of? She shook her head, feeling more timid. And what would Margrit do about it anyway? Who understands such menace even if it does come from the mouth of a man wielding a deadly weapon? Which mad wife would believe her husband capable of killing her unprovoked? Believe murderous threats from a respected lawyer in a suit? From her own husband, the father of her children for God's sake?

'Soon this will not be your home any more, maybe just as well . . .' Margrit replaced the papers, realised that her hands were shaking. Her skin had cooled unexpectedly. 'It's probably been lying here for ages. We mustn't let it distract us . . .' She tried to keep her voice steady, her nerves intact, but she felt unbalanced. Why was Dahlia so sure that he wouldn't harm her irreparably? Did a battered wife ever believe she was in peril? Isn't that why so often they stayed *till death they did part*? She felt disturbed, had a sense of growing alarm, a feeling she wasn't accustomed to, and started to search for the passports with renewed vigour.

They rummaged through the bookshelves in painstaking silence. They removed the books a couple at a time and looked in them, behind them. Eventually, after they had been searching for an hour or so, they found a manila envelope Dahlia recognised underneath a pile of law books.

'This is it.'

'Thank God!' said Margrit.

Dahlia opened the envelope and checked that all three passports were in there. She smiled as relief flooded through her. How wise she had been to get the children British passports, she thought once more. She felt herself swoon a little from the heat, the excitement and her nerves. She leaned on the desk, steadied herself, wiped away the cold sweat from her head, from the top of her lip. She puffed. 'Now what?' she asked.

'Let me take them with me . . .'

'What if he gets back from Kumasi in the meantime and looks for them?'

'Ach! But we have no choice, your flight is in two days. We just have to hope and pray he doesn't. Surely there is no reason he would?'

'I don't know . . .'

'Dahlia, listen to me, *Schatz*! We have to take this risk.'

'If he finds out he won't let me go . . . what if he . . .'

They gripped each other as the sound of a car horn, loud and impatient, reverberated at the gate. The household scurried into place, awakened from a languid spell by the innocuous, yet terrifying trumpet of Vincent's car. The maids, two of them, ran back into the house from the boys' quarters, calling out instructions to each other. The gardener, who had been on some sort of break, rushed past the window and hurriedly resumed tending a perfect border. The day watchman, already at the gate, flattened the pleats on the front of his trousers, wiped the evidence of his lunch from his mouth, and unlocked the gate, which he would be for ever grateful he had remembered to lock, even though madam had told him there was no need since Master wasn't here to make sure his rules were obeyed.

The blood had drained from Dahlia's face. She could feel neither her fingers nor her nails digging into the flesh on Margrit's arm. Her mouth had dropped and hung gaping, noiseless, while blood pounded fiercely in her ears, and fresh sweat beaded on the front of her head.

The car edged on to the drive, yards from where they stood. Dahlia's muscles loosened, her will to stand weakened. She shook as the study key, which she had been holding, clattered loudly on to the marble floor.

Margrit reached for the keys, shoved Dahlia out of the study and slammed the door behind them.

Outside, Vincent was talking to his servants.

Margrit rubbed her wet palms roughly on her dress, steadied her hands so she could put the key into the keyhole, and turned. But the Harmattan had caused the wood to warp, years of humidity, the lock to rust, and she could not budge the key.

Dahlia moaned as if in pain, stood crippled and ineffectual.

Margrit pulled the handle and tried lifting it as she turned, the only way she could lock her own front door. Nothing.

'God! He's coming . . .'

Margrit gathered the hem of her dress, covered the key with it, pulled and lifted the door once more, forcibly turned the key so hard she thought it might break, and finally felt the lock slide into place.

'Go! Put the key back. Go!' Margrit shoved Dahlia towards the central staircase. Dahlia half-ran, half-walked, holding on to anything she passed, and pulled herself up the stairs.

Margrit lifted her dress, and shoved the passports into her large cotton knickers where they could lie secured by the wide elastic around her waist. She turned to inspect a framed photograph of Vincent in his gown and wig just as he walked across the veranda and through the front door.

'Aha! Vincent, you're back, happy Boxing Day' she said. She felt a chill as her skin tightened the smile she'd plastered on her face and dared herself to keep looking at him, even though his eyes unsteadied her. The thoughts came flooding: Why? And how often? And what exactly? She had to stall them, they would show on her face, she was sure, and then he would know. She smiled harder.

He stared silently, a small furrow of curiosity on his brow.

In the ferocity of his glare, Margrit stumbled, struggled to keep looking at him. 'Dahlia . . . she had to go the bathroom, and I am just about to leave . . .'

He nodded wordlessly, looked around his home and headed towards the stairs.

'Ah . . . tell, me Vincent, ya, how was Kumasi? Ah, but I am sure you had a lovely time na?'

He paused and looked at her, his face flinched with irritation. He was immaculately dressed in a light grey suit with a red tie. His head was damp with sweat from his journey. 'Yes. I suppose so.'

'Well, we had a quiet Christmas, Kojo and I. He was mainly working, you know how he is, ever dedicated, work, work, work, all the time. You men are all the same.' She laughed too loud and tried to keep her hands from twitching. 'Oh, and someone stole my animals. You know, I really hope this government will crack down on the petty crime that seems to have become so uncontrolled, don't you?' She exhaled audibly when she heard Dahlia walking down the stairs. It was only as Dahlia came into full view that she felt some of this unbearable tension pass.

She had applied a quick dab of face powder, some lipstick, had brushed her hair and she smiled. My goodness, thought Margrit. She's masterful. She has this down to a fine art. And behind her the children followed, smiling dutifully. When she stopped they stood next to her, a living, breathing barrier of warm flesh and bones.

'Vincent, welcome home.' She walked to him and allowed him to kiss her, leaving an imprint of his too-sweet aftershave on her cheek.

Margrit's stomach contracted, forcing bile into her mouth. The way Dahlia turned her face up to be kissed, the way he stood afterwards with his hand on Cyril's shoulder, his fingers occasionally wandering over to his earlobe, how he played with a stray strand of Jasmine's hair, all of it made her sick. She couldn't talk. She wouldn't dare open her mouth and allow out the things that were gurgling in there, but she smiled until she thought her face would crack. As soon as she could, she excused herself with guilty haste from this gruesome version of family life. 'See you at the beach later then . . . or maybe you want to stay home now that Vincent is back?'

He looked irritated. 'Don't change your plans on my account. I just came to pick up something, I'm on my way to a meeting.'

Dahlia nodded, her eyes already deadening and resigned. Margrit wanted to take her, to take the children too, away from here, from this monster who didn't deserve even the whiff of family.

As she sat back into the solid seat of her car and drove off, Margrit whispered aloud, a prayer to the universe, 'It won't be long now, dear Dahlia . . .' She closed her eyes for a brief moment and sent her friend hope and strength and much luck too.

*

Eva blew air on to her nose. The entire house seemed to be perspiring; the floors were warm, the walls sticky; the windows wide open and yet no breeze came. She leant on the veranda railings. Her dress, an old loose strapless thing which she usually wore only to clean, tented around her and she parted her legs in the hope that the damp between her thighs would dry.

The garden was disintegrating under the dazzle of the sun, which had become ferocious again. There was nothing on the news about a drought, but there had apparently been little rain up country where rain was usually regular. Now there was talk of an impending famine. The shops were still empty. Even the market stalls had dried up. It seemed traders had hidden any non-perishable goods until things settled down enough for them to profiteer further.

All in all, the mood was not at all buoyant. To add to the uncertainty, there were rumours that a number of counter-coups had been quelled by Afriye and his band who were trying to cling to power. Broadcasts were frequently suspended, political bulletins regular, and there seemed to be daily edicts from the government about new appointments, policies and programs all designed to move the country along. But no one could yet see any sign of forward motion.

Eva looked wistfully at her plants, now brown and crisp, the grass wispy and pathetic, and she wished for a downpour. That would be what she prayed. Proper energizing rain that could clear the stifling air; that was what was needed to invigorate everyone and make them a lot more agreeable. A steady stretch of good rain and renewed greenness would get this country back on track, she was sure.

The water had been off for a few days and they were running out again. They were down to the last drum in the kitchen, and that was half-empty. It was surprising how many buckets full were needed to run a household. Nothing in the kitchen could be done without a lot of water, and to counter the oppressive heat she was having two or three showers a day; the kids needed at least two.

By Eva's calculations, everyone in the house washed their hands between ten and twenty times a day; a good habit in this dirty, dusty country, with disease-bearing germs everywhere. Apart from the obvious occasions that called for hand-washing, she also washed them after she returned home, whenever she had handled well-used cedi notes and, sometimes, after shaking some hands. Now that there were so many more of them, Auntie Gee, Akua, Faustina, her children Peace and Harmony, Solomon and Zachariah, who showered each morning before he left and each evening too, they quite simply needed a lot of water. And today the septic tank was scheduled to be emptied, which would mean flushing the toilets again and again while the tank was drained. There was no option, they would have to spend this morning fetching water.

She would get her chores done as quickly as possible and then they were going to the beach. They hadn't been for a while, with all the goings on. Today was doing to be a sort of festive farewell to Dahlia.

Eva had visited her yesterday and together they had sipped tea for the last time on Dahlia's cosy veranda. Eva had whispered words she hoped would give confidence, strength, courage, whatever it was that her friend needed. She had hated leaving her; in spite of Dahlia's assurances that she was fine, Eva couldn't wait to put her on the plane tomorrow.

They planned to celebrate today. She smiled anticipating the salty breeze, the refreshing water, a cool beer in the shade. Maybe some grilled lobster if the restaurant was open, but each of them would take a picnic, just in case.

Alfred wouldn't be coming, which was just as well. She had never kept anything from him in the past, but the past was still a distant place. Whenever she looked at him, she thought about

Agnes and the baby. They were yet to have that conversation, but for now, she couldn't see beyond them into his eyes, to him. And yet, she thought wistfully, she would love to be sharing his deckchair later, sitting between his legs, leaning back against his bare body, taking sips from his bottle of beer, letting him feed her bits of grilled fish or lobster as they watched the children frolic in the surf. And the way she would smile, blood warming her face further, when he whispered longingly in her ear. She pushed aside the thoughts. She had to get Dahlia off safely before she could concentrate on her marriage, try to rekindle her love for him.

Yelena arrived with the boys so they could travel together to the beach. They all piled into Eva's car. When the children complained that the leather seats were sticky and warm, Yelena told them to stop moaning and asked them if they'd rather walk. Eva told them she would speed up as soon as she could so that the breeze could cool them down, and she reminded them of the cool sweet drinks that awaited them on the beach.

The queue at the checkpoint at the Accra/Tema border was longer than usual. They rolled along, car by car. The soldiers were clearly taking their time, which was annoying.

A handful of beggars moved from car to car towards them, asking for money. Eva wound up her windows and instructed everyone to do the same. There was a chorus of protest from them. 'I know it's hot, but just do it. Leave a little gap at the top, until we get to the checkpoint.'

The first one to reach them was a young man, with an overdeveloped upper body hobbling on home-made crutches, his spindly, polio-ravaged legs unable to carry him. 'Please madam, help me,' he said through the glass on the passenger door. He was leaning on the sticks so that he could beg with his hands. Eva looked at him and shrugged. 'Next time,' she said. He looked forlorn but resigned and Eva felt a pang of guilt. There was never a next time. She rolled down her window and gave him some coins.

He grinned happily and hobbled off. As she moved forwards others came. A child with unseeing milky eyes who was holding on to a woman as her guide. Her mother? An aunt? An employer of sorts? The child's voice was plaintive and bereft of joy. She shoved some coins into their hands without looking properly at either of them. And then there was another with crippled hands and fingers, leprosy or polio? Eva gave him money trying not to touch his skin. In the back of the car, the children looked out at the beggars in silence. 'We must remember to be grateful that we are well,' she said staring straight ahead, and no one replied. Giving them money only made her feel unworthy, aware that she hadn't done enough for them, that she hadn't in any significant way improved their miserable lives.

Next to her, Yelena sat in perfect silence, her eyes straight ahead. From the corner of her eyes, Eva could see she was wringing her hands a little too hard.

'I don't like the soldiers,' said Abigail.

'Oh, they are harmless. They are just doing their job,' said Eva.

She ran through her mental checklist; her papers were in order, she had them with her, she had bribery money if necessary, and everything would be perfectly roadworthy in her new car. There would be no reason for them to harass her as they were the driver in front. He was pleading with a particularly hostile looking soldier who pointed at his tyres, kicked them, and then searched his boot. Eventually, after he had paid them some money, he was allowed to drive off.

Eva shifted into first gear, and without taking her eyes off the soldier who was motioning her forwards, eased the car into position.

'Where are you going to?'

'To the beach.'

'To swim?'

'Yes.'

'Ah!' he said with no recognition.

'You white people you like the beach, isn't it?' Another soldier said chuckling.

The aggressive soldier had gone back to sit under the tree and smoke a cigarette, clearly able to afford a well-earned break.

'Anyway do you have any contraband?' asked one of the soldiers.

Eva laughed. 'No. No.'

He peered into the back. 'Very fine childrens, very fine. I will marry that one,' he said, pointing at Abi.

'Of course,' said Eva. 'She would be very lucky to find a husband like you.'

'Anyway, so who bought you this car? Brand new Mercidis-Benz,' he said smiling.

'My husband,' Eva said. 'But it is not new . . .'

'Eh! Then it means that he loves you paah! Or it means that he has done something wrong, isn't it?' He laughed at his observation.

'Okay, anyway, you can go,' one of them said, waving her on.

She stalled as she tried to drive off.

'Ah, can't you drive it?'

She tried again and once more stuttered the engine, but on her third attempt, Eva managed to drive off slowly, carefully.

In the back of the car, the children began to shift about one by one, airing damp legs and backs that had begun to cling to the seats.

'As soon as I am grown-up, I am going to England,' said Simon.

'Me too. I want to go and live abroad,' said Joel.

'No, no,' said Yelena. 'This is your home.' She turned to Eva with a bemused expression.

'Why do you want to go abroad?' asked Eva.

'You can have a nice job. You can save, not like here where there is no point because there is nothing to buy. And everyone doesn't think you are a foreigner when you aren't,' said Abigail vehemently.

'You'd miss us,' Eva said, not sure what to think. 'Then all those things would seem empty and pointless. And it is quiet and boring there. Not so exciting.'

'But it is cleaner and nicer and safer,' said Abigail.

'Yes, but it is not perfect there either . . .'

'Well there aren't soldiers all over the place,' said Jonas.

'They are doing their job that's all . . .'

'In England people don't get shot outside your house,' said Simon, sounding unsettled.

'And it's not frightening,' said Abi.

'Yes, but this is your home, no matter how strange. Everywhere is a little strange you know?' said Yelena.

'And it's best to make the most of what you have,' said Eva. 'When you are older you can decide, but for now this is your home, there is no point wishing for something you don't even know.'

'We know what you tell us. That it is nice,' said Abigail.

'And not so hot,' said Simon. 'And the shops are full of nice things.'

And off they went: I'd have a bicycle, we'd have roller skates, we could buy ice cream with our pocket money, those big cones we saw in that film, and we could play on the streets, and we'd see our granny and grandpa who could treat us all the time, and spoil us, and, and, and . . .

Yes, it is cleaner and safer and cooler, thought Eva, but that doesn't make it your home, you darling children. This is the place you come from, the land that embraces you with fewer questions and conditions, which embraces you confidently. This is your home in spite of its frustrations and in spite of these bloody soldiers, wrecking it when it could be amazing with just a little more consistent determination, effort and faith.

Yelena and Eva set up around a cluster of thatched umbrellas. The wind whipped through their hair and quickly seemed to

331

brush away all the agitation of the recent weeks. Eva smiled and lifted her face to the sun. It was just as well that she had left Joseph at home. She hadn't wanted to bring Faustina to look after him, in case she overheard their plans, and she hadn't wanted to toddle after him in the hot sun all day.

She undressed and strolled towards the water until the impulse to run became uncontainable and her heart pounded blood into her head so fast that she felt giddy. The children splashed her. She waded in until she was waist deep in the warm water, laughing all the while. The swell was gentle, with that curative undulant motion, tugging her here and there with unseen currents, splashing unpredictably, washing away sweat and sadness. Abigail pulled her in to meet a larger wave. Together they jumped up, bracing the water with their torsos, their mouths filling with sprays of seawater as they squealed.

Later, she lay at the edge of the water and allowed dying waves to wash over her, coating her skin with healing salt, and the children to cover her feet with sand while she listened to their light-hearted chatter. The waves were mesmerising; each so different from its predecessor. She thought about Dahlia leaving and wondered what Vincent would think. How she would love to be there when he realised she had managed to get away. Ha! That would teach him, the bastard. All of a sudden she wished she could open her eyes now and see Alfred strolling towards her, looking marvellously youthful, his aviators reflecting the sun away, his shirt undone to his belly button, his bare feet kicking sand, splashing water. He would stand over her, his face radiating and laugh contagiously. Damn! She had had enough of this solitariness, she thought as she abruptly stirred and escaped from her sandy tomb, ignoring the children's cries of complaint.

After Dahlia and Margrit arrived and told the other women about their close encounter with Vincent, they fed the children sardine and egg sandwiches, and the four of the them sat at an unstable wooden table outside the restaurant.

Dahlia showed them the clothes she had had made for the children. The tailor had copied some suits from a magazine, buttoned jackets and trousers for each of them in the thickest fabric she could find. 'I hope they fit . . .' With Vincent back, she realised she couldn't take any chances and had brought everything with her to give to Eva to put in the suitcase she was hiding under her bed. 'Just a few photographs, some jewellery and these clothes. I can't afford to take any more. I have to hope that once I am in the UK, he won't mind sending the rest of our things to us. Surely he will do that, don't you think?'

No one answered. They picked at their grilled lobster and boiled rice. They sipped their beer. They listened to the swish of unfolding waves.

'England,' Eva said sighing. 'Home sweet home.'

One by one, they lifted their heads and stared out to sea, squinting, as though they might see it if they tried hard enough.

'I wonder if I'll remember how to get about,' said Dahlia. 'Heathrow, long tube ride to Brixton, then a bus to my parents' house.' She told them she had decided against calling her parents until she was in London. She bit her lip. 'I can't help thinking, what if he looks for the passports?'

'The first sign that he suspects something, you leave,' said Margrit. 'Do you understand me?' She had grabbed Dahlia's arm and was shaking it as she spoke. 'You don't wait to find out more. You leave! Even if you have to run out of the house without your shoes on, you go! Immediately!' She realised they were looking at her oddly. 'Trust me,' she said more quietly. 'I really don't think you should wait to find out what he does. Please . . .'

'Did we leave everything as we found it?' Dahlia whispered.

'Yes,' said Margrit. 'Yes, of course we did.'

'Everything is going to be fine,' said Eva. 'Let's concentrate on the plan. You tell him you are coming to mine for coffee, right?

You come dressed as usual. But you go to Margrit. I'll meet you there with your suitcase, and Margrit will drive you and the kids to the airport. You must act as if everything is normal. He won't suspect a thing . . .'

Yelena said nothing. She sipped her beer and hoped silently, which was as much as she felt able to do at this point. What options were left anyhow? What difference would it make to tell them about the man at the travel agency? They simply had to get Dahlia on the plane tomorrow, then they could relax.

Dahlia gazed out over the blue horizon and wondered how easily she would learn to live without apprehension. The thought reignited a long-dead hope and made her smile a little.

'What are you feeling?' asked Eva softly.

'I don't know. I guess I'm trying not to feel, to think. It seems less frightening. But . . . I've been wondering what life will be like as a single mother in the UK . . .' she put her hand around her neck, which felt instantly constricted.

'Don't think then,' said Margrit.

Dahlia tried to ignore the pain around her heart, the cork straining to contain her emotions. 'I did love him . . . and I wanted so much to make this my home.' She rocked herself. 'I'm afraid . . .' she whispered, and then suddenly she was wheezing and seemed to convulse as she struggled for air.

'Don't speak, Dahlia,' said Yelena, her entire body aching in sympathy for her friend.

'I feel a failure . . . running away like this . . .'

'Don't! You are a survivor, you're not running away . . . not many women would have been able to put up with what you did.' Margrit sniffed angrily. 'I know that you have not told us the worst things that happened . . .'

Dahlia let out a howl, wrenched free from the pit of her being as something tried to extricate itself from deep within her.

Eva glanced towards the children frolicking in the distant surf, suddenly grateful for their ability to self-entertain, their insatiable appetite for movement, thankful to God that they had not heard, had not seen, had not been given reason to wonder about the cause of such pain.

'I'm sorry . . . too much was bleak . . . and I desperately wanted to go with some . . . some nice memories. Of the good things about life here . . .'

'There is plenty of time for memories,' said Margrit.

There seemed nothing else to say. They sat quietly and listened to the endless swirling sea. In the distance they heard the ever delightful yelps of childish joy, the wondrous ability to be amazed afresh by something as predictable as another wave.

Chapter Twenty-Two

Dahlia was up long before the sun on the last morning in her home. She was more tired than she had been when she went to bed. She had barely slept. Every unusual sound, each unfamiliar movement jolted her, and when she dozed off her dreams were dramatic and riotous, filled with baffling events that left her drained.

Last night she had had the dream again, the one she had been having for years, which left her exhausted, yet relieved to be awake. She was always in the same place, somewhere at once familiar and mysterious, and she was on her back, immobilised. Then came the sensation that the walls were growing and tightening around her. Sure she was about to be entombed, she tried to lift an arm, wriggle a toe, jerk some part of her, but her body was frozen stiff. She panted from the effort of trying to waken, willing herself to move, but all she could do was acknowledge that she was paralysed and trapped for ever in this place.

But wasn't she awake? Was that the buzz of the air-conditioner? The harder she tried to see through grit-filled eyes, the less clear everything became. Again she tried to move her arm, a hand, a finger, but nothing budged. The wrestling was exhausting, her head spun and a frightening drowsiness overcame her, the kind that promised to lull her into permanent sleep. It was appalling, this feeling of being dragged back down towards that place where she was sure something terrifying was waiting for her.

She must have dozed off finally, exhausted from the effort of trying to waken and then slept fitfully until now.

Already she could feel the tension that had been building for days. She would wake up in Norwood tomorrow morning under a wintry London sky with the smell of damp, rotting foliage and cool December air coming through the window and wafts of toasting, sliced Hovis from the kitchen below. She tried to imagine her parents in the kitchen still reeling from her presence. She didn't have the energy now to think about their reaction to her unanticipated return, what would be the point worrying about that now? It wasn't as though she had a whole lot of choice of where to go. Besides, she would never tell them the whole truth, it would be easier to keep some things to herself.

Yesterday she had paced through the house for one last time. She had said goodbye to Vincent in her head, the distinguished-looking fellow who had winked at her gallantly in the canteen. The charming, eloquent and promising student who had swept her off her feet. She ought to hate him, she thought, and if she stayed, she would. But why didn't she already? She didn't understand that either. Did leaving mean she could be magnanimous? That she could afford to reach far into their past to the man she had been attracted to, married? Because to do otherwise, to see nothing good whatsoever in him, would that not only demean her further? Hadn't she chosen him? Admired him? Had hopes and dreams with him? And children too.

Then she pushed the thoughts away, tied them up and tried to leave them behind, for now, and instead to look forward to her parents' faces. Wouldn't there be hugs and kisses? Yelps of joy; questions later? And how would she feel? How would Jasmine and Cyril feel? Even though in a matter of hours she would be on her way to it all, somehow the chasm she had to cross to get there prevented her imagination from crystallising that part of things.

She opened her eyes and ran through the plan. It was so very straightforward, nothing could go wrong. Yet she had had to keep going through it in her mind, to make sure that they hadn't forgotten anything obvious. Margrit had the tickets and the passports well hidden in her house, Eva would bring the suitcase, Margrit would take the three of them to the airport.

She sat through breakfast for the final time. Said goodbye to Vincent courteously as he left the house. Played the starring role in someone else's life to perfection; instructed the maids what to cook for lunch, and when to have it ready by, gave Susan permission to go ahead and change all the bed sheets as usual as it was Friday, and told her which linen to use.

But as she walked towards the car, the three of them dressed as normal for a coffee morning, she struggled not to look too hard, and as had become her modus operandi, her saving grace, she continued to refuse to feel.

She drove past Eva's house. Cyril called out that she had missed the turning.

'I know,' she said without looking in the rear-view mirror so she wouldn't see his eyes, so he wouldn't see hers. On the passenger seat next to her, Jasmine had turned to stare.

'Where are we going Mummy?'

'We are not going to Auntie Eva's today. We are going . . .' She swallowed and then took a breath, shallow and unrewarding. 'We are going to Auntie Margrit's house.'

'Why?' they chorused.

She rubbed a patch of eczema that had flared up around her neck in the past few days. Her usual answers to the most impossible questions: 'I don't know', or when she was impatient or irritated: 'Because I said so', were particularly inappropriate today.

338

Weren't her children also entitled to some warning that they were being taken away from their home, the only home they had ever known? To an England very unlike the one depicted by Enid Blyton. How alien they would find it all. But what could she do? She couldn't leave them behind, she couldn't stay. She could feel the door closing; if she didn't get out now, she might never.

'We are going to England . . .'

Cyril jumped up in his seat. 'We're going on a plane?'

'But . . . but we didn't say goodbye to Daddy . . .'

'Wow! How long for?'

'But we didn't pack our things . . .'

'How long for Mummy?'

'Does Daddy know, Mummy?'

'You'll understand this one day.'

'Are we coming back?'

'How long for, Mummy . . .'

Their voices were muffled by the thick protective glass that had shielded and kept her all this time. It had allowed her to continue to exist, albeit outside of herself, her life, enabled her to put up with the humiliation, the degradation, the shame, the rejection and despair . . . tears were streaming down her face. She brushed them away furiously, and struggled to see where she was going. Not long now, not long now . . . they would take over, her friends, they would carry her the rest of the way. Margrit, strong and wise, Eva, optimistic, Yelena, fiery and so very determined. All three courageous and spirited and wonderful too; she didn't have to turn, to look, she could imagine the anguish on her children's faces, in their little hearts. Nearly there . . . the energy she had reserved for this drive was waning, she willed herself on, not long, not long, she had to hold it together, nearly there, nearly there . . .

Their goodbyes had to be efficient. They had purposely not allowed much spare time for Dahlia to get to the airport. Another opportunity not to really feel, not to fully engage, to go through the motions and hope that one day there would be enough of an imprint on her heart, something deep in her soul she could look back on and remember. Like Yelena laughing out loud, trying to be jolly, telling them that she had dropped the boys at their father's house. 'What other purpose does he have if not to help me now and very occasionally?' And how she gripped Dahlia with a ferocity that hurt and said with admirable conviction, 'We will meet again. I know we will, dear Dahlia. In the meantime, go well . . .' And how Eva had held her, then stood back, stroked her face and said, 'You are brave and beautiful . . .and I can't wait to meet you again, when you are whole . . .when you are the woman you were made to be, when you have healed . . .' And in that moment, Dahlia allowed herself to acknowledge how utterly broken she was, the shadow she had become, ashamed, unworthy, unclean . . .

As they slowed at the military checkpoint on the ring-road Margrit turned to the children and said, 'Don't say anything . . . let me do the talking. Just smile and look normal.' She stroked Dahlia's arm.

The car in front reached the soldiers. The driver had to get out and open the boot. The soldiers made him get out his spare wheel so they could have a thorough look. Two of them checked the car while a fourth looked at the man's driving licence and other papers asking him questions. His body language was pliant in anticipation of having to plead for something. Some other soldiers sat on a bench under the sprawling shade of a neem tree smoking. The women watched the driver implore and saw the soldiers mock him; one shoved his shoulder into him. Dahlia whimpered, put her hand to her mouth. The man took a crumpled wad of cedis from his back pocket, began to count, and she flinched as one of the soldiers reached to pluck the entire lot out of his hands. The raucous laughter of the men made her shiver. When the soldiers allowed him to get back in his car, she watched his powerlessness and felt his impotent rage. They looked more serious than usual, which, along with their uniforms and guns, made them menacing. Dahlia was nibbling her fingers, the broken skin bleeding some more.

'Open the boot.'

Holding on to her benign expression, Margrit got out of the car. The suitcase lay innocuously in the back. She could smell the heat and sweat beneath the man's thick dungarees, the whiff of stale cigarette and unwashed body, his power over her, like a vicious dog. She realised she was trembling and tried not to let it show.

Once he was satisfied, he nodded and walked back to his position, folded his arms and waited for Margrit to go.

Back in the driver's seat, she gripped the wheel with her sweaty hands and smiled hard at the soldiers.

She drove off, waited until she was a safe distance from them before she shifted gears and released the straining engine. She lifted one hand from the steering wheel, dried it on her lap and then the other, staring ahead the whole while. She heard Dahlia move about in the seat. She loosened up a little now, she too had sensed too much maliciousness.

At the airport, there was a chaotic crowd milling outside.

At the door to the terminal building, a soldier held on to the nozzle of his gun while he examined their tickets. 'Ah . . . where are you going then? Ejura-Wilson . . . isn't that that lawyer fellow?'

Dahlia winced. He had spoken loudly, seemed too fascinated by her name, stared too hard at their pictures. When he handed the passports to her, he nodded after looking at her face for far too long. Her hands were shaking, she pushed the children in ahead of her, stumbled, stopped, realised she hadn't said goodbye to Margrit and tried to step back out, but the soldier said, 'Only passengers beyond this point! No comings and goings please!'

She stood immobile, bit her lip and let her eyes fill. Margrit waved with both hands and mouthed 'go!' a solitary, fortifying word which seemed to propel Dahlia away from her past.

It was mayhem in the terminal building. The departure boards were not functioning and there seemed to be constant announcements that were loud and startling and were hard to understand. Every man in a suit looked like Vincent. And why was everyone staring at them? Behind her, the sound of her daughter's sniffling and her son's questions unexpectedly became too much to bear. She turned and smacked Jasmine across the face. 'Shut up!'

All the blood rushed to Dahlia's face, she grabbed Cyril by the shoulders and pulled him so hard that he yelped. 'Shut up!' she hissed again. She thought she could feel her insides weaken, ready themselves to drop out. The children were looking at her with resentment, a sense of injustice writ clearly in their expressions.

And then, over a tannoy, Vincent's name, loud and reverberating. She stopped in her tracks and Jasmine, who was still nursing her sore face, bumped into her. Seemingly the entire airport had come to a standstill and was staring at them, at the distraught looking children. Again, the name, her name. She exhaled. Of course, it was *her* name. She grabbed the children and walked briskly to the check-in desk.

Her insides were painfully knotted by the time Dahlia sat and buckled her seat belt. Her hands were sweaty and damp, her mouth was dry. She leaned back into the cocooning headrest, folded her arms and closed her eyes. She could feel every fibre of her body tight, on fire. She longed for a gin and tonic. Any form of alcohol, really. She looked to her left and to her right; a child on either side. Still and stunned. Why, they might ask, were they seated in a DC10 about to leave Accra for a land they couldn't picture, for a period of time they couldn't measure, and without saying goodbye to their father?

'You will understand why I have done this one day,' Dahlia said, reaching for their hands. 'You will soon be old enough to choose what you want, where you want to be. For now, you have to trust me. And I am so sorry that I hit you. That was utterly unforgivable of me.' Now you think that I am no better than your father, she thought.

'But I haven't said goodbye to my friends,' said Jasmine.

She turned to look at Cyril, but he was unwrapping a plastic number puzzle the air hostess had given him. She squeezed Jasmine's hand and smiled at her. 'Can you forgive me please?'

Jasmine smiled a little.

'And trust me. Everything is going to be just fine. Let's close our eyes and dream about all the lovely things we want.'

Jasmine nodded and tried to smile. Dahlia began to relax into the odours of England. She could smell dinner; mashed potatoes, some sort of brown gravy, tomato-less, pepper-less. She could hear the clink of the drinks cart. There would be brandy, Coke, nice orange juice, or even a bloody Mary, just as soon as they were up high enough. Luxurious nuts, salted cashews or smoked almonds. All served by a friendly face filled with understanding and sympathy, and maybe a little extra kindness because of their tear-stained faces and swollen eyes, universal symptoms of grief.

The pilot said something to the passengers. Dahlia opened her eyes briefly and wished they would start to taxi down the runway. She might sleep. She thought of her friends, of their association. She smiled; they had always been a club of sorts, looking out for each other. She wouldn't have made it without them.

She stirred and opened her eyes when she heard the kerfuffle towards the front of the plane. There were several loud shrieks and much hushed murmuring. Dahlia flinched when she heard someone say 'soldiers'. She heard male voices approaching and looked down the aisle. A soldier was walking through the plane with a gun across his chest, staring into the seats on either side as he walked. There were people behind him. Two or three. More

343

armed guards? The passengers cowered down, lowered their heads to save themselves from being distinguished from the rest.

'Don't look at them!' she whispered to the children.

Someone started to shout above the mumbling of the passengers, 'Everyone quiet. We are not going to harm you.' The plane hushed. 'We are not going to harm you. Sit up please.' A disbelieving quiet descended. Cyril reached for her arm and she placed a hand over his. He suddenly gripped her tightly, gouging her with his nails. Dahlia looked up, anxious to see what he had seen. The soldier had stopped by their seat and moved to the side to let Vincent in front of him.

The armed guard stood there looking about, his curiosity making him look more comic than frightening. His gun was pointed to the ceiling of the plane, but in his awe, it was clear he had forgotten why he was on this plane in the first place.

Vincent stood beside Cyril and looked straight at Dahlia with a steely stare. 'You have no right whatsoever to take my children away. I told you that you couldn't and you disobeyed me. Why did you do that?'

'Vincent, please,' said Dahlia. She was holding on to the children. Jasmine trembled as she tried to stop herself from snivelling. Cyril sat stiffly, caught between his parents, too bewildered to move.

'Please what? What kind of man do you think I am? You think I should let you go? Wave you off with my children, happy to let you steal them from me, from their country? What kind of man would that make me?'

'No . . . Vincent . . .'

'But of course, you think I am a barbarian, so perhaps you thought I might do just that. Well, you are wrong. I might not want you, but I want my children and I will not stand by and have them taken away from the land of their ancestors, away from me, their family, their legacy. And in such a bloody subversive manner too!'

'Please . . .?' Her face was streaming. Her mind had melted into a jumbled lump, unutterable words floundered about in her loose mouth; everything was thick and slow like treacle, nothing making sense.

'Excuse me sir?' said a white man sitting on the other side of the aisle.

Vincent didn't look at him, didn't acknowledge him.

'Sir, please, think of the children. This will traumatise them.'

'Please, speak only if you are spoken to,' said the soldier, suddenly coming to life. He turned slowly to face the man, adjusted his gun, which now pointed ominously at the man's torso. 'Understand that for the moment you are still in our country, and we do things in our own way here. This is our country. You understand?'

The man nodded silently.

'Come on. We cannot hold up the plane any longer.'

'Vincent!' The terror in her own voice frightened her further.

'I tell you what, since I have other children and you have none I will let you take Jasmine. Girls should be with their mothers I suppose, but the boy needs his father, needs to grow into a strong man. Cyril, get your things.'

Cyril started to sob.

Dahlia screamed. She fumbled with her seat belt with cold unwilling fingers. 'You can't do this! Please, be fair . . . for the sake of our marriage?'

'Oh please, Dahlia. For heaven's sake, stop making a fool of yourself. You had no intention of being fair when you planned this. If I hadn't had a tip off, you'd be well on your way by now with my children, hardly the work of an honourable person.'

'Please Daddy.'

'You can't make me choose . . .'

'I am not making you choose. Come on Cyril.'

'You can't separate them . . .'

'Nonsense!' He pulled his son up forcibly. Cyril clung to Dahlia with his other thin arm, until his body was stretched too far and he had to let go.

'Come on Jasmine,' said Dahlia. 'We are getting off. Get your things, quick.'

Vincent paused in his stride towards the exit. 'You are going to London. It's where you want to go isn't it?' He nodded at the soldier and then strode off.

'No!' Dahlia cried. 'Vincent . . .' Frantically she tried to gather her things. She stood and pulled at Jasmine. 'Come on . . . quick! Hurry up . . .!'

'Madam,' said the soldier who was standing next to her seat. 'Let me see your passport.'

'What? Why? Look, I have to get to my son.' Dahlia peered beyond the man's body to keep her eyes on Cyril, who Vincent was dragging down the aisle.

'The passport,' the soldier said in a less friendly tone.

'Oh for goodness' sake.' Dahlia scrambled in her bag and thrust it at him.

'Aha. British.'

'Yes, but my husband is Ghanaian. I have lived here for many years.'

'It seems your permit to stay is about to expire.'

'You have to be joking . . .'

'No. I am not joking. Am I laughing? And you are also not laughing. In fact, no one is laughing.' He shifted his gun in case Dahlia had misunderstood him in any way. 'What I can advise you is that when you get to London you should go and apply for a visa to come back and visit.'

'No, no, you can't do this . . .' she gripped his hand, shook him, jolting his gun up and down.

'Heh, mind yourself. I said this is the best we can do at this point.'

'No!'

'Sit.' He shook her off him, shoved her into her seat and started

346

to back up towards the front of the plane. 'On behalf of all of us,' he said waving his gun from one side of the aisle to the other, 'I wish you a safe journey to *abrochie*.'

Dahlia staggered up towards him. 'Please . . . don't do this to me. How can you let him take my child?'

'Madam, it is not me who has done this. Sit, please.'

'He is my baby. Don't do this to me!'

'But madam, what is your problem? As I said, I did not do it ah! Sit down right now.' He shouted at her, his face screwed together and belligerent.

Dahlia crumpled to the floor. 'I am begging you to help me . . .'

He made a loud disapproving chewing sound, turned on his heel and walked off as if he couldn't bear to see her grovelling in this way. 'The plane has to go now,' he said in a loud but casual voice as he adjusted his gun again, swinging it over so that the nozzle pointed over the heads of the passengers on the other side of the plane. 'You,' he said turning to one of the air hostesses who stood by the door, 'tell the pilot that he must go now.'

Dahlia retched. Covered her mouth. For a moment thought she would pass out. Her body went hot, cold, she slumped. She felt an arm lift her, a hand gently push her into her seat. She leaned back and stared at the headrest in front of her. She retched again, reached for an airsick bag and sat huddled as her mouth filled with painful bitterness.

She didn't look at Jasmine, but she could feel the bony shoulders of her daughter heaving. Out of the corner of her eye she could see Cyril's empty seat.

Chapter Twenty-Three

Eva felt her knees buckle when she saw Vincent striding through their gate pulling Cyril behind him. She reached to hold on to the nearest wall for support. What had happened? All manner of thoughts mushroomed in her head. Where was Dahlia? Her skin chilled rapidly and she felt as if an army of ants was crawling through the blonde hairs on her arms. She gripped her stomach.

He was nearly at the door. She wanted to run, but stood, her feet locked in position, unable to move.

'Where is Alfred?'

'Where is Dahlia?' she whispered.

He peered into her eyes. 'Get Alfred! I don't have all day.'

'What have you done?'

He stared at her silently. She gawped mutely; he must have killed her.

'Cyril?'

He was snivelling, and when she looked at him, he lowered his eyes and bit his lip, sniffing hard.

'Are you okay? Oh my God! What happened?'

'I do not have all day!' Vincent boomed, and she staggered backwards.

'I'll get him . . .' She ran up the stairs and into their bedroom.

Unable to speak slowly or clearly, swallowing much of her voice no matter how hard she tried, she told him in mangled sentences what had happened: Dahlia was supposed to have left . . . on a plane . . . this morning, I mean yesterday, with the children . . . because, you see . . . well, she couldn't take any more so we all helped, with money, you know . . . And now, now, he has gone and killed her . . . and Jasmine too . . . and it was all my idea.

Alfred shook his head. 'Woah! Slow down . . . I didn't understand a thing you just said.'

'Please just hurry up and come downstairs,' she said, leaving him looking quizzically after her. She tried to dispel the abominable connotations of Vincent's presence and ran back down the stairs two at a time, desperate to find out what had happened.

Vincent was on the veranda. He turned and stared at her, his face expressionless. Cyril sat on one of the chairs with his chin in his hands looking disappointed.

'You must come and play at the weekend,' Eva said to the boy, trying to sound cheery. She had to remain light-hearted about the situation until she had had a chance to find out what had happened yesterday. And if she could pretend that everything was normal, maybe it would be. 'What do you think, Vincent?' She felt like a traitor for talking to him, and a coward, unable to ask what she desperately wanted to.

Vincent glowered at her, tilted his head slightly, and another wave of goose bumps flared up all over Eva's skin again as beads of sweat prickled on her head.

'We'll sort something out, Cyril,' said Eva, smiling a cheerful smile at him, willing him to receive her message of hope and love and optimism. 'Everything is going to be just fine', was what she wanted to say, preferably with a hug, but she didn't like to promise things she couldn't deliver. She was oddly repelled by the idea of getting too close to him and therefore too close to Vincent.

She lingered. She had to find out what had happened. She glanced up as Alfred came down the stairs, and suddenly wished she had told him earlier what they had done. She was sure he would be on her side, once he knew the story. He hated disloyalty. Funny that, she thought, the one trait she had always believed she could rely on him for was loyalty. She lowered herself heavily onto the seat opposite Cyril.

'Could you excuse us . . .'

Something in his tone made her stand obediently and leave. 'Cyril, do you want to come with me and have a drink?' Vincent glanced at her with something close to disbelief.

'Maybe not then.' She went up the stairs and hovered at the top out of sight, hoping to listen in to their conversation, but they walked out into the garden so she could no longer hear them. Frustrated, she went and lay on their bed, comforted by the smell of Alfred's sheets, and buried her face in his pillow.

Outside, Vincent turned sharply and shouted, 'What the hell do you think you are playing at?'

'I beg your pardon?'

'After the warning I gave you, you sit back and allow your bloody wife to impede my business?'

'Do you mind? You are talking about my wife . . .'

'Well, you need to get some control over her!'

'What one earth are you talking about?'

Alfred listened, stunned, as Vincent elaborated the kidnapping plot that he had foiled, and how he had had to use 'his position of authority and power' to claw back his son. He'd been able to do so thanks only to a phone call from a trusted friend who had tipped him off about his wife's treacherous plan.

'God! I am . . .' But Alfred didn't know what he was. 'And Eva

350

had *what* to do with this?' He tried to recollect what it was she had been trying to tell him minutes ago.

'The ticket was bought by that gibbering Russian woman...'

'Yelena?'

'They were all in it together. That crazy old German woman, the gigantic one with the stupid husband and all those infested animals, was apparently at our house most days last week when I was in Kumasi. Plotting, I suppose.'

'Eva isn't dishonest or scheming ... I mean if Dahlia had decided she wanted to leave and her friends were helping her...' What *had* she said?

Vincent laughed rudely. 'To commit a crime, yes, to kidnap my children. Listen,' he wagged a finger in Alfred's face, 'you'd better get her under control before she gets you into even deeper trouble.' He spoke slowly, as if that would impart the meaning of his words more clearly.

Alfred was bursting with the many things he wanted to say, but there by the gate, in case anyone might not already know just how much power and authority Vincent had at his disposal, stood two armed soldiers chatting sombrely to Solomon. He looked at the safe, high wall he had built in which to contain his family. He looked towards the big gate and saw the shiny patches on the soldiers' green dungarees, where over the years they had been overly starched and ironed. He saw how the barrels of their guns reflected the sunlight.

Vincent was talking. Alfred forced himself to listen.

'... and if *anything* happens to Cyril I will hold you personally responsible ... do you need another warning to understand that I am not to be messed with?'

Alfred shook his head stupefied.

'They are all devious, each one of them, I am sure...' Vincent had raised his finger again and was pointing it too close to Alfred's face, making him pay attention. 'Don't think you are immune. Would you like to see the back of Eva and all your children?' He laughed heartily and put his hands up in surrender. 'Ah! Maybe you would, maybe you would. But I will stop at nothing to protect what is mine . . .'

Alfred blinked. He wanted very much to punch Vincent. His mouth filled up with anticipatory saliva. He swallowed, nodded absentmindedly. He had heard about people who were said to have disappeared, although he didn't know any personally; dissidents? He had heard about those who had been thrown in jail without charges, without trial, without any immediate hope of release; criminals? He was thinking about the many stories of those who were allegedly picked up and flogged without explanation, left too scared to name their attackers; fools? He stared at Vincent and wiped his face trying to wake himself up from these nightmarish conjectures.

Had Vincent never believed in the rule of law? Wasn't that what differentiated them from bloodthirsty military men? Vincent had had the same privileged education as he had, a better education in fact; he was an Oxford law graduate. He would have succeeded in London just as he had in Accra. Had this barbarianism lain latently all this while? Alfred tried to think, but his mind felt thick and heavy.

'I'm off now. Warn your wife. Make sure she understands. I will not be made a fool of.' He patted Alfred on the shoulder and Alfred flinched. 'For all you know she has already planned when she is leaving. For some reason they think life will be better there. They want to make fools of *all* of us.'

Alfred watched Vincent leave. He didn't get up, he didn't say a word. He was struggling to think straight. Was Eva planning to leave? Had she bought a ticket already? She had mentioned the other day that she needed to go to the doctor. Was she updating her jabs so she could travel? Would she take all the children?

He had been aware over the past weeks of a sense of something bad, something unbearable, and had been unable to dispel the thoughts. He had put it down to the strife at home, the guilt about his other child, and to the bizarre and shocking happenings recently: the soldiers, the killing outside the house. But perhaps his sixth sense had been trying to warn him all along that he was about to lose the most precious things he had.

Would Eva really do that to him? He had offered, like a gentleman, thinking it was the right thing to do, but he had never expected she would try and slink off like this. Besides, he knew she had been to see Agnes, that she had told his mother she would stay. Had she been lying? Would she betray his trust like that? Make a fool of him, as Vincent had put it, and in front of everyone? In his own country? He was tapping his feet, waiting impatiently for something.

He fetched the bottle of brandy and put it on the table. He half-filled a tumbler, drank it in one go and poured himself another measure. He realised he had been grinding his teeth and his jaw was beginning to cramp up. He fidgeted on the seat. How could she? *Why* would she? Because of a child? One child? His mind was clouding over from too many thoughts and questions.

He emptied his glass, barely letting it touch his tongue. His tummy was on fire. Knowing how much he loved her, would she really take away his children like this? Is this why she was still refusing to talk to him? 'How *dare* she?' he said out loud, rising from the sofa and knocking the table so that the bottle wobbled.

He ran up the stairs with such speed that he had to stop at the top to regain his balance and let the wave of dizziness pass. When had the ability to move fast become a challenge? What else was happening around him that he hadn't noticed? How long had his attention to detail been this slack? He could feel his grip on reality slipping. He was shaking. Is this what it feels like to be going mad, he wondered.

Eva was in the bathroom. So, she was back in their bedroom. Why now? He caught a glimpse of himself in the mirror. He had been too nice. He had been too controlled, tried too hard to hold everything together for far too long. Well, he also had a breaking point.

She came out of the bathroom still wet with a towel around her.

'I imagine you know why Vincent was here?'

Eva nodded. 'Because of Dahlia . . .'

'Because of Dahlia? *Because of Dahlia?* Is that all you can say? She tried to kidnap both of his children . . .'

'Please don't shout at me, Alfred. She had to flee, it wasn't kidnap . . .'

'I warned you about Vincent, about Dahlia. He is not someone we want to cross. Look what he did this morning, he is capable of ruining me . . .'

'This is not about you, this is about poor Dahlia . . .'

'Poor Dahlia,' Alfred said in a mocking tone. 'What exactly is so poor about bloody Dahlia?' he sneered, ignoring the shock on her face. 'And if you have any ideas about taking my children . . .' He faltered because she laughed. He could feel his hands quivering. He had never before wanted to hit her, and the raw desire terrified him now. He shook his head, trying to loosen the anger that was overwhelming him, frightening him a little.

'Where is your passport,' he said turning towards the chest of drawers where they kept their important papers.

'What do you want my passport for?'

Alfred didn't seem to hear her. He was staring into the drawer as if he was trying to make some sense of what it contained.

Eva laughed again even though she felt distinctly uncomfortable. 'Alfred . . .?'

Something in her tone made him turn and look at her, deep into her blue eyes, to try to reconnect with her, but his head was muddled, his vision blurred. She had laughed then seemed distraught, and then she had laughed again, and now look, she was smirking. Mocking him, taunting him. He turned back to the drawer and began to paw at the contents, tossing things out underneath his arms.

'Don't Alfred! Stop it,' Eva pleaded.

'Aha,' he said holding up an A5 envelope that said 'passports' like a trophy. He ripped it open and poured the passports on to the bed, but Eva's was not in there. 'Where is it?' he demanded, marching over to her. He gripped her arm.

'You are hurting me,' she wailed. 'Alfred, you're scaring me.'

'Where is the bloody passport,' he spat, shaking her hard, making her hair flutter about her face and stick to her wet face. He let go of her hard so that she fell back and caught her hip on the side of their bed.

She stayed there in a heap while Alfred started to hurl things about the room. She covered her head with her hands, not wanting to see any further destruction.

'In my wardrobe,' she sniffed. 'At the bottom, in my evening bag . . .'

He walked back into the room, held the passport in his hands where it shook so fast, she was sure he was waving it about on purpose.

She folded her arms and looked at him with disgust. 'What is wrong with you?'

Without taking his eyes off her, he ripped the passport in two.

Eva parted her lips to say something and then shut them again. She felt numb, as if she was trapped in a outlandish dream. Her hip throbbed, and her arm too, where he had gripped so hard that bruises were beginning to form.

She felt as if she was suffocating; she had to get out. She stumbled to the door, down the corridor, down the stairs. She picked up Alfred's glass and drank the brandy. She refilled it, emptied it again. Then she sat and clasped her hands, trying to tell herself that what had happened hadn't really happened. That her husband wasn't really a beast. She knew she would be eternally grateful that she had given Auntie Gee her permission today of all days, to take the children out. They had all set off early to Auntie

Gee's favourite seamstress who was going to sew some matching traditional outfits for each of them.

Eva watched him coming down the stairs. In each hand he held a piece of her passport, looking at them as if he was judging whether he might be able to glue it all back together.

Silently he got another tumbler, poured some more brandy in each glass and then sat across from her.

'Why didn't you give it to me the first time I asked you for it?' he said in a hoarse voice.

'Don't you dare blame me for this.' She laughed hysterically, horrified and assertive in equal measures. 'Do you think that all of a sudden I am no longer British? If I had wanted to go home I would have. I am here because I want to be, not because you make me stay.' She felt indignant and yet afraid. 'You spineless bastard,' she spoke with more venom now than she ever had. The brandy was swirling through her, anaesthetizing her emotions, deadening her limbs.

Alfred dropped his head into his hands and tried to think. He was no better than Vincent after all, was he? What turns a man into a monster, he wondered? And exactly when had madness overtaken his life? When he lifted his head, the entire room spun and he realised how drunk he was. How the hell did everything get so out of control? He heard the answer ringing mockingly in his ear: *one step at a time* . . .

His voice was deflated when he spoke again. 'What has happened to us? I had a bloody affair, a meaningless liaison with a woman whose name I can barely remember and look what has happened to us.'

'You turned into a bully . . .'

'Evie, I am so sorry. Vincent got to me. He convinced me you were going to leave in secret, with the children. I am so very sorry.'

'You can go to hell!' she shrieked. 'And while you're at it, why don't you go and live elsewhere?' She emptied her glass. She had never got so drunk this fast.

'No!' he shouted. 'I won't go. I love you. I don't want to live without you.' He took a long sip of his brandy. 'You . . . I heard that you went to see . . . that you said you would stay . . .'

'You went to see her again?'

'No. No . . . my mother told me. I was relieved, delighted, that I had a chance to make things up to you, that we might make a go of it. I was flustered. Vincent was altogether so sinister this morning, he scared me in fact.' He lifted his hands and whispered, his voice slurring, 'He'll stop at nothing . . .'

'He would have killed Dahlia if she'd stayed.'

Alfred shrugged. 'I don't know . . . but do you really want to leave me? To go home?'

'Yes, I do want to go home.' She was weary and drained by all the emotion and drama of the past days. 'It's been so long.'

He knelt beside her and held her hands. 'I know. And I know I can't keep you here against your will, Evie. But God, I don't want you to leave.'

'I don't want to.' She felt the tension in his fingers reduce instantly.

'I've missed you so much, Eva.'

'I hate you for what you did. Really, really hate you.' She looked at him so he could see how much she meant it. 'I gave up so much for you.' Her chest heaved painfully.

He nuzzled her ear. He stroked her arm, her fingers.

She turned to face him. 'I don't want to go Alfred. I mean, I do. I wish I could go and see my parents. So much so that sometimes it aches here, a real pain.' She put her hand on her breastbone. 'Sometimes I feel crippled with yearning. I want to smell spring rain, I want to drink a glass of cow's milk that tastes like cow's milk, I want to eat a bowl of mashed potatoes.' She shook her head. 'I want . . . to smell wet grass, I want to hear seagulls, sit by a fire, eat scones with real jam . . . but . . .' She wept. 'That isn't my home any more. I mean . . . of course it is. It always will be a "home" of sorts, where I am from and all that, but this . . . this is home now.' Her voice had dropped to a whisper. 'And that in itself is the most terrifying thing in all this. Can't you see? Can't you understand? If the place that is meant to be home feels hostile and unwelcoming, if the man that you think is your rock, the centre of your universe, shifts and crumbles, then nothing is stable any longer. Nothing can ever be relied upon to stay the same . . . I haven't been able to think straight, I haven't been able to figure out what would be right, where I belong . . . I was furious, Alfred. I am still angry . . . you let me down . . .'

'I will never forget what I did, what I ruined, what I gambled.' He looked at her earnestly.

The softening continued and she smiled at him cautiously. 'We're drunk.'

'We are . . .' He kissed her.

She was apprehensive. What would it be like? Knowing he had been with someone else. But she had spent weeks now contemplating the alternatives and none of them appealed enough. Remain with him but apart, as they had been living since she found out, leave him and set up on her own in Accra, or leave altogether. Wouldn't any one of these options be more attractive if she didn't love him?

She couldn't help it, she loved him, albeit with bruises and dents. She wouldn't know how to be apart from him. No, not at all, in fact. Categorically not for ever anyhow.

He stood, held his arms out and pulled her up. They wobbled a little and he pulled her tight, drowned out her questions against his body. He wanted to make assurances, guarantee that he would never hurt her or leave her, never forsake her, that he would take away the hurt, but each oath stuck in his throat. Words wouldn't do now.

She turned so he could kiss her. For a brief moment she

remembered how she had thought she would never be able to give herself to him freely and fully. Then she surrendered with zest to the waves of desire that crashed about her, far too powerful to withstand reason or conjecture. As she feasted her senses on him, his smell, his touch, tears streamed down her face and when he led the way, she followed him upstairs where they moulded their bodies and allowed healing in, gave hope the space to flourish.

Chapter Twenty-Four

The next morning, Eva woke with a start. She lay still for a moment, wondering what had woken her. A banging, a clattering of sorts, came from near the window. She held her breath; they were being burgled. She sat up, tried to clear the fog in her mind so she could think. She saw the shadow of a man trying to reach the window through the burglar proofing and mosquito netting. She was on the verge of calling out when she heard a muffled voice calling, 'Madam, madam!' She went to the window, opened a louver and heard Solomon say, 'Madam, please, come quick, please oh!'

'What is it?' She turned off the air-conditioner so she could hear him more clearly and she heard what sounded like a woman howling.

'Please madam. I beg oh! You just come quickly. Zachariah. Please you just come and see. Please Architect too oh, I beg.'

The sky was lightening. Eva could hear the neighbours beginning their day's work; water was being fetched, yards swept and meals prepared.

She switched on the light, and called out to Alfred. He stirred and sat up looking dazzled.

'Something's up . . . Solomon wants us to come downstairs. He sounds agitated, something about Zachariah, maybe he's ill?'

Faustina sat on one of the chairs on the veranda outside the living room. Eva had never seen her so still. Akua stood by looking fearful.

'What on earth is going on?' asked Eva.

'Madam . . . Zachariah . . .'

Eva shook her head. She dashed to the corner of the house where Solomon stood with his hands on his head. He was staring in the direction of where Zachariah usually sat to watch over them all.

She turned the corner. She saw him reclined on his chair, his chin raised to the sky, his teeth slightly bared, his hands clasped in his lap. He looked asleep. She walked towards him until her feet refused to go any closer because her eyes had seen that the dark substance beneath his chair and all over the front of his shirt was dried blood that had oozed from a deep gash in his neck.

She screamed, covered her mouth with both hands but couldn't stop herself retching, tearing everything out of her empty stomach.

Alfred ran around the house and stopped next to her, also unwilling to go any closer to the horrific sight. He gripped her, and they clung to each other.

'Dear God!' he called out over and over.

'Who would do this?' Eva yelled, looking at Zachariah as if he might sit up and tell them.

Alfred led Eva back to the veranda, where she sat next to Faustina. She listened while Solomon explained how he had been on his way to go and buy some breakfast and when he got to the gate, he called out a greeting to Zachariah. 'I said to him, "Hey, you better wake up and do your job proper, man." He didn't mind me, so I wanted to shake him and tell him to get up . . . please, it is then that I saw that he has been murdered dead.'

Faustina started to wail again and Eva wrapped her arms around herself and rocked in her seat.

Alfred went into the house to get a bottle of brandy and glasses. He poured large measures, the liquid sloshing in his shaking hands. He held out a glass to Solomon who shook his head, looking diffident. 'This is no time for politeness; it is like medicine, drink it!' Alfred emptied his glass and poured another. He welcomed the warmth that spread through his gut, eagerly anticipated how it might fortify him. 'We need to sort this out before the children get up, I don't want them to see this . . . or to ever hear about it. Is that clear?' He looked around at them. 'Solomon, you and I will go to the police station. Make a report.'

'The body . . . what are we going to do?' asked Eva.

Alfred shrugged. 'Take it to the police hospital, it's the closest, I suppose? We'll put him in the boot . . .' He paused, took a long sip of his drink, cleared his throat and then continued. 'They'll send it to the mortuary, I don't know . . . Has he got any family here?'

Eva shook her head. 'Can you please clean the . . . mess . . . before you go? The children mustn't see this.'

Faustina moaned, low and gentle. She hadn't touched her drink. She hadn't moved, in fact, and still sat huddled with her arms wrapped protectively around herself, her face set in what looked like a combination of outrage and terror. Eva put her hand on her back, patted her, and Faustina whimpered.

She looked at Alfred, 'I'm going to give her something.' She got one of the tablets Margrit had given her, crouched down in front of Faustina and made her swallow it with a mouthful of brandy. 'It will help you.'

Eva took one herself; the day's events had already been too outlandishly terrifying, too dreadful, and she had barely slept last night, thinking about Dahlia.

'Solomon drink up, we'll go now.'

Eva turned away so that she wouldn't have to watch the

indignity of Zachariah's exit. In the end his hard work had killed him, she thought sadly. Too tired from his day's gardening, he clearly hadn't moved when they crept up on him, he wouldn't have seen, wouldn't have heard his life about to end. He wouldn't have had enough time to be afraid; somehow that had to be a comfort.

She heard Alfred grunt under the weight of the body, then yelp and swear loudly. She heard the sound, rather like a heavy sack of flour being thrown into the boot of a car. She watched them drive off. She felt her already broken heart bleed a little more. How much before it could no longer be mended, she wondered?

When Auntie Gee came downstairs Eva was on the sofa in a soft daze from the Valium and the warm brandy. A hush had smothered the house. Alfred and Solomon were not back and Eva had sent Faustina back to bed, telling her to try and get some sleep. Akua was sitting shocked in the kitchen, waiting to be needed.

Eva told Auntie Gee what had happened in a tired voice, with the fewest number of words she could, with the minimum of drama or flourish: *we found the watchman dead . . .*

Auntie Gee sat in silence while the significance of what she had heard solidified in her mind. She lowered her head on to her hands and shrieked, 'Yee! This is a bad, bad sign.'

An abrupt death like this doesn't happen just by itself. There are too many outlandish things going on around here. There must be forces at play behind the scenes, working to bring it about. 'We have to get a priest to pray.'

Eva shut her eyes. She didn't have the will to try and understand her mother-in-law today.

'Where is Alfred?'

When she told her, Auntie Gee shrieked again, a shrill sound so piercing that Eva shuddered and opened her eyes.

'We have to purify the house, the garden, the car too . . .'

Eva stood up. She needed a cup of coffee. As she walked to the kitchen, she heard Auntie Gee mutter, 'Oh, Zachariah. What kind of way to die is this?'

When the soldiers arrived, Margrit and Kojo were still on the veranda having their morning tea.

'Are you Doctor?'

Kojo stood up, smiled and nodded. 'What can I do for you?'

'You are under arrest, please . . .'

'What?'

'Must be a mistake,' said Margrit rising to her feet.

'Let's go, please.'

'There must be some misunderstanding here,' said Kojo. 'I . . . what is this about?'

'We are following orders.'

'Who sent you?'

'We have been instructed. Let's go.' A couple of them grabbed Kojo by the arms and started to march him towards the gate.

They were silent and refused eye contact, which frightened Margrit. 'Wait a minute. You can't do this,' she said boldly, but aware that she didn't feel as confident as she sounded. 'What is it that you want?'

One of the men turned and glared at her. 'Are you offering us a bribe? What do you take us for? You better beware of yourself . . .'

They gripped Kojo more firmly, and he winced. Anger propelled her, and Margrit lunged at the solders and tried to pull them off him.

One of them pushed her away. The rest of them ignored her and shoved Kojo along a little quicker so that he stumbled.

'Let him go!'

'I'll be all right, darling.'

'Please tell me where you are taking him,' she said in a terrified wispy voice. The reality of what was happening was dawning on her, and a vision of what might await Kojo flickered in her mind.

'Please . . . tell me?' Waves of hot and cold rippled over her skin.

'Go to Alfred and Eva, don't stay here alone,' said Kojo.

'What are you going to do to him?' cried Margrit, and then she felt the butt of the gun hit her cheekbone and the side of her head and the pain was crippling. She fell backwards, fighting the waves of nausea and unconsciousness which sought to pull her under. In the distance, through blurred sight, she could see Kojo being pushed into an unmarked car that had been waiting on the street outside their gate and she felt a paralysing chill of fright which she had never before experienced.

This bloody, bloody country and these stupid, stupid people, thought Margrit as she stumbled to the bathroom. She stared at her face. The skin around her eye was raised and raw. Her head was tender where it felt as if they had cracked her skull. The bruise would be deep, but her eye, thankfully, was fine. She splashed water on her face, tied her hair back, dabbed the broken skin with iodine to prevent any infection and winced at the pain. Now she had a violet shadow on the side of her head. She scraped her hair into a bun, pulled on a clean dress and headed to Eva's house.

As she walked up the street, she stamped her feet angrily, held her hand to her throbbing head. She didn't have any petrol in her car and Kojo's had been parked in a queue for days now. She was fuming with herself that she had allowed both their cars to run out. And now how would she find out where had they taken her Kojo? What would they do to him? She felt her insides constrict again, felt that pull deep where she imagined her womb to be. She would never forgive them if they hurt her husband, if they took him away from her. Her feet stopped. She would kill them if they did. She gripped her arms, tried to calm herself, to hold on to some clarity.

'No, no!' she chanted, defying the idea that anything appalling might happen to her dear Kojo. She wouldn't be able to live without him.

In all their years in Ghana, nothing like this had ever happened to them. She couldn't entertain the thoughts that now flooded her mind. He was a good man. They would see that, they would realise that he was innocent, that whoever or whatever had put them up to this was mistaken. He was good, all the way through, like a stick of rock. An old English friend of theirs had said that once, and then he had had to explain what a stick of rock was, how a word was written all the way through it, from top to bottom, how wherever you broke it, you could see that word. 'That's what Kojo is like, good all the way through . . .'

When Yelena called, Eva was in a warm trance, anesthetised from the brandy that she had been drinking all morning and by the Valium too. She hadn't been able to eat anything even though Auntie Gee had asked Akua to make some toast and boiled eggs for her before she went to fetch the priest. A skin had developed over the top of her sugary, milky tea, which stood untouched on the table in front of her.

Yelena's voice had that high pitched quality of a person stressed to breaking point, and it jolted Eva slightly from her soothing haze.

'Can I come to you? Soldiers have been here, they . . .' she swallowed. 'They say that I have to close the salon. I don't understand. They say that my papers are not in order . . . that maybe I have to leave . . . that I am working illegally.' Her voice broke.

Eva sat up and tried to see through her misty eyes.

'I dropped the boys off at Wisdom's house. I thought it best if they weren't here . . . in case the soldiers come back, but now I am afraid. I don't want to be here alone if they do come back.'

'Come. Of course, come here . . . I suppose it is good for the boys to be with their father. Yes, come over. I am here. Alfred will be back soon too. He had to go to the police station . . . our watchman was murdered in the night, you see.' The words clunked and clanged and Eva, herself startled by them, shook her head as if she might be able in retrospect, to soothe their delivery.

There was a long silence at the other end of the phone, then Yelena whispered, 'My God . . .'

'Come over Yelena. Bring your things. Stay with us.'

She sat back and groaned. The house had settled into a dazed hush. Auntie Gee had gone off hurriedly to fetch the priest, taking the children with her. As she pointed out, 'with Faustina intoxicated, Eva drinking and Alfred busy carting dead bodies about, there is no one else to look after my grandchildren. Besides,' she muttered to herself, 'this place is no longer safe.'

Not long after, Eva heard the bell. She was too loose-limbed to move, but she saw Solomon heading to the gate, noted his less poised gait, and closed her eyes, sighing deeply.

She opened her eyes a little when she heard a shuffle on the veranda. Margrit's large shadow loomed in the doorway. Through the slit of light, she saw Margrit's hair was dishevelled where she had pulled tufts out of her ponytail, her face stained in indigo around a nasty bruise on the side of her head. Eva sat up, feeling everything swim a little in her head.

Margrit collapsed on to a chair, held her head in her hands and said, 'They arrested Kojo.'

Eva listened to what had happened. She battled for clarity through the dizziness, felt her hands shake, her whole body jitter. Margrit was predictably restrained with the telling, but Eva had never seen her look this weak and vulnerable; Margrit was strong, always knew what to do and what to say, calm at all times.

'Where could they have taken him?'

Eva shook her head. Nothing made sense any more if a man like Kojo could be arrested. 'Alfred will know what to do, who to call,' she said. She told her about Zachariah, and wished she didn't have to, but she didn't see any other option.

Margrit paled visibly. 'What if they kill Kojo?'

Eva moved closer to Margrit and put her arms around her. Margrit's body shook all over and she was making a whimpering sound. Instinctively Eva opened her mouth to respond, then she closed it again, too stunned and wordless. Besides, what would she say? What could she say? Of course they might kill him. After all, why not? Hadn't someone killed her kind, unassuming Zachariah? A harmless, forlorn, tragedy of a being? No, absolutely nothing had to make sense, and it was best to let go of all tenets of normality now, best to just accept that things were now decidedly arbitrary, that the least likely events were in fact, rather likely to occur.

Eva leaned back on the sofa, her hands limp between her thighs, her chin up, her eyes staring at the ceiling. The day's events had caused her brain to melt down, her thoughts had thickened to a halt. In the silence between them, she could hear Margrit breathing so softly, so imperceptibly, that Eva thought she might have fallen asleep. She tried to clear her mind, to drain the musings and wonderings that only led back to the frightening blankness, to confirmation that control and order had been ripped from them, that for now, randomness reigned.

When Alfred walked in a short while later, Eva looked up and swallowed the lump that had formed instantaneously in her throat when she saw the blood smears on his shirt and trousers. He looked ashen and reached for a drink. Eva asked Akua to make him a fried egg sandwich and some tea, then she told him what had happened to Kojo.

Eva saw how dread swamped his face, his eyes, saw how he couldn't hide it, how he didn't even try.

He went to the phone, called the police station to report the incident, see if he could find out anything, but the receptionist said there was no one available to talk to him, and could he perhaps try later? He tried other numbers, friends who might know, people in power, someone who might talk. He swore frequently, frustrated staccatos which punctuated the silence.

Finally, he got a lead. He listened helpless, afraid of his help-lessness. He tried to ignore the tone of malice as an acquaintance said, 'Yes, I heard that your wife and her friends were involved in the kidnapping of the Ejura-Wilson child . . . the wrong person to cross . . . be careful, Alfred. Watch out . . .'

Careful? Watch out? He didn't even have a watchman any more. He was dead, murdered. He felt a sudden chill and put his hand on the back of his neck where bumps had appeared all over his skin. A watchman for a daughter? He tried to get rid of the dangerous thought, this life-threatening assumption.

And when Eva mentioned that Yelena was on her way too, he slapped his head hard with his hand. 'That bastard . . .!'

The women stirred, they flicked their eyes curiously. Which bastard? Which of the many?

'Dear God . . .!' he whispered as it dawned on him.

'Alfred, you don't think he . . . you don't think Vincent had anything to do with all this . . .?' asked Eva.

'No . . . no, don't say it. Never!' He closed his eyes and tried to block out the sharp image from this morning that was replaying in his mind, tried not to think about how he and Solomon had struggled to carry Zachariah into the car. His body had stiffened, his eyes were slightly open, and when they picked him up, a moan, a puff of air really, was released through his lips, forming a small bubble of blood. Alfred had stifled a scream, dropped the body and retched. Had his throat been slit in the middle of the night because he had been unfortunate in his choice of employer? Alfred retched again and ran to the toilet.

Margrit sat like a statue and stared at the clock. She watched each second tick by while she waited for the phone to ring, for the man that Alfred had spoken to to get back to them. He had said he would, and although she had become used to the frustration of people not doing what they had offered to, she hoped, she had to. She had to imagine that it was possible that he would call back. After all, what else was there, if not hope?

When an hour had crawled past, she stood abruptly, flapped out her dress and said, 'I am going to look for him. I can't just sit here . . .'

'Hang on,' said Alfred, clearly afraid. 'Where are you going to go? I don't think that's a good idea, let's wait and see if we hear anything . . .'

'And in the meantime, maybe my husband is being flayed to death? Tortured? Killed? No, I don't think so. I have waited enough. Maybe too long already. Perhaps all they want is money, someone to come and get him.'

'But they didn't tell you where they were taking him . . .'

'No!' Margrit punched the air by her legs. 'No, they didn't, the stupid idiots.'

'So . . . where are you going?' asked Yelena meekly, trying to be kind.

'Listen, I don't know, do I? But I have to do something, do you understand?' Her face was furrowed. She started to mutter. 'I have to find him. I can't lose him. I can't just sit here and wait in case some bigwig decides to spare him. He hasn't even done anything wrong . . .' Her shoulders heaved and she wiped her cheek with the back of her hand.

Eva and Yelena looked at each other; they had never see Margrit like this.

'Alfred . . .?'

He stood and shrugged, looked at Eva in despair. But he picked the phone up and tried the police station once more. After a while, he held the receiver out into the air as if they might all hear, and said, 'It's ringing off the hook. I mean, you'd think someone would pick it up, you'd think they'd find the incessant ringing irritating?'

Margrit had paused to watch him, but now she walked purposefully to the door. 'I have to do *something*.'

'I'll come with you, Margrit. Why don't we try Cantonments police station, it's the closest big one.' He lifted his eyebrows at Eva as if to say, this is going to be a waste of time, but he held on to Margrit's elbow and guided her into the car carefully, smiled at her and said with his most reassuring voice, 'I am sure everything will be fine.'

All the way there, Margrit stared straight ahead. She had never felt such sickening dread, thick and immobilising, even the blood flowing through her had slowed, and now she couldn't really speak, couldn't really hear.

At the police station, she approached the entrance where a few policemen were milling about aimlessly on the veranda. She gripped her dress, clenching the fabric so firmly that her fingernails pinched her palm. She stood while Alfred asked the group sitting on benches on the veranda whether they had seen Kojo or heard of him. He looked at them one by one, but they shook their heads, each of them, and stared blankly, their expressions sympathetic but ineffectual.

Margrit interrupted Alfred, clasped her hands and began to plead. 'He hasn't done anything wrong. I need to find him, please help me, please?'

'Oh, madam, please don't be worried, okay? Everything will by all means be all right, okay?' said one of the men coming up to her and patting her shoulder.

'But where could they have they taken him?'

'You see now, we don't know . . . but you write your number here,' he said tearing off the corner of a used envelope and handing it to her, 'and if we have any news we will follow up with you.'

'Please . . .?'

'Madam, these days strange things are happening, isn't it? It is true, but we are not involved. If anything you should go to Burma

371

Camp, but in fact, we cannot advise you to do that today. Anyway, if as you say that your husband has not committed any treason and has not partaken in corrupt practices, by all means he will be released to you. Don't worry, isn't it?'

'I'll make some more calls when we get back,' said Alfred.

'I really should go to Burma Camp . . .'

'No! You can't do that.'

'Then what?' she asked looking at him, her face contorted. 'What would you do?'

'Oh God, I don't know Margrit. Listen . . . if Vincent is behind this, chances are he'll let Kojo go . . .'

'He killed your watchman . . .'

'We don't know for sure . . .'

'Ya, we do.'

'All we can do is hope, and wait, and pray.' Alfred thumped the steering wheel suddenly, making Margrit jump. 'But what kind of man is he anyway?'

Margrit shook her head and blinked, allowing a teardrop to roll down her cheek. 'Please be okay, my *Schatz*,' she whispered, 'please . . .'

When Auntie Gee bounded back into the house, her energy was at odds with the lethargy and depression that had settled around them. She had heralded her arrival from the gate by hollering for Solomon, for Faustina and Akua, summoning the children to follow her inside, 'And every other Tom, Dick and Harry in the boys' quarters. Now, now, please.'

In the living room, she clapped her hands, stirred them all. Slowly, one by one, they sat up, tried to focus on what she was saying, stared at the man she was pointing at. He was standing in her shadow, wearing a dog collar, and he smiled meekly at them all, nodding with hopeful anticipation.

Eva was in a daze and when she looked at Margrit and Yelena she could see that they too were woozy from too much alcohol in the stifling heat. She felt a little faint and had a sudden craving for a cold Coke, but they had run out of soft drinks.

'Please, we don't have all day here,' said Auntie Gee as Faustina made her way gingerly towards the living room followed by everyone else. She gestured to the priest. 'Reverend here has come to undo the work of the evil that has been poured out over this house and everyone in it, to purify everything. Over to you, Reverend, please.'

He was still smiling. Quite inappropriately, Eva thought, wondering if he had any idea of their collective confusion and horror, and if so what exactly he might do about it.

He spoke softly in a voice which was high-pitched. 'Thank you for inviting me into your home. You can give great thanks to Grandma here for caring about the welfare of you all to the extent that she has taken the effort to bring me here on this fine day to cleanse this house. Please, let me remind you that the occult in all forms, witchcraft and such like are very hazardous pastimes. They are not to be meddled with unless you are willing to face the consequences which can be both dire and painful and eternal.'

'Do you hear that, Auntie Gee?' said Alfred.

She looked at him with a face she normally reserved for the children.

'What we shall do now is to pray for forgiveness for the error in all our ways, to renounce all sins and turn once more to the one and only true God. And of course, we shall remember our dearly departed friend. Please, follow me.' He lowered himself on to his knees and gestured for all of them to follow suit.

The prayer went on for a while. Auntie Gee murmured periodically, the children fidgeted and Simon asked a number of times, in a loud whisper, *Is it nearly over, Mummy?* As the priest prayed for their protection, for angels and saints of heaven to protect them, to keep all evil away, Eva refused to close her eyes. She looked around at Yelena and Margrit, whose expressions had normalised, Alfred, clenching his jaw, wringing his hands. Auntie

Gee, Akua and Solomon were nodding fervently in agreement with the priest, clearly attaching their own thoughts and prayers to the wings of his. Peace and Harmony, Faustina's children, looked solemn and afraid. Faustina, who had been roused from an intoxicated sleep, looked soft and sweet, her eyes glazed. And she looked at where Zachariah might have stood. She felt her heart lurch again. She thought about his life, wretched and short, filled with so much pain, and she hoped hard, so hard, that he had realised how much she had adored him, how she had appreciated him, how she would miss him.

When the final Amen was said, everyone stood looking almost relieved. Bodies relaxed, faces too, and Faustina even managed a half-smile.

Auntie Gee stood surrounded by the entire household and smoothed down her dress, looking satisfied. 'Now I will cook some food. Everybody must eat something. And please, no further consumption of alcoholic beverages . . . if you don't mind.'

The day dragged, and then as ever, ended abruptly as the sun set suddenly, turning day to night with speed that could still take Eva aback even after all these years in the tropics. Outside, it was dark and quiet. A discernable hush descended over the house, shrouding the edginess and terror that filled them all.

Auntie Gee emerged from the kitchen and told them that the food was ready, that she had fed the children and that Akua was bathing them and putting them to bed. 'That Faustina is still intoxicated from the drugs you gave her, Eva,' she said. 'Let us hope that by morning she is back to her usual senses, isn't it?'

'She's just in shock,' said Eva.

'Yes, but not everybody is used to consuming alcohol like this.'

Auntie Gee had prepared rice and sardine stew and she insisted that everyone eat something. 'Food is essential at a time like this,' she said, handing out bowls, and then hovering to make sure that they ate some of it. She sat beside Margrit and stroked her arm.

'Just one or two spoons, my dear, then I will be satisfied. You must have some energy.'

When she had eaten a little, Margrit, who had sat silently ever since they got back from the police station, leaned back in the sofa. She held a tumbler in both hands, resting it on her belly, and sipped periodically on whatever Eva poured in her glass, first brandy and then when the bottle was finished, whisky.

Alfred had insisted that Yelena and Margrit stay the night, which they accepted. The twins could stay with their father, and everyone agreed that Margrit shouldn't be on her own at home.

The food had made Eva drowsy, she stretched her legs out, clasped her hands behind her head. She wanted to go to sleep, but she couldn't leave her friends and retire to her bed, besides, she didn't really imagine she would fall asleep with the things going on in her head. Yet, as time passed, every so often, one of them dozed off, head nodding here and there, and then the chatter of the others would wake them up.

Eva was relieved when Alfred nodded off and started to snore; he had been on the go since dawn and she could see how fraught he was from the day's events. She looked around at their heavy drooping shapes; Margrit looked worn out and Yelena anxious. She offered to make up makeshift beds, but they both refused and insisted they would stay on the sofas, hot and tired, but alert and afraid.

When the first gunshots reverberated in the distance Eva opened her bleary eyes. Alfred hadn't stirred, but Yelena had sat bolt upright and Margrit was frowning.

'Not again,' she said.

They heard shouts of terror outside, the furore of people seeking safety. Eva shouted to wake Alfred up.

'Turn off the lights,' he said as soon as he realised what was going on. And there was a quick scramble to the various switches. 'We don't want to attract them . . .'

Eva ran off upstairs to check that the children hadn't woken.

She sat on Abigail's bed, stroked her hair gently and wished she could shift the nasty foreboding she had. What else was there to lose? How helpless she felt as she realised that this, the worst day she had ever lived through, might not be over yet. If Vincent was behind the day's events, how much further would he go? Would he wish to harm her children too? Would their watchman's life not be enough? She shuddered with renewed alarm, terrified by their circumstances. We are sitting ducks, she thought, stroking Simon's forehead while he puckered his lips, moaned softly and then turned over and continued his deep, replenishing sleep.

And for the rest of the night, they sat in fright as waves of gunfire came and went. Long after midnight, a military van rumbled past the house and shots rang out too close and loud. Eva reached out for Alfred's hand.

They twitched from the lack of sleep; the alcohol and the heat had taken their toll too. Mosquito coils burned around the room, filling the air with a pungent scent, but still the insects buzzed about and occasionally one of them slapped out and scratched where they had been bitten.

Eva longed for oblivion. Anything to numb her feelings and her thoughts. Alfred was restless now, gone was the calm that allowed him to sleep earlier. He twisted and turned at every sound, kept getting up to look out the window because he was sure he heard the gate.

In the early hours of the morning, while it was still dark, there was an announcement on the radio: *Another coup. Afriye has been shot dead. Frimpong is in charge.*

'Who the hell is Frimpong?' asked Alfred. 'Where do these people come from? One minute no one has heard of them, next thing they are running our country.'

'Afriye didn't even get a proper chance to warm his seat,' said Auntie Gee.

The news remained erratic, and what little there was seemed

ridiculously trivial. The gunshots had ceased, but never had the emblem of freedom and justice had to remain so still for so long. Solomon reported that he had heard from the neighbours that there were a lot of dead people in the barracks, and the soldiers were angry and bloodthirsty.

General Frimpong made his first televised broadcast to the nation just before dawn, confirming that he was in charge, and that they were 'with immediate effect beginning the clean up of government to rid it of the infection of corruption and mismanagement that it has festered under for too long. As well as those few who have leeched our society dry and grown fat on the misfortune of the many.' He requested, although Eva thought it sounded like a command, that 'all citizens must return to life as normal today. Your country needs you to get back to productivity with immediate effect. Everyone has their part to play.' As a postscript, he added, 'I assure you that looters and pillagers will be dealt with in the harshest possible terms.'

Alfred paced about anxiously, waiting impatiently for each further snippet of news, muttering to himself the various facts, desperate to spin some sense out of the incomplete information.

Eva tried to call Vincent to make sure Cyril was all right, but she couldn't get through to their house. When she gave up, she jammed the phone in its cradle a little too hard. 'Bloody country!' she said, and went to the drinks cabinet. 'Rum anyone? We've run out of anything else.'

When the phone rang, day was dawning outside and the jingle intruded harshly. Alfred was the only one who moved. He was sore and stiff from the night, he felt tetchy. He listened, nodding, but when he put the receiver down he said to Margrit with the first smile of the day, 'Kojo is fine. They have let him go. He's coming here.'

He arrived in a taxi just as Auntie Gee was coordinating a breakfast feast with lots of fried eggs and corned beef sandwiches.

377

Margrit ran to him, her body swaying beneath her long, voluminous dress. She held him, then stepped back when he grimaced and he explained that they had used a belt on his back, which stung when she held him. She cradled his face. His eyes were swollen, his lip cut and bulbous and he smiled at her, wiped her tears away.

'Ah ah! You are such a softy, my dear. Really, you are.'

'Barbarians!' said Alfred.

'Ah, you see. They are misguided. When I was leaving, they apologised to me, the policemen. I tripped and they all jumped up to help me, they told me to take my time.' He chuckled a little. 'They were following orders I believe . . . I think that your friend's husband might have had something to do with this.'

'Do you really think he had anything to do with Zachariah?' asked Eva. They looked at each other. 'And you,' she said pointing at Kojo and Yelena.

'Seems too much of a coincidence . . .' said Margrit.

'Alfred?'

He looked at her and shrugged. 'He might have . . . I don't know, love.'

'All I know for sure is that he is not worthy of being called a man. It makes me sick to think of what he put Dahlia through,' said Yelena.

Eva was overjoyed when Cyril phoned from a neighbour's house a few days later. He told Eva how he had hidden under his mother's bed when the soldiers came for his father, how he had stayed there all night by himself, and only dared to come out when the sun came up. Eva listened to him in amazement; he sounded a little detached, but as soon as he had finished his mechanised recounting of what had happened he broke down and was inconsolable.

'Don't worry, Cyril. We are coming to get you. Stay where you are, and don't worry, my love, everything is going to be fine.'

Why had she said that, she thought, when she put the phone down. How the hell did she know what was going to happen?

Alfred went to get him, and when he walked into the house later that evening with a bag stuffed with some of his belongings, he seemed to have grown a few years and inches too. He seemed nonchalant, smiled and allowed himself to be hugged by Eva. He recounted the way his father had come on to the plane with some soldiers, and that he had taken him and said that his mother could take Jasmine. Even though the listeners expressed disgust and shock as he spoke, Cyril continued to recount the events in unembellished language, almost as though he was telling them the plot of a rather boring film that he had watched. It was only when he had finished and looked down into his lap, trying to hide his glistening eyes, that his lips wobbled and he said, 'I really want my Mummy . . .'

Dahlia replaced the receiver and looked out of the streaked window at the rain that fell in thick sheets from the grey sky. A red double-decker bus trundled past, rattling a window in its frame. Chilled air seeped through old sash windows and the gas fire glowed orange behind a metal grid. Radio Four crackled in the background along with the television. Her heart sang with joy

Chapter Twenty-Five

Dahlia had been back in Accra a few days. As soon as she had heard about the coup, she had booked tickets, sorted out visas and started packing. Within a week she was in Ghana again and had moved back into their marital home. 'It seems a waste not to, especially since Vincent is going to be away for a while.' How she had savoured every moment since she got back! She loved the warm air, the heat that seared right through to her bones. She slept without the air-conditioner so that she could wake each morning hot and sticky. She spent her time walking in her garden, smelling the flowers, laughing with the children, chatting with her maid.

During those first few days back, as she reacclimatised and made the house her home again, she barely let Cyril out of her sight, touched him often and spent half the night watching him while he slept. She hadn't imagined for a moment that she would not see him again; however, being back with him made her realise that she was lucky that things had worked out as they had. Her separation from him had been real and could easily have been permanent.

When after a few days she felt ready, she had gone to Usher

Fort, the old slave castle overlooking the sea at James Town. She had only ever driven past the large white structure and had always wondered what it was like inside, with tiny windows the size of a tea tray right at the top of the building.

In the past she would have been filled with disgust at the idea of finding out what the interior was like; however, as she walked in through the old gigantic gates, she realised she felt quite dispassionate about the fact that she was visiting her husband there.

She sat on a bench in the waiting room that had a dirty concrete floor and only one small window. The door was left wide open and a sea breeze came through. She listened to the sea and found it easy to imagine some of what it must have been like for the slaves, maybe her ancestors, as they waited in chains to board a ship. The air was dank, the stone walls thick, and she felt for a moment as though nothing had changed in the centuries since.

Vincent was surprised to see her. He seemed to be expecting someone else. He sat with his shoulders hunched and looked petulant. Dahlia knew she was looking well and sat opposite him elegantly, smiling. He had lost a lot of weight and his fingernails, which he had always kept immaculate, were broken and dirty.

She indicated a basket in which the maid had packed some food.

'Food? Good. What is it?'

'I don't know.' She shrugged. 'Susan prepared it, it was her idea.'

'Thanks,' he said, his voice thick and gruff. 'How are the children?'

'Very well.'

He stared at her. 'I shouldn't be in here. They have no right to keep me in here. This place is like hell on earth! They don't realise who I am. I mean, common criminals, pickpockets, burglars, for pity's sake. It is ridiculous!' His voice had risen as though he wanted someone out there to take note and do something.

Dahlia felt the familiar sinking sensation. She looked away. In the corner a guard sat watching them, smiling. She smiled back.

'What the hell is so funny? Are you listening to me?'

She turned back to look at him.

'I need to get out. There are rats and cockroaches everywhere, it is impossible to sleep. We have to use buckets, and I've had diarrhoea ever since I've been in here. If I don't get out soon I'll die in here. I don't deserve to be in here!'

'Maybe not, but we generally don't get what we deserve, do we?'

He looked quizzically at her. 'What did you say?'

She saw the involuntary tensing in his right hand, the fist forming. The way he stretched his fingers back out anyone would think he was about to begin playing a piano. She faced him, her one-time jailor, and stared.

'I need some fresh clothes. And send me food every day.'

Dahlia said nothing.

'I need to get out . . .'

She couldn't bear any more. She stood. 'I have to go.'

'Wait, I haven't finished. Go to see David Owusu, he will give you money.' He continued in a whisper, 'He'll tell you who to give it to. I could be out of here within days.'

She walked to the door. Turned and watched his enraged eyes search her face, the brutal expression that would precede a slap. She walked off before any of it could get to her.

But she smiled as she walked out into the sunshine and sea air towards her waiting driver. When she was safely in the car, she burst out laughing. The sound rippled over her, coating her like healing, gentle rain.

A few days later, she went back with a pot of oxtail soup and pounded *fufu*. She had to bribe the guards to let her see him as it was outside visiting hours. While he ate, slurping distastefully, Dahlia made a deal with him, the father of her children. She would bring him food, and do what she could do to make sure he had good legal representation. The latter would be a challenge; they would have to make it very worthwhile for one of the able lawyers to take on a case like this against the government. The charges were long and ferocious. 'They are even suggesting murder, Vincent . . .' He pounded his fist on the table. 'Nonsense! What proof have they got?'

She smiled briefly. She had formulated a plan. Somehow, she wasn't sure yet how she would implement it, she would make him give her what she needed. She was intent on remaining in Accra, to raise her children here, in Ghana, which was after all their motherland. But she wanted to live in her own home, somewhere she could feel safe to be herself. Besides, she wanted the children to grow up knowing their father. In spite of what he had put her through, she had tried to refrain from speaking disrespectfully about him in front of the children. She wanted to give them the ability to make their own minds up about him. She knew that ultimately they might choose to hate him, but she hoped that they would be able to forgive him. That was what she planned to do, eventually.

Chapter Twenty-Six

It was a cool Saturday in April. Everyone was grateful that the second rainy season had come after the first had failed to materialise. It was more meagre than usual, but had somehow restored the landscape to nearly normal: the shrubs had recovered some of their lustre, the dust had been driven out of the air, the skies had blued, the air cleared.

Eva stepped back and admired the tree that she had just planted for Zachariah. It was an African tulip tree, which would grow tall and slender, like Zachariah, and produce clusters of large, tulip shaped red-orange flowers. The children were patting the earth around the base of the little tree and Simon read the plaque once more, '*For Zachariah*'.

'Thank you Zachariah, you made our garden so lovely with all your hard work,' said Abi.

Alfred put his arms around Eva's shoulders and hugged her. 'That's nice guys, I think he'd like that.'

When the children had asked how he had died, Alfred had said, 'We don't actually know for sure how', and Eva had added, 'He died quite unexpectedly, and very tragically . . .'

The police had never showed up to investigate Zachariah's

death, which strengthened Alfred's suspicions. He had contacted Zachariah's other employers and given them the news. They too had no idea how to contact his family in Tamale, and it had made Eva sick to think of what would happen to his body, how long he would remain in the mortuary before he was tossed into some unmarked grave. She had told Alfred she couldn't bear the thought and he agreed that they could arrange a burial for him, which they had.

Eva, Alfred, Auntie Gee, Margrit and Kojo, Dahlia, and all the children were present in the Tekyi family's yard, sitting alongside and behind and around Yelena and the boys. Further back, Faustina sat next to Akua with Joseph asleep on her lap. Solomon was next to them in his smart white shirt with every button done up. It was tucked into his grey trousers and he was wearing his polished sandals, and Eva smiled when she noticed that he had had a haircut. She put her hand on Alfred's thigh briefly. He winked at her, making her smile. She looked over at Abigail who was proudly wearing her first pair of dangly gold earrings. Her ears had become a little infected after Gladys had pierced them, using only a needle and a cork, and for the first week she had only had a bit of black thread in her ears which had to be cleaned with hot water and turned daily.

Yelena sat perfectly straight grinning widely. Every now and then she turned to smile into Kojo's camera as he snapped away to record the day. She wore an outfit that Gladys had made for her in a pink and green batik; a long tight skirt with a slit at the side, a top with frills and bits and bows and a deep cleavage. A string of traditional Ghana beads, blue with black and green and red bits, dangled around her neck, and she had a piece of the same cloth her outfit was made from tied around her head like a headband.

'Beautiful,' Gladys said when she saw her. 'Even I could take you as my daughter-in-law.' Yelena hugged her and blinked away the moisture in the eyes. She had far less make-up on today than usual, and looked surprisingly young and vulnerable.

Sitting on the benches opposite them underneath a canopy were Wisdom and his family. They too looked proud, if a little officious. And they sparkled in gaily coloured outfits and starched trousers, their hair and make-up well presented, their hands on their laps, their jewellery glinting in the rays of sun.

The yard showed signs of having been recently swept. Eva could see the long slender arcs of the traditional brooms where no one had yet walked spreading the fine sand hither and thither once more. And much further away, near the furthest building in the compound, two old women were sitting beside large black cauldrons on coal pots which they prodded from time to time. Neither seemed aware or bothered by the ceremony going on just a few yards from where they sat. They wore house clothes, blouses with cloths tied about their waists, their hair tied beneath scarves. Chickens scratched the earth around them, a couple of dogs lay heavily, too hot to move. Eva fidgeted and hoped the ceremony would start soon, before it became stifling, and the children got thirsty and irksome.

A mature man from the Tekyi side stood up and started to speak in a soft voice. The yard hushed as everyone listened to him. He walked over to the twins, who sat on either side of Yelena dressed in elaborate woven fabric outfits, matching long-sleeved tops and trousers. They looked a little self-conscious as their new uncle took their hands and led them to face the Tekyi family.

'These are our sons. Twins. We are performing today a naming ceremony much overdue. For which we apologise to them, to our ancestors, to their mother, to all of you in fact. But we thank you for your presence here today, because as we all know, late is better than never.'

'Yes, yes,' said a number of the guests. There was even a little clapping. One of the boys looked back over his shoulder at Yelena and she waved, smiling hard.

The man gestured and another man came forward holding a calabash in each hand. 'Without a further ado, we are going to name these fine boys.' He put a finger into one of the calabashes, held one of the twins by the chin so he opened his mouth and dipped his finger on his tongue. 'You, your name is Kakra. From today you must respond to this name. When you see wine, call it wine,' he said. He did the same to his brother. 'And you, your name is Panin.' There were murmurs of consent and hushed agreement from the gathering. He put his finger into the other calabash and again into Kakra's mouth and said, 'And when you see water, call it water.' Everyone cheered, Kakra turned around and grinned at Yelena. She was wiping her face, but the tears of joy came faster than she could keep them away. He did the same to Panin and when he was finished he hugged each boy firmly. They stood there with their arms limp by their sides, engulfed in the scratchy, musty traditional cloth of their new uncle, and Yelena's shoulders heaved with the weight of pure joy. 'They have a family, they have a family,' she said over and over to Eva who had sidled over and put her arms around her. 'Do you understand how wonderful this is?'

Eva nodded. She had been thinking about the little boy, Agnes's child, and wondering whether Gladys would organise a similar ceremony for him. After all he was her grandchild too. She knew she wouldn't be included, or even informed about it. In fact, she realised suddenly, it would have taken place a long time ago. She glanced over at Alfred, who appeared engrossed in the ritual, and wondered whether he was thinking about his other son, another boy who surely also deserved an exuberant welcome by his family?

There was much merrymaking later. The guests were served palmwine and minerals; Coke, Fanta and Muscatella. They ate *achomo* and then *jolof* rice and fried chicken, and everyone made fuss of the twins. They were informed how much they resembled their late grandfather, and how handsome they were. One of

Wisdom's aunts told Yelena that she had done well raising the boys, that they were very respectful and that they showed more intelligence and humility than the average ten-year-old child, which made her cry again.

When it was time to leave, Yelena and her family were instructed to visit often, and not to forget their family-by-marriage to whom they also owed obligations of duty and respect and even obedience too.

On the way home they drove behind a lorry filled with people who were standing up close together like cattle, holding on to the railings, bumping into each other as the lorry jerked along. The lorry stopped at the roadside ahead of them and the men, who had red strips of cloth tried to their heads and arms and looked quite formidable, started punching the air and singing as they climbed over the railings and jumped to the ground.

'What's going on?' Eva asked.

'Madam, it's a clean-up campaign,' said Solomon.

As they passed, Eva tried to punch her fist in the air in a sign of solidarity.

'Mummy don't!' shrieked Abigail, tugging Eva's arm down.

In the midst of the men and women were a few armed soldiers, some of whom were carrying long sticks. Alfred said, 'Can you see the canes? They will beat the people up if they don't do a good job.'

'Well, talking doesn't seem to make the difference,' said Eva triumphantly. She turned to keep looking as they drove past. She would have loved to go and help, give a few directions here and there. 'I have been telling the people on our street for years to clean up, now they have to do it by force. I wonder whether they think I am so strange now.'

'Oh madam, please you cannot say that,' said Solomon.

'I know they laugh at me. I may not understand the language, but I know when they are making fun of me, being rude.'